*L*ucinda summoned her courage and drew a last breath for one final act of defiance. "Sushi or BBQ, asswipe!"

"Excuse me?"

Needless to say she had forgotten her carefully rehearsed speech and what she come up with was probably the most embarrassing curse she could have possibly chosen. So now she was going to die, mortified, because in the moment of peril, that was the word that came to mind. She waited. The dragon was still there.

"Sorry," she said, and could have cursed herself. She was always and forever apologizing for the wrong thing. She gave last-minute bravado a second try: "Sushi or BBQ, Thou Evil Spawned Demon of Destruction!"

There was a pause. "No," said the dragon. "I still don't get it."

Really? Lucinda took a deep breath. REALLY?

Who knew that being consumed by a dragon was going to be so much work.

Or worse feel like a test.

Or even more worse, a test she was failing.

The Dragon, Lucinda, & George

Margit Elland Schmitt
Dan McLaughlin

Copyright © 2018 Margit Schmitt, Dan McLaughlin

b
All rights reserved.
ISBN: 1983636789
ISBN-13: 978-1983636783

Dedication

Margit says:
To the Schmitt Boys, big and small, and the Library

Dan says:
To Facebook, and a much greater extent, to Vendi

Contents

	Acknowledgments	i
1	Survival Day FAQS, Participants' Edition	1
2	You Are Invited	7
3	Showing Up	15
4	The First Wave	27
5	Extra! Extra! Read All About It!	39
6	A Lesson About Dragons	49
7	In Pursuit	63
8	Headlines	71
9	The Unicorn King	73
10	The Unicorn Queen	87
11	Survival Day FAQS, Knights' Edition	105
12	The Rights of Knights	111
13	A Little Bitty Breakdown	121
14	Morning Time Daily	127
15	The Rules of Questing	133
16	Is It or Isn't It a Bomb?	145
17	Glowerflorious	149
18	Survival Day FAQS, Dragons' Edition	167
19	The Valley of the Maids and Butlers	173
20	Gathering Intelligence	189
21	The DALSED Terminal	201
22	Morning Moments Coffee, Traffic, and Weather	217
23	Too Dangerous for Children	227
24	Thursday's Headlines	235
25	Afraid of the Dark	237
26	Good Knight, Bad Knight	247
27	Sometimes You Just Ask	265
28	Gathering More Intelligence	283
29	All We Have to Do Is Everything	291
30	After the Fall	315
31	Lucy's Homecoming	335
32	One Hero Prefers to Remain Unsung	349
33	Herd is the Word	357
34	Disenchanted Dragons	365
35	Journey's End	373
	About the Authors	377

Acknowledgments

Margit says:

100% of this book would not have been possible without my mother, Carol, or my sister, Karen, or her children, Xander and Cameron, all of whom provided much needed feedback on the earliest of drafts. My husband, Mike, for his artwork, is owed many, many thanks. To my son James, thanks for his patience and support, and my youngest son, Ben, who provided the concept artwork for our draft, has been throughout my biggest cheerleader.

NaNoWriMo – National Novel Writing Month – should be a national institution; everyone should spend a month trying to write a novel, if only so that they know they never want to do anything like it ever again.

Dan says:

100% of this book would not have been possible without Margit. One evening in October of 2017 we were chatting on Facebook about **NaNoWriMo** plans for November. I had a surplus of time, but no idea, and Margit had said that she had an idea, but no time. I then asked about her idea, and she said something having to do with St. George and the Dragon. I quickly typed, "Huh, interesting, tell me more." And crack reference librarian that I am, I deftly opened another window and Googled "St. George and the Dragon."

The story, for those of you who are unfamiliar with it, is that there is a rather generic maiden left out by her village to be eaten by the dragon. George, on a horse and carrying a lance, comes across this tableau. The maiden tames the dragon with her girdle. George takes the tamed dragon back to the village, along, with, I guess, the maiden. George asks the villagers what to do with the dragon. The villagers request that George kill the dragon. George kills the docile dragon with his lance. Time passes and George becomes a Saint.

That's, uh, weird and really doesn't make a lick of sense, I thought.

Kinda tough on the dragon, and I am not sure how you get "Saint" out of it.

While I was processing all of this, Margit had detailed more of her initial idea of telling this story from a different point of view. A point of view that that is far more reasonable and results in, I think, a much more coherent story with a much better ending. [Spoiler alert: If you think the original story makes perfect sense and the ending "works" for you, you probably should put down this book now. My best guess is that you will not be pleased with what we came up with here.]

So I immediately asked to join her in making her concept a 50,000-word NaNoWriMo novel. She agreed, and we exchanged preliminary chapters to see if we could work together (i.e., accept and incorporate criticism and both agree that the work was better off for it). After determining that we could work together, we determined who our audience was (us, adults who like YA, and those who enjoy novels written by Terry Pratchett), and the time period/technology of the book (early 1990's, as exemplified by command line driven computers).

I was astounded to learn that Margit writes in complete sentences and really takes things like internal logical coherency very seriously. I really don't do either of those things. Soon, we fell into a fairly easy routine of writing and rewriting. Margit became the keeper of consistency, putting things in order and saying things like, "We really need a scene where…." I would say OK.

If left to my own devices, this book would have been considered done at about 54,000 words. The version you have in your hands is about 94,000. In general, if it's a sentence with a subject and a verb and some other kind of words in the correct order, it more than likely emerged from Margit's brain. If it has a quotation mark somewhere in the vicinity, or is in a different font, or looks like it probably was a run-on sentence at one point (AKA a rant), it more than likely started with me.

Readers of drafts at my end were my sister Maura Weber and fellow author and playwright Paula Fell, whose encouraging words and notes on form were very helpful. My lovely wife Vendi laid the book out with her customary good cheer. But mostly, I really do thank Margit for letting me hone in on her idea, and letting me rediscover the joy of collaboration.

Chapter One
Survival Day Participant FAQS

CONGRATULATIONS ON YOUR SELECTION! First of all, a BIG THANK YOU! We know you had a lot of other things that you were planning on doing with your life, things you probably are wishing that you could have been able to do, but hey, you know, sometimes life throws you a curve ball. We also know you have a MILLION questions and so we've bundled some of the most common together with answers you can use!

Excuse me. I'm not really feeling very celebratory right now.

That's OK! We get it! First the Good News! You might NOT die! True! Under the Dragon-Human Non-Proliferation Agreement, which provides the framework for the Annual Sacrifice, all you have to do is show up. If the dragon doesn't show up within 10 minutes or fails to finish consuming you within 65 minutes, you, or such bits of you that are still undigested, are home free!

That sounds fair.

YES! Of course it's fair! We're not savages, you know. And you get to keep the muslin shroud as a treasured souvenir!

Wait, if the dragon isn't obligated to show up, why am I?

Sorry, it doesn't work that way. You have to show up. The dragon doesn't.

Well, what if I don't show up?

Have you looked at your roof lately? We have painted a big red X on it and on the houses of your friends, relatives and nearby neighbors. If you don't show up, dragon representatives of the DHRCP will drop huge rocks or waves of fire on all those structures. We have also notified all those people of your selection. There are probably some of them outside your door right now, ready to help you take your place in this historic celebration. They might have pitchforks.

That sounds a little extreme.

Personally, we agree. Shrugs. But bottom line: You have to show up.

Is there an appeal process? What if I get a note from my doctor?

Doesn't matter.

A note from my boss saying I am needed for a very important presentation?

Nope.

I really don't speak this language very well and don't really understand what is going on.

You are kidding, right? You have read all of this and NOW that is your excuse? Sorry. Sigh. If you insist, the DHRCP will provide interpreters happy to guide you through the process.

I know! My eleventh-grade science project is due and ...?

Look at it this way. Either the dragon doesn't show up and you have a great excuse for having missed the whatever, or you are turned into dragon protein and you have an ever-better excuse. Either way, you have to show up.

Crap.

Yeah, we get that a lot.

Wait! It says here I have to be a virgin.

WAY AHEAD OF YOU. Virginal status is as of five days before official notification. Whatever happens between then and the date of the ceremony is entirely up to you.

WAIT! Even if I am NOT a virgin, I get eaten anyway? That sucks.

Shrugs. Blame all the people who figured that out before you. See Revised DHRCP Code 17-4-2(f). Oh, and don't even try and say you weren't a virgin. Let's just say we got ways of knowing, MAGICAL ways.

Crap.

So, anything else?

What does the DHRCP stand for, anyway?

Doesn't matter. Something in Dragon.

Is there any upside to this at all?

Aside from being able to keep the shroud, you mean?

Yeah, aside from that.

Well, nothing official, but we have found that there are plenty of unofficial perks that go with the being selected as the human component to the sacrifice. If you have ever wanted to go on a shoplifting/dine-and-dash spree, now might be a good time to do it, for instance. Temper tantrums and hissy fits in general are cut a lot more slack, in view of the situation. In many localities, parking fines and fees are waived for DHRCP participants. Please consult with your local DHRCP coordinating government agency to see what benefits you might be eligible for.

In addition, we find that many sacrificial participants bask in a lovely glow, knowing that they have done their part in making the world a safer place for everyone else in The Kingdom.

I still don't feel all that much better.

That's OK!!!! You CAN feel that way!!! We get it!!! But look at it this way: You no longer have to suffer the mystery of when your life will end. You have a definite date on which you may or may not meet your end. Embrace it! Run with it! But not too far, or the dragon will torch your family and a pretty good-sized chunk of your town. So seize this opportunity and take control of what you can, your emotional happiness!!! Like we said, in a few days, you are either going to be in a dragon's digestive tract, or you won't. Roll with it!

Anybody ever tell you that you are a real butthead?

Hey, just kiddin' with 'cha. We got a riddle that can make this eaten-by-a-dragon thing go away, forever!

Really?

You betcha. Like we said, we're not savages.

OK, so, what is it?

Ready?

Yes, darn it, tell me. Tell me.

Just wanted to make sure that you were paying attention.

ARRRRRGH!!!!!

Hey, no need to get your panties in a bunch. Here it is. Without further ado.

You really are a butthead, you know?

I get that a lot too, but here 'ya go:
"Surmount your burden great and small,
"With slender reed, plucked from a ball.
"Forsake the fire of fearsome drake,
"Your point was honed in frozen lake.
"Handless, strike the blow precise,
"With earthborn, stone and finest spice."

That's it?

Pretty much.

That's, uh, pretty obscure.

We meant it to be.

Do I get a hint, or anything?

Nope. The Poem IS your hint. Like we said, we're not savages, but we're also not idiots.

Crap.

You said that already.

I know. It makes me feel better.

OK, whatever. Thank you on behalf of the DHRCP and the rest of humanity, which will live on thanks to your sacrifice.

Unless I solve the riddle first.

Yeah, right. Unless you solve the riddle. Good luck with that.

☺!

Chapter Two
You Are Invited

LUCINDA CAME DOWN TO BREAKFAST AND FOUND HER MOTHER polishing the silverware — something she only ever did when she was upset or nervous — with the letter waiting, already opened, on her empty plate where the waffles should have been.

"What's this, Mom?" she'd asked.

Her mother, rubbing more ferociously at the spoon in her hand, didn't answer in words, but gave her a miserable look, and a sheepish, helpless groan. Mom waved a hand, polishing rag flapping, in a gesture clearly indicating that Lucinda ought to read the thing for herself.

The paper was impressive, thick, soft, with a gilded edge and texture to it. Like a diploma or a wedding invitation, something fancy, or at least trying to look fancy. Lucinda thought it might be trying too hard, especially with the curlicues and slanted writing. After all, a quick glance showed it was just a form letter.

TO HER HIGHNESS, THE QUEEN,
from the Dragon-Human Relations Center of Profundia. Respectful greetings, and preemptive sympathies. We regret to inform you that your daughter, Lucinda,

(the fancy type was slightly altered here —as if someone had been given a blank to fill out and done their best. They'd used purple ink), a virgin girl of less than twenty-nine years of age, has been selected by lottery to placate the dragon as part of Profundia's 472nd annual Survival Celebration.

There was more information, mainly about a doctor's exam to make sure no one had made the huge error of selecting a non-virgin, or a boy, or a seventy-year-old for the honor of being devoured by a dragon. Rumor had it that the last kingdom so careless had been burned to the ground and used as the dragon's litter box.
There was also a lot of stuff that covered the ceremony, costume guidelines last requests and so on. She skimmed through twice, and felt a little dizzy as she looked up again.

"Oh, Lucinda," sighed her mother.

"I hate that name," said Lucinda, who knew it had been her grandmother's name and that passing down names was supposed to be a grand tradition, especially if you were a princess, but she had always thought it sounded like it was a name with a lot more lace than she possessed even in the frilly depths of her soul. As a little girl, she'd wanted something bright or snazzy as a nickname at least, and she'd tried to get people to call her Lucy, or better yet, Lucky, but neither one seemed to stick, and she had resigned herself, doomed to be Lucinda forever.

As the lone tally on the plus side, "Forever" was turning out to be a lot less time than she'd used to think.

"Don't be saucy," said her mother, the Queen. She rubbed harder at the already shiny spoon, as if she could rub Lucinda's future away like a spot. "If only you'd gone out with that Chip Blitherington when he asked you to the cinema."

"I don't like Chip," Lucinda said. "He has a reputation, you know. They say he's like an octopus, trying to take advantage of girls. What sort of Knight asks a princess four years younger than himself to the movies? He would have…" She trailed off in the warning lift of her mother's raised eyebrows.

"Virgin," said her mother.

"Fine, yes, I know, but anyway, he didn't like me. He even told me that I wasn't his type." Lucinda, tall and skinny and devastatingly near-sighted, had never really been anybody's type. She hadn't actually talked with Chip, but she'd seen enough television to know what to expect in these situations. She could imagine perfectly well how the evening would have gone, and it wouldn't have ended with a love song and scrolling credits.

"He was only doing me a favor by asking me out. None of the other knights would be interested in a relationship. I'm sure he was the only one willing to wrap his arms around a four-eyed beanpole. I told him not to bother."

"But Lucinda, darling…What about one of his friends? There was young George, or that Bryce with the shoulders…"

"And look at the date on this," Lucinda waved the letter at her mother, which made the Queen put down the soup spoon and set to work polishing a silver ladle. "Three weeks ago. Have you been sitting on this all this time, just letting me walk around like an idiot without knowing what was happening?"

"I didn't want you to be upset," said her mother. "After all, you knew it was possible. All families have to be entered in the registry."

Lucinda snorted. It was not a princess-worthy noise. It sounded a lot like a mad camel, actually. "Other families tell each other things. They let their daughters have time to prepare, instead of acting as if everything was hunky dory. You let me enroll for that new semester of online martial arts, for Pete's sake! And all the time, Chip was buzzing around like the world's most reluctant blue-bottle, trying not to have to land on the pile of…"

"I thought he was charming, when he brought that bouquet of flowers."

"He picked them out of our own front yard, Mom, did you really not notice?"

"But just one night, sweetheart. If only…"

"Mom, forget it!" Lucinda shouted, finally jumping up from her chair, thin chest heaving with something that wasn't quite tears, but seemed a lot more like rage. "I'd rather get eaten by a dragon than ever have to go on a stupid date with Chip Blitherington or any other knight!"

"Well, that's great," snapped her mother, bitterly polishing at the silver spoon in her hand. "Because that's exactly what's going to happen to you on Sunday."

"Ladies, ladies, let's calm down a bit, hmm?" Lucinda spun and found a stranger sitting on the fold-out stool that lived in the corner, which is where Lucinda sometimes sat herself, when she helped her mother with the polishing.

"Who are you?" Lucinda asked.

"Rex," said her mother.

"Agent X.," said the man a fraction of a beat behind, and with just enough of a polite smile to imply he wasn't Correcting the Queen, and hadn't been a silent audience to the Royal Argument either. Whether he was Rex or Agent X, he was far more composed than the Queen.

"What are you doing here?" Lucinda demanded. Rex was far more composed than the Princess, too.

"Well, you see honey, Rex, I mean Agent X, is Profundia's Survival Celebration consultant."

Another smile, a polite nod. "Yes, your mother hired me to give her the best possible advice of how to get through the current crisis."

"Does Dad know about this?" Lucinda's dramatically outflung arm indicated the so-called Agent, rather than the letter crumpled up in the fist of her other hand. After all, the letter was three weeks old. Even a man as busy as the King should have found time to be notified that his daughter was about to be served up on a metaphorical platter to a literal dragon.

The Queen found another spoon to clean. There was never any shortage of spoons in the palace kitchen, especially since collecting spoons had become recognized as socially acceptable for a queen. "No, dear, not in so many words, but he has been so busy lately…"

"Why is he dressed in a black body suit?" asked Lucinda, who had plenty of glare stored up to dish some out to Agent X.

"I'm sure I don't know, dear." The Queen held the spoon up to the light and gazed very intently at the curved surface, searching desperately for any possible blemish. Agent X, or Rex depending on how well you knew him, simply sat and looked like the relaxed panther of efficiency that he was.

"To allow me to slip, undetected, into the most inaccessible of places," he said.

The spoon fell to the floor. The Queen picked it up and put more compound on her royal rag and continued to rub. Agent X smiled blandly at Lucinda.

"OK then. What's that?" Lucinda's hand shot forth in another dramatic gesture, this time in the general direction of Rex's belt buckle.

The spoon fell to the floor again. The Queen bent down again and took a moment or two before sitting once again in her chair and rubbing like crazy.

"This?" Rex said. "It's my sword." His fingers lightly caressed the pommel.

"No, I meant the other that," Lucinda flung her hand in the reprise of the first gesture.

"This is my dagger, which I often use in conjunction with my sword," Rex said, beginning to caress that scabbard as well.

The Queen tossed the spoon on the floor, and collapsed backwards, fanning herself.

"Ugh, no," said Lucinda. "I meant what is the other that? The one in the middle!" Truth be told there was noticeably less energy expended with this flinging of her arm when compared to the first, and the form was not as dramatic as before. Her arm was getting tired. She stomped her foot, and felt that restored some of her theatrical momentum.

"Lucinda," her mother began weakly, "Honey, your mother has been under a lot of stress, lately, and your father, well, he's been busy running The Kingdom…."

"This is my utility belt," interrupted Rex.

The Queen's mouth snapped shut, and she picked up an incredibly dingy butter knife.

"What do you need a utility belt for?" Lucinda asked, darkly suspicious.

"It carries the tools that enable me to successfully carry out my job," he said.

"Your consulting job?" said Lucinda.

"Yes," said Agent X. "You see, Lucinda, over the years an incredible number of rules and regulations have developed over the PSC ."

"PSC?"

"Profundia Survival Celebration," he explained. "If we can document that the dragon did not adhere to any one of those conditions in consuming, or I mean interacting gastronomically with the, er, human portion of the ceremony, we could have an excellent ground for reversing your appointment."

"Does that mean the dragon doesn't get to eat me?" Lucinda asked.

"In theory, yes." Agent X said. Lucinda felt a surge of relief so huge it made her knees wobbly, and she would have smiled at him, except that he had already held up a cautionary hand. "In practice," Agent X concluded in the same, dry tone, "it's not very likely."

Lucinda resumed her frustrated, frightened scowl. The Queen, who had propelled her self towards Agent X with the intention of embracing him in gratitude, skidded to a halt, or at least made the effort. The Queen had generated enough momentum to collapse into Agent X's arms. Immediately, with the royal training that comes with being queen, she raised a wrist to her brow in a graceful, wilting gesture.

"Oh, Rex!" the Queen declaimed.

"Why not?" Lucinda demanded.

Agent X resumed his discourse: "Well, according to my research, most violations of the traditional agreement occur in close temporal proximity to the gastronomic maiden-dragon interaction so the legal appeal tends to lack force. Historically, judgment has been more along the lines of, 'Oh well, we will do better next time,' sort of thing."

With grace and skill, he had managed to hook the nearest chair over to him with one leg, and delicately transition the wilted Queen to its sturdy frame. "Which is to say by the time we're able to prove the fault, you'll already have been at least partially devoured. Still, we'll protest."

"Really," said Lucinda.

"It's a sort of 'Ex post facto consumo' sort of deal," Rex provided the Queen with another spoon and a fresh dab of polish. "In any case, my job is to get as close to you as I can, to make sure all the rules are followed."

"Using your utility belt," said Lucinda.

"With the materials I keep contained in my utility belt I can lodge a complaint, later, safely. Of course, if I am close enough to raise a spirited protest within the traditionally specified guidelines while you are as yet unconsumed, I will absolutely do so, but as you know dragons can fly and breathe fire." Agent X held out his hands and shrugged his shoulder, looking resigned to his helplessness, and also, somewhat French.

"Can you consult with me so I'm not tied to a stake and eaten by a dragon without having my house marked for fire and destruction?"

"Not really," said Agent X.

"Mother of Felicitousness," said Lucinda.

Agent X took the Queen's hand and patted it soothingly. "Primarily, my job is also to provide comfort for those who are left behind," he said, and patted the Queen's arm in a professional manner. "The point is, you have to show up."

Chapter Three
Showing Up

IF I MUST NEEDS DIE, AS IT SEEMS I MUST, AND END MY BRIEF span of days on this earth rent asunder by dragon's tooth and claw, then let me face that fate with the dignity worthy of a Princess of Carolia.

The thought echoed through Lucinda's head, and if it had seemed a little pretentious at first, even to her, she'd had plenty of time to polish it up. The news crew and honor guard had marched out of range at the earliest opportunity; she'd heard someone suggest they go for coffee and muffins on the way back to the city, which was sensible, in a heartless sort of way. Then silence. That had been at least an hour ago. Lucinda was alone.

Somehow, she'd expected more out of the whole experience: an ode written in her honor, or a situation with chains of gold and silken blindfolds, maybe some mourners tastefully weeping from a safe distance away, but it had turned out to be extraordinarily simple, a businesslike execution. She'd been given a traditional, if impractical silken gown to wear, and had completely refused the ceremonial underwear that went with it. She was tied to a metal post with what felt like an ordinary piece of rope, and her head was covered in a muslin shroud. It had been dark when they'd unloaded her from the official (if old-fashioned) carriage, but she guessed by now, the sun had probably risen. She could see the brightness of it through the thin fabric covering her face. She heard the sounds of insects and the mournful call of birds, flying. She heard waves lapping at the water's edge. Having polished her last words, Lucinda felt a little sad that no one would ever be able to hear them from inside a dragon's stomach. Putting that thought aside, she began to run through her seven-times tables.

A cloud passed over the sun and the birds and insects went silent. Lucinda felt an intense push of air, and shivered. Her legs, which were bare, suffered a dozen small cuts from the driven sand and small rocks of the beach gravel. She could feel the weight of the dragon's enormous body as it settled.

Lucinda braced herself and waited for the blow. She refused to scream or weep (though she wanted to do both, and was afraid she might wet her pants in a completely undignified way), but it wasn't easy to hold one's breath and clench everything while a dragon looked you over. She waited. And waited.

And waited.

The roaring in her ears abated and she had no choice but to breathe. Thankfully, she managed an inhale and exhale without a scream. But still, no bite. No agonizing sear of white-hot flame. Nothing at all. Once again, Lucinda heard the small waves lapping at the shore.

What was the dragon waiting for? Was it even still out there? Was it looking her over, and thinking that her ropes and muslin and bare legs were unappetizing and unworthy? The whole point of her being here was to save the city from a draconic rampage. What if she was so unappetizing that the dragon just skipped her over, and flew off to destroy the city?

Lucinda summoned her courage and drew a last breath for one final act of defiance. "Sushi or BBQ, asswipe!"

"Excuse me?"

Needless to she had totally forgotten her carefully rehearsed speech, and what she had come up with was probably the most embarrassing curse she could have possibly chosen. So now she was going to die, mortified, because in the moment of peril, that was the word that came to mind. She waited. The dragon was definitely still there. Its voice was definitely inhuman, and yet pitched a bit higher than Lucinda was expecting. It also sounded mildly confused, rather than enraged by the insult.

"Sorry," she said, and could have cursed herself. She was always and forever apologizing for the wrong thing. She gave last-minute bravado a second try: 'Sushi or BBQ, Thou Evil Spawned Demon of Destruction!"

There was a pause. "No," said the dragon. "I still don't get it."

Really? Lucinda took a deep breath. REALLY?

Who knew that being consumed by a dragon was going to be so much work.

Or worse, feel like a test. Even more worse, a test she was failing.

"Okay," she said. "Listen. As near as anyone has been able to figure it out, the maiden who is consumed by the dragon is either ripped apart leaving only a gross assortment of bloody and horrifying bits and pieces, e.g. eaten raw, e.g. sushi, or else the remains that are found after the fact are only a pile of ash."

"Implying a BBQ," said the dragon. "On the beach. I get it now. Quite clever, really."

The dragon's tone seemed to say, "Quite clever — for a human." There was a huff of brimstone-scented breath. "Well done."

Another silence descended. Lucinda once again heard birds and insects and waves. Occasionally there was the sound of the great beast shifting on the beach rock. Lucinda remained uneaten. She was still very, very frightened, but also starting to feel a very,

very small spark of curiosity. She wished, all at once, that she could get rid of the blindfold; she would have liked to see the dragon's expression.

"Um, not to be critical or anything, but you're not really the big fierce manly dragon I was expecting."

"Well for one thing, I am a girl dragon."

"HA," Lucinda barked in surprised laughter. "That's stupid. Who ever heard of a girl dragon?"

"Well, you have heard of baby dragons, haven't you?"

This silence felt different to Lucinda, because it was. "Oh." Suddenly Lucinda was glad for the shroud that concealed her red-hot blush. "Yeah. Got it."

Then, the dragon said, "This is just awkward."

And Lucinda heard the dragon shift its — no, her — weight on the loose gravel and sand of the beach, and felt a very, very large claw pierce the muslin shroud, which tore, under pressure from the razor-sharp digit.

The removal of the shroud was actually very gentle. Once Lucinda stopped blinking (for all her brave words, most of the time her eyes had been scrunched tight), she saw what she'd known was true all along. The claw had belonged to a dragon.

It was, for a dragon, quite dainty. Not nearly as big as a mountain, this dinosaur might have fit pretty comfortably in the smallest ballroom in the castle, though she would probably have had some difficulty squeezing through the doors to get in.

Lucinda thought the dragon might be a little more than twice her own height, and much longer than she was tall (though to be honest, most of that length was made up of a long, flexible tail). She was scaled in a way that reminded Lucinda of lizards, although in this case, a lizard with an intricate, oscillating pattern that made her scales seem to ripple. Her wings were folded up at the moment, but Lucinda imagined they would be huge. She had a forked tongue, which was darting in and out, as if the dragon were particularly interested or unsure about what was happening just now.

For something so lizardish, she had an extremely expressive face, maybe something to do with her big, burning eyes. But what Lucinda noticed most prominently was that the dragon was wearing a bracelet. A particularly shiny golden chain hung around her scaled, draconic wrist, and a large red ruby, easily as big as Lucinda's fist, hung like a pendant at the center. It would have been hard not to notice; it was at the exact same height as Lucinda's head, and provided something much more pleasant to look at than all those teeth.

"Hey, cute bracelet!" Lucinda said in open admiration.

The dragon preened and arched her back. "It is, isn't it? My mom gave it to me before I left home."

"My mom gave me a bracelet, too." Momentarily forgetting she was still bound to the post, Lucinda began to raise her hand, but before she could even twitch twice, the dragon's tail whipped around and with an alarming, scissors noise, cut through the rope that had held Lucinda prisoner.

Lucinda held very, very still, and heroically held back a hysterical scream. The tail must be even sharper than the claws, she told herself, in what seemed a reasonable tone of mind. But she didn't even nick my skin.

"Show me, show me," the dragon said.

Lucinda rather slowly held out her hand. Her bracelet was also a ruby, on an intricately wrought, silver band.

"Ooh, pretty!" said the dragon, her serpent neck twisting to see the jewel from all angles. She needed to look closely, since the ruby on Lucinda's arm was only as big around as Lucinda's thumbnail.

"My mother gave it to me for, uh..." Lucinda made a rather vague gesture encompassing the sacrifice station.

"About that..." the dragon shifted uncomfortably, and settled back onto her haunches. "Erh, I don't know quite how to put this to you, but I would really rather not eat you." The dragon huffed what seemed an embarrassed little breath, and steam came out of her nostrils.

"You wouldn't?" Lucinda asked.

"Nothing personal, mind you," the dragon said quickly, but as if she wanted to reassure Lucinda against some implied insult. "I mean I could totally eat you, but..."

"But what?"

"Well, maiden meat..."

"Maiden meat?" Lucinda echoed.

It hardly seemed possible for the dragon to seem more embarrassed, but this one managed it.

"Yeah. Yuck. Even 100% maiden, which I am sure it is," she added, reassuringly. "Really isn't worth the bother."

"What bother?" Lucinda asked, too surprised to be insulted by her lack of deliciousness. "I am trussed up, or I was. And you're the dragon, fire and wings and great big-"

"Okay, it's not one maiden that's the problem. A maiden now and then is fine, if you have a taste for it, but as a principal component of a well-balanced diet..." the dragon shook her head.

"Wait," said Lucinda. "Wait. You want a salad before the entrée?"

"No, no," the dragon actually blushed, her emerald scales turning a bright, carnation pink. "I am saying this very badly."

"You most certainly are."

A dragon shrug turned out to be a pretty impressive thing to watch. Probably, it was the wings. "I know you think your kingdom is the center of the universe, but you're not. And every other kingdom is putting out maidens on trash day, and what with the flies and the seagulls and the knights, it becomes something of a chore to keep the beaches clean, you know?"

Lucinda was speechless. The dragon plunged deeper into the astonished silence.

"Of course, we want to do our part for the environment," she said. "So, we have this lottery system to select who has to go out and collect the maiden for consumption, which would be a bit of a pain, but all worth it for the greater good, and maiden meat isn't that bad if you hold your nose and use a lot of lemon, except not only do you people put out the maidens to be consumed, for some reason you then go and try and murder the poor dragon who is just trying to do his job. I mean, how insane do you have to be to do that?" The dragon glared at Lucinda, as if this had somehow been all her idea.

"But, but, but..." Lucinda put up her hands, as if to defend herself against that anger, but the dragon was clearly on a roll.

"I have lost all of my brothers to this cockamamie scheme, so when it came to be my turn..."

"Brothers as in plural?" Lucinda said.

"You mean you have never noticed that every year or so the dragon looked just a little bit different?" The dragon asked. Her voice was quiet, which was not the same as soft.

"Oh, you know what they say about dragons..." Lucinda began, so terrified that her voice came out higher pitched and faster than normal, and she was giggling with nerves.

"What exactly do they say about dragons?"

The survival part of Lucinda's brain kicked into high gear, as she noticed how absolutely still the dragon had gone. No more flickering, forked tongue, but the eyes were definitely burning. The birds and insects stopped humming and buzzing and calling to each other, and now the waves decided it was a good time to stop lapping at the shore.

Dragons, when they stare, don't blink, by the way. A part of Lucinda's consciousness filed that away. The optimistic part of her brain. The part that believed that it would be still cognizant more than sixty seconds from now and might need to retrieve that information someday. The part that hoped for a future.

"I mean, from far away, err… and with the dragon moving so fast, some of the detail can be lost so that it can become hard to, you know, um, err… see the difference. I mean everyone is running around screaming 'It's a dragon! It's a dragon!' and it really is a dragon and you kind of forget all that stuff you learn in 'What to Do When a Dragon Swoops' class and you're really not looking for any distinguishing marks of the particular dragon, other than noting it's way bigger than you are. And it is flying and breathing fire and picking up people like little dolls and they are screaming like crazy until suddenly they are not screaming anymore, and that's worse. Which is why you are really not bothering to look up to see if this dragon has a cute little birthmark, or a wreath of flowers on its head, or anything that would really distinguish this one flying lizard of doom from any other. Like that."

She spoke fast, words tripping over themselves to get out of her mouth, and the desperate explanation sounded ridiculous, even to Lucinda, who really wanted it to work.

The dragon stared.

Lucinda stood very, very still.

Nothing in the area made any sound at all as the universe held its collective breath.

Then, the dragon blinked, and let out a sigh that, while smoky, failed to incinerate anyone, even Lucinda. "Yes," said the dragon.

"I think that explains it nicely."

The world began to breathe again, and sound resumed hitting Lucinda's eardrums, and her entire brain celebrated her escape from death by making her burst into tears.

The dragon, to her surprise, said: "Oh, I'm sorry. You must be really scared." The big claw reached out and gave her a reassuringly gentle pat on the back.

Lucinda nodded, and wiped her face on the torn halves of the shroud she was still holding. She looked up into the dragon's expressive face and big, glowing eyes, and said, "Listen, do you have a name? It feels rude just to keep thinking of you as 'dragon' all the time."

The scaly head tilted to one side, and some scales or fins or gills or something spread out in a sort of lizard-bird style of interrogative. "Would you call me Ember?" she asked.

Something about that tone of voice sounded all too familiar to Lucinda. "Is that actually your name?" she asked, a little less breezy and casual, and a lot more curious and interested.

The dragon's vast, powerful body shifted uncomfortably on the gravel. Her enormous eyes glanced away, then back again. She had incredibly long lashes, for a dragon. "Not really. It's Esmeraldavinia."

Lucinda flinched in sympathy. "Mine's Lucinda."

They shared a look of true understanding, and Lucinda said, "Listen, Esmera... Listen, Ember! You don't want to eat me, and I sure don't want to be eaten, but we can't stay here, or the Knights are going to come and try to argue with you, or maybe even fight you. Neither of us wants that."

"Well I could fight them. I have been practicing," Ember admitted, with a shy arch of her long, scaly neck. "My aim's pretty good. I could just incinerate them. Dragon fire is plenty hot enough to melt their bones."

"Okay, sure," said Lucinda, pushing her glasses up more securely onto her nose, and looking around. "But we're bracelet buddies, right? We could be friends. You're the first dragon I ever met, and I think we both deserve better than this," she made a gesture to indicate the beach, the pole, and the small cloud of dust on the horizon that implied Knights on the Hoof.

"You want your salad, right? I love salad. Can't we just leave? Together? You and me? Is there a law that says you have to eat me and let the knights take pot-shots at you all day?"

"Actually, there is," said Ember. "I looked it up. The rule was signed into law by the Dragon-Human Relations Center of Profundia. They sponsored my training and everything. Sent me a badge, which I left behind, and a very fancy letter."

"HEY! You got training?" Lucinda protested. "No fair! All I got was this lumpy shroud and a ten-minute lecture about knots and how I should re-tie them in case they came loose or something!"

Ember went still, and waited. Lucinda fumed about the disparity in treatment for several moments, as the silence permeated not just her eardrums, but the whole surrounding shoreline until she finally emerged from her angry sulk, and figured it out.

"I suppose it does take a little less training to be tied to a post and eaten," Lucinda admitted, but with a certain amount of reluctance.

"Exactly. I'm the one who actually has to do something," Ember said, patiently.

"Fair enough, but do you know what's funny?" said Lucinda. "The Dragon-Human Relations Center sounds like the same group of people who signed my letter, too."

"It does seem funny that we both got letters asking us to do what we don't want to do."

"I've never actually been to Profundia. Have you?"

A shake of the dragon's head. "No, never."

From the direction of the village, they both could hear the fanfare of the horn section and horses and manly shouts suggesting a desire for revenge and dragon's guts for breakfast, or perhaps it was more sort of a brunch, but it was most definitely some sort of picnic or outdoor eating event, and the Knights setting up their first volley of more generic battle cries as they started across the big, bare beach towards the water's edge.

"What if I promise to call you Ember, and you can call me Lucy," Lucinda said. Why not? she thought. She was risking everything, right? "And we can find out where Profundia is and try to get some common-sense injected into some of these rules! What do you say, bracelet buddy?"

"I say hop up, Lucy," and with surprising gentleness, the dragon's claw reached round to pick the Princess up around the waist. Then the huge wings tore the air into thunder as she swept them down and away and they parted company with the ground.

From the sound of it, the Knights weren't pleased by this Departure from Tradition.

"Die, asswipe!" the sound drifted from far below. Both Lucy and Ember looked down and watched as a spear tumbled down into the lake below.

"Who was that?" asked Ember

"George," said Lucy.

"Who's George?"

"Just some boy."

"Just some boy?"

"Technically a knight. I've seen him around." With that Chip Blitherington, she thought dismissively. Lucy closed her eyes, because looking down was becoming a bit of a challenge.

"He threw the spear pretty well, though, even if it landed in the lake." With that remark Ember flew for a bit, her powerful wings cutting the air. Lucy felt the wind in her face, and on her bare legs, and generally, pretty much everywhere. Flying was a cold, unexpectedly breezy experience.

Then in a thoughtful, considered tone, Ember asked. "Do all humans call dragons asswipes?"

"Only until we get to know them," said Lucy. She wrapped her arms around the dragon's strong, secure claw, and held on tight.

Chapter Four
The First Wave

ON THE GRAVELLY SHORE OF THE CHILLY, ALPINE LAKE WERE TWO BOLD knights. There was also Agent X, looking not only bold, but very dapper in his black body suit, shiny boots and utility belt. Agent X looked as though he would have been at home behind the wheel of a sleek, black car, but tradition required that Survival Day Rescue Operations be performed on horseback. He had acquired a pitch-black horse. The entire picture he presented was tall, dark and mysterious, and if he looked just a little bit overdramatic, he also looked more than a little dangerous.

Beside him was Chip Blitherington, far less bold, which was easy enough for anyone to accomplish, and much more mild-mannered. Chip wore a knight's armor so perfectly traditional, one could easily assume it had been handed down over centuries, by people who had taken very good care never to expose it to dirt or battle or anything that might scuff it in any way. It was gleaming, and certainly looked as though it had cost a pretty penny. In fact, the armor was much more impressive than Chip himself. People describing Chip tended to focus a lot on his family, which was old and moderately wealthy, and his reputation, which was overly friendly. Those who knew him well thought of him as not so much bold as bland.

Next to Chip stood George, who had dismounted his horse

with a resigned sigh. He was the tallest of the young men on the beach, and wore only the most basic of uniforms, the sort routinely supplied to Knights Errant by the Agency. He was looking not bold, or bland, but just the tiniest bit irritated at the world in general and the lake in particular.

The knights had nowhere left to charge, now that they had reached the edge of the shore. Instructions had been very clear and precise:

A. Wait for the dragon to land,
B. Wait for the trumpets to sound,
C. Ride forward from the designated starting spot,
D. Shout and wave spears and swords, and if possible,
E. Slay the dragon.

It had all been a lot more waiting and a lot less charging than George had anticipated when he'd signed up for the heroic duty. Now the dragon had flown off unslain, and there was no princess around to bury or mourn, and no princess around to give them new orders. It was just an uncomfortable moment wherein they had to decide for themselves what to do next.

Agent X was looking steadily at the departing dragon, with the girl in its claws, as their shapes rapidly dwindled in the distance. Chip began to rummage through his saddlebags. George, it must be confessed, was looking ruefully at the spear floating in the lake.

"Darn," said George. "That was my only spear."

"You only brought one?" asked Agent X.

"The guy at the rental place said it was enchanted, guaranteed to always hit."

"Well, it hit the lake," said Chip cheerfully.

The three considered that bit of wisdom as they stared at the spear, bobbing on the surface of the water.

"I'd better go get it, then," said George with a notable lack of enthusiasm.

"If you want your deposit back," said Agent X.

"You didn't buy the 'swallowed by lake coverage'?" asked Chip.

"No."

"Too bad," said both Chip and Agent X together.

"My Dad used to say that rental insurance is all one big rip-off," said George.

"Until you need it," said Agent X.

George squatted down at the water's edge and scooped cold lake into his hand. He stood up quickly, shivering and shaking his hand, which didn't so much dry it off as, in the crisp morning air, make his fingers even colder.

"Hatchee Katchie! That is one cold lake!"

Even Chip had enough empathy to remain silent.

"You know this could be easier if someone had put a rope or a string on the other end of the spear, you know?" George continued petulantly.

"I've noticed in my research that a lot of people come to that conclusion right about this point in the adventure," said Agent X. "But you know what they say about hindsight."

"Always 20/20," Chip offered helpfully.

"Exactly," said Agent X with a brisk nod.

George sat down on the beach to pull off his boots before he began to wade into the water. His mother had given him plenty of advice about not swimming with shoes on, and why not to do it. She'd always told him the importance of being prepared. Come to think of it, when she had rented supplies, she had always opted for the additional coverage. She just never made a big deal about it.

Bracing himself, George stepped into the lake. He made a good half-dozen firm strides before he began to shiver.

"You'll remember this forever," said Agent X.

"I've already got a towel ready for you when you get out," said Chip, waving it encouragingly. "Oops! Wind took it out of my hands. Just bring it with you on the way back, would you, George?"

George seemed to be reconsidering his options, "Holy Fricassee of Frankincense! This is cold! That spear is really far out there, isn't it?"

"Well, you were all hyped up when you tossed it," said Agent X. In a lower voice to Chip he added, "Actually, I think he really does have quite an arm."

"Really a respectable throw, all things considered," Chip agreed.

"Kind of a shame it missed the dragon," said Agent X.

"And fell into an alpine lake."

"In spring,"

Chip and Agent X sat on their horses, experiencing the satisfaction that only comes from watching someone else do the nasty work.

"Oh well, enough of this fun," said Agent X after a minute or so. "It's time for me to do my job."

"I've been meaning to ask, what exactly your job is?" asked a mildly interested Chip, pulling out a granola bar from his saddlebag. Confounded by the wrapper, he began to wrestle with it. "George and I are knights, obviously." He checked his armor, as if to reassure himself. "But you're an agent?"

"Agent X," said Agent X.

"An agent of what, exactly?" asked Chip. "Probably you mentioned it already, but I don't have a head for details, old bean."

"I'm not an agent," was the answer. "Agent X is my name. My parents had big plans for me." And the tone of his voice made clear he considered the promise of infant Agent X to have been admirably fulfilled. "And my job is to record these events for posterity. I've researched previous adventures of the Knights, and now I'm documenting what happened to the DHRCP."

"Ah," Chip said with quiet satisfaction. He dropped a much-mangled granola wrapper on the beach and began to eat. If he knew what a DHRCP was, which seemed unlikely, he didn't say.

Agent X opened his utility belt and brought out a notebook the size of his palm, and a pen. He began to compose.

"Hey, Kid," he yelled at George, who had discovered the lake possessed a current, and was struggling against it to reach the spear, "Is it okay if I switched your battle cry from 'Die Asswipe' to 'Die Thou Evil Spawned Demon of Destruction?'"

"Whatever," George shouted back, with a regrettable lack of enthusiasm for posterity. "Just make sure you include the bit where I point out that this water is really really cold!"

Chip asked, "Why?"

"Why what?" Agent X was busy composing his report, and didn't even glance up, but Chip was curious.

"Why did you ask him if it was okay to change the account of what happened? Ooh!" Chip made a small, pleased noise as he found and began to open his second granola bar.

"Well, what I've learned is that the story is only as good as the paperwork. For instance," Agent X held up the notebook. "What have we done so far?"

"Well, we got up, and over breakfast, you flirted with Nora."

"Which one was that?" Agent X asked.

"The innkeeper's daughter."

"Ah," Agent X lifted a finger, and then used it to flip back through the pages to the correct spot in his record. "It might seem like that's what happened to you because you were there."

"Well, yes."

"But that's not really it."

"It's not?"

"History will show that after mentally preparing ourselves for the task at hand, we questioned the locals extensively for crucial intelligence," Agent X intoned.

"Then you disappeared with her for about a couple of minutes or so," Chip reminded him. "George and I had to pay the bill."

"One local informant proved to be very forthcoming in describing the local nooks and crannies where a dragon might be seen to lurk," Agent X corrected him.

"Then you took two more hours to finish your breakfast," Chip said, as he finally wrestled the wrapper away from the bar and began to chew.

"Taking time only for simple country fare," Agent X amended.

"Because you spent most of that time flirting with Alice."

"Which one was that?" Agent X brought out his pen.

"Her younger sister," said Chip.

"And gathering more intelligence," Agent X suggested. "And comforting the common people, who were relieved to know their fates were in the hands of knights of the realm."

"The two sisters were a tiny bit miffed to see you'd been flirting with them both, so we left in a hurry. Forgot the directions," Chip added. "And got lost on the way to the lake."

"Leaving no path unexplored we were relentless in our pursuit of the Evil Spawned Demon of Destruction." Agent X recalibrated.

"I say," Chip nodded admiringly. "That is clever!" He reached for another granola bar and began to negotiate with the wrapping.

George emerged from the lake shivering, icy water pouring off of him. He clutched the spear in one hand, and the sopping wet towel in the other. He threw them both to the ground, and went on cold-numbed, bare feet to see whether he had remembered to pack a dry towel in his own saddlebags.

"Oh, there's the spear," said Chip, experimentally rubbing the wrapper against his saddle to see whether erosion was an effective technique to get the granola bar out of the wrapper.

"Yes, no thanks to you!" George was without a towel, and began to dry himself off with one of the clean shirts he had packed.

"So, how was the water, George?" Chip asked politely.

"I think he said it was cold, Chip," answered Agent X, without looking up from his report.

"Ah, yes, I remember that, too, now that you mention it. And you brought the spear back. Well done, George. Have a granola bar." Chip tossed the mangled, but still unopened, granola packet to George. "There seems to be a little something off about the wrapper to that one, but you'll be able to figure it out. You retrieved the spear from the lake after all. Good show."

George snatched the unopened granola bar out of the air and took a big bite.

"Well, that's one way to open it, I suppose," said Chip, reaching into his bag for another granola bar. "Tiny bit hard on the ol' chompers, I should think, but A for initiative, old fellow."

Picking bits of granola wrapper from his teeth, George asked, "While I've been having a delightful swim, what have you two been doing?"

Chip said. "We've been playing a marvelous game. I say what has happened to us since we got up this morning, and Agent X makes it all ship-shape and form ready. Like this: 'When we finally made it back to the inn, the first innkeeper's daughter found you cuddling up with her sister and slapped you.'"

"With determination and courage, we reestablished contact with the locals," Agent X offered.

"And after her sister had told her what you said to her, she thought it was you who deserved to be eaten by the dragon, not some poor maiden," George said, immediately getting into the spirit of the thing.

"And we discovered much about the dietary habits of dragons vis a vis humans," said Agent X.

"After you got your love life straightened out," said George.

"And we found the map with the directions on it," said Chip, examining another granola bar and its wrapper.

Agent X merely nodded, "We proceeded from the inn by direct route to the lake and the ominous place of sacrifice."

"Where I tossed my spear and almost saved Lucinda," George said, limping back over to where his shoes and socks were waiting.

Agent X paused and looked up. "That's kind of strange, actually."

"How so?" George asked. "Wasn't that what we came out here on purpose to try and do?"

"To try and almost save her?" Chip asked.

"Listen," said Agent X. "Our arrival was a tiny bit later than scheduled."

"Because you had to have a second cup of coffee," said Chip.

"And because you can't seem to stay away from innkeepers' daughters," added George.

Agent X waved that away. "Or they can't stay away from me. My point is, the princess should have been chewy dragon nuggets by then, but it looked like, at least from afar, that they were just chatting," Agent X sounded genuinely puzzled.

"YOU TAKE THAT BACK!" George leaped to his cold feet. "PURE AND DEFIANT PRINCESS LUCINDA WOULD NEVER WILLINGLY CONSORT WITH—"

"Whoa, ease up, boy knight," Agent X held up his hands defensively. Clearly, the proper role and function of a princess was something of a "button" for George. "It's a good thing, actually. Shows brains; making conversation obviously went a long way to extending her life."

"It seems," said Chip, examining the granola bar wrapper in his hand, "if you grab the little tabby thing and pull in one direction, it comes off quite easily. But if you come at it from the wrong side, you have a devil of a time getting the blighter open. They should really put a little arrow on the package or something. Would save a fellow a ton of time to know which side to pull when all he really wants is a granola bar."

He demonstrated his new-found technique, dropped the wrapper, and began to eat happily.

"Listen, George," said Agent X. "Chatting takes time. Princess Lucinda chats for 15 minutes, and according to the official rules, she has fulfilled the sacrifice and no longer has to allow herself to be eaten."

"This is in the rules?" asked George.

Agent X looked smug. "It's buried deep in the records. You have to know where to look."

"So my Lucinda is saved?"

"Your Lucinda?" asked Chip

"Saved?" Agent X waved a black-gloved hand. "Oh no, most assuredly not. Oh, how shall I phrase it? 'The vile creature just wanted to eat her at more his leisure, far away from civilized men.'" Agent X was pleased with his work and posed heroically for the photographer who lived in his head. Then he added, more reasonably, "But what it does mean is that we have reasonable grounds for a most strenuously worded complaint."

"And you'll be just the man to write it," said Chip. "Excellent! This calls for granola bars all 'round!"

"No, thank you," said George. He pulled on his boot and

shivered his way towards his horse, who gave him a skeptical look as he attempted to mount.

"Come lads, not a moment to lose. Let us hurry back to the capital to file our paperwork!" Agent X looked positively dashing in the saddle and his midnight-colored horse, startled, reared in a picturesque fashion.

"Huzzah!" Chip cheered and he hastily put away his last few granola bars.

"To the city?" George asked. "Shouldn't we be going after Princess Lucinda?"

"Is that traditional?" asked Chip.

"I doubt it," said George, a touch bitterly. "I don't think anyone's ever been made a dragon's prisoner before."

There was silence, as Agent X mulled over the appropriate course of action. Without the crinkling and gnawing that was Chip's awkward consumption of granola bars, the gentle sounds of nature began to return to the lakeside. It was almost peaceful, if you didn't pause to consider where they were, or why they'd come here.

Slowly, Agent X turned to give George a thoughtful look. "You mean, go after her to see whether she is still alive enough to sign the complaint herself?" he asked.

George hesitated. "Yes?" On a scale from 1 to 100 with 100 being totally certain, George checked in at about a 65.

"Brilliant, lad!" cried Agent X. "To be honest, I never suspected that you had such a talent within you."

"Indeed!" said Chip, bolstering George's spirits by giving him a hearty slap on the back.

Agent X was grinning, ear to ear. "History will show that our mighty Company spared no thought for the danger, but spurred onward in hasty pursuit of the Princess Lucinda, and her valid signature with photo ID."

"If only we are not too late," said Chip.

"Let's get going already," said George.

"Seriously, though," said Agent X. "We need to stop and drop off this report. It's on our way," he added, in the face of George's expression.

George didn't answer, and neither did Chip. The three horses galloped off toward the city, and on the lonely beach of the alpine lake, a handful of crumpled granola wrappers scattered in the wind.

Chapter Five
Extra! Extra! Read All About It!

The following headlines and articles were taken directly from issues of the Carolian Star-News: *"Local News Your Way"*

"FIE ON THEE, DRAGON ASSWIPE!"
These were the last words heard from valiant Princess Lucinda as she was carried away to almost certain consumption.

Kingdom of Carolia mourns and gives thanks for royal daughter, who, it seems, did not go down easily.

"I just ate some asparagus and brussels sprouts, so I probably taste pretty nasty," were penultimate words thrown at rapacious dragon, as reported by Sources.

Royal brussels sprouts growers society begs to differ. Strident complaint to be lodged (about the Princess. Not the brussels sprouts. Nothing can be done about them.)

"ROYAL BRUSSELS SPROUTS GROWERS SOCIETY OFFERS FANTASTIC RECIPES FOR TASTY AND VITAMIN-PACKED VEGETABLES"
Experts recommend you bring plenty of butter to this year's fall-foliage-and-farming festival, as the local farmers feel they have something to prove.

"We certainly feel sorry for the poor girl with the glasses," said one Farmer Brown. "But when one of the royals starts slandering the cruciferous vegetable community, it stinks."

"DETERMINED PURSUIT BY VALIANT KNIGHTS SOON TO CONFIRM CULINARY FATE OF BRAVE PRINCESS, AUTHORITIES ATTEST
by Special Sacrifice Correspondent, Earl Barret

(the Castle) "Fie on thee, Dragon Asswipe," were the last words hurled by brave Princess Lucinda Merrie Periwinkle Grottweiler Rotunda Doorstop, asserted official heralds at the Palace last night.

"I always knew the girl had spunk," reported a sad, but slightly proud father, King Doorstop.

"Yes, dear, but I am not quite clear where she picked up 'asswipe,'" added her mother, Queen Doorstop (nee Grottweiler) and keeper of the Royal Spoons. "Do you have any notion?"

"Er, no. That doesn't matter. So, The kingdom is saved. Let us all rejoice," the King began.

"No dear," the Queen said. "That is not quite right."

"Er, celebrate?" the King offered.

"No, dear," the Queen said.

"Um, reflect?" He was clearly guessing at this point, but our loyal populace can forgive much of a man who is deeply struck by grief.

"Mournfully reflect," the Queen was clearly certain on this point

"That's it, splendid. Let us mournfully reflect on the...sacrifice?" said the King, emboldened by his relative success, and displaying a higher degree of confidence in his tone.

"Heroic sacrifice, dear," the Queen said.

"Yes. Let us mournfully reflect on the heroic sacrifice selflessly rendered by my daughter."

"Our beloved daughter."

There was, one regrets to say, a rather uncomfortable and lingering pause.

"Louise?" He drew out the word with regal bovinity. Clearly, he was back to guessing.

"Lucinda, the one with the glasses," the Queen said.

"Isn't she the one with the braces?" When you look up the word "befuddled" in the dictionary, this is tone that they mean.

"No dear, Lucinda is the one with the glasses," the Queen said.

"You're certain of this?" When you look up "determined" in the dictionary, this is pretty close to the tone they mean.

"Remember, dear, the little memory game I taught you LGTBEA."

"Yes dear, Lucinda glasses, Tracy braces, Edwina acne. Well anyways, that one, the glasses one. Let us mournfully reflect on the heroic sacrifice selflessly rendered."

"Randomly selected to selflessly serve," the Queen said.

In a later press conference hastily called by the Royal Herald, Rosemary Scrunch clarified the entire Royal Family was in a genuine state of mourning for Princess Lucinda Merrie Periwinkle Grottweiler Rotunda Doorstop, the one with the glasses.

Ms. Scrunch went on to explain that by using her wits and a hitherto unrevealed talent for brilliantly defiant repartee, Princess Lucinda had avoided immediate consumption. According to reports generated by the infamous Agent X, while the Princess has delayed her in-person tour of the dragon's digestive system, the dragon has clearly broken with tradition by spiriting Princess Lucinda away to a dining room, whose location is currently unknown. Agent X, in the company of two unnamed knights, is in pursuit.

"Good morning. This is Mindy Maxim-Fnort, on a special castle correspondence here at the Palace Carolia. Today, I'm meeting with the sisters of that most surprising celebrity, Lucinda Merrie Periwinkle Grottweiler Rotunda Doorstop. I'd like to thank the guards for their escort, and their Highnesses being willing to spare the time as we finally get a chance to find out 'Who really is Princess Lucinda?'

"This part of the palace is reserved for just the family. Here we see the annual portraits hanging opposite the window. An elegant arrangement, and perhaps where Princess Lucinda spent much of her time when she was younger."

Mindy Maxim-Fnort paused, while the cameras captured the rows of pictures, the piano at the end of the long hall, and the half-circle of comfortably plush chairs near the fireplace. They'd only been granted access to this single corridor, and Mindy meant to make the most of her time here.

"Lucinda's childhood has certainly been a mystery. Like most of the Princesses, she has been hidden by crowds of retainers and a rather deep, crocodile-filled moat. It has been difficult for outsiders to get to know the girl we call Princess Lucinda, the one with the glasses, who was going to be eaten by the dragon.

"What we do know is that like most Royals, she rode horses very well, and that she showed a greater tolerance than most teenagers could be expected to show for the Queen, her mother's, legendary interest in spoons. The Princess was, in spite of her youth, recognized as one of Carolia's leading authorities on the care, maintenance, and history of spoons. Unfortunately, her growing independence and blossoming interest in the area of forks was cut short by her joyously random selection as Sacrifice this past week-end.

"Lucinda was born the seventh of nine children, the fifth daughter. Lucinda always seemed to be the skinny one, with a scab somewhere. As you see in these family portraits, she can be found sullenly scowling from the fringes with her arms crossed. The King and Queen, and the crown prince, were unavailable this morning. However, in this unprecedented interview, the royal Princesses have graciously gathered together to talk about their presumably incinerated and consumed sister.

"I'd like to begin with the eldest: Princess Dana, what would you like to tell our viewers about Lucinda?" Mindy offered the microphone.

Dana had a regal smile. "Ah, Lucinda," she said. "In so many ways, she was like a sister to me, although my clothes never fit her very well. Her body was all wrong for them, you see."

"Wrong how?" asked Mindy.

"What I think my dear sister means is that Lucinda had a way of making everything she wore quite her own," said Princess Pacifica.

"And the good news is that because she basically trashed every hand-me-down she got, I got all new stuff all the time," said Princess Edwina. "I'll miss her. She was also the one who knew all the rules to the board games, too, and wasn't too busy to play."

"Our viewers will remember that Edwina is the only one of the royal sisters who is younger than Lucinda. Would you say the two of you were very close?"

Edwina opened her mouth to answer, but was interrupted.

"She did have a temper," said Princess Tracy, braces gleaming. "If you told her to do something, and she asked why, and you told her, and she didn't like it, boom! Out would fly the boot and away she would run."

"Like if you said, 'That's the way Princess Perfect does it,'" said Edwina.

"She means Dana," Pacifica explained.

"It's so simple, really. I'm the eldest and I know the right way to do things," said Dana.

"Naturally," said Mindy in a soothing tone. "The eldest Princess would set an example she would like all the others to follow. Would you say that Lucinda ever showed an inclination to set any trends of her own?"

"She seemed mostly focused on not doing what I told her, and spending all those hours with Mother, counting spoons," said Dana.

"Of course, Mother did say that if she was going to kick everyone she disagreed with, she was going to have to wear soft-soled shoes," Pacifica remembered. "Those were certainly very comfortable."

"And soon, simply everyone was wearing them," sighed Dana. "Instead of what I wanted them to wear."

"Oh good lord, remember the 'Lucky' phase?" Tracy said, a question that was answered with peals of laughter from all the sisters.

"A lucky phase?" asked Mindy. "Would you mind telling our viewers what that was about?"

"Oh, it was nonsense," said Dana. "For almost a whole year when she was about six, Lucinda insisted on being called 'Lucky.'"

"Just as she insisted on her 'lucky' socks," Edwina said.

"And her lucky t-shirt," said Tracy.

"And her lucky food." There was another round of genteel laughter from the sisters. "A bowl of spaghetti with a lucky pat of butter. A lucky apple, cut into eight lucky slices. With a chocolate bar for dessert."

"She was such a willful child," said Dana. "Back in those days."

"I wouldn't call her Lucky," said Tracy. "But I did call her Picky."

"Of course, it really is just as well that 'Lucky' never really caught on," Mindy said gently, watching the faces of the sisters. "Given the events of this past weekend."

"Yes," said Dana. "Considering how she ended up. The lottery completely passed the rest of us by, all these years, but Lucinda…"

"Not really 'lucky' at all," said Tracy.

"Sad, really," said Pacifica.

"Quite," said Edwina.

"Rather more unlucky, I suppose," said Tracy.

There was a pause. The cameras scrolled round the faces of the princesses, capturing the emotions there, and then panned out to take in the grandeur of the room. The portraits on the wall were all posed and perfectly symmetrical. The piano, elegant, had no music waiting on it. It looked as though it had not been played for some time.

"How do you think Lucinda would want to be remembered?" asked Mindy, and the cameras returned to the Princesses.

"We are going to have the loveliest ball in her honor," said Pacifica.

"We will all get to wear pointy hats," said Edwina.

"And Papa will waive all parking and traffic violation fines for the entire weekend of the ball!" Pacifica said. "Free parking throughout the kingdom!"

"So Lucinda's legacy will live on?" said Mindy.

"At least through the weekend," Dana said.

"Was Lucinda particularly interested in the parking problems through the city? I understood she wasn't quite old enough to drive yet."

"Well," said Dana. "No."

"But I'm sure Dadsie will name something after her," said Edwina.

"A boat perhaps? I hear the Navy is getting a new one," said Pacifica.

"I think they prefer you call them ships, sister," said Dana.

"Why do we have a navy anyway, we're landlocked. Aren't we?" asked Tracy.

"It's the principle of the thing," said Dana.

"But landlocked, sister obtuse, which means there's no point to even having a navy," said Tracy.

"It's the principle, sister dimmest, which means—" began Dana.

"Sisters, dearest ones," said Pacifica. "Remember we do have the lovely lake, and boats and ships are perfectly capable of sailing on it."

"There," said Edwina, triumphantly. "You see. Dadsie will buy a boat."

"Ship," said Dana.

"For the Navy," continued Pacifica. "And how grateful they will be to have two boats at last."

"Ships," said Dana.

"Then, we will have a big party," explained Tracy. "And we will look sad when anyone says Lucinda's name, and we will waste a perfectly fine bottle of Champagne when Mumsie does the smashing bit."

"Christening," said Dana.

"Is there anything else you need, Miss Maxim-Fnort?" asked Pacifica.

"No, I see the guards have returned to escort us away, but I think I have everything I need."

"Got it all?" asked Tracy. "Good. To sum up: We're heartbroken, but onwards and upwards, stiff upper lip, and so on. Oh, and we hope that someone else's family is picked next year..."

"...Is blessed with the signal honor of her joyous selection as sacrifice participant, sister," said Dana.

"Of course," said Mindy Maxim-Fnort. "One final question."

Dana assumed it was going to her, and waited expectantly.

"Edwina," said Mindy. "Next year will be the first year you'll be eligible to be the Survival Day Celebration participant. How does that make you feel?"

She made a signal to the cameraman, who kept the film rolling, so that as peals of laughter erupted from the elder Princesses, they were able to capture the image of Edwina, the youngest Princess, who sat in silence and clenched the arms of her chair.

Chapter Six
A Lesson About Dragons

LUCY WASN'T THE SORT OF GIRL WHO HAD EVER DREAMED OF FLYING. She wasn't scared of it, precisely, but her dreams had been about more ordinary things: math class, riding lessons, counting spoons. Flying? She hadn't given it much thought. With dragons infamously cruising the coastlines, and prices more than sky-high on airlines that had to insure themselves against airborne predators, she'd just figured it was more than unlikely she'd ever get a chance to fly, and the skepticism must've translated itself into her dreams. But it turned out that she liked the view from the sky a lot, and wasn't at all bothered about heights. Maybe she was feeling just a tad proprietary about her new dragon friend, but it seemed to her that Ember was really good at flying.

She didn't care much for the wind, however. They were moving fast. So fast that the wind was a gale-force, tangling her hair and her shroud, which was all she had as protection against the chilly air. Her hair and shroud were whipping up in all directions. She would have liked to do something about it, but needed both hands to hold on for dear life to Ember's claw. They were so far above the ground just now, and her hair was so very much in her face and mouth and eyes, that everything was a blur.

Or maybe that was just because she had tears in her eyes.

Lucy, huddled against Ember's thorax, felt a vibration, and realized it wasn't the first one; Ember was trying to talk to her, but while she could feel the vibrations in Ember's throat, they were moving so quickly, the words were whipped away before they could get themselves into anyone's ears.

"What?" asked Lucy.

Another rumble, and it was strong enough to shake her bones. It was a little like trying to discern lyrics from the party music when you were too young to attend the ball; your sisters were in the ballroom downstairs and kept the bass turned up full. Mainly, it sounded like thumpy-whump-bump.

"What?" Lucy asked again, and then again: "WHAT?"

Ember tilted her head down in a sinuous way only something halfway between snake and bird could manage. "I said, I'm going to try and land somewhere safe so that we can talk."

The safe place turned out to be the top of a snow-dusted cliff, looking out over the ocean. Waves crashed below — a long way below. The air was cool, and if someone wasn't gasping for breath after a near-death experience and possibly a near-death rescue, too, well, they might look out over the water and find the rolling fog beautiful enough to cause a different sort of gasp. There were tall rocks, sea stacks, both on the top of the cliff, and at the bottom where someone accidentally falling might land on them and regret it, but not for long. Though she was very glad not to be flying hair-first into the wind at the moment, Lucy didn't know if she felt all that much more safe. There was still wind, but it was being blocked by the dragon's body, instead of propelled by it. There was solid ground, even if it was covered with slippery frost and lichen. Lucy's eternally scraped knees were testament to her ability to trip and fall, even when the footing was not this treacherous.

"You've got a little smudge, right there," said Ember helpfully.

Lucy felt like at this point, she might be accurately described as one big smudge. She did lift both hands, numb from holding onto

Ember's claw for an hour, and she did try to shove her hair up out of her face and untangle her glasses and her ears.

"No, not there, on the…" Ember cocked her head to one side. "What is that thing you're wearing?" Ember tilted her head to the other side, and blinked in curiosity.

Lucy looked down at herself, and discounted the Traditional Sacrificial Gown as being the cause of concern. "It's my shroud," she said.

"Shroud?"

"Well, it's tradition," Lucy admitted. "When we die, we're buried by being wrapped in a shroud. It's just fabric, and so nobody minds if it gets buried, but it holds all the yucky bits in."

"Seems a waste of protein," said Ember. Dragons really were excellent at shrugging. "But if it's tradition."

"But see, since the person sacrificed isn't expected to live through it, it's tradition to just send the maiden off with her shroud, because there probably won't be enough left over to bury later, and it's very important to make sure things are Properly Done."

"It is?"

"Especially with princesses," said Lucy. "They do seem to fall into the lottery more than other sorts of people."

The dragon sniffed, and Lucy flinched. Was it preparation for a flaming ball of fire from those enormous jaws? Or worse, a preparation for sarcasm? Whichever was meant, the dragon managed to restrain her baser impulses.

"There's something caught in your burial blanket," said Ember.

Lucy turned her head now, not birdlike or snakelike or even regal, just confused. "Huh," she said. "I guess there is, but…" She squinted, and twisted, and pulled and finally found the place where the loose edges had knotted themselves together mid-flight. After a lot of wiggling and pulling, she managed to get free of the tangled shroud.

Lucy said, "I got a whole bag of things they left me with." She sat cross-legged on the rocky ground and forgot for a minute that she was afraid of the precipice, of dragons, and bird droppings (there were plenty of those to spare on top of the cliff).

"Look at this. Flashlight, crinkly, reflective emergency poncho, water bottle, shoe insoles, granola bars, applesauce tins, and for Pete's sake. The only thing nice in this whole bag is some fancy underwear." She dumped the whole pile out onto the dirt. "They wanted me to wear it, back at the beach, and when I wouldn't, they must have shoved it into the bag."

"About that," said Ember.

"Yeah?"

"I'm just thinking. The only other people out there were those idiots in their combat riot gear."

"Knights," said Lucy. "We're supposed to call them knights. Valiant is optional."

"Whatever," Ember's tail lashed dismissively. "I just don't think that they were interested in this stuff. Was anyone else there?" The dragon continued. "When they dumped you on the beach?"

"Dumped seems harsh," Lucy said.

"What did they call it, the ones who brought you?"

Lucy thought about the flurry of fancy words, the hour of speeches in the city, and the farewell recording played at the beach, all of which basically meant, "Tied you to a post and stuffed a bag over your head. Now we'd better scoot before the you-know-what gets here." She shook her head. "Never mind," she said. "Dumped is about right. And I didn't see anyone there." Because of the bag over her head.

"Naturally, they wouldn't want to be very close to the Beach Clean-up crew, while we were engaged in very important litter removal," said Ember.

"Excuse me?" said the so-called litter.

"No offense," said the dragon, with an airy wave of one claw. Lucy ducked. "But we do a very important and dangerous job that helps protect a special ecological niche and maintain water purity." She hesitated, claw still raised midair. "Erm …."

"You got that from your form letter, didn't you?" said Lucy.

"Maybe," said Ember, a bit defensively. "I just wonder whether there's a crew on your end," she added thoughtfully. "A human crew, because obviously dragons are meticulous and honest in their reporting, but I suppose if someone human is disposing of royal maidens over and over, they'd at least need some kind of crew on hand to make sure the dumping ground was clear for the next one."

"And you think this stuff might be swag for the cleanup crew?" asked Lucy.

"Don't you think so?"

"I don't know," Lucy said. "I'm good at math, so I help my father with paying the bills, and I can tell you that the men and women who run the refuse-pick-up and keep our streets clean earn a pretty good wage. Plus," she wrinkled her nose at the pile on the dropping-crusted ground. "I guess when I unwrapped it, I thought it was something like a bonus for the knights, so I could thank them properly if they got there in time to save my life."

"Thank them with bottled water, underwear, and granola?" asked Ember.

"No, probably not," sighed Lucy. "But it is nice underwear. Although…" she picked it up, and made a face. "A girdle? It's so weird. What's it for, I wonder. In case I'm not svelte enough to appeal to your appetite? You'd think they'd want me to look more plump and juicy, not the other way around."

"So, it seems we have a new question."

"Why a girdle?" suggested Lucy.

"Well, that is a good question, but it only makes sense in a wider context," said Ember.

"You mean a wider context such as what kind of society thinks it's necessary or even appropriate for a fourteen-year-old girl to be given a girdle?" Lucy said with not-at-all-deceptive sweetness.

"I don't think we really have the time or resources to answer that question here, and it requires one to have a basic understanding of what a girdle does," said Ember, who didn't, but wasn't about to admit that. "But we can reduce that question to a smaller, easier-to-answer question that in answering might bring us back to a larger truth."

"Brilliant! What question is that?" Lucy asked.

"What do flashlights, water bottles, ponchos, shoe insoles, granola bars, applesauce tins and girdles all have in common?" Ember asked.

"I know, all something you can buy at corner convenience markets!" Lucy said.

"Except a girdle."

Lucy frowned. "They can be used by just about everyone?"

"Except a girdle."

"If you don't clean your car out very often, they can usually be found under the front seat?"

"Except a girdle. I think. I've never been in a car or had to clean one." Again, that sinuous head-tilt, indicating Ember was becoming thoughtful. "That suggests an even smaller question as the springboard to the hidden truth."

"Brilliant! What is that?" Lucy was beginning to get cold, so she reached over and slipped the poncho over her head. It rustled and felt like nothing but a portable itch, but she was immediately warmer.

Ember lifted her head, and looked like a very scholarly dragon. "What does a girdle have in common with all those other items?"

Lucy waited. "Brilliant. What's the answer?"

"I don't know."

"Less brilliant! Unless you can tell me who would know?" Lucy suggested, when Ember looked crestfallen.

"I would suggest an infinitely wise creature possessing compassionate empathy."

"Where would we find something like that?"

Ember adopted a lofty air (easy enough for someone who could fly). "I was thinking about consulting a unicorn. As you are a maiden, they are honor-bound to answer you."

"Really, Ember?" said Lucy. "Unicorns don't exist. They are mythological creatures. Their supernatural abilities are just stupid myths."

Ember gave Lucy one of her dangerously long looks, and one of her thoughtful blinks.

Lucy swallowed and said weakly, "Listen, I've grown up with dragon lessons, but even at school, they tell us unicorns aren't real. Flying dragons? I can understand that. The wings are right there. But fire-breathing? Don't get me wrong. I'm relieved to know that was just a stupid myth, too!"

Suddenly, Lucy felt the whip-steel strength of Ember's tail wrap around her waist, and felt the immense pressure of suddenly being lifted straight up in the air. The optimistic part of Lucy's brain made a mental note to self to delete the phrase "Stupid myth!" from her vocabulary, especially when she was anywhere near a dragon. The poncho billowed like a horrible, rustling parachute and Lucy instinctively grabbed and pulled it close. As she began to fall Lucy was treated to an all-too-close-up view of the edge of the world, which went a long way down before the crumbled stones and icy waters would swallow her up. She drew breath for a scream, but before she could make a sound of her own, Ember's tail pulled her close, and she found herself pulled tight against Ember's throat, secure again in Ember's claw. The dragon's body was not just solid, but warm. Very warm. In fact, it grew steadily uncomfortable, like being cuddled by a teakettle about to boil, and when Lucy risked a look, she saw that Ember's throat was actually glowing.

She felt it when the dragon began to exhale, and from Ember's mouth shot a stream of white-hot flame. The dragon fire streaked out on a blindingly bright path over the edge of the cliff, across the water, and with pinpoint delicacy, melted the stones on one side of one of the sea stacks into solid glass. Ember turned her head slightly, drew another breath, and Lucy turned, too, to watch the dragon blow a second stream of flame, this one less full of condensed fury, so that it could rebound artfully off the reflective surface of the melted stone, crashing down against the churning waters below, where it made a spectacular geyser of steam. With her other claw, Ember lifted a stone the size of a football and showed it to Lucy. With a glance and a raised eyebrow, Ember indicated a shrub clinging to another stack even farther across the water. Once she was certain Lucy was looking in the correct direction, Ember pursed her lips as if she were about to whistle.

Instead, she threw the stone in her claw and at the same time, blew out a ribbon of flame. The rock arced up and over the water, and the flame chased after it. The fire was merely orange now, no bigger around than Lucy's wrist, but Lucy could feel the heat of it like a sunburn. The flame hit the rock and ricocheted back, incinerating the shrub, which was easily a good hundred feet away.

"Sometimes," Ember said gently. "We don't breathe our fire because we don't want to. It doesn't mean the fire isn't real."

Ember's claw uncurled from around Lucy's waist. For a long,

very long, moment, the world, the waves, the bees, and even the birds in the distant forest were absolutely silent, giving Lucy all the time she needed to realize how much power the dragon actually had, and the way she had taken great care to show it off without actually putting Lucy in any danger.

"Er," said Lucy. "Nice flame."

"Thank you."

"And, uh, very nice demonstration of mythological abilities."

"Thank you, again."

"When you think about it, there really is nothing stupid about being able to breathe fire."

"I'm glad you think so."

"I can think of hundreds of ways it could be useful.'"

"That's the way I've always considered it."

"So," Lucy said briskly. "Now we're going to see a not at all mythological unicorn!"

"If that's okay with you?"

Dragons have expressive eyebrows when arched.

"Oh, no-no. I mean yes. Yes. Excellent plan."

Mollified Ember nodded and gathered herself up, wings outspread to a formidable degree, and stretched out her claw to catch Lucy up and fly away.

Lucy stepped back in a hurry. "Err… excuse me," she said. "I don't mean to complain, but it is rather chilly flying with you in all that wind."

Ember looked at Lucy. "For something not a complaint, it certainly sounded like one," the dragon said.

Lucy was about to apologize, to deny it outright even, but then shut her mouth with a determined snap. "Fine then, it is a complaint. When you fly, I get cold, and I get things in my eyes." Lucy squared her shoulders. Dragons weren't the only ones who could have attitude. "We shall walk to the unicorns. I decree it! I am princess!"

Ember gave Lucy a thoughtful look. "Human princesses do a lot of walking, do they?"

"Oh yes, the palace is quite large and in most places we are not allowed to take the ponies at all. I'll just pack up here." Bending down, Lucy used the shroud to wrap all the strange contents together, and tied it around her shoulder, as sort of a sling. It worked, and didn't take long, which was for the best. Lucy did not want to lose momentum.

"Walking is really quite simple," she said. "Like this, see?" Proud of her own initiative, Lucy began to stride confidently in a way she imagined capable of leading countless armies and parades to all kinds of fates. The dragon sat and watched, silently. That wasn't important. What was important, in Lucy's mind, was moving away from the edge of the cliff.

After a hundred yards or so, just as she reached the first shade of the first trees of what loomed impressively like a forest, she turned and glared over her shoulder at the dragon. Ember hadn't moved. She still sat with her tail coiled around her front claws, as if she had been mesmerized by such an expert display of pedestrianism.

"Well?" Lucy demanded. "What are you waiting for?"

With a small cough the dragon turned her head to the northwest, where two monolithic chunks of granite stood pale against the dark trees, one of them on either side of what was clearly an actual path through the wood.

"I knew that," Lucy said, with more spirit than honesty. "I was just making sure that you knew the way." She realized she was sounding a great deal more like a Lucinda than a Lucy in that moment, and lifted her chin, waved a hand in a more friendly way, and added: "Come along. We're burning daylight."

It was one of her father's favorite expressions. Thinking of him, of home, made Lucy have to blink hard and force back some unworthy tears. There wasn't time to miss her parents, she told herself, and it wasn't a good idea to miss a family who didn't do anything to try and rescue you from your fate. You had to rescue yourself.

After she'd seen that the Princess had a fair handle on the correct direction, Ember hopped into the air and landed close to Lucy. Glad she didn't have to be brave entirely by herself, Lucy politely affected not to notice the rain of sticks and pebbles caused by the landing of a graceful and delicate, but still ballroom-sized, being in the forest. Ember stood still and watched as Lucy continued to walk away. Then Ember hopped again, showering Lucy with more sticks and pebbles. Determined not to notice, Lucy pressed her lips together and continued to march, despite the slight ache blooming in her calves and thighs, which were not opposed to walking, as a concept, but had absolutely no experience with rough terrain over a long distance as a practical matter.

The path grew narrower. It wound in and around the trees, and then weeds and brush seemed to take it over. When Ember next leaped and landed with accompanying cascade of sticks and pebbles, again, she said: "I think we need to veer off a little to the west."

"Thank you." Lucy said with precision.

Another hundred yards, another leap, another landing, and the accompanying shower of debris. Ember took a breath and nodded her chin towards a burly oak tree. She said, "You need to go more over that way a little bit."

"Thank you." said Lucy in a voice that was part sing-song and part "off with their heads." "I think I have got this now," and she picked up her pace.

Another hundred yards. Another leap. Another landing.

Another shower. Ember took a breath, but before she could say anything, Lucy said, "Would you please quit it with the sticks and pebbles? Please? How do you expect anyone to get any place while being bombarded by forest bits every ten feet?"

Lucy felt a little better. It was good to snarl at someone, standing her ground instead of trying to be polite. It also felt good to just be standing! Her legs were seriously regretting agreeing to accompany her on this journey to the mythical (sorry real, very real, definitely real) unicorn-town.

"I'm sorry." Ember shuffled away from Lucy, and her enormous, expressive face looked more than a little embarrassed. "These trees are so close together, I'd knock them down if I tried to walk between them, and it just seemed kinder to not destroy the forest and make these little hops. I can see it makes you uncomfortable." She looked as sheepish as a dragon could, and Lucy, taking the cue, brushed acorns and leaves out of her hair.

Ember said, "I was thinking. Maybe I could fly holding you in my claw, and we could use some the big leaves or a piece of bark to keep the wind off you."

Lucy looked at Ember. She really did seem to be sorry. Part of being a good princess was knowing when to let other people help you, she realized. Lucy smiled. "Well, yes. That would be acceptable to me," she said. "Thank you."

And it turned out that figuring out which tree had bark one could peel in a solid enough chunk to be any good as a shield, and just how many pine boughs would make sufficient insulation against the wind, was rather fun. Ember was very good at peeling trees, and her claws were surprisingly deft. Lucy taught her how to weave the pine branches into wreathes, and soon they were both sporting crowns of forest green, and giggling and joking with one another in a way that came surprisingly easy.

"Look! I am Jane of the Jungle!"

"You look like a slug with a very sturdy shell."

"We call those snails," said Lucy, whose lofty tone was spoiled entirely by giggles.

"This particular frond," said Ember, who was learning a lofty tone of her own, "will give you most elegant fangs."

"I vant to suck your blood," said Lucy obligingly. Then she stopped and gave Ember a worried look. "Wait, are vampires real, too?"

Ember shook her head. "No, those really are made-up. I've never seen a real one, not at any of the magical creatures union meetings, or even my parents' coffee hours."

"Because I wouldn't want to make fun of one of your friends."

"I know," said Ember.

Lucy suddenly giggled. "I can't help but wonder what sort of teeth a vampire might have, if it wanted to drink dragon blood."

"Sharp ones," said Ember, giggling, too.

"Fireproof," suggested Lucy. "Dis blood ees too hot. Owie. I vill drink eet cold. On dee rocks even."

Ember laughed, and was struck with new inspiration. "Here, let me wrap you totally up."

"Oh, I am a mummy." Lucy held out her arms straight in front of her again, and her voice dropped an octave. She paused. "Oh, are those—"

"Historical, but not mythological, and definitely not anyone I've met." Ember snorted scornfully, accompanied by a little puff of disdainful smoke. "Mummies," she said.

Lucy held out her arms again. "I'm the stupidest monster ever because this is as fast as I can go and all I can do is moan and nudge you with my hands. Very scary."

"Oh no. Oh no," said Ember, in mock distress, and in a voice several octaves higher than normal. "I am being pursued by a bandage-encrusted moaning thing that might eventually touch me. Oh, the terror! Oh, the horror! Whatever shall I do?"

Waving her front claws in a dramatic and Princess-worthy fashion, Ember flipped on her back in the middle of a convenient meadow, and very carefully rocked back and forth. "I am doomed! DOOMED!"

Lucy lumbered against Ember, hitting her with her outstretched hands.

"DOOMED," wailed Ember. "And I am being nudged by a mummy."

Lucy moaned and giggled, bumping into Ember like a wind-up toy hitting a wall.

"DOOMED," giggled Ember.

"Know the terror of the mummy," intoned Lucy.

This went on for quite longer than it really needed to.

Later, bundled up safe and secure in Ember's claw, Lucy took a moment to meet her new friend's warm gaze.

"I'm sorry I said you couldn't really breathe fire," she said.

"That's all right," said Ember. "I'm sorry I said you were just litter."

"That's all right," said Lucy.

And then, they were off to meet the unicorns, which were not mythological or stupid at all.

Chapter Seven
In Pursuit

"Greetings, Champion! We at the World Health Alliance for Damsel Safety (WHADS) welcome you into our elite corps of educated bodyguards, beauticians, and wellness coaches. Your aptitude scores have already placed you in the top 5% of student applicants in terms of scholastic and athletic achievement. With the full payment of your tuition, you will have access to a caliber of training that will pave the way to not only a unique and fulfilling career with the archaic nobility of our great nation, but which offers you a chance to mentally and physically excel.

"WHADS is unique in the Healthcare Services world in that our students engage in the vigorous pursuit of excellence in academics and art, as well as the customary dedication to sports and medicine. Whether your calling is to reassure a fading queen that she is still the fairest of them all, or to keep a despotic emperor in gilded splendor, our courses will see to it that you have the confidence of knowing you are top of your craft, and worth every penny of the exorbitant fees you charge (5% of which shall be the modest fee rendered back to the WHADS Alumni Fund as testament to your gratitude). As a bodyguard or a masseuse, a Chief Torturer, or Chief Seneschal, you will know you are ready to provide your local monarch with an exceptional degree of unwavering support. It's not for nothing that people have looked at our graduates and said, 'What a WHAD!'

"If, after the completion of your training program, you desire further study and glory, WHADS is one of only two institutions on this continent licensed in the training of Kindred Noble, Intervention and Guardianship of Heirs in Trouble (KNIGHTs). These specially trained infantry and calvary units are famous for their televised appearances during the Lottery Seaside Festival and Sacrifice, but few realize they are also employed amongst the nobility as long-term bodyguards, warlords, assassins, and chiropractors. We only accept the top applicants into this prestigious graduate program, but invite you to awaken the sense of Honor within you and Apply Yourself...."

George folded up the much-thumbed page into his wallet, and stuck the wallet into his back pocket. He felt a little bit stupid poring over the old acceptance letter, but he'd also minored in Sentimentalism, so it seemed appropriate to take a few minutes while they were setting camp to look over the mementos he carried with him to remind him of how far he'd come. He wasn't a spindly little bookworm anymore. Six years of blood, sweat, and tears, combined with healthy calisthenics and an earnest desire to do the best that he could in any situation, had brought George to a broad-shouldered, well-moussed sort of ease with himself, and given him a plethora of usefully archaic trivia to call upon in need, and also somehow, miraculously gotten him to the top of his class.

His mother would have been very proud. But George had been thoroughly instilled with a sense of responsibility for WHADS, and had respectfully accepted the assignment to accompany Chip Blitherington — himself a graduate of the four-year program — on a mission to rescue Chip's true love. George didn't see it himself. The Princess was only a girl, and the girl was (by all accounts) just a girl. Admittedly, he didn't read the society papers much. He had too many pushups to do, generally. But what his mother used to say to him on their weekly phone calls had indicated that the Princess Lucinda was subject to an unfortunately chronic case of foot-in-mouth disease.

Naturally, since she had been chosen in the lottery, the media had been flooded with any and every camera shots they could find of her, and interviews by people who vaguely knew her. George didn't begrudge the camera-people and yet he couldn't help but feel sorry for a young girl no one but Chip Blitherington seemed to know well enough to like.

Feeling sorry for Lottery Winners was encouraged among the Knights. Granted, part of George's pity was engendered by having been in Chip's company for much, much too long. He had done everything short of actively peeing on the young woman in public to try and stake his claim upon her hand. He would let none of the other Knights or even any of the other members of the Nobility within arm's length of the Princess.

Perhaps it was just her proximity to the throne, but George had an idea that at least some of it might have to do with her Ugly Duckling sort of bearing. There was always the potential (though it wasn't realized as often as people wished) that she might grow into her scraggly hair and stick-out ears, and become ravishing. It hadn't happened yet, but George was willing to give the girl another ten years of hormones and the benefit of the doubt. Maybe Chip had noticed the way Lucinda's eyes, behind the thick glasses, were sky blue. Maybe he'd noticed that the color of her hair was the same shade as melted brown sugar, when you poured it over your mother's perfectly made oatmeal on a cold morning.

"Did you dig the latrine yet, good chap?" asked Chip, breaking in on George's musing.

George looked up, blinking a little at the intrusion of reality on his Sentimentality. He didn't get up, but remained crouched by the new-lit campfire. It was considered poor manners to punch your teammates in the schnoz, and George had gotten top grades in Manners.

"Not yet," he said. "Do you need something that the side of a tree can't provide?" A full latrine seemed overly intricate for a quick camp, and they'd all seen the dragon fly off with Princess Lucinda (the someday could-be-fair) in its vile grip. "We'll be leaving at first light, and need to get all the rest we can."

"Yes, yes," said Chip. "Before the girl's been given place of honor in the animal's larder. I understand. The thing is, George, I really do need to take a dump."

George got to his feet and went into the brush with the shovel, reflecting that it was just as well a knight wasn't encouraged to judge a book by the number of times it crapped in the woods. Constipation, he reminded himself, was not the hallmark of nobility, but it certainly had an upside in the field.

After a longer pause than would typically be considered appropriate, or even comfortable given the circumstances, Chip returned from the latrine with a thoughtful expression on his face.

"Say fellows," he began, "I had a thought."

This was unusual enough to make Agent X actually look up from his notebook.

"Oh, a thought," he said. "How did you recognize it?"

"Oh, you know, it has a beginning, middle, end. Premises, hypothesis, conclusion. All in one coherent package. You know, a thought." Chip looked about expectantly. "Thingie," he added, somewhat undercutting his authority.

Agent X and George looked at each other. They were stuck in the woods and there was nothing else, really, to talk about. George mentally drew the short straw. "What was your thought, Chip?"

"Thanks for asking, old chap. It all started when I was sort of wondering what we are all doing here."

George said, "In an existential way?"

Chip looked blank. "Not ringing any cognitive bells."

Agent X said patiently, "Like, what is the meaning of life?"

Chip gave it a try, then shook his head from side to side. "Sorry. A bit like rubbing two damp sticks together. No spark. No matter."

"No," said George.

"Well, this was my thought," said Chip. "Here we are, going after this Lucinda chappess. Yes?"

"To rescue her," said George

"And to get her signature," said Agent X.

"Indeed, but why has this Lucinda not already been et? That's the truly remarkably thing!"

"Well..." said Agent X.

"She's been taken away," said George.

"Whisked away," clarified Agent X, with some hurried scribbling.

"Kidnapped and taken to suffer a fate worse than death, probably to add her bones to the dragon's treasure pile to serve as a grisly warning to others who dare try and challenge their destiny." George was a quick study.

"Or to be fed to the little baby dragons back at the lair." Agent X had a competitive streak.

"I daresay," said Chip, who wasn't following their discussion, but waiting placidly for his turn at the conversational wheel. "But there is another alternative. It seems this Lucinda princess was something of a firecracker, loose cannon sort, yes?"

"Yes." George allowed, but with reluctance, as the idea of

Lucinda as a loose cannon did not mesh well with his idea of what princesses in general were meant to be.

"I suppose," said Agent X, who had met the young lady, and also was really regretting that he hadn't thought up 'loose cannon' for himself. "I wonder if 'unbridled spirit' would work as well," he thought.

"It's only that every time we have seen Lucinda and the dragon together, it doesn't seem that she is under any restraint at all." said Chip.

"We only saw them from a distance," pointed out George.

"And then, they were flying away," said Agent X. "Who knows how much struggling she did, while clenched in the grip of those rapacious claws." He began to scribble again.

"Yes, yes," Chip waved his hands ineffectually in the air. "The point is, we have never seen her tied up since the sacrificial pole. We haven't heard her scream. As far as we can tell, she has made no attempt to escape." Chip was indignant, and resembled in that moment something like a very thoroughly manicured poodle trying to prove itself a real dog by staying en pointe.

"Exactly what are you saying?" George asked.

"Maybe instead of being kidnapped by the dragon, Princess Lucinda is escaping with the dragon?" Chip asked. "Why do you think she might do that? It certainly makes me wonder."

"That is one of the stupidest ideas that I have ever heard," said George, turning back to the fire in disgust.

"That seems to be a bit harsh," said Agent X.

"Might as well suggest that the Princess has kidnapped the dragon," George said.

"Why would Princess Lucinda want to run away with a dragon?" asked Agent X.

"Dragons eat princesses; everyone knows that," said George.

"But this one hasn't, don't you see?" Chip persisted.

"What about the liquified rocks we found this morning along the coast?" asked George. "And there were definite signs of a struggle in the forest."

"Actually, Chip has a point," Agent X said. "There is a seldom invoked sub-clause of Dragon-Human Accord that allows for just such a contingency."

George felt like everyone around him was going nuts. Chip thinking? Agent X agreeing with him? "The contingency where the dragon inexplicably decides not to eat the maiden and carries her off to who knows where instead?"

"Precisely."

"But just because there is an official form for it, doesn't mean that it's true in this specific instance," George said.

"Of course not, but why hasn't she escaped? We've been following her for three days now and haven't seen a sign of struggle, a smoke signal, or even heard the echo of a call for help. Why? We know they've landed, but she hasn't even piled up rocks in a cunning arrow-shape to help us track her," Chip said. He didn't seem triumphant, just confused by this fact.

"Nonsense," said George. "Of course, she is kidnapped. She is a Princess with a Dragon. Any other story is just madness."

"Well," Chip said. "From where I sit, I think it's an open question until we see a pile of bones and a burping dragon."

"Well, listen Knighties," said Agent X. "We won't be able to resolve this tonight. Let's get some sleep and go princess hunting—"

"Rescuing," said George.

"Pursuing," said Chip.

"Tomorrow," said Agent X.

Margit Elland Schmitt & Dan McLaughlin

Chapter Eight
Headlines

Message series from the Royal Library Newspaper Archives:

PRINCESS LUCINDA KIDNAP VICTIM OR???

SPECULATION SWIRLS ABOUT WHY SHE HASN'T BEEN ET YET.

"SHE REALLY COULDN'T BE THAT BAD TASTING," ONE EXPERT EXPLAINS.

"GOD, YOU ARE SUCH AN IDIOT!" EXPLAINS ANOTHER.

GOD IS NOT AN IDIOT, ONE EXPERT ASSERTS.

I PUT A COMMA THERE, ASSWIPE. PAY ATTENTION.

ROYAL HERALDS INSIST THAT SHE IS THE VICTIM HERE.

SHE THE PRINCESS, NOT SHE THE GOD.

PALACE UNABLE TO PRODUCE SHROUD.

GALLUPED POLL SAYS THAT 37% BELIEVE PRINCESS

LUCINDA IS "IN" ON IT.

"IT" NOT CLEARLY THOUGHT THROUGH, ALL SIDES AGREE.

OF THE 37% WHO THINK "IT", 84% ASSERT THEIR RIGHT TO THINK "IT", "NO MATTER WHAT."

THE REST ARE UNSURE, OR DON'T QUITE UNDERSTAND THE QUESTION.
OR THINK THAT PEOPLE WHO ASK POLL QUESTIONS JUST MAKE IT ALL UP ANYWAYS.

PALACE BLAMES THE MEDIA.

Chapter Nine
The Unicorn King

Secure in Ember's claws, protected by a shield of wood and pine, Lucy had forgotten fear and uncertainty. She had, in fact, fallen asleep, sure that her friend would never drop her. She was still pretty tired. Being sacrificed, dragged through a wind-tunnel for hours, and then hiking through a forest for most of a day could really take it out of you. She wondered what had changed enough to wake her up. When she felt as much as heard the subsonic rumble of Ember's chuckle, Lucy realized she was being talked to

She mentally shook herself awake and looked around. Being carried by a flying dragon, she thought, is pretty fun.

"WHAT?" she yelled. "WHAT did you say?"

Ember did what Lucy was beginning to think of as "the twisty thing" and brought her face close to Lucy's. "We're almost there."

"Oh, okay." As much as she could, Lucy stretched.

Ember landed. This was much more comfortable when you were in the dragon's care than when you were just standing next to the dragon. Almost cushiony. Hey, I could get used to this, Lucy thought.

Gently, Ember deposited Lucy on the ground and stood still as Lucy tried to remember how her own legs were supposed to work. They were still protesting after an unwelcome day of hiking in the woods, and then an extended dangle, but after a few moments, seemed to have decided to give her another chance. Clenching one of Ember's claws for support, Lucy asked, "Where are we?"

"We are in the Pasture of Perpetual Wisdom," said Ember. "This is the safe sanctuary of the unicorns."

Curious, Lucy peeked between the talons. A gently sloping meadow was generously dotted with shade trees and wildflowers. The greenery rolled away from her startled gaze. Sparkling pools and burbling streams dotted the meadow. She definitely detected a waterfall or two.

"It's beautiful," whispered Lucy, too awed to speak out loud.

Something came towards them, capturing her attention, as well it might. A unicorn was cantering through the meadow, his sturdy hooves beating a strong tattoo that resonated through the ground beneath their feet, but was still gentle enough not to disturb the blossoms of even the smallest wildflowers. Lucy found herself trembling as the magnificent creature approached.

"Relax," Ember whispered. "It will be okay." But Lucy could tell her dragon friend was nervous, too. When a dragon trembles, you notice. Holding Ember's talon, she waited for the unicorn to arrive.

The unicorn, a starry white, jammed his forelegs into the soft turf before them. He reared up onto his powerful hind legs, and tossed his gleaming mane. His horn, his crowning glory, was bright gold, and seemed to attract sunbeams, which wanted to glitter on it. He came to rest, looking at Ember and Lucy with infinitely wise eyes. He exhaled in a particularly thoughtful manner.

It was all the girls could do to restrain from applauding. Instead, they swooned.

"Welcome, Esmeraldavinia." The deep, majestic voice didn't so much sully the air as gracefully waft itself into their ears.

"You know my name?" asked Ember.

The unicorn nodded his regal head. His eyes were warm, as if he knew every one of the dragon's faults, from her ticklish temper to her prickly tail, and still accepted her, just as she was. "Of course."

Ember bowed her head. Lucy stared. She'd never seen her friend at a disadvantage before.

The unicorn brought his gaze over to Lucy, and she felt the weight of it like a golden blanket, priceless, heavy, irresistible. "And this must be Princess Lucinda Merrie Periwinkle Grottweiler Rotunda Doorstop,"

"Yes, Your Unicorness." She dropped a perfect curtsey, one that would have surprised her tutors.

"The one with the glasses. Such a long title, to encumber one so young."

His chuckle was warm and inclusive. Both girls felt welcome and at peace. Whatever was going to happen to them here, a quick, shared glance confirmed they both agreed they weren't in any danger. From behind the King of the Unicorns, for this is who it must surely be, came the sound of a slightly less thunderous rumble of hooves, and a splaying of turf. Then a pure voice, rich and sweet as honey, spoke.

"Who is it, Daddy?" she asked. "Who is it, who is it; is it a dragon? A real dragon? May I see? May I see?" From the sound of it, whoever owned the voice was actually bouncing up and down.

With the grace of infinite wisdom, the King of Unicorns stepped aside to reveal: "My daughter, Connie." Connie was a unicorn foal, as delicate as a fawn and as bright as a sunbeam, with a mane like silken joy, laughing, long-lashed eyes, and hindquarters dappled with what were probably, technically, the equivalent of unicorn freckles — radiant spots along her withers and backside, somehow combining adorableness and magical beauty in a way that made Lucy involuntarily say: "Awh!"

The unicorn filly didn't notice. "Oh! Oh! Oh!" she was saying, her delight punctuated by the height of her bounces. "It truly is a dragon. Oh, and a human too?" Lucy felt herself blushing, and feeling as if somehow, against all odds, she were as impressive as Ember. "Oh, Daddy," said the unicorn filly. "Just look at how hungry they are!"

Lucy felt her face go hot, but it was true. Her stomach was probably growling loud enough to be mistaken for a dragon. Her last meal had been her "last meal" before being tied up at the post, and that had been a long, long time ago. True, she had granola and applesauce, but in all the flying and fear and chaos, there hadn't been time to tuck in for a bite.

"Be wise, my heart," said the Unicorn King. "These maidens came of their own will, to ask for help, wisdom, and guidance." His gaze was kind. "And so we should treat them gently. A picnic would not come amiss. After all, these are our guests," said the Unicorn King, and he bent his powerful neck to nuzzle his foal with undisguised fondness.

"I wish I could manifest the food for them." Briefly Connie hung her head and her tail drooped. It had to be said that even her regret was adorable, but her father touched her gently with his horn and she brightened right back up.

"Allow me," the King said, and made a gesture with the tip of his horn.

For a moment, light seemed to hang in the air, the pattern that he had traced, and then, it dispersed, and became a blanket upon the ground, and two bowls. One was clearly for Ember, because it was the size of a wading pool. The other was for Lucy. Both of them were filled to the brim with salad.

"Thank you!" said Ember in delight.

"Yes, it's wonderful!" said Lucy, and it was, probably, the best salad in the world. Not just lettuce, but every kind of green mixed together with citrus, apples, and berries, which blended together to make a sweet sort of dressing, and there were crunchy bits, too, nuts and carrots. Lucy realized about halfway through the bowl that there hadn't been any forks included, but the unicorns didn't seem to mind that she was eating with her hands, or that she had to wipe her face and fingers on the picnic cloth afterwards. The King and Connie simply admired the enthusiasm of their guests, and the unicorns politely grazed on the brilliant meadow blossoms nearby until Ember and Lucy were finished.

"That's better, isn't it?" The King asked, whisking the picnic blanket and the empty bowls away with a tiny gesture of his horn. Ember was nodding, clearly glad to have had her salad at last, and Lucy couldn't stop smiling.

"Yes, thank you, Your Majesty. I didn't realize how hungry I was, but I feel much better now."

"And now, we can move on to the purpose for your visit. You seek the wisdom of the unicorns," said the King.

Lucy got to her feet, which seemed a good beginning, only then, she stalled. "I don't know the right way to do this," she said.

"Worry not about the form of the question, my child, for truth can reach us on many different paths. Ask us what you will, and we will render what aid we may." The Unicorn King was calm and serene in a way that Lucy's father, who was always overworked and preoccupied, would have admired. Just behind his withers, Connie gave a twitter of anticipation through her horn. It sounded like a baby bird.

"Okay," said Lucy. She drew a breath, and then untied the shroud, which had become a sling, from around her shoulder. At home, Lucy knew her place in the family hierarchy. She wasn't oldest or youngest, but muddled in the middle. Unfortunately, Lucy was self-effacing enough to find herself, in all practical ways, last in line. This was especially true when it came to conversation. In Lucy's experience, if you wanted to be heard, you had to get to the point quickly. "Ember was drafted, and I was sacrificed, and we got this stuff, do you see?"

She lay everything out onto the emerald grass of the meadow. "We don't know what it's meant for, and we don't know who gave it to us. It's like a puzzle and one of the pieces clearly doesn't fit," said Lucy. "Water bottle, poncho — I'm wearing that part — insoles, flashlight, granola, applesauce, and… girdle."

The King of the Unicorns and his daughter studied the pile. They seemed grave, and said nothing, and Lucy felt obliged to fill the silence.

"So we think the girdle is the outlier, but we're not quite sure of it, and if it is, what does that mean? We were kinda hoping that…" Lucy trailed off, and as the unicorns were still involved with the collection of tchotchkes, risked trading a glance with Ember.

The dragon looked as uncertain and confused as she felt.

"An intriguing question," said the Unicorn King, almost after they'd despaired of a reply. "One well worthy of contemplation." At the very least, he sounded intrigued. "Flashlight, poncho, water bottle, insoles, granola, applesauce, and a girdle."

Lucy shifted her weight nervously from foot to foot. She couldn't help but notice that Ember was doing the same thing.

"Connie," the deep voice filled the air. "You are several hundred years old." The King looked with infinite fondness at his daughter. "It is time for you to demonstrate your wisdom."

"Goody!" said Connie. "Oh, thank you, Daddy! Thank you!" Connie began to prance in a circle, swinging her mane and tail. With every step she took, flowers bloomed upon the ground and stardust sprinkled from her silver horn. The effect was just the tiniest bit spoiled by the fact that she was singing, too.

"I get to be wise. I get to be wise. I get to be wise."

It wasn't that the little unicorn's voice wasn't tuneful. It was. It was like a flute, a harp, or some other musical instrument where even the most incorrect notes couldn't help but sound beautiful.

"I get to be wi-ise! Oh, I get to be wi-ise. Oh, I get to be wi-ise." Somehow the song had morphed into a rhumba and Connie was prancing about waving her tail in time to her beat.

"Connie…"

Her enthusiasm, which was youthful and charming, and so earnestly given with the whole of her heart, made it so that one couldn't help but love her, even if one were, at the same time, searching for a few wads of cotton to stuff into one's ears for just a tiny moment of silence.

"I get to be so wise. So wise, wise, wise. I get to be so-so wise." Now, a tango.

"CONNIE…"

The little unicorn paused, mid-prance. There was a breath of peace. "Sorry, Daddy." But Lucy couldn't help but notice that the way she said it made it obvious that she knew without a shadow of a doubt that her father would love her beyond any fault or error. She adored the little unicorn in that moment, and she envied her, and she shoved the uncomfortable conflict of emotion down under the more pressing business at hand.

The Unicorn King said, "Please, dear. A moment's thought while you study the mysteries before you."

"Yes, Daddy," said Connie. She stared intently at the pile of stuff Lucy had put onto the ground, concentrating so hard that her little horn began to fizz and give off sparks. Abruptly, her posture changed. Her head shot up, "Eureka!" she squealed in delight.

"That means I've got it," she added kindly, for anyone who might not understand. Her mane shimmered through the air, a ripple of delight. "A stick in time save nine," Connie cried triumphantly.

"Stitch, honey," said the Unicorn King.

Connie didn't miss a beat, but proclaimed, "With these ingredients and a decent length of vine, you could make a telephone system for your fifth-grade science project. I do believe you'd get an A! So wise! Oh, so wise! Wise-oh!" And she rhumba'd away.

The unicorn, dragon, and human watched in silence, as Connie danced away.

"Infinite wisdom does not always come easily." The deep voice filled the two girls' brains with a gentle sigh.

Lucy exchanged a glance with Ember, and then gave her respectful attention back to the King. "I can't help but notice most of these things would be useful if someone was going on a journey."

"Really?" asked Connie, suddenly back at her father's side, her big, dark eyes gone wide with delighted surprise. "How is that, exactly?"

"Well, they are things you could eat, and drink," suggested Lucy. "Things that could keep your body warm, or protect your feet."

"I didn't know that humans ate flashlights," said Connie with real delight. "Did you, Daddy? Daddy, did you?" Connie bounced delightedly on all four hooves. "I bet you already knew that, Daddy. You are pretty wise."

"No," said Lucy hurriedly, while the King of the Unicorns maintained a dignified and noble bearing, fondly gazing down at his young daughter and definitely not rolling his austere eyes, even the littlest bit. It was an amazing display of self-control, thought Lucy. "Not the flashlight. That's to help people see in the dark."

"You can't do that anyway?" Ember and Connie asked in unison, several vast octaves apart.

"No, human sorts of people can't, and we don't eat grass," Lucy added quickly, as she sensed Connie was revving up for another question. She directed her attention back to the king. "I thought at first that these things were meant for the Knights to find... um... afterward. But that doesn't make sense."

"Mmm?" the Unicorn King rumbled encouragingly. Lucy plunged on.

"Because they come from the local garrison. I mean, if they were successful and killed poor Ember on the beach, just like previous Knights had killed her brothers ...." Lucy put a hand on Ember's claw, offering what she knew was only a thimble-sized comfort. "They wouldn't need to sneak away by night. They'd be made into heroes and could pretty much parade back tootling on trumpets."

"I wish I could tootle!" said Connie, wistfully.

"You will someday, dearest," said the Unicorn King.

"Oh, joy!" said Connie. Lucy reflected with suitable awe that she was probably the first human being ever to actually witness what a baby unicorn looked like when gamboling in honest delight. It was every bit as heartwarming and adorable as one had any right to expect.

"They were made for you," said Ember, suddenly. She leaned her big head down to more closely examine the items spilled on the ground. Her expressive, dark eyes were twice as big as the humble pile of stuff. "You were put out there before the sun was up. They always litter the beach in the dark — probably so the authorities don't catch them at it."

"Again," said Lucy. "Not litter."

"I thought you were the authority," said Connie to Ember. "Just think! You might have got applesauce with your maiden meat, if you hadn't been such a picky eater." A butterfly had landed on the tip of her silvery horn. In the awkward silence that followed, the butterfly opened and shut its wings a few times in a picturesque way, and then fluttered off.

Ember said, "I'm guessing someone hoped you would be able to untie yourself and sneak away before dawn."

Connie pranced over to join the inspection of the goods. "Then you would really need the flight-lash."

"Flashlight," said Lucy.

"Yes, that," said Connie, with honest gratitude for having been given the correct word. "You'd need it to help you not fall into a lake."

"Unless I were just going home." said Lucy.

"And the food so that you didn't starve to death on the way," said Connie.

"But my kingdom is right there at the lake. I should have had plenty of time to walk back without starving," Lucy said.

"Whoever left these things didn't think you'd be going home," said Ember.

"About that," said Connie. "Why aren't you?" To their blank stares, she gave a flick of her silken mane and one of her direct, supernaturally adorable smiles. "Why aren't you going home?"

Lucy hesitated, and shared another glance with Ember. It was surprisingly easy to share an intimate glance, even with a creature several times her own size. Neither of them wanted to be the one to shatter the young unicorn's innocence.

The silence stretched out. In the end, her father, the Unicorn King, had to break it. "Because, my heart," he said gently. "Her parents were the ones who arranged for our young friend to be tied up on the beach in order to be eaten by a dragon."

There was a horrified pause. "That wasn't very nice, was it,

Daddy?" whispered Connie.

Her father was likewise quiet. "We cannot know the reasons for others' choices if they do not tell us," he said. "We can only judge their actions."

"You would never do that to me, would you, Daddy?" asked Connie.

"No, I would not," said her father.

"Unless," said Lucy, with the clipped precision of suppressed emotion. "Unless you thought it might save the lives of everyone in the kingdom?"

The King's response was lost as Connie nodded, a surprisingly brisk move for such a graceful, supernatural creature. "It's a sad story, and needs a happy ending. This is what I'll do. I'll go along with them and help them find the place where they are going. It will be an adventure, and we'll become the best of friends. I can eat all the grass, and Lucy can eat all the applesauce and lat-fishes."

"Flashlights, and I don't..."

"And Ember will have to find something new to eat besides maidens," Connie blithely concluded.

"Well," rumbled Ember, rubbing her scaly jaw in meditative thought, or possibly hunger. "Besides a good salad, I've always been fond of chili peppers and chocolates."

"Huzzah!" said Connie, and celebrated the new menu by kicking up her heels until glitter rained down all around her hooves. "We shall be happy as moonbeams! You don't mind me going, Daddy, do you?" she added, nuzzling up to her regal father and touching her horn to his in what (Lucy guessed) was a version of a unicorn kiss.

"It will be a long and dangerous journey," he said.

"Danger grows your wisdom," said Connie.

"It does?" asked Lucy, surprised.

"Oh, yes," said Connie. "It gives you memories of how bad danger is and why you don't want to be in it anymore, which is wise. You also get to find out whether you are brave or cowardly. I hope I'm brave, don't you?"

"We don't even know where to go," pointed out Ember. "Or how long it will take to get wherever it is."

"We'll be going to the Hall of Wizards, won't we?" said Connie, genuinely astonished that anyone might choose to go anywhere else.

"Will we?" asked Lucy. She looked at Ember. "Do you know where that is?"

Ember nodded her gigantic head, but with obvious reluctance. "Only in the most general terms," she said. "But it's supposed to be a long, difficult journey, and my parents always said it was better to stay away from it entirely. I'm not really sure I understand why we even would want to try to go there."

"We have to go," said Connie. "To see if one of them wizards put the magic spell on the girdle."

"What magic spell?" asked Lucy and Ember together.

"It's all covered in magic," said Connie, frisking over to the pile of goods and turning one of the applesauce tins over with the tip of her horn, as an entomologist might flip an interesting beetle over to see whether or not it had wings. "Everything else is mostly normal, but the girdle is just dripping with magic. I can see magic, can't I, Daddy?"

"It's your natural talent," he said, with understandable pride.

"What about cuteness?" asked Lucy.

Both unicorns turned to look at her. There was a pause, then the King said, "Connie's cuteness is innate."

"At least the water in the bottles isn't poisoned," said Connie. "Did you know unicorns can purify water?"

"Can you tell what the girdle does?" asked Lucy.

"We unicorns can sense poison," Connie assured her. "We can also cure someone who's been poisoned if we dip our horns in —

"But the girdle?" persisted Lucy. "Magic?"

"It's a girdle," said Connie, who switched conversational threads with ease. "It makes things smaller."

Lucy realized that the Unicorn King's ability to not roll his eyes was not born of supernatural patience (i.e. innate), but of long practice (i.e. learned). She took a deep breath, and that helped. Ember, clearly, needed deeper breaths and more practice. Or maybe because her eyes were so big, it was easier to see when they started to roll. To her credit, she didn't seem to mind the wise little unicorn's silly comments. Instead, she bent her head over and touched the girdle with the razor-sharp tip of one claw.

"I suppose it's the elastic," Ember said, but whatever she meant to add to that thought was lost as she suddenly gave a dragon-sized gasp, and a roar.

Things happened very quickly. The girdle moved. It seemed to leap up and wrap itself around Ember's extended claw-tip, to crawl or slither and wrap itself around the dragon's forelimb. The clasps on it were hook-and-loop style, and they moved as fast as snakes striking, fast as squids in the deepest ocean, like tentacles wrapping, catching, holding.

There was a flare of darkness, like a camera flash in reverse, sucking the light out of the air around them, and Ember let loose a fiery breath in self-defense. Lucy, Connie and the King of Unicorns ducked, and the torrent of flame took out a quarter of the forest just behind them. It did Ember no good.

Ember shrank.

One moment, a ballroom-sized dragon stood on the hillside. The next, it was only a sitting-room-sized dragon.

When Lucy felt brave enough to look up from where she crouched near the smoking ruins of the forest, holding her hands up to protect her head and the singed ends of her hair, she saw that Ember was only half the size she had been before, and still getting smaller. As they all watched, horrified, the dragon shrank and shrank again, in fits and bursts. It went on and on, for what seemed a long time, but was really only a minute or two, then the process seemed to be slowing. And then, it seemed to have stopped.

They waited. The dragon, once as big as a house, was now only the size of one of Lucy's sister's spoiled dogs. Everyone stood frozen for a moment, afraid to move, in case it might cause another surge of shrinking. Then, Ember gave a smoky belch, and looked up, and up some more. Her head was on level with Lucy's waist.

"Oh, fewments," said Ember.

"What are fewments?" asked Connie.

"Dragon droppings," Ember explained.

"I feel wiser already," said Connie.

"This is great magic. The only way you will ever find out if your young friend is cursed to remain diminished for the rest of her days," said the King of Unicorns, "is to ask the wizards, for only they know the answer."

"Do you think they will tell us?" asked Lucy. "If they put the girdle in here, they must have wanted the magic spell to work. Why would they want that?"

"There's only one way to find out," said Ember.

"Hooray!" said Connie. "A Quest!"

Chapter Ten
The Unicorn Queen

"That was weird," said Ember, experimentally extending a much smaller foreclaw and then looking up at the concerned faces around her. "I am guessing by the way you are all looking down at me that I have gotten smaller rather than you have all gotten bigger?" She looked directly across at Lucy. "Has your knee always had so many nicks and scabs on it?"

Lucy was afraid, but fourteen years of experience as a princess with sisters had taught her that you could hide just about any feeling, so long as you kept busy. In this case, her specific activity was frantically tugging at the girdle. "That's what I have been trying to tell you, but don't you worry. Oh, Ember, let me just get this stupid girdle off of you. I have opposable thumbs, you know, and I am quite clever with my fingers. Everyone says so. Let's strip this girdle off of you like it… No, that didn't work. Well, maybe we can pull it up over… No. Or down and…" To be honest, she was also babbling. Her fingers fumbled with increasing urgency, but there was no appreciable uptick in results.

"Ember," said Connie. "This magic girdle just snatched you up and shrank you down. It didn't even say please. That is really not very good manners."

"The important thing is not to panic," said Lucy, though she could tell from the tone of her own voice that she was already wobbling on the edge of panic, and looking off over the side. "There, there," she said. "We will get you all nice and big again."

"This girdle made me small?" Ember asked, uncertainly.

"Oh no!" said Connie. "It was the magic the Wizards put in the girdle. I did tell you that a magic girdle would make you small, and here you are. You barely touched it and then zip-zap, thank-you-jack, you were mini-Ember. Well, not before you singed the meadow a tiny bit."

Even Connie could not help but be a little sad as she looked across the burnt landscape, but unicorns can be forgiving creatures. "I expect you were surprised."

"So I'm small now because of the girdle," Ember said, still trying to put the pieces together. Magic, it seemed, could disconcert even the most level-headed dragon.

Lucy flung up her hands in frustration. "This darn thing! It's got way too many of these twisty bits. Girdles are so stupid! It's too tight, and my hands are shaking. I never thought I'd miss the palace, but at least at the palace we have maids to handle things like this!"

Ember, frowning, looked from Connie to Lucy and back again. "So is the girdle causing the earthquake, too?"

Lucy realized that her friend was right. It wasn't just her hands shaking, but her whole body, and a large part of the landscape, too. It was a significant measure of how used to Ember's landings she'd become that she hadn't really noticed it. Ember, though, had never felt a shaking like this, and seemed to be having difficulty staying on her feet.

And then, a herd of unicorns came racing up the hill. There weren't just dozens of them, but almost a hundred, beautiful, supernatural creatures of strength and power and beauty. It was magnificent, and terrifying. The King and Connie turned to face

The Dragon, Lucinda and George

the charging herd, which came to a dramatic stop, tearing up the turf beneath their hooves.

Ember made a small sound, and Lucy bent down to help the surprised dragon begin the unaccustomed task of picking bits of grass and dirt from where they'd landed between her scales.

The largest unicorn of the group was a mare as cool and bright as new snow. She tossed her mane and stamped her perfect hoof. The ground shook with the force of the blow. No one in her right mind could doubt that this was Connie's mother, the Queen of the Unicorns, for she had a regal stature and bearing equal to the King's own.

"Frank," she said. "Have you been letting Connie play with her chemistry set again? I distinctly remember we had a talk about it, after what happened to the wheat field last spring."

"Hello, Mummy," said Connie.

"Hello, Helen," said the Unicorn King, who was also Frank.

"Mummy, Mummy," Connie said, unabashed. "It wasn't me! It was the dragon."

"The dragon," said the Queen.

"Here she is." Connie pointed with her horn. "Her name is Ember and this is her friend, Lucy. Lucy is a human," Connie added, in case this were not obvious.

The Queen spared a glance for the miniaturized dragon, the tattered and windblown princess beside her, and the ashy remains of what had once been a picturesque hillside in bloom. Her regal gaze returned to her husband the King.

"Frank," she said, very quietly. "What exactly is going on here?"

The wisest creature in the world, the King of Unicorns, hesitated, no doubt to make sure that his words were the wisest words possible. The pause extended itself uncomfortably, and the Queen of Unicorns began to tap her hoof impatiently.

"Frank, I'm waiting."

The King of Unicorns took a deep breath and began to speak in rich and rolling tones, "And Lo, unto the valley of wisdom came two young emissaries from distant lands. Sisters in spirit, though different in species, each was filled with the spirit of inquiry and sought the ultimate treasure: Wisdom," he said.

"Cut the crap, Frank," interrupted the Queen. "Why is a full quarter of the meadow suddenly blackened ash?"

"Mummy, it wasn't me this time!" said Connie. "And it wasn't Daddy, I swear! Ember did it!"

"I wish you'd let me intone it, dearest," protested the King.

"Frank?"

"It sounds so much more impressive."

"Frank!"

"All right," The King sighed, clearly disappointed. Lucy looked at Ember — they were both a little disappointed, too, but either the Queen was in a hurry for answers, or those supernaturally resonant tones of the King had to be reserved for special occasions. He gave the rest of his explanation in a much more casual way. "You see, Nell, these two came into the valley with a pile of rubbish, trying to figure out what to do with it."

"And then Ember the dragon touched the girdle, even after I told her it was magic," said Connie, eager to finish the story. "And Ember got scared because the girdle magicked her. And a lot of flame came shooting out of her." Connie, clearly, was impressed. "I mean, like a lot of flame, and it was kind of cool except for the burning of the meadows part, and then ding-dong, all-gone-wrong, she was teeny." Connie looked over at Ember, and then added. "And adorable. Can we keep her?"

"No, darling," said the Queen. "Dragons are beings, not pets. You are a dragon, then?" Nell peered down the length of her horn at Ember. "You seem rather small to have caused all this disturbance."

"Yes, I'm a dragon," said Ember. "Your Highness."

Lucy blurted out, "This is only how she looks under the curse. When she's large you wouldn't believe how big she is! Ginormous! And all we have to do is get this darn girdle off of her, so that she can be herself again."

"And quite capable of incinerating the entire valley," added Ember, helpfully. "I can assure you, it would really be no trouble at all."

"And all we need is someone like a maid to help get this girdle off," Lucy finished.

At the word "maid", the air around Queen Nell became distinctly chilly. Actual frost began to form on the seared ground where Ember's flame had destroyed the verdant landscape. King Frank saw this, and looked rueful.

"A maid, Frank?" said the Queen. "Really?"

"The girl mentioned it, and you know as well as I that unicorns are magical creatures. We can recognize a spell but not undo one. Now, it seems the wisest course would be to send them to Maid Valley."

"I remember we had a maid once!" said Connie. Both her parents turned their heads sharply to look at her, but the little unicorn was addressing this remark to Lucy and Ember.

"I didn't know unicorns could have maids," said Lucy.

"This was a long time ago," said Connie. "I was very little. Her name was Suzette and she had the fluffiest tail and she wanted to be something other than just another Unicorn in the Herd, so she decided to be a maid. She would wear the cutest little hat and apron and hold a feather-duster in her teeth. Luckily, we don't use our mouths to sing, because Suzette was always singing while she did whatever it is the maids do."

"Dust the boulders?" suggested Lucy.

The King looked at Lucy and said blandly, "A maid can be good for something more than housekeeping chores," he said, which earned him a very long look from the Queen.

Connie said, "She and Mama-Queen had an argument, didn't you, Mama?"

There was an infinitesimal pause. The frost around Queen Nell's hooves began to spread, with a crackling sound, like thin ice, breaking. "I had no quarrel with Suzette's ambition to make something greater of herself," she finally said. "I only disagreed with her choices."

"How so?" asked Lucy.

The King found this a particularly good time to heroically gaze into the middle-distance.

Queen Nell met her gaze. "I fail to see why being a member of the Herd wasn't enough for her."

"And then she went away to Maid Valley to be with all the other maids, who aren't unicorns," said Connie. "And now she gets to do maid things, whatever they are, all day long."

Lucy, who was actually used to the subtle sub-currents of tension within her own family, picked up on the look Nell and Frank exchanged.

"Wise Queen Nell," Lucy said. "I am the one who asked for a maid. At the palace they are skilled at getting complicated bits of clothing like girdles to do what they are supposed to do. My mother, the Queen, has three of them wandering around her closets all day. Well, they do other things of course, but the point is we need an expert to get the girdle off of Ember, before her small size becomes permanent. I hope, if you can, you will help us, Your Majesty, by showing us the way to the Valley."

Lucy's tutors would have been proud. Well, to be honest, they would have been astonished at the precision and grace with which Lucy dropped her second curtsey of the day. Ember, now smaller, certainly had a better perspective from which to appreciate the skill, so she added a discreet puff of smoke in support.

"It would only be kindness to send them to the Valley," said the King in an under-voice. "Whoever they spoke with would be sure to offer them help, even if it were not…" he trailed off in the face of another frosty glance from the Queen.

"The maid." the Queen said.

"Suzette," said Connie.

"Oh, was that her name? I had quite forgotten." This was said by the King in the tone usually reserved for expressions like "One lump, or two?" or "No, no, after you, madam," or "I had no idea I was going that fast, officer." This caused the Queen of Unicorns to raise both an eyebrow and to flick her tail to a distinct and precise degree. The King, proving his wisdom yet again, thought it prudent to say no more.

"Thank you, my dear," said the Queen. She lost some of her icy air and became merely brisk. "Now, young ladies, this is how it shall be. You two," she indicated Lucy and Ember with the tip of her horn. "You shall go to the Valley of the Maids and seek what help you may find there. I shall not be surprised if you discover that Suzette has taken charge of the place, but if she has, I am certain she will remember my daughter fondly."

"Mummy, may I?" Connie asked.

"Yes, Connie," the Queen said. "You may go along with your new friends as far as the Valley of the Maids. As for you, Your Majesty," she inclined her head towards King Frank in a gesture that had absolutely nothing of humility in it. "I feel certain you will be well occupied with personally cleaning up this mess. A housekeeping chore worthy of a king, don't you think, dear?" Needless to say, she did not wait for a response, and the King wisely offered none.

There was a moment of silence, from everyone save Connie, however. Because the littlest unicorn was prancing and leaping about the remains of the meadow in a clear state of excitement. "A quest!" she sang. "A quest, a quest! I'm going on a quest!" Her eyes widened, and she said, "Oh! I'm going on two quests! I'm going to the Wizards, and I'm going to the Maids! From none to two! Wow!"

Both Nell and Frank took a very deep breath. Unconsciously, they moved to stand shoulder-to-shoulder, presenting a close and united front.

"Yes, daughter. It is time for you to leave your home and acquire the wisdom that only can come from a quest." Frank cleared his throat impressively, and abruptly, Connie stopped singing and sprinted to stand proudly in front of her parents.

"Oh goodie, it's the," for a moment, Connie dropped her voice in a fair imitation of her father, "'Go forth and do the herd proud,' speech!" Her voice went up to its normal range, "Only this time it's for me!" Connie danced in a way that seemed to put her on the very tippy toes of her dainty hooves.

Queen Nell smiled fondly at her youngest child, but this did not disguise the incipient tears in her eyes. King Frank, perhaps because he had performed this ritual before, did a better job of hiding most of his emotions behind a regal attitude of benediction.

"For it has long been our way, to leave the safely of the meadow and classroom, the security of hearth and home, the serenity of certainty and answers."

Ember looked up at Lucy, who glanced around and saw that the entire herd of unicorns had moved silently to stand in a circle around the Royal Family. This, it seemed, was one of the special moments for which his most impressive tones were saved. As the King spoke, the other unicorns began to move, heads bobbing, tails waving in the breeze like living banners, bodies gently swaying, as if they could hear some music behind the King's words that Lucy's human ears were unable to pick out. This was obviously a ceremony they knew well, and loved.

"The herd has protected and taught, instructed and nurtured...."

A large silent tear ran down the snow-bright face of the Queen. Her horn began to glow with a lovely light. Connie was staring at her father, silent for perhaps the first time in her life, her expression one of rapt adoration.

"The herd has guided and instructed, listened and learned." A small ripple of laughter went through the herd. The king seemed to smile. "The heard has not only taught you, but been taught much by you, dear Connie. Together, we all become wiser."

Here, the great King paused. The herd looked up, directly at the King, and Ember and Lucy realized that he must have departed from the traditional ceremony. Something unusual was about to happen.

"In my eyes, you have been the brightest flower to ever grace this meadow," the King said. "You have always brought light and laughter wherever you go, and brought joy to what could have been a rather joyless pursuit of truth. You serve as an example that wisdom is often found in surprising places, and that... Well," his voice was full of fond laughter. "There's never anything certain when you are around, right, honey?"

The Queen smiled bravely and then rested her head against the King's strong neck, which gave her a chance to wipe her eyes. The King blinked heavily a few times, but when they raised their heads again, the royal eyes were clear at last.

The King drew a deep breath. "Connie, my heart, we send you out into the world, with the wisdom of the herd in your past, our hopes for your future, and our hearts ever in your present."

The herd gave a heavy snort in unison, and every right forefoot gave a powerful stomp of approval.

Lucy and Ember felt a tremendous release of tension from the herd, as they universally relaxed.

"You did very well, you old goat," the Queen whispered to her husband. She wept openly, and didn't seem at all embarrassed by this. She might have said something more, but then Connie, who couldn't contain her enthusiasm a moment longer, crashed into her parents. A fullback would have been flattened, but her parents didn't flinch. A beat or two later, the rest of the herd was pressing into the family's circle, and it was clear that all unicorns were, in some way, part of the same family, and all of them wanted to be part of this last embrace.

It was such a poignant, private moment, in spite of involving a hundred other beings, that Ember and Lucy both decided to take themselves elsewhere. They moved away down the hillside, Ember gliding on outspread wings, and Lucy walking.

"This going-away ceremony was a lot different from the one my kingdom threw for me," Lucy said, trying for a dispassionate, non-judgmental tone. She thought she managed a not too shabby effort.

"Oh, was it?" Ember seemed willing to adopt a neutral tone, too.

"Yes, in part because my parents couldn't attend personally. My sisters were there, but in the royal box, rather than on the dais. Most of the ceremony was symbolic. The official castle spokespeople did the talking and answered questions from the television and newspapers."

The Dragon, Lucinda and George

"Hm," Ember nodded. "I didn't see any television crews here today," she remarked. "That certainly is a marked difference."

"Did your parents give you a going-away ceremony?"

"Not exactly," Ember said. "It works a bit differently. They did ask me to be careful, and my mother reminded me to chew every bite thoroughly."

"Ah," said Lucy.

There was a pause, not precisely uncomfortable, but long enough to remind both of them that there were some hurdles they still had to climb over in their new friendship.

"Well, it's nice to see that some of the trees managed to survive your flame," Lucy said with diplomacy. "You were right, you certainly do have an impressive range."

"This one seems to have escaped entirely," Ember said, and they stopped under the shade of one tree with spreading branches.

"Do you know what sort of tree it might be?" Lucy asked.

"I didn't make a great study of trees," Ember confessed. "But I believe it's an elm."

"It gives good shade," said Lucy.

"I think it is rather unusual to find this type of elm tree so far to the south," said Ember.

"Oh, really?" said Lucy. "I do like the shape of its leaves."

"Oh, yes," said Ember. "Very distinctive."

From the sounds coming from the direction of the herd, it seemed that further conversation was warranted.

"Unfortunately, the only tree I can recognize on sight is the dogwood tree," said Lucy. She hesitated, then plunged recklessly on: "I know it by its bark."

Ember hesitated, but Lucy, pretending to be disinterested, thought her friend was trying not to laugh. "Oh, certainly. And have you ever heard that there's one side of a tree that will always have more leaves than the other?" the dragon asked.

"No," said Lucy. "Is there?"

"Indeed," said Ember. "The outside."

Lucy made a small choking sound, like a smothered giggle.

"I believe much wisdom may be derived from a close examination of the way the bark has peeled away from the tree," offered Ember, at her most scholarly.

Lucy tried to adopt a similar tone. "They say no tree ever shed its bark the same way twice."

"Oh, really?" said Ember, with the hint of a smile. "You don't say."

"Well, no, I don't." Lucy was smiling, too. "It's they who say."

"They could be right," Ember volleyed with a giggle.

"In what they say," Lucy nodded sagely.

"Right," Ember said, and then they both dissolved in peals of laughter.

Lucy put her arm around Ember, careful not to disturb the motion of the dragon's wings. "You know, I've been trained in how to have a conversation almost since I learned to talk, but I never really enjoyed it before. I guess it helps having a friend with a sense of humor."

"Ahem," interrupted Queen Nell. "If you young questers can spare a moment."

"Yes, your majesty!" said Ember. Lucy dropped another perfect curtsey, courtesy of all those years of practice. Ember dipped her wings and gave a flourish with her tail that seemed to accomplish the same effect, with more natural grace than study.

"Don't worry about all that etiquette fiddle-faddle," said the Queen. "Come, and let me take a look at you." Her haughty head turned this way and that as she took in Lucy's extremely travel-worn appearance. Lucy had no access to a mirror, but she knew she felt mucky, and could imagine what the Queen saw. There was the wreck of her hair, which had suffered from the windy flight and probably besides being as tangled as a bird's nest, was full of pine needles and twigs from their efforts to build the wind-screen. Then, there was the delicate sacrificial gown, which had not been intended for long journeys on land or through the air and had suffered as a result. Lucy's legs and feet were still bare, and so were her arms, though she had sort of wrapped the pieces of the shroud around the stuff she'd been given, into an improvised pack, and tied that around her shoulders. She supposed she didn't look very much like a noble quester, let alone a princess.

"This sort of thing usually goes to fairy godmothers," said Queen Nell, "but if you don't tattle, I'm sure no one will mind if I bend the rules just this once." She made a complicated flick with her horn, drawing a symbol in the air, one that seemed to hang there for a moment, only to vanish when Lucy blinked. But in that same blink, the pine needles and sticky sap had vanished, and so had the sensation of being grimy and exhausted. She felt warm and comfortable, and surprisingly well-rested, considering she couldn't remember the last time she'd slept in an actual bed, rather than on the ground or hanging from a dragon's claw. A single glance was enough to confirm that the wreck of the sacrificial gown had been replaced by warm and sturdy clothing, denim, flannel, and wool, even a corduroy jacket! Her bare feet were now safely closed into a pair of walking boots, just her size. Lucy didn't mind at all that they weren't made of glass; they seemed much better suited for hiking than dancing. She put a hand up, and yes, the mess of her hair had been combed out, and woven into a braid.

"Am I dreaming?" Lucy asked.

"If you are, you must be talking in your sleep," said Ember.

"And all of this was made just for me," Lucy said. Her voice was a whisper, as if she was afraid speaking out loud would disrupt the magic.

Meanwhile, the Unicorn Queen had turned her attention to the miniaturized dragon. As if to herself, she said, "Dragons don't need much, generally, but, I want to get into the spirit of the thing." Again, the slight twitch of the horn, another pattern in the air.

Lucy blinked. A sparkling cloud had seemed to surround Ember, and when it dispersed, Ember emerged, looking bright, sleek, and more vibrant than ever, as if her colorful scales had somehow been washed and buffed. Even her wings shone, and her claws had been polished, gleaming as brightly as if diamond-coated.

"You look beautiful," said Lucy.

Ember twisted her long neck in the snaky way of dragons and admired her new look. She gave a snort of fire, clearly approving of what she saw "I feel rejuvenated," she said, and lifted her head to meet the Queen's gaze. "Thank you, Your Majesty."

The Queen did not seem to wish to be thanked. She was still in organizing mode. "Now, you young people do seem fond of rushing about without a plan, but here among the unicorns, we still do quests the old fashioned way. This means each of you should bring provisions for the journey, but you may only take what either you or your horse can carry."

"We don't have horses," said Lucy. She was surprised she even had to mention it.

"If Ember were her full size, I'm certain it would be no trouble for her to carry everything you might need for an importan journey," said the Queen. "But until the three of you complete your quest to undo the curse of the girdle, we will just have to make do." She didn't swish her horn this time, but instead blew a melody through it, clear and true, and soon, cantering gently up the hill, were three of the biggest horses Lucy had ever seen. They were draft horses, beautiful, glossy creatures, with feathered hooves and broad, strong backs. As Lucy watched, each of the massive animals presented themselves on one, bent knee before the Queen, in what was clearly a bow.

"My friends," said the Queen. "I ask you to accompany our Connie, and these two ladies upon their quest. It may take you into danger, and worse, may take you to the Valley of the Maids and Suzette."

Behind her, the King was wise enough to leave certain thoughts unspoken.

"... or even beyond the Valley," continued the Queen, smoothly. "I feel certain the questers will need the strength of your backs, the speed of your legs, and the sureness of your hooves. They will need your help to carry what they cannot during the journey. Will you go?"

Lucy had ridden a pony in her life as a princess, but she had not thought much about the intelligence of her steed. These three seemed to be something entirely different. They listened to the Queen with gazes that seemed almost as wise as a unicorn's, and they nodded their heads quite clearly in answer to her request. Lucy had the impression that if the horses hadn't wanted to go on the quest, they wouldn't have been forced along. The Queen gestured with her horn again, and two of the horses were suddenly laden with packs. The third had a perfectly sized saddle, and Lucy realized it was meant for her.

"The packs contain a change of clothing and some clean socks," Queen Nell said, "as I know that human feet can be very delicate and need protection. But most of what these horses will carry for you is food and water, and even a few little treats for along the way."

Lucy was about to thank the Queen for the fine gifts, when she heard a familiar squeal of delight.

"Oh look!" Connie called. "It's Boots, Scoots, and Skipper! My ponies!" She came over the hill at full speed, only checking herself at the last minute, and skidding to a stop beside Scoots with only inches to spare.

"Are they coming on the quest too, Mummy? Are you coming, Scoots? Are you coming, Boots? Please say they will come with us!" Connie's supernatural powers seemed to include advanced wheedling, and as if she were already confident in her success, the little unicorn didn't wait for an answer, but turned at once to talk with Lucy, "Scoots is the nicest pony, and she is ever so gentle, and she will never ever buck you off. Will you, Scoots? But you might want to give her an occasional apple whenever you have one, because she is really quite fond of them, and if you are eating an apple and you don't share, that isn't very—"

"Connie," the King of Unicorns looked very noble, with the wind blowing through his mane and tail. The meadow went silent in anticipation, even Connie, which was noteworthy all by itself. "Connie," King Frank said. "It is time to start your quest."

Connie looked very young and very small as she gazed up at her parents. She stared for a long time, and Lucy wondered whether the little unicorn was trying to commit this moment to memory. Connie stepped forward and gently nuzzled her mother's shoulder, then her father's.

"Your companions are good ones, Connie," Queen Nell said. "I have looked into their hearts and they are true." The King and Queen glanced over to Lucy and Ember. Without a word being spoken, the girls knew they being asked to take care of Connie. They both nodded in answer. It was a responsibility they were willing to take on.

"Be safe on your quest, Connie," said King Frank.

"A gentle breeze brushed though the meadow. Then:"OK! Time to go!" Connie said. She kicked up her bright heels with glee. "Love you, Mummy. Love you, Daddy! Bye-bye! See you when I'm wise!"

Without ceremony, Connie turned and dashed off into the unburned portion of the forest.

"Connie, WAIT!" Lucy shouted. She scrambled to get on Scoots, who was much taller than her pony had been at home. Ember and the other two horses were already racing off after Connie.

Lucy could hear Ember calling: "CONNIE, THE FIRST RULE OF QUESTING IS THAT WE ALL STICK TOGETHER!"

Chapter Eleven
Profundia Survival Day FAQs, Knights' Edition

Congratulations On Your Selection As Part Of The Security Component For Profundia Survival Day! It Means So Much To Have You Here. For Most People, Survival Day Is A Time Of Reflection And Sacrifice, But For Knights It's So Much More.

Whoa, whoa, what's with all the upper and lower case?

Too Much?

Kinda.

Sorry. This better?

Much, thank you.

So, where was I?

Something about Survival Day and knights?

Oh yeah, thanks. Ahem. For most people, Survival Day is a time of reflection and sacrifice. But for knights it's so much more.

Triple overtime?

No. Well, ok. Overtime yes, but also the opportunity to do something that you have always wanted to do.

Double-dip the pension?

No, not double-dip your pension. Well, ok, if it's legal go for it (Hint: you want to be an employee, not a consultant), but we were more publicly thinking of slaying the dragon, rescuing the Princess, winning half a kingdom deal. You know, knight stuff. Now before you go out looking for trussed up damsels or swooping dragons, let's go over some of the basic ground rules and regulations of the Profundia Survival Day (PSD) as are laid out in excruciatingly vague detail in the DHRCP

DHRCP. What's that?

Doesn't matter. Something in dragon.

Listen, why do we need rules? They're coming into our neighborhoods and eating our maidens. I say, bugger the rules and let's get us some dragon hide! Dragon hide! Dragon hide! Dragon hide!

Listen, calm down. We'll get to that soon enough. And the sooner we get through this, the sooner we can go outside blow something up.

Blow something up! Blow something up! Blow something up!

In the meantime, please help yourself to the bacon and pastries on the table over there. Um, the orange has been there for a couple of months, so I would avoid that.

We don't eat, we don't meet! We don't eat, we don't meet! We don't eat, we don't meet! We don't...

Yeah, we heard you. Settle down. Settle down. Thank you.

Great bacon.

Thank you. Now, where was I?

Why don't we just slay the dragon?

That's an excellent question. Let me bottom-line it here for you. Your primary responsibility is not the SD/RM protocol (slay dragon/rescue maiden protocol), but rather the MASTERS strategy (make absolutely sure things end-up relatively similar). Now here is the dirty little secret that no one really speaks out loud. Dragons are big, and generally could kick our butts, and if they are happy with one maiden, shrug, you know greater good and all that.

Greater good, how does that work here? Could we get some more bacon?

Of course. Gentlemen, we discussed this in your training. In an emergency, like an earthquake, or in this case a dragon, you can't stop and help the first person you see. You have to do a wind-shield survey of your area so we all know where help is needed most. It can be tough if you're in the first house, but works in the end for the greater good of the whole kingdom. Same thing here. We have to make sure that the overall rules are followed so the dragons don't have an excuse to drop the hammer on us.

They're carrying hammers? Bad enough when they were just breathing fire!

No, not real hammers, it's just an expression. Oh look, more bacon!

To be honest, we're men of action. This diplomacy stuff is not our strong suit. Just point us toward the scrambled eggs and the bazookas, and we'll be fine.

Again, this is where all that training comes in useful. You'll remember you had archery lessons, and sword swinging, and for some of you, advanced axe mechanics. You won't be issued bazookas or guns or laser-strike-engines.

Wait, what? But we're fighting dragons?

Yes, and dragons have distinctly sensitive ears and are very respectful of tradition. If you start shooting at them, they'll only get angry.

But dragons.

Angry dragons are extremely destructive dragons, and our experts have determined that a princess/maiden per year, more or less, is an acceptable risk for the greater good. Need I remind you that the battleground is too near population centers for us to be willing to risk the lives of all those innocent men, women, and children just to make your job easy. I'm sure you wouldn't want to take unnecessary risks with their safety.

Dragons, though! With hammers!

Have you tried the roasted potatoes? Very festive. Have a double helping, and a waffle. Now, needless to say, we won't leave our security team — yourselves — unarmed in a state of crisis, and while explosives and projectiles are considered inadvisable, we do have some tracking systems that might help with targeting. Our point is, gentlemen, that we realize you will be engaged in an extremely complicated enterprise, and that as the muscle of this traditional ceremony, you shouldn't be required to also figure out strategy. That's why we provide knights on assignment with a certified agent to do any industrious comprehension activities that might be required.

"Compre-who?"

The thinkie parts.

But we still get our snacks, right?

Of course you do! And please feel free to take anything extra from the food table to take home with you. Now, let's go blow something up, shall we?

Blow something up! Blow something up! Blow something up!

Margit Elland Schmitt & Dan McLaughlin

Chapter Twelve
The Rights of Knights

"It would be nice for once," remarked George conversationally, just loud enough to be heard over the sound of the horses' heavy breathing and thundering hooves, "to just leave a tavern like a normal person. Don't you think that would be nice, just for a change of pace?"

From much too close for comfort, the sounds of angry pursuit bruised the predawn stillness. A vengeful saucepan whizzed by them, hitting a tree with a considerable clang.

"Nice arm, but without control, it's just wasted effort," said Chip. "And that was a cooking pot of some quality."

"We might have had a good breakfast there," continued George, with an increasing edge to his voice, "if we'd been able to stay at the tavern long enough to enjoy it."

"She threw it hard enough to scar the tree bark," said Chip, looking over his shoulder.

"Poor tree. Wrong place; wrong time." George shook his head.

"Another thing for people around here to remember us by," said Agent X. His smug tone reignited George's temper.

"As I was saying, it would be nice if we were able to leave a place without leaving a permanent mark on the landscape. A knight's rule is, 'Take only information; leave no memories.'" One of the skills George seemed to be picking up on this journey was the ability to make air-quotes while riding a horse at high speeds.

"Just as well I'm not a knight," said Agent X.

"It could be worse," said Chip. "There is something to be said for an early morning ride to get the day started. Quite invigorating, you know."

"Shouldn't the yelling be further behind us by now?" asked Agent X, who had accumulated considerable experience in these sorts of things.

George risked a glance over his shoulder, "Oh, look. They have a truck."

"Clever chaps," said Chip. "Non-traditional, but clever."

"Duck," said George, and as if connected by the same string, all three riders dipped lower in their saddles. A flight of arrows whizzed over their heads and pierced only the local foliage.

Chip said, "Horses do have a bit of an advantage in wooded terrain, don'cher know."

Sitting back up, George simply glared at Agent X, who returned his glare and doubled it.

"Listen." Agent X was getting annoyed. "If you guys did your share of Gathering Intel from the local population, we wouldn't have to leave posthaste!"

"What do you mean by that, old chap? Ah, veer left," said Chip.

In fluid synchronization, the trio turned their horses sharply to the left. One arrow actually stuck itself into George's saddlebag. This did nothing to improve George's mood.

"My bad," said Chip. "I meant the other left."

Agent X continued his complaint. "I'm just saying that typically problems only arise when I am forced to Gather Intel from two different sources. Usually, but not always, they turn out to be sisters, and then they find out that I have been Gathering Intel from each other. Now, if either of you two gentlemen were to also Gather Intel …"

The Dragon, Lucinda and George

"Duck," said George. They ducked, and no one was hurt. " … Gather Intel," said Agent X. "Then when the wenches in question compare notes, there would be—"

"There would be two chappies asking the questions, and the ladies would have no reason to be enraged and we might catch a few extra hours of sleep," Chip triumphantly concluded.

"Or something," Agent X added.

"Very clever notion, old chap," said Chip.

"Or you could just keep your Gathering Intel efforts to daylight hours and public spaces," George said.

"Veer right." The three of them veered right and easily avoided the arrows. "Because the way you go at it now doesn't seem to have anything to do with intelligence."

"We are Knights, lads," said Agent X.

"Except you keep reminding us that you aren't," Chip pointed out, determined to be helpful.

Agent X pretended not to hear. "Intel Gathering among the wenches is part and parcel of life in the field, and furthermore, it is expected of us. Or at least me. Indeed, the wenches would be disappointed if we didn't Gather their Intel." Somehow, Agent X managed to pose and flex while riding his horse. A pair of enraged, if distinctly feminine, screams could be heard from the pursuing forces as he did so.

"This batch seems a bit more persistent than usual," said Chip.

Agent X looked over his left shoulder. "It seems both wenches had betrotheds, never a good combination," he laughed. "I believe we will be riding hard for a bit longer, lads."

"Veer right," Chip sang out.

Obediently, they veered right. Another arrow appeared in George's saddlebag.

"My bad, other right."

George was seething. "Have you ever considered trying to find out whether there was a mother, a father, a brother, a sister, a significantly irritable other or any possible combination of the above before you started to Gather your Intel?"

"That seems an excellent notion," said Chip.

George rounded on him: "And you, THIS is RIGHT and THIS is LEFT. GET IT?"

"I can see you're frustrated, old chap." Chip didn't seem offended in the least. "Some of us are just not morning people," he added to Agent X in a perfectly audible whisper.

George gritted his teeth. There was no point in shouting at Chip, who meant well and hadn't wanted to miss breakfast either. George sighed and muttered, "Fine, be that way about it."

Eventually, the crash of metal against rocks, and a distinct cut in volume, indicated that the people shouting and shooting at them had decided Agent X had been driven far enough out of town.

Eventually, the sun rose.

Eventually, hours later, they came across a narrow road, one which led to a town that had an innkeeper who cooked a savory, hot breakfast for reasonable charges, and (better yet) had no daughters at all, only a lunkish, lout of a son, who cleaned the taproom floor. Even Agent X was persuaded to sit down for breakfast, and dawdle over the third helpings. He was drinking a lot of ale and singing, but George didn't have to listen. He had finished his single helping and gone outside the building, prying the arrows out of his saddlebag and patching up the holes left behind. From this distance, Agent X's singing was only slightly horrible.

In spite of himself, George began to feel a little better. Maybe it was the warmth of the sun easing the stress out of his neck and shoulders. Maybe it was the thought that a few arrow holes in the saddle's surface might actually make it look like it belonged to someone who had seen adventures, rather than someone who was just starting out in the knighting biz. Maybe it was because a full stomach and a moment's privacy went a long way towards easing what had been a pretty uncomfortable couple of days.

They ought to put warnings on adventuring gear, he thought: "One sleeping bag. No actual sleep included."

"Worrying about your saddle, old chap?" asked Chip, appearing almost out of nowhere, or in this case, the door. "Why don't you ask your father to get you a new one? Oh, I'd forgotten."

George shrugged, being used to the fact that while Chip had a remarkable memory for arcane genealogy, he had little room in his head for the things George thought were important. "Right," he said. Which wasn't the same as saying it was all right.

"Dash it, I ought to have remembered the whole orphan thing."

"Yes."

"Especially since I was just at the funeral with you."

"Yes."

Chip clapped George on the shoulder. "Buck up, fellow! Before you know it, we'll have rescued the maiden and brought her back before Agent X has a chance to mistake her for a local and try to interrogate her."

"What?" George blinked, a little horrified. The thought hadn't occurred to him. "He wouldn't, would he? Not with a princess!"

"Well, there's no telling with that fellow." Chip's patrician nose wrinkled and he rubbed at it thoughtfully. He looked to be a bit in pain, but George realized it was just because Chip was listening to the yodeling coming from the inn. "He's a man with secrets. For example, I didn't even know there was a third verse to that song, let alone that it had a turnip in it!"

Chip went back into the inn, and through some means better left unexplored managed to stop Agent X from singing the fourth verse. For a long while, George was happy simply grooming the horses. They were good, solid animals, strong and capable, but they were designed for brief, courageous charges into danger and out again. The sustained getaway gallops from the last few inns had taken their toll. These were valiant beasts, but beginning to show signs of stress.

"What you need," George said to the horses, "Is a good long rest in a nice, warm stable, plenty of food and water, and no baggage to carry, and no death-defying races to run for a while." He reached into a little sack he carried, and offered handfuls of oats for each of them to lip over.

Pretty much by default, George had been in charge of the horses since they had left the WHADS citadel. Partially, this was because it never would have dawned on Chip or Agent X to offer, but more than a little, this was because George knew neither Chip nor Agent X had the least idea of how horses were cared for -- whereas, George, a scholarship student, had been working off his student loans in the stables almost from when he'd filled out the ream and a half of paperwork to get the darn things.

It was true that George was an orphan. He'd been lucky to get a scholarship at Knightsbridge Academy, owed not just to his own studies, but to his father's influence. George's father had been an academic, a teacher of very good repute, great mind, and noble family — all of which combined to give him some pull, at least in scholastic circles. He'd wanted George to be educated the same way he was, and so that had been arranged.

George's memories of his father were strong and warm and laced with unexpected sparks of humor, much like the man himself.

"You are very like him," George's mother would say. At the time of his father's death, George had been only fifteen, fearing that the growth spurt he'd been hoping for would never come, and that he'd always be pudgy and undersized, with a natural ability to bump his elbow against any hard edge. George couldn't have imagined anyone less like his father than himself. His father had been a big man, not just half a head taller than the other academics, but broad in the shoulders, and capable of filling a room with the quiet confidence of his presence. He'd had a big smile, and made friends easily.

He'd been fond of sport, too, which was something George did not pick up until he finally entered school. His father would take to the fields on afternoons and weekends, a powerhouse with a ball in hand, mowing down the opposition with such a cheerful grin that no one ever took their losses personally. He was faster on his feet than such a big-boned man ought to have been. Looking back on it, George could see now that his father must have taken at least a little training as a knight. The moves had all been there.

It was only now, after his own schooling and all those years of enforced exercise, drills, and calisthenics, that George sometimes surprised himself, seeing the memory of his father looking back at him from out of the mirror.

"You are very much like your father," his mother used to say. "He was brave, and honorable. He was kind."

George hadn't argued — one didn't with his mother — but he'd always suspected that his case was one where her sharp mind and keen judgment were just the tiniest bit askew.

His father's death, a fatal heart attack on the tower steps at the Academy, had taken George completely by surprise.

His mother's death, three years later, had devastated him. Like his mother, his grief refused to be ignored and would reach up and stab him in unwary moments. George sometimes admitted to himself that it was one of the reasons he was willing to spend so much time in company with Chip.

Young Blitherington, self-absorbed and oblivious, had not been very likable when they first met. He'd been asked to look after George when George first came to school, and through a sense of duty, or more likely (George suspected) a complete lack of imagination such as might lead him to consider a change of routine, maintained a mild sort of friendship with him over the years. Spending time with Chip was tedious at best, and annoying at worst, but it did distract him from missing his mother and wondering whether she would finally be proud of what he had made of himself. And one of the benefits of Chip's acquaintance was that Chip never taxed one's brain. He only ever asked the most superficial questions, and then forgot the answers immediately. If he hadn't been borne aloft on an impenetrable, Blitherington fog, George suspected that Chip would never have graduated, let alone entered into the competitive and exclusive Knights program. It was rumored someone had paid for Chip's grades.

But that was one of the lessons George had learned in school: the exact difference between the amount of influence afforded to someone like Chip Blitherington, of impeccable lineage, and the tolerance afforded to George Gerontius, who was definitely not of nearly so exalted a bloodline.

"It's the way of the world, George," his mother had said. Like his father, she had been tall and dark, though she had been beautiful, without even a trace of his father's famous mustache. Even before she was a widow, she'd worn black all the time. Serviceable or sleek.

"It behooves the likes of us, who are not of royal blood, to watch the way the world works. We don't have to go along blindly. We only go if it suits us," she said. Looking at his mother, he could absolutely believe she was capable of stopping the irresistible tide of the future. So far, George hadn't mastered the skill of not being swept along.

Everyone had said he took after his father. It was only now and then (and especially now, on the road) that George thought it would have been useful to have a little bit of his mother in him as well.

In George's experience, the world had its own expectations, and when you didn't go along quietly, it slapped back. His mother had her own specialized sort of weaponry to deal with that kind of thing, and he found himself feeling the slap now and then. Just as he found himself worrying about Princess Lucinda, the one with the glasses, and worrying about whether this surprising escape from death was going to bring more trouble into her path. That is, if one could imagine such a worse trouble than being kidnapped by dragons and forced to rely on Chip Blitherington for rescue.

The horses, nudging him in hopes of more oats, or carrots, or apples, or really any treat at all, broke George out of his reverie. He couldn't do a single thing to help Lucinda if the world were gearing up to slap at her, except to decide he wasn't going to let himself be the arm of that slap. But he could make a decision on behalf of the horses here and now.

So when Chip and Agent X finally wandered out to the street from the inn's doors, it was to see that instead of having their mounts saddled and ready to go, George had gone down the street to the rental station and picked up —

"A car?" Chip was goggle-eyed with disbelief.

"Yes," said George. "And a full tank of gas. We'll go faster than the horses can, and catch fewer bugs in our teeth."

"But tradition, old man!" said Chip. "What about tradition?"

"The horses are tired," said George. "They aren't made for running all day, and to be honest, I'm a little tired, too. I'd just as soon take the car. It needs only one driver, so no one will get lost if he is temporarily distracted and can't remember which left is right."

"Well, that could be useful," said Agent X drily, to no one in particular.

"And it has steel sides and windows, in case there's some reason irate townspeople and innkeepers might choose to follow after us shooting bows and arrows," said George.

"But tradition," said Chip.

"Well, I know that tradition says we're supposed to head out on horseback to rescue the Princess or die trying, but since I don't want to die, and I do want to rescue the Princess, I can't help but think that the car has the benefit of an extra seat. We only brought three horses, after all, and it's been a long ride already. I don't know how much you gentlemen remember about our 'riding pillion' lessons, but I thought it was pretty darned uncomfortable."

"That's true," said Agent X. "She could sit in the back seat, and I could sit next to her and Gather Intel about her experience in the dragon's maw."

George shuddered, and hoped he'd be able to arrange things so that such a fate for Lucinda could be avoided. "I've already got our luggage packed and loaded," he said. "So the sooner you both get inside, the sooner we can catch up with Princess Lucinda and rescue her!"

Chapter Thirteen
A Little Bitty Breakdown

It turned out that when you were Questing with a Purpose, rather than just being swooped up spur-of-the-moment-like, but actually planning to go to a specific place with supplies and comfortable shoes and a warm coat, and a big, beautiful horse to ride, in those circumstances, Questing was actually very nice. At least, that's what Lucy was thinking.

The sun was shining, and Ember, so much smaller than before, was a much easier companion, able to zip and dive between the forest trees, and swoop and swing around the horses, or even perch up on the baggage Boots was carrying, so that she and Lucy could chat now and then.

Connie was prancing at the front of the line close enough that they didn't have to chase her or worry her, but definitely ahead of them. The little unicorn was unflaggingly cheerful, bright, and delighted in leading the way with a song.

"Oh, who are the people in your meadow?

"In your meadow?

"In your meh-heh-dow!"

She didn't just sing. She warbled, enthusiastically.

"The people that you'll meet today!"

Boots, Scoots, and Skipper were probably used to the sound: they were nodding their heads in time with the beat.

It was actually very pretty, and almost soothing, and gave Lucy, in particular, time to think, which was something she hadn't had since picking the letter off the breakfast table a week ago. She wondered whether her father had found someone to help with the accounting, now that she was gone. She wondered whether any of her sisters would help her mother polish the spoons.

"Oh, a squirrel jumps from tree to tree," Connie sang.
"He's looking carefully to see,
"If there's nuts or berries in a bunch.
"Enough for him to eat his lunch!"

She was so cheerful, Lucy thought. Ember and she had agreed that their new friend wasn't just cute, but courageous, too. It was her first trip away from her family, and it didn't seem to bother her at all to be far from home. She wasn't scared. In fact, her little hooves weren't just prancing. They were dancing. Nothing seemed to bother her. Of course, nothing bad had ever happened to her.

Lucy took off her glasses to polish them on the corner of her shirt. One of the hinges was loose, and she tried to use the tip of a fingernail to twist the screw more securely in place. If she'd been back at the palace, Dana could have showed her exactly where the screwdriver was, and how to fix the glasses. Pacifica would have even fixed them for her. Instead, her glasses slipped from her hands and the world became a vague blur. Damn it!

"The squirrel is a person in the meadow!"

"A person that we met today!" Connie sang. Even without her glasses on, Lucy could see that the little white blob was adorable, and happy to be on this adventure. She was cheerful. She probably had flowers in her mane. Again. And some butterflies were flying around her horn, Lucy just knew it.

"Lucy, why are you crying?" It was Ember.

"I am NOT crying!" said Lucy, who was not just crying, but whose whole body was shaking with an effort to stop. But the tears kept coming, and her eyes were streaming, and her nose was running. Ember fluttered over to Lucy's saddle, holding something. She pushed the shroud into Lucy's hands, so she could blow her nose, which Lucy did in a messy, horrible way that didn't really help, because her nose kept running, and she was getting snot all down her face, and it was hard to breathe between sobs. Lucy tried to blow her nose again.

"Oh, no!" said Connie, and as Lucy slid off of the saddle, the unicorn was already looking in the grass around and between Scoots' hooves.

"I didn't ask for this!" wailed Lucy.

"Lucy, have you lost your glasses?" asked Connie. "Let me help you look."

"I can find them myself."

"Maybe if we sang the Finding Song we could all find them together."

"GO AWAY AND LEAVE ME ALONE!"

For the first time in her life, someone had yelled at Connie in anger.

"Do you want me to—" Connie began do a little dance, and stepped on Lucy's glasses. The tell-tale crunch brought everything to a halt for a single moment. Then Lucy began to wail again.

"My dad gave me those glasses. Go away. I told you to go away, so just go away before you break anything else, you big baby."

Stunned, Connie looked at Ember.

Lucy said: "Let me tell you something, little Miss Dancing Hooves. When my mom and dad let me be put on a stake for a dragon to eat me, it's not because they didn't love me. They had to or the dragons would come and eat more people and destroy the whole kingdom. They had to do it, and I am a princess and sometimes princesses have to do things they don't want to do because it's their job. We have responsibilities. We can't be cute and pretty little dancer-bell singing things all the time. We have to do things, hard things, so don't you dare think that my parents didn't love me because they did." The words coming out of her now were the angry thoughts she hadn't dared to let herself so much as think. "You... You silly little unicorn! I hate you!" Lucy picked up her broken glasses and threw them at Connie. They missed entirely, which just made Lucy even angrier. "You have no idea what you are talking about."

Connie deflated. Her tail and her horn drooped.

"I'm sorry."

Lucy lost it. "You don't get to be sorry for me." She began to weep in great, wracking sobs. "My parents do love me. They do. They do. They DO."

Connie didn't flinch. She just came closer and leaned gently at her new friend's side. Ember curled herself around Lucy's other side.

Lucy's sobs became even louder and, if possible, messier. "My parents do love me. They do!" she wailed. "They love me. They had to give me up, and they didn't want to, even though I am not as pretty as Dana or make everyone feel good like Pacifica," she wept. "And- and- and- Daddy never called me his little ray of sunshine."

Lucy rubbed her face against Ember's scaly hide, and saw Connie and howled. "I'm not cute. I'm not cute like YOU. Your daddy would never send you away! Mine did. Mine sent me away to be eaten by a dragon. He didn't love me enough. They didn't love me enough." Lucy's tears brought on an attack of hiccups, which made them even more painful.

Ember began to rock gently against Lucy's side. "It will be okay," she said. "We love you."

Connie met Ember's gaze, and nodded. "We do, Lucy. We're

not going to send you away. You're with us, and we love you."

"But they sent me away. They sent me away to die and I did nothing wrong."

"I know, Lucy, I know. Just cry, Lucy. It's ok."

"I did nothing wrong."

Gradually, Lucy's spasms grew less intense, the crying less painful. Ember produced the much-abused shroud. Lucy took it, blew her nose thoroughly, and in the quiet that followed, asked: "Why?" She looked at Ember. "Why?" she repeated.

Ember took a deep breath and gave the only answer a friend could give. "Lucy, I don't know why your parents made their choice, but I do know that once we get this girdle off and I can fly us there, we're going to go to Profundia and make darned sure no one else ever has to go through this again."

"And then we will go home and see your mummy and daddy," said Connie. "And they will be so proud of you, 'cause you make things better for everyone, which is what a real princess does."

"We will?"

"We're best buddies, aren't we? And here, I think these are yours."

Connie's dainty hoof very gently nudged Lucy's glasses.

Lucy dropped to the ground and put them on her face.

"Ooh, they're fixed. But how?"

"I can be more than just a singer of silly songs," Connie said.

"Yeah. Sorry to be such a…"

"An asswipe?" asked Ember.

Lucy choked, halfway between a sob and a laugh. "Yeah," she said. Quietly. "Crying like that is not very Princess-like."

"You cried perfectly, Princess Lucinda Merrie Periwinkle Grottweiler Rotunda Doorstop," said Ember. "Nobody could have possibly done it any better."

Margit Elland Schmitt & Dan McLaughlin

Chapter Fourteen
Morning Time Daily

"Good morning, viewers. Welcome back to Morning Time Daily. I'm your host, Artifice Draught." Under the bright, hot lights, and expertly applied makeup, Art smiled warmly, with just the right amount of twinkle in his eyes. He had six trophies for Most Endearing Smile sitting on his mantel at home, and was considered a shoo-in for a seventh at this year's Celebrity Celebration Awards

"And I'm Ambrosia Waters." Art's co-anchor was still new to the program, a bare six months into her tenure, and was still having to wean herself from a tendency to rely on the facts when she was discussing one of their stories. It wasn't that facts were unimportant, but the producers had made it clear that their viewers (and more importantly, the sponsors at Big Time Suds and Soap and Morning Moments Coffee) preferred their information to be gently watered down with friendly conversation, light banter, and a lot of inconsequential chitchat.

"If you're just joining us," said Artifice, "We're here in the studio with expert statistician, Doctor Armando Blatterborp, to discuss his take on the surprising events that occurred just three days ago during the Survival Day Surprise. Welcome Doctor Blatterborp."

"Thank you, Art. I have to say, big fan of the show."

"And we appreciate that here at Morning Time Daily. I think I can say that everyone here appreciates what you have done for us in the past by providing numbers."

Everyone shared smiles all around. Art's was the most endearing, but it had to be admitted that Ambrosia was a quick study, and likely to be nominated for Charm and Compassion. She wouldn't win, not in her first year, but it was an honor just to be nominated.

"Doctor Blatterborp," said Ambrosia, leaning forward just a little. "We know you've analyzed this surprising event. Can you give us some statistics about the likelihood that Princess Lucinda might still be alive?"

"Well, Ambrosia," said the doctor, fidgeting with his coffee cup. "It isn't a pleasant sort of thing to contemplate. After all, history tells us that 100% of princesses who left their stakes in the company of a dragon did so inside the dragon's stomach. This is a unique situation, and dozens of mathematicians and statisticians at the university have been wearing their pencils down in a feverish desire to answer your question."

"Those are some great minds," said Ambrosia.

"Thank you."

"And sharp pencils," added Artifice, chuckling.

"Have they actually solved the question yet?"

"No, not yet. But we're confident that a solution is available."

The camera switched to Art again, smiling. "Let's go for a moment to one of our reporters in the field. Mindy Maxim-Fnort is at the Center for Electronic Design Improvements. How's it going, Mindy?"

Mindy did not have a warm smile, but she did have Great Hair, and more than twenty years of interview experience. The magazines said that she preferred field work to being in the studio, although the blogosphere hinted the reason had less to do with stuffy studio lighting than the fact that she and Artifice couldn't be in the same room without arguing.

"Artifice, I'm visiting with Brian Johnson, one of the engineers at CEDI, who have been designing an important part of the Princess Care Pack for almost twenty years."

"That's impressive, Mindy. Was it the water bottles?"

"No, Art."

"The granola bars?"

"No, Art."

"I've always thought," with his endearing chuckle, "that there was something very well engineered about the combination of grain and seed and honey we call the granola bar. I mean, how does it stick together so —"

"It's the tracking device, Art. The GPS monitor." Mindy managed not to make the interruption come in an exasperated shout. She was a professional. "This is how the Knights have been following the Princess without having to keep the dragon in their line of sight."

Dead air was the worst thing a morning show host could ever incur on his program. It was the host's responsibility to keep the talk flowing easily and well. Later playbacks would show that the stunned silence in the studio lasted for a full, horrifying, five seconds.

"Frankly," said the engineer, Brian, with a little nervous laugh that was naturally endearing, and therefore did not read well on camera, "We never thought it would come in handy. It's a grandfathered project. What with dragons and flight zone laws and so on, there's only a half dozen working satellites even up there, and most of them are taken up with television broadcasts. I had to call in one of the old guys to explain to me what was happening when we started getting a signal. Fortunately, the data is simple enough, just automatic location signaling, longitude and latitude and rate of travel and elevation from sea level, so there's all kinds of interesting data we're getting."

"And the Knights are getting the signal, too," said Mindy, helpfully.

"Oh, yes," said Brian. "They have a transponder wired into their gear. As long as they have the gear with them, they'll be receiving the telemetry data. I'm pretty sure—" He hesitated, and sounded a little doubtful. "I'm pretty sure that they're still trained in translating the readout data stream. I mean, they would be, right?"

"Right," said Mindy, and she smiled a real smile, which was only a little triumphant and not at all relatable, except to Women 35-50 a significant marketing group which made up 40% of the audience of Morning Time Daily. "Art, you'll be glad to know that I've arranged to get an additional transponder for Morning Time Daily's exclusive use. As soon as I get back to the studio, we'll be able to see exactly where the Princess is, and can start interviewing people on her path to see what is happening!"

"You mean, why she betrayed her people and joined forces with the dragon?" Art asked, rallying at last. No one, thanks to the geniuses in Makeup, would be able to say they had seen him sweat.

"Well, Art," Mindy was clearly the victor in this interview, not that it was a contest. We're all friends at Morning Time Daily, even if rumor held that Mindy was hoping to get a job on Evening News Facts Nightly. "I think that after all our questions, it will be nice to finally have a way to get some answers."

"George," said Agent X from the back seat.

"I can't stop him snoring," said George. "I've tried shaking him, but the Blitheringtons have an impenetrable snore generating gene, that isn't just dominant, it's aggressive."

"Not that," said Agent X. He was pretty pleasant company, in the confines of the car. Or maybe that was just George's impression now that he wasn't forcing them to run away from angry innkeepers and jealous tavern-maids. Or maybe it was just that of the three of them, Agent X and George were the ones currently not snoring loudly enough to rattle the steel frame of the car.

"What then?" asked George. He hadn't been driving since he underwent the obligatory training at 18. He actually liked it almost as much as he liked the horses.

"Your helmet is beeping."

Chapter Fifteen
The Rules of Questing

AFTER EVERYBODY HAD A GOOD CRY, IT WAS JUST A matter of traveling through the dark, green shadows of the forest, toward the gap between the mountain that King Frank had assured them was the entrance to the Valley of the Maids.

Lucy was learning a lot on the journey. She learned that she liked trees. She hadn't ever had a chance to see them growing wild before. The palace had an orchard, but it grew in straight lines, and only included apricot trees, and out here in the world, trees grew all different sorts of fruits, nuts, and leaves, and they leaned any way they could to catch the sun or stay out of the wind. Not to mention the plethora of bushes and vines and wildflowers, that made tangles of the ground and tripping hazards of the path, but looked so beautiful, you couldn't really complain about it, except in the moment where you were being scratched by thorns. She learned that mosquitoes loved princesses as much as princesses loved chocolate cake -- maybe more. She learned that sitting on a saddle for hours on end was every bit as painful as walking for hours, even if the horse was gentle. She learned that dragons who had been shrunk could hover like bees, but that it made them tired. She traded off with Ember on Scoots' saddle, only one of them perched on it at a time, and the other one walking.

And she learned that Connie loved to sing.

"The first rule!" warbled the young unicorn from the front of the line.
"The first rule of Questing, the first rule, Hi-ho!
"Is that we all stick together! Hi-ho!
"Together, together
"In any sort of weather! Hi-ho! Hi-ho! Hi-ho!"

They had agreed early on that it was best for Connie, so bright and easy to see, to keep to the front of the line. When she was behind them, it was too late to see where she had run off to when she got distracted. In any case, she was a cheerful addition to the forest, and she kept good time with her singing Lucy and Ember both agreed that Connie's clever little dance was especially endearing.

"The second rule of Questing, the second, Hi-ho!
"Is that we find fresh water, Hi-ho!
"We drink it, don't sink in it.
"We drink the fresh water, Hi-ho! Hi-ho! Hi-ho!"

"I see it, Connie," called Ember, who was currently perched on top of the luggage, carried on Boots' back. The dragon fluttered down to join Connie at the edge of a chattering stream. "Let's be careful not to fall in this time, don't you think?"

"Yes, let's be careful," said Connie, with a cheerful flick of her tail and swish of her mane. "I did not like falling into the last two streams. They were cold, and water is wet."

"You are definitely getting wiser," said Lucy. She looked around the area while the horses and Connie and Ember all bent their heads and drank from the stream. It was a nice little space, flat ground, and lit with faint sparkles of golden light from the setting sun. "Do you think this might be a good place to set up camp?"

"The third rule!" Connie lifted her head up eagerly, and began to prance around the clearing.

"The third rule of Questing. The third rule, Hi-ho!
"Is we set do not set camp, Hi-ho!
"In the damp, the damp
"We do not set camp in a place cold and damp! Hi-ho! Hi-ho! Hi-ho!"

"Well, this place looks warm and dry," said Ember. "As long as it doesn't rain tonight."

"And as long as none of us falls into the stream," added Lucy.

"I won't," promised Connie.

Ember used her wings to help her scale the tall, overspreading trees and to confirm that there were no clouds in the late afternoon sky, and the three draft horses seemed to take it as a given that this was going to be where they stopped for the night, because they were looking at Lucy in a very significant way.

"I suppose you want to be comfortable, too!" Lucy said,

She reached up and began unbuckling the straps that held the saddles and packs onto their backs and dragged the packs one by one over to the area circumscribed by the circle outlined by Connie's dancing hooves. She saw that Ember had already come down from the trees and was busy using her small, sharp claws to clear part of the forest floor of debris.

"Connie," said Ember. "Would you roll some of those rocks over here? I'd like to make a circle inside the circle."

"Hooray!" Connie said, with her usual enthusiasm. "Is this a new game? I'll play." She began looking for rocks of the correct size.

Meanwhile, Lucy opened one of the packs at random. "Let's see whether there is food for you in here. I hope so." She untied the knots, and looked inside, and yes, in one of the packs there were feed bags, already loaded with grain for the horses.

"Num-num," said Lucy, as she got up to try and hook the feed bags onto the horse's heads. They had to bend down on one knee and lower their heads for her to do it, but all three horses seemed interested in dinner. "I know I'm supposed to rub you down, too, but I'm afraid I didn't spend any time at all in the stable. I'm not sure what that is all about."

"Look for a brush!" suggested Connie, busily nudging stones out of their holes in the ground and adding them to Ember's circle. "There should be a brush. All you need to do is brush off the dirt and sweat. They'll feel so much better if you do, won't you, Boots? Won't you, Skipper?"

Lucy found a brush, and a towel, and thought she could probably use both to take care of the horses. Except that it took a long time because the horses were so large. But Lucy had to admit that they didn't have hands and couldn't comb their own legs. Standing on a big rock that Connie rolled over helped. "And since you've been so nice to carry Ember and me all this way, we do kind of owe you a nice treat at the end of the day. It's only fair."

Fair or not, Lucy's arms and legs and back were not at all happy with her by the time she had toweled and combed all three horses and put away the empty feed bags. The clearing was dark. Lucy was sore, especially in places that had never had to do any work at all in her ordinary princess days, but she also felt pretty good about her accomplishments, because Boots, Scoots, and Skipper looked relaxed and happy, and Connie was dancing and making cute little whistles and peeps with her horn.

"Look, Lucy! Look! We made a circle of stones. Isn't it pretty? Ember helped, but I did most of it. Ember did stack the wood up in the middle," Connie added, as one trying to be fair.

"Now, watch this," said Ember, coiled up next to the circle of rocks. Pursing her lips, as if she were about to give a dragon-y whistle, she let out a silken ribbon of flame that kindled the wood and brought a comfortable glow back to the clearing. "I heard you humans prefer your food cooked, and I thought this might help."

"It's lovely," said Lucy, and she found herself smiling.

"It's the best fire I can do, when I'm this small," Ember said, regretfully.

"A bigger one would burn down the whole forest again," said Connie. "We might run out of forests if you kept that up."

Lucy found blankets for the horses in one pack, and in another, three blankets for Connie, Ember, and herself. With those, was an assortment of fruits and vegetables. The fire lit up the clearing so that the trunks of the trees around them seemed to glow, keeping out the shadows and darkness that extended in long directions on all other sides. It was very comfortable, if you would let it. The salad had been long ago, and Lucy actually was very fond of roasted apples and roasted carrots and roasted potatoes, so she thought they would have a very tasty supper. She was sure she would sleep well, even if it was on leaves and twigs and the ground.

"The fourth rule of Questing! The fourth rule, Hi-ho!

"Is we build a fire on the ground, Hi-ho!

"The unicorn with shiny horn

"Puts stones all around! Hi-ho! Hi-ho! Hi-ho!" sang Connie.

From out of the shadows of the forest came the sound of a howling wolf. Boots, Scoots, and Skipper lifted their heads all at once, and their ears swiveled forward. They seemed nervous, but Connie was clearly not.

"The fifth rule of Questing. The fifth rule, Hi-ho!

"Is to brush the fuzzy horses, Hi-ho!

"Head to hoof, hoof to head,

"So they are ready to go to bed. Hi-ho! Hi-ho! Hi-ho!"

A second howl, and then two more, rang out. Lucy couldn't see anything out in the darkness beyond the firelight, but the horses, as big as they were, looked very, very nervous. Their eyes were rolling, and they shifted their weight from foot to foot, as if they wanted to run, but could tell there was nowhere safe to go.

Ember jumped up into the air, wings beating madly, and flew off into the darkness. Lucy wished she hadn't gone. It was nerve-wracking without her. What if the dragon couldn't steer between the trees in the darkness? What if the wolves got her?

"The sixth rule!" sang Connie.

"The sixth rule of Questing! The sixth rule, Hi-ho!

"Is when wolves are in the wood, Hi-ho!

"They howl and they prowl

"Are they bad? Are they good? Hi-ho! Hi-ho! Hi-ho!"

Lucy turned her head in surprise. She'd given up listening to Connie's endless singing, but suddenly it turned out worth listening to. Lucy gasped, her heart lurching. Looking past Connie, into the shadows, she saw the glint of eyes, reflecting the firelight: a wolf!

"There are eight of them!" Ember flew back into the center of the clearing, breathless from her hurry. "They're on all sides of us."

"What should we do?" asked Lucy.

"I don't think they want to come into the firelight," said Ember.

"What if we run out of wood? Or fall asleep? What if the fire goes out?"

Just as suddenly, Lucy was wishing that more of the Royal Curriculum had been devoted to the burning characteristics of different types of wood than to the relative depth of curtseys due to different ranks of nobility.

"I'll go say hello," said Connie and pranced away.

"Connie wait!" Lucy called, jumping to her feet, but before they could stop her, Connie pranced into the darkness of the forest. Ember wrapped her tail around Lucy's leg to try and stop her from following, but she had forgotten she was much smaller than she used to be. The dragon got dragged a few yards forward before Lucy stopped. Tripped, rather, and fell on her knees in the dirt.

"I think," Ember said. "I think she knows what she is doing." Even so, the dragon was worried. Lucy could tell by the way Ember let out a warm-up puff of flame. She couldn't see her friend's expression, though, because when she fell, her glasses had fallen off. The world was just a soft blur of light and dark.

Leading the wolves away from them, Connie was just a white patch in the dark wood, but the wolves seemed drawn to her, as the most vulnerable of the group. Lucy and Ember, Boots, Scoots, and Skipper all watched her progress with dread, and froze when more wolves leaped over the stream bank so that Connie was surrounded. She was still humming, and didn't seem nervous at all, only breaking off her tune when she took time to count all the wolves, as if making sure they were all present.

"Eight! Eight wolvies!" she said. "You are so cute! Have you come to play with us?" She tilted her head, to look more closely at the lead wolf snarling in front of her. "I have to ask: Wolfie, are you a good wolf or a bad wolf?"

The growling sound intensified. One of the wolves behind her darted in and nipped at her heel.

"Connie, look out!" called Lucy.

"Bad wolf!" squealed Connie. She kicked with her hind legs at the wolf who had snapped at her, killing it instantly with her sharp hooves, and sending it soaring gracefully over the campsite in a high arc. Ember, bathed it in a sheet of flame as it passed overhead. Apparently she did have more firepower than she'd supposed, and it landed, smoking, on the far side of the stream bank.

"Tsk!" said Connie, and she turned back to the other wolves surrounding her. "Are you a good wolf?" she asked again. The wolf in front of her lunged, and she skewered it with her horn and tossed it aside. "Are you a good wolf?" A third wolf went roaring for her throat, and she reared up, stabbing with her needle-sharp horn and the razor quickness of her front hooves. "You?" Another wolf leaped, and Connie gave an easy toss of her head and flicked it into the lifeless body of its neighbor.

"Bad, bad, bad, bad" she said. "Four more bad."

Connie reared and crushed and skewered and kicked, and soon there was only one wolf left, one who crouched, snarling, on the very edge of the clearing, barely visible in the flicker of firelight.

Connie looked down her bloodstained horn and considered the wolf for a long moment.

Lucy realized she was holding her breath.

"You're very cute," said Connie softly, still leading with the behavior she would like to see. "But are you a good wolf or a bad wolf?"

The wolf snarled and whipped its tail back and forth. Hesitating only a fraction of a moment, the wolf took a few steps back, then turned tail and ran off into the darkness.

"Hooray! He chose cuteness." Connie gave a nod of approval. Then with a little shake, she trotted cheerfully down to the stream, where after a few moments of delighted splashing, she emerged completely clean, no longer covered in wolf blood and effluvium.

"The seventh rule! The seventh rule of Questing!

"Is that we kill bad wolfies dead,

"Poke then with the pointy horn

"And kick them in the head. Hi-ho! Hi-ho! Hi-ho!"

If you hadn't heard Connie singing that song all afternoon, you might not have noticed that the little unicorn was swinging her hips just a little bit wider and swishing her tail just a little more aggressively.

"She just kicked some major wolfie butt," said Lucy, in the tone of one who was trying not to freak out.

"All the while looking as cute as a button," added Ember, striving for the same even and fair tone.

"You know, I'm never going to hear that song in the same way ever again," Lucy remarked.

"I think the correct answer to the question, 'Are you a good wolf or a bad wolf?' is 'Good wolf,'" Ember said.

"If you are a wolf," Lucy said. She was still having trouble catching her breath.

"Interested in living," Ember said with a nod.

While Ember was speaking, Lucy got to her hands and knees and crawled around in as dignified and princess-worthy fashion as possible. She was trying to find her glasses, but when she did, gave a small sigh of regret. They had fallen too near the horses, and Boots, Scoots and Skipper, concerned with the wolves, had broken them into bits and ground those bits into the dirt with their big, nervous hooves.

"I won't be able to wear these anymore," she said. "I think they're so broken that even Connie can't fix them."

"We can watch out for you," said Ember, always supportive.

"My mother would have been able to make you new ones," Connie said. "I'm not old enough for that yet."

"Well, you're old enough to save our lives," said Ember.

"Yeah," said Lucy in the general direction of her two friends. "You seem like you did a lot of growing up tonight."

"Hey, maybe I did," said Connie, and the filly took a deep breath. Her horn sparkled and glowed, and suddenly a pair of Bakelite pale green oversized glasses with embedded rhinestones appeared spinning around Connie's head.

"Oh, pretty!" The glasses circled at a variable rate. "Oh my, I'm getting dizzy."

"Connie!" said Lucy.

"Oops, sorry."

And just as suddenly, the glasses appeared on Lucy's face instead.

"Connie, that's not what I meant!" Lucy's hand went up to her face and touched the glasses. "Hey, I can see better…" She looked around. "Wow!" Lucy looked over at Ember. "These feel cute, are they cute?" asked Lucy.

"Yes, actually, they are. They look good on you," answered Ember.

"Oh," said Connie, full of excitement again. "Oh yes, they are adorable!" Connie was simply bursting with excitement again. Her horn glowed, and a small hand mirror appeared in front of Lucy. She caught it before it could fall and break, and considered herself.

"Hey, they are cute. Can I keep them?" she asked.

"Oh my goodness, yes! They are so cute on you. Green really is a good color for you!" Connie said.

"Well, thanks, but really Connie… Ember… " Lucy took a deep breath. "I want to make one thing perfectly straight."

Connie looked up, excited, "Is this a geometry lesson? I love geometry. Do I need a protractor?"

"No, not that," Lucy said, disconcerted. "Let me level with you."

"Oh, civil engineering, I love civil engineering, it is such a useful art."

"Connie, now it would be wise to be quiet," said Ember. "Again."

"I just want to say thank you, to both of you," Lucy said. "For saving us from the wolves, and for being with me when I really,

really needed good friends." She gave Connie a big hug, and gave another one to Ember, and the three girls giggled the rest of the night away.

Chapter Sixteen
Is It or Isn't It A Bomb?

Even though the roads were almost empty, George decided to pull over in a deserted side-road before examining the noises that had been emerging from his helmet in the trunk of the car. Part of that was because he was naturally cautious, and another part was because he could see a creek bed nearby, and if the beeping was coming from a bomb, he thought he might like to dive into the water before it exploded. Also, he wanted to wake Chip up, because if the beeping wasn't what was giving him a headache, he felt confident that the snoring deserved at least a little of the blame.

It took shaking and, it must be confessed, gently banging Chip's head against the door frame, before the Knight awoke, with a sputter and a yawn. The silence when the snoring stopped was profound. George would have liked to have felt all the muscles he'd been clenching against the sonic assault relax, except... the bomb.

At least, they presumed it was a bomb.

"Who would have set it?" asked Chip. "Do we have any enemies?"

"Except each other?" asked George. But it was true that with the ongoing digestive war between dragons and humans that had engrossed them all for generations, there hadn't been much going on in the way of kingdom-to-kingdom combat.

Fortunately, they had Agent X, who had trained for this,

among many other mysterious emergencies. Sleek in his black jumpsuit, he leapt out of the car and flung open the trunk while Chip was still stretching. Agent X (Never just Agent, and never just X, and only Rex if you happened to be the Queen) had found the helmet and was turning it over in both hands, thoughtfully. Agent X prodded a few places in it, and it gave him a small, electrical shock. Agent X yelped. George braced himself to dive into the creek.

There was no explosion.

"No one else's armor seems to be doing this," Agent X said, holding it out to George. "But it looks like an electronic gizmo. I've made so many modifications to my gear, I'm not surprised a wire or two might have come loose. I'll look it over when we have more time, but it just seems like a message, not anything dangerous."

"Why doesn't mine have a message?" asked Chip, looking for his own helmet in the back of the car. It would take some time to discover it in a casual search, thought George, since he remembered (if Chip did not) that Chip had deliberately left his helmet behind at the Academy, because he preferred to let his hair blow artistically in the wind. He hadn't really thought there would be any danger on the beach mission — if he had, he might have accepted that saving his skull could be worth a little helmet-hair.

George let Chip do the rummaging, and Agent X made a small gesture, as if giving permission for George to put the helmet on. It was kind of him, George knew, not to just stick his own head in there and see what the noise was about — the helmets were one size fits most, and he could easily have done it, so giving George a moment, in case the message (if it was a message) was private, was a surprising act of consideration.

Or a precaution against having his own head blown up, in case he was wrong and the message turned out to be "Boom!" or something similar.

There was no explosion. When George put the helmet on, the beeping (which was not loud) was right by his ear, and adjusting the helmet's buckle for security, clicked some kind of receptor so that almost at once, the beeping stopped. Instead, a genteel voice, one he recognized from the voicemail system at the Academy, said: "George Gerontius, incoming message stream for your attention. Please enter your pass code to continue."

There didn't seem to be a keyboard in the confines of the helmet, but after some awkward trial and error, Chip discovered that the pass code had to be rapped with a knuckle against the side of the helmet — while it was on George's head — and was "shave and a hair-cut, two bits."

"Thank you. Spooling data now." There was a whirring sound, and George wondered whether he was about to be treated to a message about an overdue Academy library book — there was one sitting on his desk back in his room, because he hadn't expected to be gone this long — but it turned out not to be a message at all, but a command of some sort to another part of his helmet. He thought, for a moment, that something was caught in his eye; all at once, the lens he was looking through had discolored, and there was a flickering.

No, not a flickering, an arrow. George blinked, and realized he couldn't exactly focus on the arrow itself, but if he turned his head in that direction, he got a brief message, scrolling across the glass. It took him several tries before he got all of it — he hadn't worked with any sort of data packet since his earliest training days, and had thought the idea of a helmet-feed was just theoretical.

"It's a map," he said. "Or... directions. Yes, that's it. A direction and distance. To the Princess."

"What?" said Chip.

"Evidently when the dragon took her, she still had the direction tag on or with her. No way to tell now whether she's in good health, but at least we have a signal to follow."

"That's wonderful!" said Chip. "So we can arrest her and slay the beast. Heroes all!"

"You'd better let me drive," said Agent X, closing the lid of the trunk.

"That's a good idea," said George. "I don't think I can control the car and keep track of where we're meant to be heading. If you don't mind my navigating, I can…"

"Point to the right," said Agent X, deadpan.

George grinned in answer, and deliberately pointed left.

"Close enough. The job is yours."

Chapter Seventeen
Glowerflorious

"Oo-oh, who are the creatures in your forest?
"In your forest. In your fo-ho-rest?
"Say, who are the creatures in your forest?
"They're the creatures that you'll meet today!" Connie had picked up a new verse.

"I never knew there were so many interesting creatures living in the forest," sang Lucy.

"In this forest?" sang Ember. Both the dragon and the princess had learned that singing with Connie was better than just listening to Connie.

"Yes, in this forest," sang Connie, her tail happily emphasizing "this".

"They are the creatures you will meet,"

"When you're walking on your feet,"

"The lovely creatures that you'll meet today!" they chorused. It was a good chorus. Connie had added a harmony that was actually harmonic. Even the horses seemed to enjoy the tune, bobbing their heads in time to the music.

Ember looked ahead. "And who is that in the middle of the road ahead?"

Connie and Lucy obediently began to sing: "In the road ahead…"

"No guys, cut it out. There really is someone up there on the path."

They stopped walking. Lucy, conscious of her new glasses, squinted a little. "It's awfully small. Are you sure it's not a rock?"

Dragons have very good eyesight, even when they have been miniaturized. Ember tilted her head a little, as if for a better angle. "It looks like a kitten," but she sounded uncertain.

"A kitten all by itself in the middle of the road?" Connie looked alarmed. "Oh no!" With typical impulsiveness, she took off, going from a standstill to a full run with nothing but a flying leap.

"COMING, KITTY!" she called. She twittered on her horn like an urgent sparrow.

"CONNIE!" Lucy shouted. "WHAT IS THE FIRST RULE OF QUESTING?" The horses were slower to respond than any of them would have liked, but Ember launched herself into the air almost instantly. To their surprise, Connie stopped her mad rush, skidded to a halt, and waited.

"The first rule is that everyone sticks together," she said. "HI-ho. I know." She gave them an agonized, urgent look. "But it's a kitty."

"This is a dark and dangerous forest. We've been singing all day about the creatures we found in it, and they included deadly vipers, growly bears, and a cranky wild boar."

"Yes," said Connie. "This is why I was hurrying to rescue the kitty. I've never seen a kitty before, but I know they are cute and fluffy."

"Boots and Scoots and Skipper did not like having to run away from the bear."

"But…"

"Ember did not like having to wrestle the deadly viper."

"But…"

"The kitty, which could actually be just a kitty-shaped-rock, will still be there if we take our time." Lucy scolded. "I have seen kitties, and if it's sitting there, it will probably sit there a while longer. We don't have to rush."

"Oh, all right," Connie muttered, but she wasn't singing anymore.

Lucy considered it a battle won. They moved forward. Connie's ears and tail remained alert, and they soon began to make out details.

"It has adorable little whiskers!" Connie announced. "And a fluffy little tail."

"It doesn't seem to be a very friendly kitty," murmured Lucy to Ember, who nodded. What awaited them in the middle of the road was actually a little, hissing fuzzball of wrath.

"It has green eyes!" Connie cooed. And it did. They were wide, and the pupils were narrowed into vengeful slits as it watched them approach.

"And orange stripes!" Connie said. This was also true, although the fur was sticking out in all directions, as spiky as it was stripy.

The cat yowled, a drawn-out agonizing caterwaul that made Lucy stop in her tracks. She shivered. Even Connie, technically with her fellow questers, but definitely in the lead, hesitated for a moment.

"Hello, kitty," Connie said. "Are you a good kitty or a bad kitty?" She paused only a few paces away from the kitten, which hissed and spit in response.

Lucy jumped down from Scoots.

"Be careful, Connie," Lucy said. "Don't talk to it. I think it's magical."

"Because it's so angry?" asked Ember, fluttering over to look.

"Well, a little bit, but more because it's floating!" Lucy pointed, and it was true, that the angry, yowling kitten was hovering just a few inches above the ground.

"That's different," said Ember. "I didn't think cats did that."

"They don't," said Lucy.

"I think this is a bad kitty," said Connie, lowering her head, and moving her beautiful, and occasionally deadly horn in smaller and smaller circles. "Bad, bad kitty." She was focusing on the little cat, but didn't seem to notice that every time she said the word "bad" it was growing bigger.

Whoa!" said Lucy. "Connie, let's rethink this. We can just go around!"

However, Connie only braced herself in the road, muscles twitching. It was as if Connie's long-lost psychotic twin had suddenly emerged. "Bad kitty," she said. The kitten grew. It was almost the opposite of what had happened to Ember, Lucy realized.

"Bad, bad, bad, kitty!" sang Connie.

"It's time to crush the evil kitty,

"Once it's dead it won't be pretty.

"Bad, bad, bad, kitty, BAD!"

Lucy put her arms around Connie. "Don't touch it," she said. "Can't you see that it's magical?"

Though Lucy tried her best, the unicorn filly shook her off as easily as she would shake away a fly.

"Bad, bad, bad, kitty!

"Throw it into the lake with a bag of rocks!

"Or into the ocean from the longest dock!

"Bad, bad, bad, kitty, BAD!" sang Connie.

The kitten grew.

"Ember, help!" Lucy said. "Connie is being enchanted, and her song doesn't even scan!" Lucy reached up and tugged at Connie's horn, tying to make it point anyplace else but at the hissing, growing kitty. Ember flew over and began to tug on Connie's mane, to no avail. Either unicorns were stronger than they appeared, or there was some other force holding Connie.

Boots, Scoots, and Skipper shared a glance, then went to the other side of Connie, put their shoulders against her quivering hide, and pushed. This, at least, got a result. While Connie was still rigid and focused on the kitty, the three draft horses managed to push her inexorably to one side, though her hooves left great gouges in the roadway.

"Hi-ho, Hi-ho,

"Let me go!

"Bad, bad, kitty needs to be squished-squished-squished!

"That is my fondest wish-wish-wish!"

"Err… Hi-ho! Hi-ho!"

They got several meters away, and Ember said, "Well we've moved her and she still seems to be equally as bewitched, so that means it's not a spatially distinct spell imposed from the outside."

Lucy gave her a blank look. "What?"

Ember gave her a small, almost bashful smile. "Well, I can't cast spells, but I have read about them."

"Oh. But what does it mean?"

"It means that whatever is causing the magic isn't in the ground or the cat. It must derive its power from inside Connie."

"Connie," screamed Lucy. "Think of something nice!"

"Bad kitty. Bad, bad,

"Bad kitty, stop your pushin'

"Dead and skinned, you'll make a cozy cushion!

"Hi-ho, Hi-ho!" said Connie to the growing, glowering kitty, who was now the size of a mountain lion, and whose tail was whipping back and forth as energetically as Connie's.

"Connie, think of lollipops, cotton candy, soap bubbles," pleaded Lucy, hanging from the horn.

"Meadows, butterflies, babbling brooks," said Ember, tugging on the mane.

Boots, Scoots, and Skipper, pushing mightily from the side and having the most effect, paused and stamped their left hooves in unison, and then resumed pushing.

"The HERD!" Ember said.

"Your MUMMY and DADDY!" said Lucy.

Suddenly, Connie's straining muscles went slack, and everyone else went sprawling and staggering at the abrupt release in pressure.

"I'm dizzy," said Connie. "And my head hurts, too."

"Oh Connie," Lucy picked herself up off the ground and gave the unicorn a big bear hug. "I'm so glad that you are better!"

Connie looked over at the incensed kitty, still spitting and snarling with an arched back and lashing tail. "Is that the kitty?" she asked, uncertainly. "She got big quick."

"Don't get any closer, Connie," Ember zoomed in to block Connie's line of sight, in case the little unicorn tried to approach the road again. "We don't know what effect it might have on you if you get closer."

"Well, it's obviously unhappy," said Connie. "And full of magic. We can't leave it here."

Lucy and Ember exchanged glances. Lucy shrugged.

Ember said. "Well, the cat does seem to be pretty much rooted to that spot. Maybe it's a spatially contiguous spell."

"You just said it wasn't," said Lucy.

"It's not a spell that works on how close you are to the kitten," said Ember, carefully. "We found that out because it worked even when we moved Connie away. The spell was affecting Connie's mind."

"And the kitty's, too," said Connie, helpfully.

"Yes, but probably it has something to do with that space in the road, more than you or the kitten."

"That means one of us has to try and move it, right?" Lucy said, carefully.

"Without getting close enough to be affected by the spell," Ember said.

Everyone looked at the snarling, hissing, spitting bundle of feline hatred for a long moment. Though still technically a kitten, it was also still the size of a small lion or a tiger, and did not invite much sympathy from anyone except the supernaturally kindly Connie, who seemed to have gone back to her normal self. Lucy made a face. Skipper stomped her hoof.

"Oh," Lucy said, "good idea!" She went to the draft horse's side and began to rummage through one of the packs the Unicorn Queen had packed. "Just hang on, guys, I'll be right there. I have an idea. Please just make sure the kitty doesn't go anywhere."

"Sure," Ember said with an understandable lack of enthusiasm. "I'm on it."

"Maybe if 'bad kitty' makes it grow, 'good kitty' will make it shrink," said Lucy, her voice somewhat muffled from inside the pack. "And I just remembered when we caught those fish for breakfast yesterday. We have this!" Lucy emerged from behind Skipper, bearing a net with a telescoping handle and beekeeper outfit.

"OK. I'm good to go! This should help me catch the kitty without even having to step on the road. Be sure to thank your mom for thinking of everything, Connie!"

Lucy cautiously approached the snarling, spitting bundle of fury, edging closer to the side of the road, and watching her feet to be sure she didn't trespass over the verge.

"Nice, kitty, good kitty. Oh, so good, good kitty," Lucy cooed at the really not very nice at all kitty. She was nervous, but it was encouraging that every time she said the word "good" the enchanted cat shrank a little bit, and then a little bit more. Soon it was back to cat size.

Among the useful things princesses were trained to do was to say the same thing over and over and still sound sincere. Usually, it was simple phrases like, "How do you do?" or "Welcome to the palace," or "What an intriguing piece of legislation," but in this case, it was "Good, good, good kiddy." Lucy's tutors would have been stunned to see their lesson applied with such skill by a pupil who had been so "difficult" or (more tactfully) a pupil who "represented such a unique challenge."

"Here, let me just pick you up and take you to some, place nice and safe, and we can try to break the magic spell."

Suddenly, Lucy lunged with the net and scooped up the kitty. The kitty, once again just kitty-sized, was stunned to have actually been touched, and was quiet for the briefest of moments.

"It worked! I am a Kitty Whisperer!" Lucy exclaimed, prematurely as it turned out. She shifted her weight to carry the kitten out of the enchanted road and bring it to her friends. The world was quiet, just for a moment, and then the kitty became an outraged whirlwind of teeth and claws. Lucy tried to contain the kitty and move away from the road, but that only seemed to make things worse. The kitten, already enraged and enchanted, became something much more savage, though it was difficult to recognize graduations of ferocity at this point.

The kitty tore through the net, and Lucy, acting on instinct rather than rational thought, caught the creature in both hands.

When constructing the timeline of what went wrong later, this act was highlighted as "Where Things Got Really Bad." Catching the enraged kitty was filed under "Things to Never, Ever Be Done Again."

But absent the lessons of hindsight, Lucy caught the cat, which bit and scratched and clawed, as if it were some sort of animated buzzsaw, up her arms, and lunged in a bloodthirsty, murderously fluffy way for her face. Lucy's beekeeper's outfit was shredded by the magical claws, and her skin suffered as well.

Fortunately, the facial helmet survived and the kitty clawed its way to the top of Lucy. Then, with no change in its ferocious cries, obeying some inner call, the kitten abruptly launched itself into space, and landed in the road again, as near as anyone could tell, in the exact spot it had been previously. Yowling madly, screaming in blood-curdling fury in the air, the kitty landed on all four feet, sat and quietly began to clean itself.

"Aw," said Connie. "Kitties are so cute!"

"Holy Mother of Felicitousness. That hurts," Lucy was shaking. Her hands and arms and other body parts stung fiercely. She was bleeding, and felt like she would never really be much of a cat person no matter how old or lonely she got.

Ember looked reflective. "Okay, that didn't work. We won't break the spell that way."

"You think?" Lucy looked up from her shredded skin. "You really think so? What next?" Sarcasm mixed with a liberal dose of princess fury made for a forceful delivery. "Maybe we should find an enchanted fire hose and try and try and soak the magic out of it. What could go wrong with spraying a magically enchanted cat with water?"

"No," said Ember, thoughtfully. "That wouldn't work."

"Oh, really?" asked Lucy, with an exaggerated politeness born of pain and frustration and leftover terror. "Why is that? Do you think, just maybe, that interfering with the magic might make the kitty a tad miffed?"

"Yeah, probably," agreed Ember.

"Well, I wish someone had thought of that earlier," Lucy grumbled.

Connie reached down and lightly touched Lucy with the tip of her horn, and the scratches immediately began to heal, which definitely helped improve Lucy's mood.

"Thanks, Connie," she said.

"All right," said Ember. "According to one school of thought, magic is simply a metaphor brought to life. To counteract that magic then, all we simply need to do is find the basis of that metaphor, and then counteract it. Somehow. We simply don't have enough data."

Boots stomped her hoof and shook her load.

"Good idea, Bootsie," exclaimed Connie.

"Oh yeah," said Lucy. "Let's look through the stuff from my Survival Packet," Lucy went to get the shroud and the items she'd rolled into it from Boots' pack. "One of the items was magical enough to transform a whole dragon. Maybe something here will help with an angry kitty creature."

Skirting a wide half-circle around the dangerous kitten of doom, Lucy crouched next to her two friends, and dumped out the contents of the Packet. "Flashlight, water bottle, shoe insoles, trail mix, and applesauce tins," she said. Attracted by the falling materials, the kitty stopped grooming, and looked up with kittenish curiosity.

"Aw," said Connie.

"It looks like my sister Pacifica's pet cat, Mister Rumbles," said Lucy.

"It's so cute," said Connie, with a wistful sigh over the kitten in the road. "Its whiskers probably tickle."

"They stab," said Lucy, who had reason to know. "But, I do have a weird idea." She bent down and scooped up the trail mix, and shook the packaging. It was bright red and gold, and she had to wrestle with it.

"Are you hungry?" asked Connie. "Maybe you should take a bite of lishflat."

"Flashlight," corrected Lucy automatically. "I'll need that, too, but not yet." She finally managed to open the packet of nuts and seeds and cereal, and dumped that in her lap, only to spread the plastic wrapper out and try to smooth it. She pulled the cap off of one of the water bottles.

"I thought we agreed that it wasn't a good idea to get the cat wet," said Ember.

Lucy actually smiled. She passed the cap to Connie. "Can you poke a teeny hole in the middle of this, please?" she asked. Connie's horn was up to the task, certainly, and Lucy slid the red plastic wrap from the trail mix, over the top of the flashlight, and covered it with the cap and its pinhole. "Watch this. Back home, my sister used to play a game like this with her cat all the time."

Lucy turned on the flashlight, and immediately, the light through the pinhole and the red film made a bright red dot appear on the roadway in front of the kitten. Lucy jiggled the flashlight, and the dot seemed to dance, like a firefly or a fairy. Immediately the kitty froze. All its attention was focused on the light.

By shaking the light so that it flickered one way and then another, Lucy was able to keep the kitten's attention, and eventually, it forgot to be angry, forgot everything but a desire to catch the red dot. It crouched down, looking ready to pounce, but in a kittenish way, Lucy was relieved to see, not a "death to all mortals" way. Keeping an eye on those terrible claws, Lucy teased the cat, and gradually, steadily, lured it away from the road.

"That does look like fun," said Ember. Lucy looked up and saw that while the kitten was transfixed on the dot, Ember and Connie couldn't take their eyes off the kitten. It was almost as adorable as Connie now, and looked perfectly harmless as it pounced and whirled and pawed at the air. Even Boots, Scoots, and Skipper seemed to be enjoying the show, and quite honestly, no one but Lucy seemed to notice that the kitty was getting further and further away from her spot.

"Can I try?" asked Ember.

"Sure," said Lucy, and passed the flashlight over into Ember's claws. Laughing, Ember continued to play with the kitty, making wider and higher circles with the moving red dot, causing the kitty to jump higher and farther. Ember sent the red dot high into the air. The kitty leapt up, and began to grow.

"Oh, no," said Lucy, bracing herself for bloodshed.

Following the red dot, the kitten kept going up into the air, and it kept growing. Larger than a lion, larger than a bear, it grew and elongated, and continued to rise. Its orange-striped fur became orange-striped scales. It sprouted wings, and as it continued to grow, its neck elongated, and so did its tail.

"Holy Mother of…" whispered Lucy.

"Felicitiousness!" whispered Connie.

The flashlight fell from Ember's claws, and everyone stared upwards at what was without a doubt the biggest dragon any of them had ever seen. Larger even than Ember had been before the girdle. Orange and gold, the dragon let out a mighty roar, of relief or rage, they couldn't tell. A tremendous wall of flame shot out.

"Bye-bye kitty," said Connie.

"Farewell forest, too," said Lucy.

"Wait," said Ember. "I know that dragon."

Ember's wings beat mightily and she darted upward before Lucy could suggest a more cautious approach. As she rose into the air, Ember let out a much smaller version of the dragon's roar, and what looked like a purely decorative dart of flame. She had gotten much better at fine-tuning her fire since she'd become enchanted, and it was clear, at least to Lucy and Connie, that she was just trying to get the big dragon's attention. Lucy hoped the big dragon would see it that way.

The big flying dragon looked down and saw Ember and folded his enormous wings. With terrifying speed, the dragon plummeted downward, screeching madly. It was probably just as well that Lucy, Connie, and the draft horses were frozen by the spectacle, so they were standing firmly rooted to the spot when the dragon, instead of crushing them like mosquitoes, landed gently to one side of the smoking hole where his flame had reduced the kitten's spot in the road to a crater. Ember, still flying, was less fortunate. The mighty rush of wind from his wings sent the much smaller dragon tumbling backwards, head over tail.

"Esmeraldavinia," the big dragon called. "Are you here? I thought I heard you."

Ember had righted herself, and she was flying back at top speed. She seemed as miffed as the kitten had been, which Lucy found frightening. "Burn it, Glowerflorious, do you always have to land like a ton of rocks? Always?"

The other dragon squinted down at Ember, who was hovering furiously.

"Esmeraldavinia," he said. "It is you. What's happened? I'm a little fuzzy about the last few days, but I remember that even when you were small, you were not this small!" The big dragon laughed, and Lucy couldn't help thinking that she'd come a long way when hearing a dragon laugh loudly as thunder was more comforting than scary.

"Do you know this kitty, Ember? And who is Esmeraldavinia?" asked Connie, dubiously.

"I think it's safe to say the dragon is the kitty," said Lucy. "And Esmeraldavinia is the long way to say Ember's name."

"Oh," said Connie. "Like mine is Confidantina."

"Yes, I know this big lug," said Ember. "This is Glowerflorious. He was one of my big brother's best friends when they were growing up. They went off to eat maidens a year ago, and never came back."

Fluttering her wings, Ember lifted herself up to eye level with the bigger dragon. "Glowerflorious, do you know where Charrtonio is?"

The large dragon settled on the verge, and folded his claws in front of him. He was motionless, thinking, and everyone else became aware of how exactly still a dragon could be when it wanted.

"I wish I could tell you," Glowerflorious said. "But we got separated even before we made it to the snacking spot. I had hoped that Charrtonio had eaten his maiden, destroyed a knight or two, and gone home safely, but I got drawn off over the forest by a strange light. The next thing I knew, a wizard stood in front of me with a magic wand. I was frozen in place by a bright light, and then… Poof!" He blew a picturesque puff of orange smoke. "Enchanted kitten. It was horrible." The dragon shook his enormous, scaly head. "All I knew was that I had to stay on this spot. I couldn't move, but as long as I stayed there, I could feel…" He gave a slow shake of his big, scaly head. "I was being drained. I don't know how to explain it. There was food and water. I wasn't too hot or cold, but something, some important part of me, was being leeched away."

"That sounds awful," said Lucy, sympathetically.

"It was," agreed Glowerflorious. "If only they'd left me in my dragon shape, it would have been the easiest job in the world to escape. I don't mind admitting that I was afraid for my life. It's why I started attacking anyone who came near." He shifted his wings, and proved, at least to Lucy, that he was every bit as good at shrugging as Ember.

"I was a kitten. If I'd been myself, I could have done it. One whisk of fire, and they'd be ash and cinders. One nibble, and they'd be lunch." He sighed. "Kittens lack any sort of arsenal. The best I was able to manage since my imprisonment was a maiming or two."

"You seemed to do all right with what you had," Lucy said, feeling a tad less sympathetic.

"Well, I'm not sure where the idea came from, but it seemed to me that if I could only kill one intruder, I'd be free of the enchantment. Maybe because when the intruders attacked me or called me names, like 'bad kitty'," he nodded in a friendly way to Connie, "I was able to get closer to my original size. I think if I'd managed to kill you, the curse would have been lifted, but we'll never know."

"Actually, we do. Because this time you were playing with people who were being nice to you," said Ember. "And all that niceness broke the spell. When that happened, you reverted to being yourself again."

"Wow," said Glowerflorious. "When I'm wrong, I'm really wrong. But Ember," he turned his head to examine her more closely. "What's up with the itty bitty dragon act?"

"It's not an act, unfortunately," said Ember. "It's a magic girdle. The enchantment makes me small," she added, with some degree of bitterness.

"And we are on our way to the Valley of the Maids, because maids know how to take off girdles and stuff like that, and then Ember will be Regular-sized Ember, not Mini-Ember," Connie said.

"We're on a quest, actually." For some reason, Lucy felt she needed to insert herself into the conversation.

Glowerflorious peered down at her. "Ah, yes. You're the one

who made the red light that broke the spell. Thank you, maiden."

"Lucy," said Lucy.

"She's my best friend, Glowerflorious," added Ember.

"Lucy," he said. "I am sorry I shredded your white suit with my enchanted kitten claws, and I am forever in your debt for the rescue." Glowerflorious bowed his head, which still left him considerably taller than Lucy.

"I helped, too!" piped up Connie.

"And this is Connie, my other best friend," Ember supplied.

"I'm a unicorn," Connie explained. "Are you going to travel along with us to the Valley of the Maids to free Ember from the spell? And then to the deep, dark, whatsis of Profundia so we can tell the wizards to stop what they're doing? Then dragons won't eat maidens anymore." Connie's tail twitched with pride as she finished her recital of the summary of the plot.

"Connie," said Ember. "Glowerflorious has been trapped in the body of the kitten, forced to not be able to devour people. I'm sure he would rather not—"

"Yes, I'll come," Glowerflorious said.

"And be our boon companion?" asked Connie eagerly, displaying her questing vocabulary.

"I wouldn't miss it for the world," said the big dragon.

"Hooray!" Connie gleefully began to caper around the still-smoking crater. "The kitty is coming with us as our new best friend!"

Glowerflorious seemed to find the unicorn as amusing and adorable as she found him, but for the moment, his attention was focused on the only other dragon present. "Don't worry, Ember," he said in what, for a dragon, was a quiet and reassuring voice. "We'll find out what happened to Charrtonio, and if it turns out he's become enchanted someplace, well, I'm not going to bet against you and your friends. You'll find a way to save him, too."

Chapter Eighteen
Profundia Participant Survival Celebration Day FAQs, Dragon Edition

Congratulations on your selection! You are now an integral part of one of Drangondom's most hallowed institutions, the Profundia Survival Day, a day that continually gives purpose and meaning to our lives as dragons, both as individuals and as a people. Together, we (well, mostly you, to be honest) protect a unique and irreplaceable ecological niche, maintain water purity in a very difficult environment and promote the general welfare. Once the task is accomplished you will have a lifetime of satisfaction knowing you have done your part for dragon society. Pat yourself on the back! Or have someone do it for you because our arms are so small! We know you have a MILLION questions, so we've bundled some of the most common together with answers you can use!

Arrgersddd frogler?

Why you? Excellent question! You were selected because you are incredibly (items noted below): CitAdmnCde DHRCP 4 sec.13 9(c-e)
X Young

Intelligent
Agile
X   Available
Have a strong stomach
Have superior social skills
Come from a good family
X   Come from a family
X   Can fly and breathe fire at the same time

Have displayed an aptitude with these extracurricular activities:
School Play
Musical Instrument
Sports, Soccer
Sport, Anything Else
Student Government
Volunteer Work
With Homeless
With Aged
With Disabled
Debate Team
X   Hovels and Humans
Art
Anything Science-y
Highest Score in <u>DAT 920 (adequate enough)</u>

Cccrrrttghh 'DHRCP'?

Doesn't matter. Something in human.

Grrought. Srrogh, grrrumblegrough greesele rtuurtuu?

Good question! It's really very simple. As part of their fiendish plan to destroy the world and steal every dragon's hoard, humans leave their excess maidens on the shore. They don't care that they are thereby ruining a perfectly dragon-friendly habitat. Meaning it's our (meaning is this specific case, your) job to swoop in and eat them. Easy Peasy, right? Once you do that, only good things will come your way!

Cccrrrttghh fgggghhtty kkkdfgtpmtt rtuurtuu?

Ok, for one thing, it looks GREAT on a resume! Put a maiden in your belly and under your belt and watch yourself go right to the top of the Clan. Maybe even all the Clans. It's the Crème de la Crème of Community Service! Now, we're not going to say anything OFFICIAL, but it is pretty much the worst-kept secret in Dragondom that those who have completed a tour of Beach Clean-up Duty receive access to a special valley populated with juicy, fat deer who have little legs and breed like rabbits. We've heard that the caves around that valley are already stocked with gold and jewels.

Most dragons don't even come back; they munch one maiden and settle back for the good life.
Cccrrrttghh "Easy Peasy"?

Oh, it's a human expression meaning roughly gggrrrffhrth rrrgggffhrth.

"Crème de la Crème"?

Oh, that's human too. It's like cklllats ckllats.

Grrought. Wweewjjwejgh wwwpppwpppgthom rtuurtuu?

You want specifics? That's great! That's the spirit! Starting first thing on Monday, you'll begin an intensive training program in the necessary Maiden Devouring and Knight Fighting skill courses. But wait, there's more! You'll also receive a free 10 oz. supply of Maiden Detection Spray and Skin Moisturizer. The secret formula in this bottle makes sure that what you find tied to a post on your assigned beach is a genuine maiden (i.e., making sure there is no embarrassing error on our part). You just hop within two feet (dragon feet, not human feet, VERY IMPORTANT) of the officially designated maiden and spray her. Then:

If the shroud stays grey, fly away.

If the shroud turns blue, chomp or burn is what to do.

As a bonus, top performers in the training program will get to choose the flavor of their Maiden Detection Spray (Fall Nutmeg; Winter Spice; Spring Blossom; or Summer Splash) as well as a delightful array of additional sauces and spices to make the requisite gobble a delight you won't soon forget.

(Although, to be honest, some dragons prefer just a simple sprig of a lemon tree squeezed, then served on the side. Which is cool. We've got greenhouses.)

Cccrrrttghh kraughtywqqq grrrroogh?

Nope, that's pretty much it. Oh, wait, there is a badge too, but most dragons usually don't bother with it. Just swooping down and snatching up the maiden is usually enough ID to establish your bona fides, but otherwise it's really a piece of cake.

Don't bother asking. Something human, approximately meaning tyyyyootemmmrrrgh yggghhther.

Chapter Nineteen
The Valley of The Maids

IT WAS LATE AFTERNOON WHEN THE TRAVELERS FINALLY arrived at the entrance to the Valley of the Maids, but at first they didn't realize that they had reached their goal. They were distracted, in part, by the fact that standing in the middle of the trail was an austere, mahogany podium, and next to it, an elaborate rope of crimson velvet, with a gold tassel. The podium was empty. The rope stretched up to the highest branches of the trees, where it vanished from sight. Beside the podium was a glass-cased, black felt-board with "Valley of the Maids Daily Activities" listed in elegant calligraphy. It read:

Welcome.
Sunrise Room: Sunrise 6:34 A.M.
Sunset Room: Sunset 7:45 P.M.

"Doesn't seem like they like to keep too busy," remarked Ember.

As usual, Connie was at the front of the procession. She looked along the road, stepped delicately around the podium and examined the felt-board of activities (such as they were) with interest. "Hello?" she called into the apparently uninhabited forest. "Is anyone here?"

There was no answer, not from birds, squirrels, snakes, or any other inhabitants of the forest neighborhood.

"What should we do?" asked Connie.

"It does look as if someone is supposed to meet us here," said Ember.

"I could try lighting it on fire," offered Glowerflorious, wanting to be helpful.

"Try pulling the rope," suggested Lucy. She had far more experience than any other member of the party with castles, hotels, and fine houses in general.

"If you think that will help," said Connie. She took hold of the rope in her teeth, and gave it a tremendous jerk. The company braced for a gong worthy of a rope that size. Unfortunately, they were disappointed. Instead of powerful resonance that would shake them down to the bones and leave their ears ringing, they heard a distant tinkle. And that was it.

"What now?" asked Connie.

"Now we wait?" said Lucy, who wished she wasn't the authority on fancy bell ropes.

They waited. They settled down. They let Boots, Scoots, and Skipper graze in the grass next to the road. Connie grazed companionably alongside them.

"The rope tasted pretty dusty," Connie said.

Glowerflorious landed carefully and edged himself into the shade of the big trees. Ember perched alertly on his foreclaws. They waited some more.

Finally, Connie got a little anxious. "Do you think they heard us? Um, Hello?" Connie directed her question down the pathway. "If no one's going to come and meet us," Connie said, "maybe we should just go around and let ourselves in to—"

Suddenly, the butler appeared.

He was tall, dressed impeccably in a black suit with a shirt so white it was almost Connie-bright. He was totally bald on top with only a fringe of hair around his ears, and a small precise mustache on his face. His expression did not seem welcoming, but then, it was so completely bland and neutral, it didn't seem to qualify as an expression at all.

"That will not be necessary, Miss," the butler said. His tone was cool.

"Oh, you surprised me!" said Connie, and she tilted her head winsomely at the butler. Lucy was impressed. She found him more than a little intimidating. "We didn't think anyone was coming at all."

"Yes, Miss," said the butler. He looked down his nose at her, and did not seem charmed by the unicorn filly at all. "This is the south entrance. Uninvited visitors usually travel round to bother us from the north entrance." He had the air of one stating the painfully obvious to the pitifully ignorant, politely but with obvious disdain.

"Today being the day for dusting, we were all much occupied in the main house. When you rang, I was obliged to traverse the entirety of the north-south axis of the valley in order to request that you leave your message succinctly and then be so kind as to go away," he added.

"We're sorry," murmured Lucy. She shared a glance with Ember, who was looking chastised at the thought of having made this fastidious and precise person go out of his way. Glowerflorious seemed affected, too, and even the three horses were hanging their heads, as if embarrassed.

Connie, though, seemed immune: "Oh goodie!" she said, with genuine delight. "I suppose you got some exercise, then? Did you have to run? Was it the most delightful surprise you had all day?"

"Indeed, Miss," said the butler, looking not at all delighted. "Now, if you would—"

"It must be nice to have two doors to answer," said Connie, with a giggle. "In my valley we don't have any doors. All that running back and forth. Wouldn't it be fun to have a race?" She twitched her tail and gave one of her cute little prances by way of demonstration. "We can go back and forth—"

"Indeed, Miss," said the butler.

"—Back and forth, and back and forth again!" Connie said.

"Indeed, Miss," said the butler. "Now, if—"

It was an unwise venture forward. Connie hadn't finished. "Unless," she continued cheerfully. "You have four doors to answer. An east and a west door, too, do you see? Then you could just keep going in a circle! Do you have to answer two doors, and then another two doors, too?"

"No. Miss, just the two," he said.

"Wait!" Connie giggled again. "Did you hear what I said? Two-too! One two like the number, and the other 'too' means also." She flicked her mane and tail and turned to her friends. "Did you hear that, Lucy? I said two-too! Ember, did you hear?"

"Most amusing, Miss," said the butler, valiantly trying to return to the point. "Now in regards to the reason for your visit." There was an increasing note of desperation in his tone.

The rest of the company had, by this point, completely lost any sense of intimidation and indeed, Glowerflorious was sprawled quite comfortably in front of the podium, and both Lucy and Ember were using him as a sort of couch while they waited. It was clear to them all that the butler had thoroughly underestimated his opponent. Even the horses had gone back to contentedly grazing, their tails gently swaying from side to side.

Connie was attacking with sheer, deadly charm and aggressive good humor. "Our visit?" she said. "Do you mean when we rang the bell by pulling on that big rope over there? Actually, it was me that did it. There wasn't a sign that said not to, and we thought someone would come to help. I thought a big rope would be attached to something that would make a really big humongous

BOOM! or CLANG! But it didn't. We only heard a teeny little tinkle. Was that anything like what you heard?"

"I heard a tinkle, Miss." A slight sheen of perspiration could be detected on his forehead.

"Of course, I meant tinkle the sound, not the other tinkle. You meant tinkle the sound, not the other kind of tinkle, right, Mr. Nice Mustache Man?"

"Tinkle the sound is what I meant, Miss, now if you would simply…"

"We wouldn't have rung this bell, if there'd been a sign asking us politely to go 'round to a different bell," Connie continued. "Because we are friendly and polite, although we're also tired, and have been walking a long time, and it doesn't seem nice to make us go even farther when you don't even know why we came. But you did hear that we were here?"

"Yes, Miss," said the butler.

"I did it again," said Connie, with another giggle. She danced in place with her own cleverness. "I said here and hear!"

"A witticism indeed, Miss," said the butler.

"Here like the place, and hear —"

"Why is it you've come to visit us, Miss?" the butler ventured.

"What is it you heard?" asked Connie.

"A tinkle, Miss," he said.

"What sort of tinkle?" Connie asked.

"A teeny tiny tinkle," said the butler, utterly defeated. "I'm sorry, Miss. So very sorry." He was practically pleading with her now.

With the apology, Connie relaxed her adorable power-stance, and became much more natural, and consequently, much more unaffectedly likable. "Yes, thank you," she said. "We've come to see Suzette, please. She's the unicorn maid."

"We all know who Suzette is," said the butler, and then froze, as he became aware that his answer might not be taken in an entirely positive way. Connie's unblinking stare probably had something to do with this realization. The butler's face contorted in a fleeting look of horror and he began to babble as he hurried to make things right. "No-no-no, I didn't mean it. No disparagement of the lovely, warm, and wonderful Suzette was ever intended, especially if she is a friend of yours. Er, is she?"

"Indeed," said Connie, with a surprising amount of dignity.

"You understand," the butler said. "I'm highly proficient in disdainful silences and meaningful glares, but I never have the opportunity to use my skills. It isn't anything personal, and I offer my sincerest, most abject apologies. Of course, we welcome any friend of Suzette's to our Valley." He bowed, and extended a welcoming hand, inviting them all past the barrier.

Connie dropped her affectedly cute pose and the butler gave a large sigh of relief.

Lucy applauded, politely. Connie bowed her head in shy acceptance of the accolade, and they all moved forward into the Valley.

"So that's a butler," said Ember.

"He did pretty well for his first full Connie," offered Lucy, judiciously.

"I don't know, I was expecting someone who was a bit more…" Ember sought for the word.

"Pompous? Starched? Determined?" suggested Lucy.

"Someone who could have lasted a few more rounds, perhaps," Ember said.

"Well, the poor man had no idea what he was going up against," Lucy pointed out.

"True. Our Connie can be quite a force of nature." Up front, the unicorn overheard them, and preened herself just a little at the phrase "our Connie." The butler flinched. "To encounter her with no prep time or warning. That's just nasty." Ember shuddered.

"Remember that girl at the washing well?" Lucy said.

"The one just yesterday? Who recommended which inn would accept customers of 'our sort'? That girl?" Again, Ember shuddered. It was impressive, as always, even on her new smaller scale.

"Yeah, that was just painful." Lucy shook her head in sympathy with Ember and the memory of the initial encounter.

"After the first hour it was, certainly, but until then it was pretty entertaining," Ember said.

"Thank goodness that she ended up falling in that well," Lucy said, looking more innocent than the situation warranted. "Otherwise we still might be standing there watching the two of them try to out-cutesy each other."

"I still wonder what caused her to tumble over so suddenly," Ember said.

"Do you?" Lucy affected polite surprise. "Really?"

"Well, I have had time to puzzle it out," Ember allowed. "And now I wonder whether it might have had something to do with her sudden spasm of coughing."

"Wouldn't it be more precise to say it had something to do with how forcefully someone patted her on the back when she cleared her throat?" Lucy asked.

"I had to act decisively and forcefully to make certain the cause of the sudden cough was not something stuck in her throat," Ember pointed out, nobly. "It's possible I saved her life."

"Er, yes," said the butler. "Delightful story that, but…"

In that moment, a Rubenesque unicorn arrived, almost out of the blue. She was very striking, an attractive, older unicorn, but what Lucy chiefly noticed as unusual was that she was wearing a maid's uniform. It couldn't have been more traditional: black skirt, white apron, and a little black and white cap settled between the unicorn's ears. It definitely created an impression as she swept forward.

"Connie!" said she.

"Suzette!" Connie sprinted over to greet the One Who Had Made a Grand Entrance.

"Ah, ma petite Princesse. I thought it would be you. So many giggles from ze south entry. Who else could it be? Only ma chère amie from ze herd?"

Connie giggled. This giggle had not been weaponized, but the butler still flinched.

Suzette turned to him, "Ah Robert, you were naughty to ma mignonne Connie, and so she had to teach a lesson to you, oui?"

"Naughty? Never," said the butler, Robert. "I was merely correct."

If Suzette had possessed hands and a fan to hold in them, she would have snapped it shut. Instead, she stamped a hoof. "Bon, it seems you have learned your lesson well. Now why are zeez people, friends of my friend, still in the lobby?" The question had more than a hint of steel in it.

"I beg your pardon, Suzette," said Robert. "But I have been rather busy sorting things out and…"

"And mon Dieu! What is a dragon doing over ze head of Suzette?"

Connie stepped forward. "Oh, I'm sorry," she said. "I was so excited to see you again, I forgot to introduce everyone. Suzette, these are Boots, Scoots, and Skipper. They are my friends and very strong."

The horses nodded their heads gravely. Suzette nodded back.

Connie took a deep breath. "This is my good friend Lucy, who was supposed to be eaten by a dragon (boo!), but she wasn't (hooray!), and this is our good friend Ember, who is a dragon. She was big once, and she was supposed to eat Lucy (boo!), but she didn't want to (hooray!). Ember's small now, because a magic girdle made her tiny (boo!). Up there is Ember's friend Glowerflorious, who used to be a not-nice little kitty (boo!), but then Ember and Lucy broke the spell and snip-snack-fire-crack he turned out to be a wonderful dragon. Hooray!"

Lucy stepped forward, "And we're here because I was hoping, Suzette, that the maids of this valley would be able to help us. Connie said you were very good at what you do, and the maids who work in the palace where I'm from would know how to take off an ordinary girdle. I thought maybe you would be willing to tackle a magical one."

Suzette beckoned Ember forward with a preemptory wave of her horn. Ember hesitated. She wasn't usually shy or nervous, but something about the maid's brisk attitude of superiority was intimidating.

"Come-come, child," said Suzette with surprising gentleness. "Do not be afraid. I do not bite, but I would have to see zis girdle before I can know what may be done with it."

Gathering her courage, Ember presented herself, and her girdle. A pair of reading glasses appeared on Suzette's nose, along with a large tape measure and a rather large needle between her lips. Her expression was no longer free and flirtatious, but serious and focused.

"Do you carry a secret, my enchanted garment? A girdle, is it? To make one small. Hmm. Bon. Turn around, petite." Obediently Ember rotated. "Bien. Good. Stop here. Look at zis stitch work. No concern to ze garment itself, only what ze garment is supposed to do. Pathétique. Imbecile! Where is ze style? Where is ze panache? All form, no substance. Zey might as well have ordered it from ze Dollar Girdle Emporium section of Ze Wals Mart. Zis is ze garbage! I spit on it!"

She spat.

Ember back-winged away quickly, out of range. "Please don't. I mean, how about you just spit near it?"

Suzette was too outraged to listen. "Did I say ze Dollar Girdle Emporium? But no! Even zey would spit on such a garment as zis." She spat again.

Ember adroitly moved out of the way as another glob of unicorn saliva sailed through the nearby air.

"On such a piece of tripe as zis, I, on behalf of all self-respecting seamstresses in ze world spit again!" said Suzette, with fervent zeal.

"How about that you don't spit at all?" suggested Ember.

"Suzette was always the best spitter in the herd," Connie said, with obvious pride.

"Probably because she's French," said Ember.

"Yes, I see," said Lucy. "But even if she hates the girdle, can she get it off of Ember?

"Pfft," Suzette stopped spitting and tossed her mane. "Eet eez a child's play to take a girdle zis horrible off of a dragon. Come." Suzette motioned Ember closer.

"No more spitting, ok?" asked Ember.

"Certainement," said Suzette, and she became intent on her work. Tilting her head this way and that, and without relying on the reading glasses she'd donned (perched daintily on the tip of her nose, they were nowhere near the unicorn's eyes), the unicorn maid studied Ember's girdle. With a casual air, she asked Connie, "Do tell me, chérie, how is mon grand general?"

"That's unicorn maid for Daddy," Connie explained to Lucy and Ember. She was beaming, "He's really awesome. When he did the 'Do the herd proud 'speech, he did a special section just for me.

He said I was his brightest flower in front of everyone!"

"Bon," said Suzette. "He sounds as wise as I remember him to be."

There was a pause, while Suzette continued her inspection of the magical girdle, one that stretched out tautly with expectation, until Connie, not surprisingly, was the one to break the silence.

"Mummy is doing awesome too," she said. "She—"

"Aha!" interrupted Suzette, who clearly had no interest in the how the Queen was doing. "I have it now. Eet ees to laugh. Zo simple even a queen should have been able to figure it out," and so saying, she hooked the needle held within her teeth into a certain place on the girdle, one that looked to Lucy just like any other place. Except that the needle stuck, and as Suzette tugged loose a thread, the girdle began to come undone. Even as it was coming off, Ember was growing, expanding claw by neck by tail. Released from the magical pressure, the dragon stretched luxuriously, flapped her wings, and began to fly.

"Hooray!" shouted Connie. "Bye-bye, itty-bitty-Ember."

"Wait!" shouted Lucy, reaching out involuntarily. "Ember, wait."

Suzette gave Lucy a shrewd look. "What is ze matter, ma petite Princesse? Is zis not what you wished me to do?"

"Yeah," said Lucy. "Yes. It is, but I didn't get a chance to say goodbye." Lucy felt embarrassed and on the verge of tears. "I know it's silly. She's not gone. She's still herself. I just got used to having her down here with me."

"Oh, I didn't get a chance to say goodbye, either," said Connie, and her tail drooped. "It's going to be much harder to play tag, with Ember big again."

"But we're happy for her," Lucy said, quickly. "We're happy she's free of the spell now. I just didn't think about how different it would be." Connie leaned against her side, and they shared a hug of mutual sympathy.

Robert, the butler gave a mournful sigh, and Lucy looked over to see him dabbing a tear from his eyes with a pristine handkerchief. "This is what comes of acting without forethought," he said.

"Imbecile." said Suzette. Above them, the dragons were circling, Ember was back to her full size, and she and Glowerflorious looked very impressive as they looped loops around one another and rode on the air currents in lazy circles.

Suzette tilted her head slightly, pointing her horn skyward, and from it came a piercing whistle.

Connie was impressed. "That's almost as good as a tootle!" she whispered to Lucy.

"Allo, Dragons!" called Suzette. "You up zere. Come down from zere rapidement. Oui, both of you. At once." She stomped her hoof and waved her tail like a bossy flag. Obediently the two dragons began to descend, landing with the customary shower of sticks and pebbles. "Zis one," Suzette gestured to Lucy with her horn. "She has ze something to say to you."

Blushing furiously, Lucy still couldn't let this chance to speak go by. She realized that she might never have another chance. "Ember, I'm glad that you are free of the spell. I just wanted to tell you that even though it was an enchantment, I think I'll miss having you down here with me."

Ember's enormous gaze was somber. She nodded her massive head. "I will miss it, too," she said, and her voice was deep and resonant, but still feminine, just as it had been the first time Lucy had heard it.

"And I will miss it, three," said Connie, and the unicorn filly burst into tears, which made Lucy start to cry after all, and even Ember's big, glorious eyes were welling with steaming-hot teardrops.

"We're still friends," Lucy said, in the sort of thick, blubbery voice you get when you are trying hard not to dissolve into sobs. "That hasn't changed."

"Oh mes enfants adorables," said Suzette. "Stop ze crying. S'il vous plait." She then waited for the tears to subside, but not for very long. The unicorn maid simply didn't have the patience for it. "Oh, for ze love of ze Pete." She tilted her horn and blew a whistle, even louder than before. The glass covering the daily activities message board shattered.

"Oh dear," sighed the butler. "I really should just order in bulk."

"Now you crybaby children, listen to Suzette!" said Suzette. "Do you think zat Suzette would be zo stupid as to do somezing zo dramatique and zen walk away? Ze role of ze maid is to make things better, everything put in its place. Now you, give me ze claw. Now. At once. Rapidement. Ze lizard gigantique "

Slowly, an intimidated Ember extended a claw.

"What is zis? Do you think a silly little unicorn can hurt une grande dragonne? Hold steady, chérie. Now vous, you come here at once!"

"Um, me?" asked Lucy.

"No," said Suzette sardonically. "Ze other human princess with a zumb opposite, how do you say? Opposable thumb. Oui you, ma petite Princesse." Some maids have an authoritarian streak, which, frankly, some people like.

"DID I SAY MOVE ZE CLAW? NON! Keep ze claw like ZIS!"

Right now, Ember and Lucy were not feeling it.

"Bon. Now with ze thumbs, Princesse, you will take ze guiding zread. Non, not zat one!" she snapped, when Lucy touched what looked like the correct thread, though how to tell one shade of ecru from another was anyone's guess. She moved her hand a fraction of an inch and tried one that seemed a little more shiny, unless she was imagining it. "Oui. Better," said Suzette, so maybe Lucy wasn't imagining it after all. "We are going to gently remove zis zread from ze rest of ze girdle. Use ze needle… Pull… More. Now ze snip." Suzette turned to the butler, who smoothly produced a pair of scissors. "Bon, you are almost useful today, Robert."

"Thank you, Suzette."

"Now, Princesse, tie up ze zread-fabrique again."

Still not sure she knew what she was doing, Lucy snipped the single piece of thread she had teased away from the girdle, and then held it out to Suzette. Suzette let out a dramatic sigh of operatic proportions.

"Non, and non!" If she'd had hands, Suzette would have thrown them up in despair. "Do not tie it upon me! Do I want to be smaller? Non! I do not. Suzette eez ze size perfection for Suzette. Everyone, zey know of zis. It is for ze dragon, chérie! Tie it around ze claw of ze dragon."

"Oh," said Lucy. "The dragon. Okay." And she turned her attention to Ember's extended claw. Tying it on wouldn't be much of a challenge; Ember hadn't dared to move her claw as much as a fraction of an inch after Suzette's last command, but she still hesitated. "If I tie it onto the bracelet she got from her mother, won't that be more sturdy?" Lucy hesitated. "Otherwise, I think it might break."

"Bon." said Suzette. "Is a good zought. Well done, ma petite Princesse. Now you, la grande dragonne magnifique. You have ze string."

"Yes," said Ember.

"It is on ze beautiful ruby bracelet you received from your mother, non?"

"Yes," said Ember.

"Give to ze bracelet a twist. Like zo. To ze left, when you would like to be small. To ze right, when you would like to be big again. Comme ça!"

Ember's expressive face lit with comprehension. "Yes, I see. The single thread possesses only a small fraction of the power of the original girdle, and is hence more manageable." She gave the bracelet a good twist and promptly became the size of a hummingbird.

"Oops! Too much, I think," said the high-pitched voice of the Micro-Ember. It took several attempts at resizing, swells and contractions everywhere from bumble bee to blue whale before Ember was able to find a proportion she liked, one that put her eye to eye with Lucy.

"Now vous," snapped Suzette. "Ze other dragon."

"Glowerflorious?" asked Connie. "That's an awesome idea!"

"Oui," Suzette preened. "Zere are two dragons, and enough zread for both of zem to make good use of zis bad magic. Same for you. Depechez-vous."

Lucy took the needle and scissors, and bent over the girdle again, and once Glowerflorious was given a loop of the string, he was able to twist it and experiment with size himself. Soon Glowerflorious was standing shoulder to shoulder with Ember, looking 'round at the assembled group with friendly interest.

"I've been looking at the tops of your heads for a while now," he said. "It's a much better view eye-to-eye. You all look very nice. Beautiful." But Lucy couldn't help noticing that while the compliment was technically addressed to all of them, Glowerflorious couldn't seem to tear his gaze away from Ember.

Whether Suzette noticed or not, no one could tell. She had whisked away the rest of the girdle in some complicated maid clean-up effort, and now was anxious to get everyone back onto her schedule. "Bon," she said. "Everyone is happy. Now to bed with you all and tomorrow we will decide what you must do next upon your quest!"

Chapter Twenty
Gathering More Intelligence

GEORGE PULLED THE UTILITY VEHICLE INTO THE PARKING lot of a small town's civic center and turned the engine off halfway between the library and the city hall. Chip was snoring. It was a measure of how the drive had gone that he was inclined to think the snores were getting softer. It wasn't enough to just go by decibel level anymore. George was becoming something of a snore connoisseur, measuring amplitude and resonance and how much Chip's nasal passages actually sounded like angry dogs.

The instant George turned the key and the engine rumbled into silence, Chip also went silent. He sat up, blinking. "I say, where? Who? What?" he said.

"We're here," said George.

"So I shall repeat: where, who, what?" Chip said.

"An extremely small hamlet," said Agent X. "Princess Lucinda, and to investigate, report, and track."

"I say, good fellow, I know everyone thinks you are the most clever chap, and you are definitely the hit with the barmaid set and all, but could you unpack it a bit for the rest of us, eh?" Chip was not exactly annoyed, his breeding prevented it, but he had clearly woken up on the wrong side of the car.

Agent X and George simply smiled at each other.

"Sorry, Chaps, it's not really my fault. It's just that cars lull me to sleep, always have. When I was just an infant, the slightest sign of discomfort on the Chipster's brow, and off I'd be bundled into the nearest car and taken for a spin around the park. Fall asleep, problem solved, smiles all around.

"'Fetch the Rolls,' Mummy would say, and off to dreamland I'd go. Or was it the Bentley? No, the Bentley was always in pieces in the garage. As was the Austin-Martin. And Reggie's MG. Oh good grief, I don't know how the poor fellows in the garage managed to keep the parts separate. They all look pretty much the same you know. Things sticking out and holes where they stick other things in. And belts, I can recognize a belt. Looks like a belt, don't you know."

Chip stretched and yawned. "There were always parts strewn about, so finally they decided to have one car that would actually work, they would have one car for every day of the week. There was Mummy's Rolls Monday; Tuesdays was Daddy's Rolls; Wednesday, the Bentley; Thursday, the—"

"Right," said Agent X. "We're here to see if we can get any more information first-hand about the Princess."

"What about the MG?" asked George.

Agent X gave George the look that Shakespeare had in mind when he wrote "Et tu, Brute?"

George shrugged. "I'm curious."

Chip said, "Ah, the MG. Fifth Sunday of the month if the weather was nice and you didn't have to actually be anyplace too far to walk back from."

Agent X, ostentatiously ignoring Chip, had pulled paperwork from his utility pouch. He consulted it and said, "Well, the report says there are two primary witnesses to the incident. Sisters, so I think I will take that part of the investigation."

Both Chip and George responded with enough pointed silence to cause Agent X to look up at his two fellow Knights simply staring at him.

"I say, old duffer," began Chip.

"The memo we got from the Bureau of Customer Service, Public Relations, and Complaints, was rather clear on that manner," continued George. "No interviewing sisters by yourself."

"Have to hand it to you, old man," said Chip. "I've never seen an entire memo in all caps before. Ten pages of it. Remarkable!"

"No matter what their occupation," George recited.

"And a lot of it with that clever drop-shadow font-fellow effect," Chip said.

"Or how crucial the information."

"Now, I'm sure that when it comes to bureaucratic mumbo-jumbo, you two have figured out the Chipster's old noggin turns to guacamole, don'cher know. But in this case, the point was pretty clear. You—"

"Don't interview sisters by yourself," Chip and George concluded in unified chorus.

"Of course, I meant with some back-up from you, George. Ready to watch how an old hand interviews sisters?" Agent X knew when to fold 'em.

"Yes, sir. Thank you, sir," said George.

"And you, Chip. See what the Chief Constable has to say."

"Yes, I think he's a distant cousin or something."

Moments later Agent X and George were escorted into a rather pleasant reception lounge in the civic center. One of the constables (the town boasted two) had summoned the sisters, and Agent X automatically identified them as the Pretty One and the Other One.

"Good afternoon, Ladies, I am Agent X and this is my colleague. George. We're Knights investigating the Survival Day incident. Now, we understand you had an encounter with Princess

Lucinda the other day."

"Oh, we did, and it was awful," said the Pretty One. Her lower lip quivered and her eyes sparkled with unshed tears.

Immediately Agent X was at her side, laying a comforting arm around her shoulder and an equally comforting hand on her knee. George recognized the pose as fig.1 from the "What Not to Do" portion of any sexual harassment workshop. The illustration had been included specifically in the recent memo from the Bureau of Customer Service, Public Relations, and Complaints.

The Pretty One (George saw in the records that her name was Annmarie) looked ready to faint, and rapidly fluttered her eyelashes. Still, she was coherent enough to struggle more securely into Agent X's increasingly comforting arms.

"I can't go into the details in front of all these people," she murmured, waving a shapely hand at her sister, who presumably knew all the details already, and George, who was the only other person in the room. "Could we go somewhere more private?"

"George," said Agent X, promptly. "It seems that this witness here needs some time to compose herself. I shall escort her to a place of safety so that I can take her statement when she is ready to give it."

Since technically the memo only addressed Agent X interviewing two sisters, George merely shrugged his shoulders. Agent X and the Pretty One left, leaving George with the Other One (whose name, according to the report, was Rachael). The silence was undeniably awkward, and to break it, they both turned to each other and spoke at almost the same time.

"I should apologize. We've had training but… Oh, I'm sorry," said George. He could feel himself blushing.

"I should apologize. This happens all the time and…Oh, I'm sorry," said Rachael. She was blushing, too.

The Dragon, Lucinda and George

"Oh, I'm sorry," said George. "Please, you first."

"Oh, no, no," Rachael protested. "That was rude of me. You go first."

"No," said George. "You go first, I insist." He managed to blush and be forceful at the same time.

"Well, this happens all the time, actually," said Rachael, with a sigh. "She sees something she wants and she cries, or bats her eyelashes or giggles, and then, here I am." She made a simple "ta-da!" gesture with both hands. It wasn't, George realized, that she was unattractive. It was just that her sister was so aggressively capital-P Pretty that it overshadowed everything else in the room.

"Well," George grinned. "He sees something he likes and soon thereafter I'm dodging flying saucepans and rolling pins. Care to trade?"

Rachael, the Other One, let out a surprised laugh, thankfully not a giggle, and her embarrassed face was suddenly much more lively and engaging.

"I had never considered it from that angle before. No, on the whole I think I prefer not to dodge rolling pins, not that I'm sure he doesn't deserve them," she said, with much more spirit.

Instead of blushing, they both laughed.

"Well, I suppose I could ask you some questions," George said, as if making a suggestion.

"Are you really a Knight?" she asked. "You look so..."

"Young," supplied George. "Yes. First rescue. First interview."

"Oh, then that means you'll always remember me," said Rachael. She might or might not have blushed after that. George didn't seem to notice; he was industriously focused on getting out the appropriate forms.

"I think we should start with your name," he said, even though he'd already looked up her name. It was traditional to ask, and sometimes traditions were comforting. By the time he looked up, they'd both had time to compose themselves.

"Rachael Broadwin," the Other One said promptly. Part of her was glad there really was going to be an interview, and she folded her hands in her lap and sat up straight in her chair.

"Thank you, and you were there when the Princess encountered your sister?"

"Yes," she said. "I was there and saw it all."

"Can you tell me in your own words what happened?" he asked. "You're certain it was Princess Lucinda?"

"We've seen pictures of the Royal Family. She's the one with the glasses, right?"

"That is correct," said George.

"Yes, her photo's been on the news a lot lately. It was her," said Rachael. "She had this cute pair of wraparound sunglasses with the little feathers on the sides. Very attractive and the sort of thing you'd expect a princess to wear." She hesitated. "My sister wanted a pair just like them," she added dryly.

"Yes, that would be her, please continue." George marked a box labeled simply "Glasses" on his form, and made a brief note of the description.

"Well, there were three of them," said Rachael.

"Three pairs of glasses?" asked George.

"No, three girls," she answered. "There was the Princess, the little dragon in a corset, and a unicorn."

"I'm sorry, what was the color?"

"Of the unicorn?" Rachael blinked. "White, I—"

"No, sorry. The feathers. You said the sunglasses had little feathers. What color were they, if you can remember."

"Oh, orange. Burnt orange with a black outline around the edge. Like the rest of the eyeglass frame."

"Thank you. For the form, you see. Just give me a sec here." Rachael waited patiently as George worked on his form. He didn't have Agent X's facility with a pen. "Got it. Sorry. Please continue."

"Like I was saying, there were three of them. The Princess, the little dragon in a corset, and a unicorn."

"I beg your pardon?" George looked up from his form. "Little? The dragon was...small?"

"Oh, yes," Rachael nodded. "I was expecting something bigger, actually, what with everything they say about the history of Survival Day."

"How small, exactly?"

"Oh, like a big dog," she said. "Maybe a small pony, but it could still fly."

"Did the Princess seem to be being held against her will in any way?"

"Oh, no."

George ticked a box on the form. "Did she seem drugged, or under any spell of any kind?"

"No, honestly, she sort of seemed to be the one in charge," Rachael said. George ticked another box. "She was asking directions and watering their horses and things like that. The dragon seemed quiet, not at all fire-breathing or roaring, and the unicorn was busy being cute."

"Cute?" asked George.

"Believe me. She was cute, and I know cute when I see it. Let me tell you, done right, it's a full-time gig."

"I see, go on."

"Anyway, my sister and I, Annmarie. That's her name, Annmarie,"

"Thank you," said George, continuing to take notes.

"We were just hanging out by the washing well. It wasn't like we didn't have a washer or dryer at home, but it's picturesque, which

Annmarie likes, and historical, which I like, and... Well, there is not really a lot to do in a place as small as Little Daytonia. It was a nice day. We were enjoying the sun, and up the road came this little dragon, and Princess Lucinda, and the unicorn."

"You're sure it was Princess Lucinda?"

"I couldn't imagine any other princess who would have a dragon with her just now. I mean, it's been on the news," said Rachael.

"I see."

"And isn't she the one with the glasses?"

"Yes," said George, miserably. He wasn't liking the implications of this.

"Well then, it was her. She had on the cutest pair of glasses. They were Bakelite pale green ones, oversized with embedded rhinestones on the frame."

"I thought you said..." George looked anxious.

Rachael shook her head, smiling. "They were here for a while, do you see? She was wearing the sunglasses when she came into town, and put on the other ones as it was getting dark."

George looked down at his form in dismay. "Can you draw me a picture of the glasses?" he asked, finally. "Both of them?"

"Oh sure." George gave her another piece of paper and a pencil, and Rachael began to draw.

"Hey, you're good," he said, watching two pairs of glasses take shape on the page.

"Thanks," she seemed engrossed in her task. "I like to look at stuff and draw it later."

George took out another piece of paper. "Can you draw the small dragon?"

"Sure."

"So, Princess Lucinda rode into town?" George prompted, after he had secured the drawings away for later study.

"Oh. Right. The Princess and the dragon and the unicorn arrived, and Annmarie said, 'Let's have some fun with this one.' I don't think she knew quite who they were. She wanted to see how long it would take for her to out-cute them, and I said 'I dunno, Annmarie.'"

"Out-cute?" George asked.

"The truth is, we were bored and there's nothing I can do or say to stop her when Annmarie gets cute on the brain. Soon enough she and the unicorn were in the most competitive cute contest any of us had ever seen. Annmarie would bat an eye and the unicorn would shake her tail, and then one would toss her mane and the other would jiggle and then one would prance. People gathered around, because who doesn't like to watch a real cute battle? Especially around here, where we've got Annmarie, 'cause she can pretty much can beat anyone."

"And did your sister out-cute the unicorn?" asked George.

"No!" said Rachael indignantly. "How can a human being be cuter than a unicorn? Annmarie was holding her own on points, but we all knew she would have lost eventually. Probably on a technicality. So I could see Annmarie was going to make a last push for the win. She has a trick that always works. She does this little, cute cough," she demonstrated for George, resting her fingertips against her throat and giving a dainty "hem-hem" sound of distress.

"When she does that," Rachael said. "Everybody flutters around trying to make her feel better. It always gets her drinks at the pub on Friday night. Except that she barely started her adorable sputter when, right out of the blue, the dragon went and pushed Annmarie into the fountain. Just pushed her. It was so unfair. She was just getting started."

"What did the Princess do?"

"Oh, not much as I recall. I think she offered a towel, but like I said she sorta seemed in charge and she was grinning like a banshee as Annmarie hauled herself out of the fountain."

"Then what happened?"

"Well, of course then Constable Blather showed up, and he was useless. He wanted to hand out tickets. Annmarie had calmed down and being cute demands that you don't make an overt fuss, so both the unicorn and Annmarie teamed up and started being cute at him."

"Really?" asked George, writing 'Weaponized Cuteness' on his form.

"He lasted all of 2 and a half seconds before he was telling everyone to move along, and that there was nothing to see."

"And then?"

"Annmarie hates not having the spotlight, but funny thing; it was like Annmarie and the unicorn could respect each other after that. They shared a look. You know the sort," she said. "As if they were saying 'You got game, girl.' They started giving each other their cute tips and Annmarie's father and mine owns the Only In Town Inn, and so they stayed the night, and rode out the next day."

"When you saw the Princess with the others in the inn, was she always with the dragon?" asked George.

"Oh no, they were just going about their business, like normal folk," said Rachael.

George frowned down at his form. He didn't like what it was telling him. "Thank you very much, Rachael. You have been very helpful."

"Is that all you need?"

"Yes, I think so."

There was an awkward pause while George packed his form away with Rachael's drawings, and secured the whole pack together. He looked up and met her gaze.

"So, there is nothing really to keep you here, I suppose," said Rachael.

"I'm sorry, Rachael, I am a Knight, and a Knight's got to go where the quest takes him."

Rachael blinked. Her eyes didn't sparkle when she had tears in them, but her nose did get endearingly red. "I did mention that our Daddy owns the Inn?" she said.

"I'm sorry," said George. "It's better for everyone if we keep moving."

"You have to rescue the Princess," said Rachael, a trifle flatly.

"Yes," said George, though the forms in his pack seemed to be growing heavy. "At least, I have to find her."

"I will always remember you, George. You were the first Knight I ever spoke to."

"And I will always remember you too, Rachael. Remember me when the wind comes whistling through town on a lonesome night."

"And remember me when you see a lantern in a window in a distant cottage when you just keep riding by."

"You take care, Rachael."

"You too, George."

"If you're ever in these parts again," she said. "Look for me?"

"That's a promise." This time, the pause in conversation wasn't awkward in the slightest. In fact, it was pretty comfortable. George broke it at last, getting onto his feet and calling into the back room, loudly enough to disrupt whatever Gathering of Intelligence was going on back there. "Agent X," he shouted. "It's time to ride." Then, to Rachael, he said: "Ma'am."

If he'd been wearing a hat, he would have tipped it, but his helmet was still beeping, and loudly enough that they generally left it in the car.

Margit Elland Schmitt & Dan McLaughlin

Chapter Twenty-One
The DALSED Terminal

It turned out that when you were hosted, given supper, and put to bed by an entire village of professional maids and butlers, it was a truly memorable experience. There were no dragon maids or butlers, and Suzette was the only unicorn that Lucy saw, but besides the humans, there were troll maids, and elfin butlers, and one of the gardeners was definitely a centaur. Certainly, people, or people-like things, were called from all over the world by the mysterious need to learn the secrets of dusting and polishing.

There was the meal, first, atop a table big enough to park cars on, laid out with gilt-edged plates and platters and gleaming silverware (Lucy's mother would have loved to see it!) in all shapes and sizes, which at this particular table was an impressive assortment. With their expertise, the maids and butlers were able to provide a full set of formal dinnerware of the sort Lucy had only ever seen at state occasions, and also what looked like the world's most elegant trencher for Connie, and two dragon-sized platters, one for Ember, and one for Glowerflorious. There were candles, gleaming, and white tablecloths, and literally hundreds of servants in black and white livery.

Lucy had never seen so many butlers and maids in one place before. It was like being in the presence of the world's politest army. It was also a trifle unnerving, because as it turned out, Lucy and her friends were the only people being served. All those eager eyes, waiting for the chance to offer a bit of help or advice, to pick up a napkin or serve another helping of rice pilaf, were intimidating, to say the least.

Somewhere in the background, behind closed doors but put on their mettle, must have been a hundred chefs, because Lucy and each of her friends was served an impressive array of food. For Lucy, there was salmon and the almond rice pilaf, just the way she liked it, and a salad, and fresh, hot bread, and butter, and jam, and apple juice to drink. She couldn't remember how long it had been since she'd had such a well-cooked meal. It was definitely better than granola bars.

Connie seemed happy with her supper, too. Some of it was definitely hay and oats, but it had been arranged in fanciful shapes and patterns. There were apples for her, and what looked like an enticing array of edible flowers.

Ember had a salad of her own. She and Glowerflorious were enjoying their meals, too, and it was a huge tribute to the talent and tact of the Chefs that two dragons could eat their fill with gusto, and not leave their fellow diners spattered with …remnants.

Afterwards, there were baths, in private, with warm fluffy towels, and (at least for Lucy) soft flannel pajamas to change into afterward. There was cocoa at the bedside, which Lucy imagined Connie would like the most, because it was served in a precious teacup. Lucy didn't drink it, though. She thought she was tired enough already to sleep without its soothing.

Except that after they wished one another goodnight in the hallway, and the doors to their private rooms were gently closed for the night, Lucy found that she couldn't sleep. She lay in the dark on a soft, comfortable bed, beneath a warm coverlet, with her eyes wide open. Her mind kept turning over the events of the day, and wondering why, when everyone had seemed so kind and helpful and capable, even in the face of Connie's aggressive cuteness, she still couldn't relax.

Maybe it was just because Suzette had run away from the rest of the Herd. To Lucy, that the unicorns, who (the ceremony had clearly shown) were all about love and family, in a way that still brought tears of wistful envy to Lucy's eyes, was ideal. She couldn't imagine someone wanting to leave that beauty and security for a place where they had to iron and fold and dust all day long.

Or maybe it was the way the unicorn maid had treated all their travels like a very big joke. That grated on Lucy (who had too many sisters who teased her to tears and then told her they were just joking) and her possibly oversensitive nerves. Or the way Suzette had removed the girdle so easily and then remade it into something, somehow, that Ember could control. How, exactly? It didn't make sense, and they still didn't know where the girdle had come from, or where it had gone to, or whether it had been meant for Ember or for Lucy herself. Why would anyone want a tiny princess? It still made no sense.

She was feeling more than a little useless and out of sorts, and wished she had something to do. Since beginning this journey, she'd had to overcome one problem after another. Maybe she had been angry and tense for so long that she'd forgotten how to relax, and was looking for problems that didn't exist.

With a sigh, Lucy got out of bed and drank her cocoa. Somehow, it was still at its most perfect temperature. Maybe cocoa wasn't so bad after all.

At some point, she must have fallen asleep, because Lucy eventually woke, with a heart-pounding start. Nothing was wrong, but she could see by the dainty clock at her bedside that it would be better to get up than try for more sleep.

A maid came to help her dress, and combed her hair, which turned out to be very soothing. At breakfast, everyone was eating. When Lucy arrived, Connie had been showing her friends that the Maids had, in a burst of creative pampering, painted her hooves with ruby-red hearts and flowers.

"Zo, my little ones," began Suzette, "You want to go to zis Profundia place to stop ze dragons from being forced to snack on ze maidens. Bon. Do you know where zis place might be?"

There was a longish pause, and the girls exchanged glances with each other.

Connie tossed her mane and tail in a way utterly lacking of conviction, and said, "North?"

"North?" asked Lucy and Suzette. Lucy looked at the Maid, and wasn't sure how she felt about being in sync with the bossiest woman in the place.

"Why north?" asked Lucy.

"Well," said Connie, "In most quests bad things only ever come from the north, especially if it is frozen, and Profundia seems to be a bad place, so I thought we would just go north and look for signs of frostbite."

"North," finished Ember.

For a moment, it looked like Lucy was going to say something, perhaps less than complimentary, perhaps even a trifle snarky, but she met Suzette's eye and subsided. Glowerflorious had the good sense to remain impressively bland and polite. Lucy was sure he was only pretending to be so thoroughly engrossed in his breakfast.

Slowly, Lucy said, opting for solidarity instead of reason, "Well, it is a plan."

"You mean signs, like road signs?" asked Ember.

"I'm not really sure," answered Connie, hesitantly. "Maybe yes?"

"Or maybe back-track all the instances of evil to their source? Is that what you mean, Connie?" Lucy suggested.

"Maybe, yes?" suggested Connie. "Maybe no? I don't really know."

The travelers considered their options as they chewed on their breakfast, which was grapefruit. Only grapefruit. Suzette and the butler, Robert, gave no real reason why there was such a change in menu, only that it was Grapefruit Tuesday. Lucy supposed that the Valley of the Maids (Resort and Spa) could occasionally try to do something vaguely health-conscious and trendy. Supposedly, grapefruit contained nutrients of a sort.

Connie and the horses had a large barrel into which they would lower their heads and pull out a grapefruit to chew. Well, that is what the horses did. Connie would toss her grapefruit into the air and bounce it about with her nose and her hoof. After she'd had enough of playing with her food, she would catch it in her mouth with a cheerful snort, spear another grapefruit, and begin another round of her game. It did take a lot to get a unicorn down. Honestly, since she had been the only one who had made an actual suggestion so far, she seemed content to rest on those laurels.

"If you don't go north," said Robert, with a discreet cough, "what would you do?"

"We could…" began Lucy. "But oh, no, that wouldn't work. Ducks don't do that."

"We could…" began Ember. "But oh, no, that wouldn't work. Iron rusts."

"We could…" began Glowerflorious. "And this could totally work, if you'll bear with me. First, we get all bitten by radioactive earthworms and then each one of us would develop a super power, like the ability to see though dirt. Naturally, we'd all get amnesia and wake up in the middle of a huge forest watched over by a wise, old gnome who speaks only in limericks, like, 'There once was a dragon from Bamber,' only he does them backward. Get it, backward? Then all we'd have to do is go backward in time to when Profundia really did exist on this earth, and change history so the dragons and the princesses can be friends! Let's do this! Who is with me?"

Everyone, including the horses, were staring at Glowerflorious. No one moved for a long moment, then with equine shrugs, the horses resumed chewing on their grapefruit. Connie lowered her head into the barrel and speared another orb to play with.

Undeterred, Glowerflorious continued. "Hey guys, we can do this! First step, find a radioactive worm to bite us." He looked around expectantly. "Who's got one?"

Robert cleared his throat, and said, "I'm afraid, sir, that the larder is completely bare of radioactive worms."

Glowerflorious noticed the lack of reaction to his proposal, and sulked, but expected no one would pay attention to that, either.

"All we really need is a radioactive worm or two," he muttered. "How hard could it be to get some of those?"

"Excuse me," said Robert the butler. "We do have a DALSED terminal." He made a vaguely theatrical but restrained gesture to a hitherto unnoticed corner of the room, where a work station stood. It had been dusted, but that was all Lucy could say recommended itself to her.

For the dragons, the effect was instantaneous. At the word 'DALSED', Ember and Glowerflorious had whipped their heads around. If DALSED had been edible, whatever was on the other side of their eager gazes would have known it was toast.

"A DALSED terminal," exclaimed Ember. "Wow!"

"It's a 238," said an enraptured Glowerflorious. "I thought this version wasn't supposed to be released until March."

Two dragons stared at one butler.

"How did you score one of these?" asked Ember.

"The Valley of the Maids Resort and Spa has had the honor of being designated a beta test site for DALSED."

"Hooray!" said Connie, who was enthusiastic about enthusiasm, even if she generally had no experience with anything in All Caps. "What is a DALSED?"

"DALSED," dismissed Suzette, "is a box zat zinks she can zink." She gave a derisive flick of her tail.

The DALSED terminal was indeed a box. It had a large screen, like a television, fit into a polished, mahogany cabinet. The butler pulled out a hidden shelf in the cabinet and revealed a keyboard.

"It looks like it weighs a ton," said Lucy.

Robert reached out and pressed one of the keys with an elegant, gloved hand. The key gave a distinct clicking sound. "We've never had an opportunity to test the keyboard before, but the company representative informs us the system is certified 'Dragon-Proof'." He gave a benign not-smile to the two dragons. "I wonder whether you would be willing to assist us in verifying the matter?" he said.

If the maids and butlers had not been so assiduous in their cleaning, the scramble as the dragons rushed to be first at the keyboard would have left a cloud of dust in their wake. Ember turned out to be faster. She was poised firmly in front of the keyboard, with Glowerflorious hovered over her shoulder looking at the screen. Ember's claws were sharp, but also surprisingly nimble. She was already furiously typing.

"DALSED," said Robert over the clicking sounds, "stands for Data and Literature Stuff Electronically Delivered. It is an extremely complicated, state-of-the-art artificial intelligence system. It is highly sophisticated, a technical tool of the highest order. Only a technician with years of training can successfully navigate—"

"We're in," Ember said, shortly. She was still typing.

"Hooray!" said Connie, celebrating achievement.

"Unless you're a young dragon, it seems," said Robert, somewhat deflated.

"It's a box. What's so intelligent about it?" asked Lucy.

"It can tell you what time a movie is starting," said Robert, who had clearly read the accompanying brochure and was trying to recapture the magic of being the oracle of the box.

"Oh," said Connie with a noticeable drop in enthusiasm.

"So can a newspaper," countered Lucy.

"It can help you write a letter."

"So can a pencil," said Lucy.

"An advanced user can program the DALSED such that, if you are typing a big word, like 'bureaucratic', all you have to do is type in the first few letters, like B-U-R-E-A and it will finish the word for you," said the butler with an increasingly desperate air.

Connie and Lucy exchanged a glance, too polite to express how often that circumstance had ever been useful, or even interesting, hitherto in life.

Glowerflorious and Ember were hunched over the keyboard and staring at the screen.

"You can play games on it," Ember said.

"Games?" Connie brightened up immediately. "I like games! What kind of games?"

"Hovels and Humans," said Ember. "We just started a new round."

"Check for traps," said Glowerflorious, and Ember typed.

"No traps," said Ember.

"Enter the room," said Glowerflorious, and Ember typed.

"There is a bed, a desk, and a mirror," said Ember.

"Go to the bed," said Glowerflorious. Ember paused.

"Not the desk?" she asked.

Connie leaned over and whispered to Lucy: "This is a game?" She looked forlorn. Lucy wasn't sure of the answer, and merely shrugged her shoulders.

"Oh right. Good. Go to the desk," Glowerflorious said, and Ember typed.

"You are at the desk," said Ember.

"Check for traps," said Glowerflorious, and Ember typed.

"You found a trap," said Ember.

"Oh no!" said Connie. "A trap!"

"Disable the trap," said Lucy, and Ember typed.

Somehow the other two girls had been drawn over to join the dragons. All four of them surrounded the screen.

"You have disabled 70% of the trap," said Ember.

"What does that mean?" asked Lucy.

"That means there is a 30% chance that something bad will happen if we go ahead and open the desk drawer," said Ember.

"Like one of the characters could get hurt or die," added Glowerflorious.

"Well, disable the trap again," said Lucy.

"You can't do that," said Ember.

"It's a rule," explained Glowerflorious. "You get only one chance to disable a trap, or climb a wall."

"Or detect poison," said Ember.

"I can detect poison," said Connie, cheerfully. "I can do it as many times as there are things to detect about it. This isn't poison," she said, tapping the DALSED's cabinet with her horn. "This isn't poison," tapping Ember's bracelet. "This isn't poison," tapping Lucy's shoe. She moved off through the dining hall, apparently deciding that making her own game of This Isn't Poison was more fun than Hovels and Humans.

"You're not poison," she reassured Robert.

"In the game, you only get one chance," said Glowerflorious.

"That's a stupid rule," said Lucy. Ember and Glowerflorious just shrugged.

"Rules are rules," Ember said.

The cliché wasn't any more palatable to Lucy just because it was coming from a friend, but in the interests of playing the game, Lucy suggested: "Let's open the drawer anyway."

"What, and risk three of my half-lives? I only have five left," Ember protested.

"I say we go for it!" Connie said, from where she was checking whether the grapefruits were poisoned. They weren't. "It's a game. Let's have some fun."

"You heard the unicorn," said a smiling Glowerflorious.

Ember typed. "You are able to open the drawer."

"Hooray!" said Connie. "An open drawer!" Clearly something actually happening in Hovel and Humans had trumped the attractions of This Isn't Poison, and Connie was back by the terminal.

"Inside the drawer is an envelope."

"Double Hooray!" said Connie.

"Check for traps," Glowerflorious and Lucy said together.

"And poison!" added Connie. "I bet there is lots and lots of poison!"

"Children," the butler was polite, but definite with his interruption. "While the games are a popular part of the appeal of DALSED, it has many more useful features, such as GlobalScan 360."

Lucy happened to glance over at the Maid. Did Suzette's expression seem a bit strained?

"GlobalScan 360 is a service that can plot a route to anywhere on the globe," the butler added.

"Oh!" said Lucy. "Switch to the GlobalScan 360 channel. Go there, Ember, go there."

"It sounds perfect!" Connie pranced over on her shining hooves. "It can show us how to get to the north!"

"Remember to save the game," said Glowerflorious.

"Let me just ..." Ember, typing even faster, opened the envelope, noted its contents, and then saved and shut down the game.

Soon she was typing again, this time on another screen, which showed a box for dialogue and an artistic image that almost resembled a globe, if the globe was a chunky circle with an arrow stuck in it.

Marlou H.
Welcome to GlobalScan360. May I know your name to address you better?

Guest1
Ember.

Marlou H.
Hi, Ember. I hope you are feeling well today, Welcome to GlobalScan 360. My name is Marlou H. and I am your personal travel agent to anywhere you want to go. How may I help you?

Ember
My friends and I want to get to Profundia.

Marlou H.
I do understand, please hold on.

"It's telling me to wait," said Ember.

"This is so exciting," said Connie. "What has it done so far?"

"Asked me my name."

"And Ember is such a good name. I hope you get extra points for it. This is just as much fun as the other game. The one with the desk! Check for traps!" said Connie.

Marlou H.

Thank you for your patience, Ember. I hope you are feeling well today, and my concern is to fix the issue that you are getting and for us to do that, I need your cooperation to narrow down the issue and fix it.

Ember
Uh, OK.

Marlou H.

May I confirm if the issue is regarding with the wishing to arrive at Profundia ? If yes, type "Yes." If no, please type "No" and retell the issue.

Ember
Yes.

Marlou H.

Please bear with me. When would you like to arrive at the destination of Profundia?

Ember
As soon as possible.

Marlou H.
Thank you, Ember. May I confirm if the issue is regarding with the wishing to arrive at Profundia as soon as possible ? If yes, type "Yes.". If no, please type "No" and retell the issue.

Ember
Yes.

Marlou H.
I do understand, please hold on.

"She's asking me to wait," said Ember.
"Who's she?" asked Connie?
"Marlou H."
"That's a pretty name," said Connie.
"She talks a little funny," said Ember.
"Dragons must have good ears. I can't even hear her," said Connie. "Ask her if she wants to go on the quest, too."
"Er, maybe." Ember shared a glance with Glowerflorious. "If I get a chance."

Marlou H.
I do understand and thank you for your patience, Ember. May I confirm if the issue is regarding with the wishing to arrive at Profundia as soon as possible? If yes, type "Yes.". If no, please type "No" and retell the issue.

Ember
Yes.

Marlou H.
Thank you for your patience, Ember. I hope you are feeling well today, and my concern is to fix the issue that you are getting and for us to do that I need your cooperation to narrow down the issue and fix it.

Ember
OK.

Marlou H.
I do understand, please hold on. Ember, please tell me the number of people in your party.

Ember started to type, but then paused and looked up from her keyboard. "Connie, your quest was to get us here to the Valley of the Maids. Do you want to keep on going to Profundia?" Ember hastened to add, "Marlou H. wants to know."

Connie looked crestfallen. Her head and her tail drooped. In a small voice, she asked, "Don't you want me to come with you guys anymore?"

"Yes, we do," said Ember, firmly. "But it's going to be dangerous, and I don't know if your parents knew what all would be involved in going to a kingdom of total evil."

"No. We're questing buddies," said Connie, firmly, returning to her customary enthusiasm. "Through and through. I'll explain it to Mummy and Daddy when we get home."

"I was just asking," muttered Ember as everyone else glared at Ember for making Connie sad. "Marlou H. made me do it, anyways." She resumed typing.

Marlou H.

I do understand and thank you for your patience, Ember. May I confirm if the issue is regarding with the wishing to arrive at Profundia as soon as possible with a party of three horses, two dragons, one human, and a unicorn ? If yes, type "Yes." If no, please type "No" and retell the issue.

Ember
Yes.

Marlou H.

I understand :) No worries, I will make sure you get there in the most economically and timely manner possible. While I compile the results of your trip request, I just want to inform you of what other perks of having GlobalScan 360 might interest you. There may be a slight add-on charge.

Ember
That's OK.

Marlou H.

Please bear with me. I see that you are logged in from one of our Select Beta Sites, and therefore I would be able to waive most, if not all, fees that may accrue.

Ember
That's OK. Thank you.

Marlou H.

:) I just want to make you feel comfortable in our chat session. Are you ready for your itinerary of the wishing to arrive at

Profundia as soon as possible with a party of three horses, two dragons, one human, and a unicorn ? If yes, type "Yes." If no, please type "No" and retell the issue.

Ember
Yes.

Marlou H.
Thank you for choosing GlobalScan 360 and giving us the opportunity to assist you. Our customers are our business. We exist to provide our clients with 110% support 100% of the time. Once again, this is Marylou H. Have a wonderful day!

From the base of the cabinet, a steady, mechanical ratcheting sound began, and a slip of paper began to ease slowly out of an almost invisible slot: evidently, the map with its directions.

"Looks like we'll be waiting a while," said Glowerflorious.

"Let's play some more 'Check for Traps!'" said Connie, and soon the four questers were back together in a command line world of traps and locks, adventure and friendship

Chapter Twenty-Two
Morning Moments Coffee, Traffic, and Weather

"Happy Wednesday, Carolia, it's just another beautiful *Morning Time Daily Report*. We've got some haze and fog outside right now, and we expect it to be sunny and the temperature to top out at about 78 later today. Tracy will have your Morning Moments Coffee *Morning Time Daily* Weather Report about eight minutes past the hour, or about eight minutes from now," said Artifice.

"And Good Morning to you, Art. The traffic on the Duke's Highway is backed up heading into the castle district, but no surprise there. Otherwise we're looking pretty good on the highways and byways out there. Yvonne will have more in your Morning Moments Coffee *Morning Time Daily* Traffic Report, coming up about eight minutes from now," said Ambrosia.

"Or eight minutes past the hour," said Art.

"Got me there, Art," said Ambrosia.

"But first, to the story that has the entire kingdom talking: the kidnapping of Princess Lucinda. We're in Day 5 of the Survival Day Surprise." Behind the desk, a Survival Day graphic appeared on the display. The graphic was a broken pair of glasses with "Day 5" written large in the upper right-hand corner. "Shock at this unprecedented departure from tradition has wracked the kingdom, and we still have many more questions than answers," said Art.

"You're certainly right, Art," said Ambrosia. "While there is no new news, there has been lots of speculation, and we have full team coverage. Our very own Mindy Maxim-Fnort is in the Lucinda Watch studio with what's latest." Viewers at home were treated to a split-screen view with Mindy in one half, and Ambrosia and Art at the familiar studio in the other. "Mindy, it seems that there is quite a lot of speculation concerning the Princess and the dragon," said Ambrosia.

"Well, that certainly is an understatement, Ambrosia," said Mindy. "People at the palace have issued a statement saying they are very upset with the situation, and in particular with public reaction, which seems to be turning against the Princess."

"How is the mood at the palace, Mindy?" said Art, reading off of his cues. He realized belatedly that he was a beat behind. "Oh, concerned you say?"

"Yes, Art, very concerned." Mindy had been in the field for some time. She was used to not being listened to.

Art gave his award-winning smile, and said: "We have some tape here taken just a few hours ago at the palace. Let's have a look. This is palace spokesperson Bonita Allen."

"Thank you," said Bonita, as the screen switched over and her broad, earnest face was clearly visible. "Thank you very much for coming out on such short notice. This is an incredibly fluid situation so I am going to start with a brief statement, and then take a few questions. I will not discuss any operational details of any Knights in the field, but I have a statement. 'The King and Queen are saddened and outraged by the abduction and non-consumption of Princess Lucinda. As they have stressed ever since the beginning of this tragedy, since Princess Lucinda was not consumed she simply needs to be restored to her rightful home at the palace. Their Majesties insist that any dragon or dragon sympathizers holding the Princess return her to the loving arms of her family at once, or Their Majesties will take all measures necessary, including military action, to rescue their daughter.' Questions?"

There was the sound of cameras clicking and many voices raised for attention. One of the reporters raised a hand. "Are you saying that Carolia is going to war with the dragons?" he asked.

Bonita said, "Even as we speak, the King and Queen are in constant contact with members of relevant royal agencies evaluating intelligence and formulating contingency plans. We cannot overstress how serious Their Majesties take the kidnapping of a member of the Royal Family."

Another reporter rose. "What about the rumors that Lucinda is a willing participant?"

Bonita frowned and shook her head. "The insinuation that somehow Princess Lucinda would take part in a rampage is an insult to both the Princess and her family's proud legacy."

There was another flurry of sound, cameras, and people, and Bonita called on a different reporter. "Jack," she said.

"Thank you. There are reports that a select group of Knights are close to the Princess, and that they are poised to rescue her. Is this true?" he asked.

"I think I said at the start that I would not discuss any operational details of any potential Knights in the hypothetical field. I think that question clearly is in that area," Bonita answered, coldly.

There was the sound of lots of cameras, and more people shouting.

"Yes, Billie?" Bonita called on another reporter.

"Thank you. Is it true that the Knights have a tracking device attached to the Princess, and the fact that she has consistently moved away from Carolia is said by some to be evidence that she is escaping with criminal intent?"

"Well, Billie, I believe I said at the start that I would not discuss any operational details of any potential Knights in the field, and

I think that the first part of your question falls into that category. I will say that the notion that Princess Lucinda would ever have any voluntary association with a dragon is, on the face of it, ludicrous. The fact that she is consistently being taken away further from Carolia, is simply reflective of the fact that she is the victim here, being held against her will."

"Another question," over the sound of lots of cameras, and people shouting. "Wendy," called Bonita.

"Thank you. There have been reports of increased dragon activity along the border and at the Sacrificial Spot. First, have you been in touch with any Dragon Kingdom representatives, and second, how do you view their increased presence?" asked Wendy.

"That is an excellent question, Wendy, and I thank you for bringing it up. Their Majesties can categorically state that at no time has any dragon or anyone representing the dragons attempted to contact them regarding the fate of their daughter. Indeed, the fact that the dragons have not offered any explanation at all for their unorthodox behavior strikes us, quite frankly, as worrisome. We urge in the strongest terms that the dragons explain their behaviors and actions before, during, and after the abduction of Princess Lucinda before we take irrevocable actions that could have unfortunate consequences," said Bonita.

The chaos of sound increased: people, reporters, photographers.

"Bonita, is that a threat to the dragons?" someone called.

"I think that statement stands on its own and needs no further qualification," Bonita replied.

"Are we going to war with the dragons?" Another voice from the crowd, but Bonita ignored it, and called on a reporter elsewhere in the throng. "Marcus."

"There are some who say the aggressive Castle response is an attempt to divert attention from allegations that Princess Lucinda is a voluntary companion on this 'kidnapping.' What would you say to those critics?" asked Marcus.

"Well, Marcus, I would say those people are grievously wrong. We, and by that I mean all the people of Carolia, are the victims here. If you could see the anger in the King's eyes, and the genuine anguish the Queen is feeling, you would know that there is nothing diverting about this situation. I think that we're done here. We will do our best to keep you apprised as to what I have said is a rapidly evolving situation," and Bonita shut the microphone off.

The image returned to the home studio, and Ambrosia said: "So that's the situation as seen by the palace, where as we have just shown you, officials are extremely concerned."

"Well, sorry to break in, Ambrosia, but it's time for Yvonne and her Morning Moments Coffee *Morning Time Daily* Traffic Report," said Art, cheerfully.

"With Traffic by the good people at Morning Moments Coffee, Where Every Morning ...," said Ambrosia.

"... Deserves a Good Moment," said Art.

"Well thanks, guys. Looks like war with the dragons. That's unusual," said Yvonne, as she stood in front of the traffic map.

"I suppose it is," Art agreed.

"Well," said Yvonne. "The good news is that if the dragons were planning to take either the Duke's Highway or General Patatoraie Memorial Expressway, they are not going to conquer anyone any time soon. It is jammed up both ways due to not one, but two overturned big rigs," said Yvonne.

"Two," said Art. "Wow, what were they carrying?"

"Eggs and flowers, Art. Eggs and flowers."

"That is gonna be some big pancake, Mindy," said Art.

"It's Yvonne," said Yvonne.

"I can only imagine the syrup dispenser," Art continued.

"No, flowers, Artifice. F-L-O-Wers. Flowers that bloom in the spring. Not flour; white stuff you bake with." There was general laughter in the studio. They always seemed to have such a good time. Even Yvonne was laughing as she was joined by Tracy. "Come on, guys! Too much fun," said Tracy. "And if it's gonna be war, the dragons are just gonna love our weather for the next three days."

The traffic map behind Tracy dutifully became a weather map, and the camera cut away from Yvonne. As soon as the red light of the camera gleamed in her direction, Tracy began to talk and move at the same time. "That strong ridge of high pressure last week giving us the warm offshore flow is going to continue to break up, so as you can see when we put the maps in motion, that will reverse the offshore flow and give us much more of a nice onshore flow, which you know any dragons flying in are going to just hate. And better air quality. I'm Tracy,"

"And I'm Yvonne." Yvonne walked back into to the weather board

"And this has been your Oh-eight weather."

"And traffic update."

"Brought to you by Moring Moments Coffee." They said this together, in a well-practiced unison

"—Where Every Morning …" said Ambrosia.

"…Deserves a Good Moment. Thank you, Tracy and Yvonne, the best Weather and Traffic team in the Kingdom. We will see you in another eight minutes," said Art. "At 16 past the hour."

"You know, Artifice," said Ambrosia. "That's a lot of conflicting news to take in about the Survival Day Surprise. And to help us sort it all out, we have a guy who does nothing but sort things out, in his mind at least. From the Carolia University Philosophy Department, Professor Zeldo Zaida. Professor Zaida, welcome to the Morning

Time Daily Report," said Ambrosia.

"Let me jump in to say that Professor Zaida comes to us via the good people at Big Times Suds and Soap," said Art. "Where the big brown lump..." said Art.

"... Is not a potato. Welcome, Professor," said Ambrosia.

"Thank you, it's very nice to be here. I have to say, I have never seen this show before, but you all seem very nice." Professor Zaida was a thin man, with a narrow face and thinning hair just a little on the long side.

"Well, thank you, Professor, we like to think we are." Art said, sharing a laugh with Ambrosia. "We hope you feel the same way after the interview. Just kidding. Now as I understand it, you think that philosophy can help sort out the troubling state of the kingdom."

"Oh, I get it," said the Professor. "'Is not a potato.' Very clever. A disharmonic polynome. Very good." Professor Zaida beamed.

"I don't think we have ever been called that before, Art," Ambrosia said with a laugh.

"I am not even sure I know what that is, Ambrosia," Art laughed.

"It's a very simple concept, really," said the helpful Professor. "You see, you have reality, or at least one version of it, -"

"I'm sorry, Professor, we're just having a little fun with you here," said Ambrosia.

"That is quite all right," said Professor Zaida.

"You see, Professor, the palace officials have asked that we bring you on our show this morning to explain why philosophy can help us understand what is going on with Princess Lucinda. They told us that you are going to tell us how Princess Lucinda is a cat? Do I have that right?" asked Ambrosia.

"More like a spitfire, I'd say, or at least a very wet cat," said Art, with a warm chuckle.

"No, I think that the situation with the Princess is more accurately akin to the famous conundrum of Schrödinger's Cat," the Professor said.

"Schrödinger's Cat, I see." Art winked at the camera.

"How can you break that down for us simple laypeople, Professor?" asked Ambrosia.

"Who have to break for commercial in two minutes," Art said.

"Schrödinger's Cat postulates a state where there is one being in two mutually exclusive states at the same time. The metaphoric cat is in a hypothetical box, and we know it will die in the box, but from the outside of the box one has no idea whether the cat is either dead or alive at any particular moment. Likewise, Princess Lucinda, who is either being kidnapped or in collusion with the dragon, is like the cat in the box. Because we cannot see inside the box—"

"Schrödinger's Cat," Art supplied, helpfully, but again a beat behind.

"Well, it really doesn't matter whose cat it is for the example to work," said Professor Zaida. "Because—"

"Well, I certainly hope it is Schrödinger's Cat, because if he is putting someone else's cat in a box—" said Art.

"I think what he means is that the cat is just a metaphor, Art," said Ambrosia.

"Schrödinger's metaphor," said Art.

"Yes," said the professor. "Precisely. Until we can see the Princess and speak with her, we cannot know her state of being."

"Oh, I see, said Art. "Very clever. I still have one question, though."

"Yes?" said Professor Zaida.

"Whose box is it? I mean, if it is Schrödinger's box, we could just shake the box," said Art.

"No, it's a very heavy box. Schrödinger says there is no way you can tell from the outside what is going on. That's the whole point. You simply do not know, and should not just assume that you know," Professor Zaida insisted. "You don't have enough facts to be sure of—"

"Oh, I get it," said Art, as an intern pressed a cup of Morning Time Coffee into the professor's hand.

"You sure?" Ambrosia asked.

"It's like with me and my fish," said Art.

Ambrosia chuckled. "Oh, you and your fish stories." She waved a hand at him and shook her head.

"It's like when I turn out the light in the living room and go to sleep. It's dark and I can't see the fish in the tank. I don't know if any of the fish might be belly up and going to meet the great toilet in the sky," said Art.

"That's actually very astute!" said the Professor. He seemed surprised. "It is precisely that same state of not knowing that is analogous to the state of Princess Lucinda. It would be much more convenient if we could turn on the night-light to see whether the fish are alive or dead."

"Or what about," Art paused dramatically, "Catfish?"

"Catfish, good one," Ambrosia laughed.

"I'm sorry, catfish?" Professor Zaida said.

"Princess Lucinda is a cat. Big fish eyes. Glasses. Schrödinger," Art explained. "Am I right?"

"I don't know," said the Professor, clearly floundering.

"Oh, I see," said Ambrosia, helpfully.

"But the catfish don't!" laughed Art. "They are bottom dwellers and can't see much of anything!"

"Artifice, you are on fire this morning," said Ambrosia. "Give me five." They exchanged a quick and cheerful high-five.

This was the precise moment when the idea of putting Professor Zaida on the *Morning Time Daily Report* was attributed to Zoe the Intern. She was promptly fired, just as soon she finished the photocopying. Later, because there was no one else who wanted to fetch coffee and do the photocopying, she was reinstated.

"It's not all me, Ambrosia," said Art. "This Morning Moments coffee is so good, good, good this morning! What more does the Philosophy Department have to tell us about catfish, Professor? Do you like them fried, grilled, or deep-fried?"

"All Schrödinger is saying is that people should not be so quick to pass judgment on the Princess," Zaida said, as he struggled to regain control of the narrative. "We have no evidence by which to judge her actions."

"We couldn't agree more, Professor, that's why we here at Morning Time Daily are pleased to announce that we are setting up a tip line for anyone who has seen Princess Lucinda and the dragon," said Ambrosia. "The number is on your screen."

"We're gonna shake that catfish out of the box, Professor," said Art.

"Thank you very much, Professor Zeldo Zaida of the Philosophy Department at Carolia University for coming to the studio to chat with us," said Ambrosia. Professor Zaida looked dazed, and he held onto his coffee cup as if it were the only solid thing left in the world. It was just too bad that his fingers covered up the Morning Moments logo.

"And we'll be right back to the Morning Time Daily Report, after we pay some of the bills around here," said Art, "by showing you a few messages from our sponsors."

Having displayed a mastery of the medium, Art leaned back and drank his coffee. Ambrosia nodded in approval, as she restocked her paper notes.

Chapter Twenty-Three
Too Dangerous For Children

Lucy was so angered by what she had just heard that she accidentally swallowed some of her grapefruit. A catfish? she thought. Not a leaping salmon or a cute little dolphin, but they called her a catfish, probably the ugliest fish in the world. Bad enough when they had ignored her, dismissed her as "The one with the glasses," but now they were LAUGHING about her and calling her a CATFISH! Ha-ha-ha! It was on the news. It would be on every channel!

Fortunately, the room was full to overflowing with Butlers and Maids, all of whom had been formidably trained in first-aid techniques, and were willing to pat her on the back until the choking stopped.

"I'm confused," said Connie.

"About what?" asked Ember.

"Why are they so surprised that Lucy is still alive? It's called Survival Day! They said so!" She cocked her delicate head to one side, and her silken mane rippled. "Where is the surprise?"

"It's because no one has ever survived before," said Glowerflorious, his draconic expression rather grim, even for a dragon. "Either the dragon or the Princess, or usually both, dies every year."

"Shouldn't they call it Carnage Day, then?" asked Connie. "Or Selective Slaughter Day?"

"Marketing, I suspect, and I suppose they already had all the banners printed," said Ember, but a little bit absent-mindedly, because she was concerned, not so much about the purple shade Lucy had turned, but the way she was almost buried by offers of help. However difficult it was for her to breathe, though, the girl had been raised in a palace and had plenty of experience in politely declining things. Already, Lucy was recovering enough from her shock to wave away any further offers from the Maids and Butlers to provide aromatic hand massages, haiku-scented oxygenated water, and the opportunity to be turned upside down and slapped until the offending piece of pulp dislodged itself, though that one Butler did get a look.

"Are we really on a rampage?" Connie asked.

"Well, you were pretty hard on that poor girl in the village," said Ember thoughtfully. "When you extra-cuted her half to death. And the wolves."

"They were bad doggies," said Connie, looking meek and darling and practically incapable of tearing a pack of playing cards to shreds, let alone ravenous wolves. (So long as you ignored the sharp, pointy horn at the center of her brow and the sharp hoof on the end of each dainty, but incredibly powerful leg.)

"You were pretty hard on me, too," said Glowerflorious, though the big dragon seemed to admire the little unicorn's attitude.

"I can't believe," said Lucy, when she got her voice back, "that they think this is all some terrible plot. Plot against what? Being eaten?"

"I can't believe they didn't seem happy to find out you're still alive," said Connie. "Even if you are part of a rampage."

Lucy sniffed, and reached for one of the handkerchiefs offered by the legion of butlers and maids in the room. "Oh, I can believe that," she muttered, but mostly into the handkerchief, so everyone else could be forgiven if they pretended not to have heard the bitterness in the remark. She was grateful to her friends for not mentioning the catfish comments, and resolved to put them behind her forever.

She wiped her face, and then looked from Ember to Glowerflorious and back. "What do you think the dragons will do, if they take my parents seriously? Is Carolia in danger?"

"Not immediate danger," said Glowerflorious, after some careful thought. "I think they'll want to see what's happened to Ember first, and whether she's kidnapped you, or you've kidnapped her."

"But eventual danger?"

"Not as much danger as the three of you seem to be in," said Suzette, joining the group of them with serious concern in her gaze. She was so upset, she had forgotten her faux-French accent. "If they are sending hunters and spies and television crews along to capture one or both of you, you don't dare waste another minute getting on the road to Profundia."

"If that is still where you intend to go," said the Butler, with a question mark gently applied in his attitude, if not his tone of voice.

"Well, I don't know," said Lucy. "We know it's north, like Connie guessed. But we don't know what we'll find there."

"Actually," said Suzette. "We do."

She was treated to expressions of disapproval and horror on the discreet faces of the Maids and Butlers in the room, but shook her head saucily. "Oh, relax, all of you," she scolded. "We hoped they would come up with the answers on their own and want to go, but there isn't time for that now. We have to tell them."

"Tell us what?" asked Ember.

"Is it the secret recipe to the chocolate chip cookies you served after dinner last night?" asked Connie, bouncing on all four hooves. All the collected stares, human, dragon, Maid and Butler, turned and focused on her, but nothing as simple as a lot of attention could possibly wilt a flower as bright as Connie. "They were Yummy Super Delicious, and the Chef said it was a secret recipe!"

"It is not that," said Suzette, without even a trace of exasperation (possibly a unicorn super power). "It's the truth about Survival Day, and what it means."

"It doesn't mean saving the beaches from the horrific invasion of flies after human beings have left all their litter tied to posts on the shore?" asked Ember.

"It wasn't like that," said Lucy. "I wasn't litter."

"I know," said Ember. "But that's what we were told in our form letter from Profundia. That we were saving the ocean, and helping the planet to survive. Survival Day."

"And it was certainly interesting that garbage day for the humans seemed to happen at the same time every year," said Glowerflorious.

"Again," said Lucy, "not garbage!" She was finding it much better to be indignant about unimportant things than to spend any more time wishing her parents loved her more than they did.

"But your letter," said Ember. "Was from Profundia too."

"What did it say?" asked Connie.

"It said I had to be tied up on the beach to appease the appetites of the dragons, or else they would destroy the city. That I was doing it for everyone else's survival. Survival Day. But you were never intending to destroy the city."

"No. It sounds exhausting to try, and your city is full of Knights. Besides, people don't taste all that great, anyway. No one really wants to eat them. Ugh," said Ember.

Lucy laughed. "I'm glad I'm not delicious."

Ember laughed, too, accompanied by little smoke rings.

"But children," said Suzette, firmly. "To get back to the point, whoever has been living in Profundia - and we aren't certain, but we think that it is an evil wizard, or maybe a group of wizards - has been luring dragons and princesses to their forest kingdom for almost a century now."

"A century?" gasped Lucy.

"Maybe longer. That's when the Valley of the Maids and Butlers was founded, and as far back as our records go."

"Why do they want the dragons and the princesses?" asked Ember.

Robert shook his head gravely. He did have an excellent solemn expression, and seemed willing to make use of it whenever possible. Now that the questers had spent more time around him, they also recognized a deep concern for others underneath it all.

"We don't know why they do it, because anyone who gets close enough to their stronghold to find out vanishes in horrible circumstances."

"How do you know they are horrible?" asked Connie. "If they've vanished, you don't see them again. Maybe they've vanished in wonderful circumstances. "

"Connie ..." said Glowerflorious, attempting repression. It failed.

"Maybe they're all at a party there, having a wonderful time, with balloons and cotton candy, and a bouncy house. I've always wanted to visit a bouncy house, but I never could. If I had a chance to go to a bouncy house, I would bounce and bounce, for hours and hours! But Daddy says unicorns are too big for bouncy houses, and I say that they just don't know to make a bouncy house for a unicorn, but if we tried, and tried really hard, I just know that we could..."

"Connie!" said Ember and Lucy together.

"Sorry," said Connie. "Make a bouncy house for unicorns," she added quickly, under her breath.

"They vanished," said Suzette. "In mysterious circumstances." She gave a steely glare at the three girls.

"Oo! Mysterious circumstances," Connie shivered dramatically. "That's totally different."

"But we think that your friend, Glowerflorious, is our best clue as to what has happened to them," Suzette continued, smoothly.

"You mean," said the big dragon, several of his scales going grey. "What happened to me might have happened to them?"

"Yes," said Suzette. "I think they might have been en-kittened." As dire pronouncements went, it was rather spoiled by Connie's response.

"Aw! I love kittens! Almost as much as bouncy houses."

"But Glowerflorious is not a kitten any longer," said Ember.

"No," agreed Suzette. "Your use of the experimental flashlight and red-wrapper dot pointer that we included in your Survival Day baggage worked more effectively than we could possibly have hoped."

"Experimental?" said Ember.

"Yes, of course! You don't think we spent the last hundred years just dusting and sweeping and washing dishes, did you? We've been hard at work developing methods intended to help rescue princesses and dragons for a long time now."

"You sent the bag?" said Lucy.

"Yes," said Suzette. "I'm sorry we couldn't be more explicit in our instructions. We weren't entirely sure who was complicit in the plan to capture dragons and princesses and who was just obedient to tradition."

"And to be honest," said the Butler, Robert, "our methods have never been this successful before."

"I'm relieved you all made it here safely," said Suzette. "But I'm sorry, girls, now that we know our experiments do work, we'll have to take the bag back from you and use the devices ourselves to go to Profundia."

"No," said Lucy. "No, that's not right."

"You have to give us the recipe for the cookies first," said Connie.

Lucy laughed, surprising herself. "No, I don't mean that. I mean that what's changed isn't your bag of tricks, but it's us. The news has talked about knights before, or dragons flying away, or princesses who got away, but what's different now is that it's all of us. A team. Ember and me working together, with Connie helping in ways we didn't expect. Your bag is useful, because we're using it in ways you aren't expecting. So if you took it from us, it wouldn't work nearly as well for you, and you'd be disappeared."

"And Ember and Lucy would still be criminals," said Connie, helpfully.

"And Connie would still be rampaging," said Glowerflorious, who was really getting to like the little unicorn.

"No. It's too dangerous a task for children," said Suzette. She said it firmly. She put all her authority as Head Maid of the Valley behind it, but Lucy was a princess, and princesses overruled maids all the time.

"We're grateful to you for helping Ember with the girdle," Princess Lucy said. "But we really do have to do this ourselves."

Suzette paused for a moment longer than a well-trained maid might have done, but at last ruefully said: "Robert, give them the printout of the map. Bon voyage mon petite generals. Take care and it has been a privilege to serve."

"Hooray!" said Connie. "A rescue mission!."

Margit Elland Schmitt & Dan McLaughlin

Chapter Twenty-Four
Thursdays Headlines

PRINCESS LUCINDA ASSAULTS POOR SERVING WENCH!!!

PRINCESS CRIME SPREE REACHES HINTERLANDS.

"SHE WAS IN TOTAL CONTROL OF THE SITUATION!" EYEWITNESS CLAIMS EYES WERE BATTED.

"THOSE GLASSES SURE TO BE NEXT NEW THING," ASSERTS MORNING TIME DAILY'S AMBROSIA WATERS.

Chapter Twenty-Five
Afraid of The Dark

THEY WERE NOT SO MUCH PACKED AND PROVISIONED FOR THE JOURNEY AS bundled out the door with whatever happened to be in the sacks nearest to it. To Ember, who only needed her own scales and wings to be comfortable, and was still wearing the thread from the magical girdle besides, it was easy to find the whole thing amusing. The maids and butlers were efficient in a way that implied they'd been doing nothing but training for emergencies their whole lives, but they were clearly not used to being surprised. While they did everything they were supposed to do (for instance, Ember didn't see anyone running around with pillows over their heads, screaming in panic), she kept catching surreptitious looks passing between them, as if the maids and butlers, in passing, were making sure that everyone else approved of what was being done.

"They do like to scurry," said Glowerflorious in a draconic whisper, which was comfortingly like the rumble of a far-off storm. "Why don't we wait outside? I feel as if I'd like to be dragon-sized again, and we'd only be in the way while they're packing."

It was true. The hall was grand and polished and gilded with attractive glints that hinted at long-term investments tastefully not-flaunted before any guests, but at the same time, it had an unused, sterile quality. It didn't look as if they often had guests. In the same way, the formidable facade of the building and the formal garden stretching before it looked excruciatingly well maintained, but not precisely lived in.

"It's no gem-studded cave near a toasty-warm lava-river," said Glowerflorious. "But they do seem to take good care of the place. Not like those foolish humans in the big cities."

"Remember," said Ember. "That wasn't really litter on the seaside. It was people."

"Mine was rescued by a bunch of obnoxious fellows in rattly armor, I do remember that," said Glowerflorious. "They had some sort of device that tore a bloody great hole in my side, and I was dripping ichor all the way north in my attempt to escape."

"I'm sorry," said Ember, coiling herself comfortably around the decorative fountain. It had a sculpture in the center, of a number of maids, stone arms held aloft, while the water splayed out like the fronds from crystal feather-dusters. "We were all worried about you, when you didn't come back from your tour." Ember remembered her brother had moped around the lair for months. She'd been almost as bad; although Glowerflorious had never been her particular friend, when she was a youngling, she had always admired him. "That wound must have hurt, and still you flew all that way. Were you frightened?"

"I probably should pretend I wasn't," Glowerflorious said, with a scaly grin. "But that's not true. I was afraid for my hide most of the way. Of course, now I realize that it was all part of whatever magical spell the wizard people cast on me. All so that they could turn me into a kitten." His eyes gleamed with admiration. "You fared much better, Ember. There's more gold to you than grit," a high dragon compliment. "Something special to you, and not just in those shiny scales of yours."

She blushed at the compliment, her scales rippling all over in shades of flame. "Oh, that's just because the maids keep polishing anything in arm's reach."

"I'm not so sure," he said. "My memory of my ignoble kitten days is more than a little foggy, but I remember my dragon time perfectly well. In particular, I remember my friend's pretty sister tagging along whenever we'd go lava-sliding. You haven't changed that much, Ember, except for your name. Though you're right about the maids and butlers. They polished and oiled and trimmed everything twice over, and every time I yawned last night, someone jumped in to brush my teeth again."

Ember laughed, with accompanying smoke rings. "Well, they aren't any more used to us than we are used to them," she said. "Lucy's the only one who knows about maids and butlers. We don't have them."

"Why should we?" Glowerflorious shrugged. "Dragons don't have clothes that need buttoning or shoes that need tying."

"No, I know," she said, though privately, Ember thought a maid might be nice to have around when it was time to shed her skin, someone to get into those itchy nooks where it was so hard to reach! "But I was just thinking that from what I've heard about them, this bunch seemed a little strange."

"How so?" he asked, giving her a thoughtful, curious look that would have flustered her to pieces if she were still a little girl dragon and not a grown-up adventuress.

"Just that they seem to be so thoroughly experts in everything around the place, especially the technology —"

"That was an excellent DALSED terminal they'd rigged up," agreed Glowerflorious

"— but what I notice is that they all seem to be waiting for someone to ask them for help or to tell them what to do. They know how to do everything, except how to decide to do it, if that makes sense."

"It does, actually," he said, after taking a gratifying moment to think over the implications. "All potential and no direction. Here they come," he added, his gaze shifting to the big, heavy doors of the building.

Ember shared a look with him, and out of consideration for Lucy and Connie, the two dragons used the power of the girdle thread to shrink down to a size more suitable for human conversation.

"You've made some good friends, Ember," Glowerflorious murmured, before Lucy and the unicorn skipped over. "Your brothers would have been proud."

Fortunately, there was no time to say more, and if Lucy was perceptive enough to notice that Ember's scales were scintillating in rose and gold and carnation - shades of delight and embarrassment - she was also too tactful to say so. Ember was resoundingly grateful, and offered to carry the big, heavy bags of whatever it was the Maids and Butlers had decided was essential to their journey.

"Even if I'm only human-sized," she said. "I still have dragon-strength. You and Connie will be less tired if you don't have to carry anything new."

Naturally, Connie's equine companions were still carrying most of what had been provided by the unicorn herd. All Connie, cute little thing that she was, had to bear was her own attitude, but that would have exhausted a lesser being days ago. Lucy still had the bag made out of the shroud, the same one she'd been given to die or escape in that day on the beach. It seemed ages ago.

"How are you feeling?" Ember asked. She couldn't help but notice that her friend was off her color, too. Humans didn't have scales to show what they were feeling, but over time, Ember had learned to read Lucy's emotions in the shifting of her expression and (in this case) the over-bright sparkle in her eyes, behind those attractive glasses.

"It's all so weird," said Lucy. "I was just the least memorable sister in the family, just a few days ago. Now I'm a wanted fugitive, a personality rather than a person."

"A legendary princess, kidnapped against her will," said Ember, tilting her head a little to one side.

Lucy smiled in answer. "I like thinking of myself as a rebel with a loaded dragon."

"Not to mention your batflash." Ember nodded approval. "Wait till they get wind of the fact that we have Connie with us. The threat of a unicorn unleashed at terminal cuteness velocity is liable to bring the world to its knees."

"I hope so," said Lucy. "Even if it's only that small part of the world currently under the management of evil wizards. What I want to do is save all those dragons and maidens who weren't as lucky as us."

"Let's get to it, then," said Ember.

By this time, Connie had already convinced Glowerflorious to accompany her at the front of the procession. She was threatening to teach him all the verses of the questing song. The unicorn princess had already said her farewells to Suzette, and now was prancing into the dark and scary forest without a care in the world, accompanied by a noble dragon. Ember thought it was adorable how quickly the unicorn and her brother's friend had hit it off. It was still unclear which one thought the other was his or her special pet. Maybe the feeling was mutual. Ember was having fun watching them figure it out, from a safe distance.

"How are you feeling?" asked Lucy, as they entered the forest. "Does it bother you, the idea of having a magic spell on you?"

"Another magic spell," Ember pointed out, lifting her claw, where the thread from the girdle was still tied in a jaunty bow around her mother's bracelet. (You had to hand it to the maids. When they tied a bow, it stayed tied!) "When I shrank, it was sudden and scary," she added.

"I remember. You burned down lots of that forest."

"This is scary, but in a different way. It's more subtle. If the magic of these wizards twists us dragons around and brings us north to be enchanted, how do I know I'm not under their spell right now?"

"Connie was the one who suggested north, and the DALSED box just confirmed it."

"Still," said Ember. "It makes me wonder how much of what I'm thinking is really my own thought, you know?"

Lucy considered it, one hand resting lightly on Ember's side. Ember was glad they could walk together like this, almost hand in hand, though of course dragons didn't have hands. "Except that you're something special," Lucy said. "All the other dragons got swept up in the moment and ended up enchanted somewhere, or killed by Knights, or picking bits of maiden out of their teeth."

"Yuck," said Ember.

"But you stopped long enough to talk to me," Lucy went on. "And ignored whatever the magic was asking you to do until you'd made up your own mind about me first."

"Do you think that's because the magic has been going on for so long it could be getting weaker?" Ember asked.

Lucy shook her head. "No, I don't," she said. "I think it's just exactly what I told the Maids and Butlers. You're special. I'm special, too."

"I'm special, three!" said Connie, who could sneak up on someone pretty well, when she chose not to sing her questing song at full volume.

"Yes, we all are," said Lucy. "I think maybe it's destiny that we came together. I think we really do have a chance to stop this, so no one else has to ever get another form letter from Profundia again."

"Down with the printing press!" said Connie.

"Let's not get crazy," laughed Lucy.

"I don't entirely object to crazy," said Ember, in a dragon's whisper.

"Whoa." said Connie, unnecessarily. Boots, Scoots, Skipper, and Glowerflorious had all come to a sudden stop at the base of a high hill. No one had seen the hill before, because it was almost entirely concealed by the forest, which grew in thick, choking tangles all around, as if making a deliberate attempt to block the way.

But the road they were traveling, the road to Profundia, led directly through the hill, by means of a deep, dark, spooky-looking tunnel. Even Ember, who loved a nice cliff or a warm, cozy cave, couldn't help but shiver at the sight of that lightless gap in the earth.

"Are we going in there?" asked Connie, in a small voice.

"I think we have to," said Lucy.

"Boots and Scoots are afraid of the dark. They don't like it," said Connie, again unnecessarily. The pack horses stood as if they were doing everything in their power to turn themselves into iron and root themselves to the spot. Their eyes were wide and rolling.

"Glowerflorious and I could grow big again, and carry everyone over the top of the mountain," said Ember. "It might take two trips, but we probably could do it."

"Skipper is afraid of heights," said Connie, looking a little green around the nostrils.

Ember and Lucy shared a glance. "Is it possible that some unicorns might be scared of the dark, and of heights, too?" asked Ember gently.

"Hypothetically speaking," said Lucy.

Connie wilted, a pitiful sight. "It's possible," she said, in a meek little voice, and she scuffed one polished, cloven hoof in the dirt. "I never really did have any experience with all-the-way darkness, you know. In the meadow with my Mummy and Daddy, there were always stars at night, and the moon, and unicorn sparkles. This looks like the sort of darkness that happens when something big and scary picks you up and swallows you down whole. But I'm also not a bird, you know? I don't have wings like you do, Ember, and I don't know how to do long-way-downs and landings."

"Which one scares you less, Connie?" asked Ember. "Walking into the deep, dark tunnel in the middle of your friends?"

"Who have a flashlight," offered Lucy.

"And can breathe fire," said Glowerflorious.

"So it won't be entirely, totally dark," said Ember.

"Or would you rather be flying high up in the sky with your dragon friends," asked Glowerflorious. "Looking down on all the birds and trees."

"And wolves," said Lucy.

"Have you ever tried singing from up in the air?" asked Ember. "Just think how far your melody could go!"

That seemed to cinch the matter. Connie perked up, just a little, and although it didn't look as if the horses thought the solution was any kind of improvement, they were in no condition to resist when Glowerflorious grew to his full size and picked one horse up in each claw. He was very careful with Boots and Scoots.

Ember's job was to pick up Lucy and Connie in one claw and Skipper in the other. She did her best to remember the lessons she'd learned about carrying Lucy the first time, and shield them from the wind. Unfortunately, Connie didn't get a chance, once they were in the air, to experiment with her singing. But at least they were all able to reassure the little unicorn later, when they were safely on the ground on the other side of the hill, that it had absolutely been the most adorable torrent of unicorn vomit ever to rain down upon an unsuspecting countryside.

Chapter Twenty-Six
Good Knight, Bad Knight

The following is the only independent account of the now infamous Heigh-Ho Wolf Incident. This interview took place at the Thornton Forest Knight station. Translations of wolf transcriptions are available on request.

Agent X:
Thank you for coming in, Mr. Afraid.

Wolf:
It's Alfred.

Agent X:
Sorry?

Wolf:
The name is Alfred, like the king. Not Afraid, as in a mouse.

Agent X:
I'm sorry, the intake form here is quite clear, it says you are Afraid.

Wolf:
Alfred. A. L. F. R-

Agent X:
Mr. Fraid, I'm going to have to ask you to calm down.

Wolf:
OK.

Agent X:
Or we will have to put a muzzle on you in addition to the leash.

Wolf:
OK. I said OK, geeze, calm down. What a hard-ass.

Agent X:
What was that Mr. Fraid?

Wolf:
Nuff'n.

Agent X:
Very well, Mr. All Afraid. Again. Thank you for coming in.

Wolf:
I didn't come in. I was drug in. There's a difference.

Agent X:
Maybe to lawyers, Mr. Fraid, maybe to lawyers. But to you and me, here in this little interrogation room right in the really nice local Knights' office, not so much. No shrugging, Mr. Fraid.

Wolf:
I don't have to tell you nuff'n.

The Dragon, Lucinda and George

Agent X:
We'll certainly see about that. This here is Knight George. He will be observing. Is that OK, Mr. Fraid? (sound of shuffling) I'm sorry, Mr. Fraid. We are recording this, and a shrug is not sufficient to constitute a reply. Nor is that gesture at all appropriate. And stop slouching. Need I remind you, Mr. Fraid, that this is a Royal Investigation and that we are Knights?

Wolf:
Whatever. I'm still not saying nuff'n.

Agent X:
Whatever indeed. Now, according to the statement attached to your intake form, you were part of the pack that threatened Princess Lucinda's party Tuesday last, yes?

Wolf:
You mean the bean pole with ears? Looks like a slug with glasses? I mean, maybe, I'm not saying nuff'n one way or the other.

Agent X:
Royal Princess Lucinda, you mean.

Wolf:
She ain't my Princess.

Agent X:
Listen, you snotty little dog-faced—

George:
Actually, he's right, Agent X. Wolves are a Democratic Republic,

and certainly not recognized in the tax codes as citizens of the Empire.

Wolf:
Yeah, what he said.

Agent X:
Well if you know so much, why don't you take over, Knight George?

George:
May I, Agent X? Thank you. Mr. Alfred, I really should apologize for my colleague's behavior. I'm afraid since you are not a barmaid, he's rather at a loss at how to proceed. Please, Agent X, why don't you go and take a break.

Agent X:
You sure that you're going to be OK with this mangy creature?

George:
I'm sure I will be fine, thank you.

Agent X:
Fine, but we're not done yet, wolf.

(sound of Agent X leaving)

Wolf:
What an asswipe.

George:
Really. Now let's get this leash off of you. I'm so sorry they put it on you in the first place. A complete mistake on our part. "Treat you with kid gloves," it says, right here in your file. There we go, leash off. Is that better?

Wolf:
Much better, thanks.

George:
I happen to have a bit of extra rabbit. Care for a bite?

Wolf:
Wouldn't mind a bit of rabbit.

George:
Here you go.

(sound of massive jaws quickly devouring rabbit bits)

George:
Well done.

Wolf:
Been a while since I've had a nice bit of fresh rabbit.

George:
Would you like some more?

Wolf:
Wouldn't mind.

George: (over intercom)
Constable, could we get some more rabbit in here, please? And maybe a chicken. Thank you.

Wolf:
Still don't have to say nuff'n.

George:
Of course not. The law is quite clear. Ah, here is the meat, dig in.

(sound of massive jaws quickly devouring rabbit and chicken)

George:
Better?

Wolf:
Yeah, thanks.

George:
So, you've been without a pack for a bit now, haven't you?

Wolf:
Yeah.

George:
A little rough.

Wolf:
A little, but I'm doing OK.

George:
Oh, sure you are, I can see that, clearly. You know, I lost my mum and dad a few years ago. It was pretty rough, too.

Wolf:
Oh yeah. (pause) How did you get a new pack?

George:
It was tough, I've got to tell you. You have to be careful.

Wolf:
Yeah, that's what I figure. You know, I'm like weighing my options now. Don't want to make the wrong choice.

George:
It's a big decision.

Wolf:
Yeah.

George:
Now I'm not promising anything, but if I knew a fella who knew a pack that was needing a young, cautious wolf like you, would you be interested?

Wolf:
Could be. Maybe. Yeah. I'm still a little hungry. Any of that rabbit left?

George:
Rabbit is something there is never a shortage of. They breed, you know. (over intercom) Constable, could you please bring the

rest of the rabbit?

Wolf:
And the chicken.

George:
Yes, and the chicken, too, please. Thank you.

(sounds of more crunching and devouring)

Wolf:
Thanks.

George:
No problem, Alfred. Now if you have just a moment, I was wondering if you could help me out.

Wolf:
Sure.

George:
You see, everyone we've talked to so far about this Princess Lucinda has been all ga-ga over royalty, so we haven't been able to get the view of someone as clear-headed and realistic as you.

Wolf:
I could see that, sure. They do go all in a frenzy about them Royals, they do.

George:
So, I could really use your help. You know, if you tell me what

you know happened that night, it would help me out more than a little.

Wolf:
Well, if I were to help you out, and you know someone who needs a new wolf for the pack, maybe we could work out something— you know, what do they call it?— a quid pro quo.

George:
Absolutely. You have my word as a Knight.

Wolf:
OK, yeah, I'll tell you what I saw. OK, it was like, just a normal day in the woods. Me and the pack, we were doing nuff'n, having a few laughs. When like off in the distance, we hear this singing.

George:
Singing?

Wolf:
Yeah, singing, you know Hiiiii-ho Hiiiii-ho, da-dum de-dum Hiiiii-hooooo

(sound of several men entering the room)

Constable 1:
Everything OK, Sir?

George:
Everything is fine and in order, Constable. Thank you, gentlemen. Thank you, you may go now.

Wolf:
Sorry.

George:
Oh, no problem. Um. You do have an excellent singing voice, Alfred, it carries wonderfully, but from here on out, you don't need to sing anymore.

Wolf:
All right. So anyways, there we was, just minding our own business, and we heard this singing, so we said to ourselves, "Let's sing too, like back at them, all friendly like."

George:
All friendly, like that howl you just gave?

Wolf:
You know, howling, singing, it's all the same, isn't it? Oh yeah, just like that. Nice and friendly, like I said.

George:
Sure.

Wolf:
So, we says to ourselves, "Wonderful, a party. Let's go have a look, shall we?" and off we scoot, all friendly like.

George:
I see, scoot.

Wolf:
"So, what's singing without dancing?" says Reg. That used to be our pack's motto, so as we gets closer, we starts dancing.

George:
Dancing?

Wolf:
Yeah, dancing, like a circle dance, everyone gathering together, all nice and together and friendly like. See?

George:
I quite see.

Wolf:
So like then we appear, "Surprise! We're at the party, too."

George:
Surprise, like a birthday party?

Wolf:
Exactly, you got it. Like a birthday party. Only like, it's no one's birthday.

George:
No, of course not. Then what happened?

Wolf:
So there we sees them. There was this cute little white unicorn at the head, all singing and dancing like she's the leader of the biggest parade ever. She didn't even notice us and she kept dancing and prancing, but the others, they, like, froze.

George:
Froze?

Wolf:
Yeah, like as in frozen in surprise. Delight.

George:
Or fear.

Wolf:
Fear and delight. Two sides of the same coin, yes?

George:
Interesting notion. Then what happened?

Wolf:
Well, they froze, but the white one, she keeps dancing and prancing, and so we figured, she's still dancing, so we should do our friendly circle song and dance around her.

George:
Around just the unicorn?

Wolf:
Well, yeah, seeing as how she was the only one still singing and dancing. It would have been rude to ignore her.

George:
Rude? Wolves?

Wolf:
I know, right? We're the most politest creatures of the forest, wolves are, ask anyone.

George:
We have.

Wolf:
So anyways, there we are singing and dancing around this cute unicorn, and all sudden like, she stops singing and dancing. And she looks at Reg and says like, "Are you a good wolf or a bad wolf?" real sweet and nice like. And then Nick, he decides to have a little more fun, you know, to show he's a good wolf, he like darts in like he's gonna take a little nick out of her back ankle.

George:
Just playful?

Wolf:
Oh. Of course. I mean his name is Nick, so what can you expect? Because that is what he likes to do for fun. Of course, sometimes he gets carried away and it's more like a bite, and once in a while he sorta accidentally severs a tendon and leaves them more sort of crippled than anything else, but that's just Nick, you know. Nick nicks.

George:
It's just his way. I get it. Then what happened?

Wolf:
Well, then little Miss Corny went bonkers on us. One little kick,

and Nick is sailing through the air, deader than a doornail. Then the little dragon in a diaper gives him a kiss of flame as he sails by. And like all he did was like lunge in for a little nick. It was totally uncalled for.

George:
I see. Then what happened?

Wolf:
Well, then it was a whirling bit of kick, bad. Stab, bad. Kick, stab. Bad, bad. Stab, toss, bad. Stab, toss, bad. Kick, kick, kick. Bad, bad, bad. And the pack is flying through the air, completely dead and in some cases completely burnt, just to add insult to injury, and suddenly I am staring at the business end of a unicorn horn, and she is asking me all calm and pretty like if I am a good wolf or a bad wolf. Totally psycho.

George:
So, what did you say?

Wolf:
Oh, we talked for a bit, you know.

George:
Friendly like.

Wolf:
Precisely. You got it. Friendly like, and then we parted company, all palsy-walsy.

George:
I see. It seems clear. I just have a few more questions for you, if I may?

Wolf:
Sure.

George:
So, the unicorn started it?

Wolf:
Oh yeah, totally. The friendly wolves, just singers and dancers and party-people, and then wham!

George:
And Princess Lucinda, what did you notice about her?

Wolf:
You mean aside from how she seemed to be under the impression that all the singing and dancing wolves were about to rip her to shreds? Mistaken impression, I mean.

George:
Yes, aside from that.

Wolf:
Not much.

George:
And what about the dragon?

Wolf:
You mean aside from the fact that she was pint-sized, or that she was wearing some sort of clothes, and sending out a small wall of flames that was spit-roasting the pack?

George:
Yes, aside from that.

Wolf:
Not much.

George:
Did the Princess seem to be under any state of captivity or any stress while you were in her presence?

Wolf:
You mean aside from being surrounded by a party-sized pack of wolves?

George:
Yeah, aside from that.

Wolf:
Not much. Honestly, I was mostly focused on the little psycho with the horn. That's all I know, Knight. So, you'll put in a good word for me with your friend in this other pack?

George:
Of course, Alfred. You have been very helpful. Wait right here and I will get the paperwork squared away.

(end of interview)

When George left the interview room, it was to find the hallway filled by a crowd of grinning constables, who burst into spontaneous applause.

Chip was the first to speak. "I say, old fellow, best rendition of good cop/bad cop I have seen in ages. And first time through. Well done."

"I was thinking maybe I went over the top with the bad cop, but I was just making sure that you would be a better good, but I shouldn't have worried. You were great, kid. Just great," gushed Agent X.

"I liked the part about the barmaids," said one constable, to gales of manly laughter and back slapping.

"Thank you, thank you. You were perfect, Agent X, I was thinking all the time about the stuff you told me. It was very helpful. Well, here is the name of the fella who knows of a wolf pack," George said, and suddenly found himself the focus of a dozen shocked stares.

Chip was the first to speak. "You actually know a fellow…"

"Why yes, a knight would never lie, after he has given his word, I mean." George's sentence was half question, and half statement.

There was a long and increasingly uncomfortable pause.

Agent X said, "Speaking as your mentor, maybe I have been remiss in explaining the finer points," he began.

Chip lay a hand on Agent X's arm. "He did such a good job," Chip said. "Let's give it to him."

"That's what I was going to say," concluded Agent X, weakly, and there followed a rather confused cheer.

Margit Elland Schmitt & Dan McLaughlin

Chapter Twenty-Seven
Sometimes You Just Ask

AFTER BYPASSING THE TUNNEL OF FOREBODING FEELINGS, and blazing through the Bog of Intestinal Discomfort and navigating through the Glen of the Pounding Pain Behind the Eye, the merry band of questers were glad to be on a flat stretch of road, singing merrily. Connie led the way, twittering on her horn.

"Can you tell me where's the tree," she sang.
"The tree with a bee on Concordia Street.
"There are blossoms and branches there,
"Waving themselves in the springtime air,
"And the bees making honey they don't like to share!"

Lucy leaned over to Ember, who had made herself small and was perched on Skipper's saddle beside Lucy. "I'm so glad you didn't gobble me down. This is so much better."

"Than being eaten?"

"Yes, so much more has happened than I expected."

Glowerflorious' voice cut through the crisp air. He had a lovely and clear Irish tenor, that blended well with Connie.

"Can you tell me where's the cake,
"The cake in the lake on Concordia Street.
"The mermaids throw a party
"Their laughter's very hearty
"I wouldn't want to be tardy!"

Connie giggled with joy, and Scoots, Boots, and Skipper bobbed their heads in time and snorted as if they had just eaten a particularly nice bit of clover.

"That concludes verse 74, I think," Ember said, a trifle dryly.

"Glowerflorious and Connie got to be good friends very quickly, don't you think?" said Lucy.

"I'm sure they're both very friendly beings," Ember said, looking somewhat stonily off at a suddenly interesting tree. Or rock. Or hill. Or something.

Lucy laughed. "Oh no, silly, are you jealous? They're just friends. Glowerflorious couldn't be in love with even the cutest unicorn in the world. There's only one creature on this quest who really interests him."

Ember turned her head, and once again Lucy was reminded how quickly dragons, even small, cuddly, hug-sized ones, could move when they really wanted to. And how they didn't blink when they stared. And quite frankly, how terrifying that was for any creature that had been small and totally unable to defend itself from being snatched up and consumed in one gulp at one point in its evolutionary development, no matter how big its brain was now and was quite clever with building things and organizing things like complex societies....

Good thing it was just two friends talking, so Lucy could relax.

"How do you know?" Ember asked. "And don't say it's some maiden instinct, or I swear, Lucy."

She nudged Ember. "No." Lucy smiled and looked around to make sure that no one else was listening. "I just asked him."

"Lucinda Merrie Periwinkle Grottweiler Rotunda Doorstop," hissed Ember. "Tell me you did not."

"Of course I did. What else are besties for?" Lucy asked. "Sometimes you just have to ask."

The Dragon, Lucinda and George

"Lucinda Merrie, I swear sometimes you are just as bad as Connie."

"Maybe I am," said Lucy, who didn't mind the accusation much at all. "But don't you want to know what he said?"

"Yes! What did he say?"

"You have nothing to worry about. He thinks she's a badass little pony. I asked Connie about Glowerflorious, too. She thinks he's nice, nothing more, but she also thinks clearly he is interested in someone else." Lucy tried waggling her eyebrows, and was happy to see that Ember had started to blush.

"Oh."

"Yes, oh. And so do I."

"Who?"

Lucy laughed. "For a wise and witty dragon, you sure can be stupid sometimes."

"What do you mean?"

"I don't know," said Lucy, who was enjoying herself. "Let's try and solve this logically. Dragons like logic, right? First question: Every time you go flying, Ember, who drops whatever he is doing and goes to fly with you?"

"He does, but only because I'm the only one here he can fly with," said Ember.

"Yeah, right. That's why. But let's go on to the second question: Who does he let strike first when the two of you hunt?"

"Well, me, but that's just because he's bigger and would throw me off if he went first," said Ember, but she sounded a little more doubtful, and there was the hint of a smile at the corner of her mouth.

"OK, third question: Who does he make sure is watching when he does all his stupid flying stunts, like the other day when he flew backwards into the lake?"

"Well me, but—"

"And who gives you a hug and sits with you when you're thinking of your brothers even though you're not saying anything about it?"

"He does."

Lucy waited. She tilted her head a little and lifted her eyebrows, and even looked at Ember over the tops of her cute glasses. "And?"

"Do you really think he's noticed me? I mean, noticed me noticed me?"

"Esmeraldavinia, has he noticed you? Good gravy," laughed Lucy. "The only way he could be noticing you more is if you were tattooed on him!"

"He is dreamy, isn't he?" Ember whispered.

The two girls looked over. The object of the conversation had come up with another verse.

"Can you tell me where's the ark,
"The ark in the dark on Concordia Street.
"There are lots of aardvarks there
"Doing what aardvarks do,
"But what that is I have no clue!"

"Hooray!" Connie cheered.

"He is just the cutest," Lucy said, though part of what she liked about Glowerflorious was the way he got along with everyone in the party. Even the horses liked him.

They were bobbing their heads and waving their tails in time to the music. He wasn't afraid to sing along with Connie. He just seemed like a genuinely nice, friendly dragon. No wonder Ember liked him so much.

"I like the way he flies," said Ember, softly. "He really pushes against the wind."

"Did you see that splash when he hit the lake?" asked Lucy, who didn't know much about flying technique, but had been impressed by the size of the splash. "It was totally awesome."

"You ladies have gotten kind of suddenly quiet and whispery over here." Glowerflorious had stopped his singing and was now directly behind them. "What are you talking about?"

Ember and Lucy shared a glance, then exploded with laughter.

"Hey, I have sisters and I know what it means when they get together and talk like that," Glowerflorious said.

"I can promise you that your sisters have never had this particular conversation ever!" Lucy said, which made Ember giggle, in spite of herself.

Glowerflorious suddenly realized they were talking about him and began to edge away. Now boy dragons, as a rule, are pretty fearless, willing to face armies of the undead, or battalions of knights, but two girls obviously talking about him and then giggling would make any dragon look for the nearest exit posthaste.

Ember noticed, and the sympathetic part of her brain checked in, "Don't go," she said.

"No, go," countered Lucy. "Especially if you're going backwards or going to fly." She was attacked by another case of the giggles.

"Lucy, knock it off. Listen, Glowerflorious, we were just goofing around. It wasn't anything serious. We were talking about," Ember looked around for something plausible. "Uh, that bat."

"What bat?" asked Glowerflorious and Lucy.

"That bat," said Ember, with a tone of voice that implied her eyesight was better than anyone else's.

"I don't see a bat," said Lucy.

"That's a bat?" asked Glowerflorious.

"It's just a very small bat," said Ember.

Connie abandoned her song to skip over and join the gathering. "Hey, who invited the bat?" she asked

"What bat?" asked Lucy.

"That bat!" said the other three.

"That's not a bat," said Lucy. "It's a dot."

"It's moving."

"It's a moving dot?" suggested Lucy.

"You need new glasses," said Connie, and instantly a circle of glasses began to rotate around Lucy.

"Oh, I like that one," Lucy said, and grabbed another pair, this one with hot pink frames, purple flames, pink rhinestones, and a tiny mirror on the bridge. "You're getting really good at making glasses out of thin air, Connie!" As the glasses settled on her nose, Lucy was better able to focus. But still, she asked, "They're cute, right?"

The consensus was that they were cute. Lucy then focused on the matter at hand: the dot. "Oh, that bat! I thought it was a dot, but it is a bat. A bitty bat."

"The bat seems upset," noted Ember.

"It really does look like the little thing is trying to say something," said Glowerflorious, thoughtfully.

"Oh!" said Connie. "Is it a questing thing? It is!" She began to cavort around the road. "It is, it is a questing thing. I just know it!" She danced on the tips of her hooves with excitement.

"Try not to crush the questing thing, Connie," suggested Glowerflorious, but Connie had already closed the distance between herself and the bat, and probably wouldn't have heeded his advice, even if she had heard it.

"Are you a good bat or a bad bat? Tell us something quest-y," said Connie, gently nudging the bat with her horn. "Uh-oh, this bat seems to be broken."

"Poking it with your horn really isn't helping," said Ember.

"I know," said Lucy. "Let's get out the questing kit."

There on the road, she poured out the strange items she had considered as part of her kit, since discovering that the maids and butlers had sent them. The flashlight, water bottle, insoles, trail mix, and applesauce tins lay on the dirt and didn't look very helpful at all. The questers looked dutifully down at the rather forlorn pile, then looked over at the even more forlorn bat, and then returned to the pile.

Ember began. "Honestly, I've always wondered what this is." She delicately touched the shoe insoles with the tip of a claw, understandably wary, but the shoe insoles attacked no one and remained inert. Whatever special powers they had, they weren't intended for dragons.

"Those are shoe insoles," Lucy explained. "You put them on the inside of your shoe to stop your feet from getting tired."

"Are they magical?" asked Connie.

"I think they're just filled with jelly. They make the shoe feel gooshier inside," Lucy said. "But in a good way. I think maids in our castle wear them."

"Why," asked Ember, "would you want jelly in your shoes? Isn't the whole point of shoes to keep things away from your tender human skin?"

"Well, generally yes, but sometimes if you have been standing all day, because you are making beds and folding laundry, or maybe because you had to go out and spend the day waving at the parade and there was nowhere to sit, your feet start to kill you and the insoles make them more comfortable."

Connie looked at the insoles with obvious disapproval. "They aren't very pretty."

"They're not meant to be pretty, they're meant to make your feet feel good."

The unicorn and the three horses shared a glance, and somehow managed to communicate the thought that four feet were far superior to two. The dragons also exchanged a glance, clearly of the opinion that flying beat walking any day.

"I see," said Ember, clearly deciding that for the peace of the quest, it was better to let certain thoughts remain unsaid. "Good questing fact to know. Thank you, Lucy. So, the purpose of the insole is to comfort and restore."

"Yeah, I guess you could put it like that," said Lucy.

"Maybe if we wrapped the bitty bat in the shoe insole, that would restore and comfort the bitty bat," said Ember.

"It does look unhappy, poor thing," said Connie.

There was a pause while Lucy stared at the bat and the items on the ground, and when she looked up, she blinked in surprise. "Why are you all looking at me?"

"You're the one with an opposable thumb," said Ember.

"You've evolved it, you grab it," Glowerflorious added with one of his grins.

"That was the kind of thinking that got my arm shredded by you!" Lucy protested.

"See, now you've got the experience, too!" His grin was even bigger. "Perfect."

Lucy sighed, and unfolded one of the insoles into her palm, "Oh, for goodness' sake, come here, bitty bat," she said, and using the power of her opposable thumb for good, scooped the flopping bat out of the road and into the middle of the insole.

"What's happening?" asked Connie, after a bit.

"I don't think anything's happening," said Lucy, though she could hear the squeaks of the bat. It sounded irritated, or in pain. "The bat does seem a little more agitated, but that might be because it's been surrounded by giant monsters and forced into something that's supposed to be worn on the foot."

"Ah," said Ember. "This does not seem to be working. Release the bat."

Lucy carefully opened the cup of her hand, and the bat flopped out and into the dust of the road. Instantly, it began flopping and writhing again. Lucy frowned.

"Take it off the road," said Glowerflorious, suddenly. He didn't wait for Lucy or her thumb to do it, but bent his head down and picked the bat up with extreme delicacy in his claws, trying not to touch the road himself. "I don't want to tear its wings," he said, and Lucy had her hands out to catch the bat as he dropped it.

The bat lay still a moment, dusty, with its tiny chest rising and falling rapidly. Absently, Lucy picked up the water bottle and wet the insole, which sucked up the water like a sponge. She began to bathe the bat. "Hey," she said. "I think it's thirsty. It's drinking the water."

"The water isn't poisoned," said Connie, knowledgeably. "It will probably be good for the bitty bat."

"Maybe it's hungry, too," said Lucy. "Would it eat granola, do you think?"

After a moment, they decided that no one, especially not the bat, would be desperate enough to eat the granola.

"What else is there?" asked Ember. "We don't have salad."

Lucy glanced down, "Applesauce tin?"

"What's applesauce?" queried Connie.

"Apples that have been mashed up into a sauce," said Lucy. "It's sweet. Bats like fruit, don't they?"

"Or insects," said Glowerflorious.

"We don't have insects in our kit," pointed out Lucy. "Just applesauce and granola."

"I like sweets," said Connie. "And apples. Maybe I should test the sauce to see if I think the bat will like it."

Knowing that resistance was futile, Lucy put the bat down onto a mossy bit of ground in the shade, several steps away from the road. She opened the tin of applesauce. She held it out, and Connie's delicate, unicorn tongue slipped into the tin and she took a taste.

"Ooh, yummy!" said Connie. "It's not poisoned at all. I'll share with the bat. I think there's enough for two of us to —" she had already emptied the applesauce, and her voice, with her nose in the tin, echoed a little.

"Wait," said Ember. "I know what to do. Lucy, trap the bat under the tin."

Without hesitating, Lucy flipped the tin upside down and trapped the bat. The high-pitched sounds of an extremely annoyed bat became not muffled, but amplified.

"There, it worked!" Ember said, proudly.

"Did it?" said Glowerflorious, supportive, but dubious. "What worked, exactly?"

"The empty applesauce tin is acting as an amplification chamber, so now we can hear the bat," Ember said. She gave her bracelet a twist, and shrank down so that she could put her head quite close to the tin. "Hello!" she called. "Can you understand us?"

Listening intently, Ember said, louder, "I'm sorry I can barely hear you, could you please speak up?" To the others she said, "Fortunately, bat and dragon come from the same language group: Things that fly but aren't birds."

"Oh, I certainly hope we get some clues or hints on how to deal with the evil wizards." said Lucy.

"Can you tell me where's the wiz," sang Connie. "The wiz of bad biz on Concordia Street." Connie let her body begin the familiar dance.

"Connie, please, this may be crucial," said Lucy.

"Oh, sorry. Crucial questing thing. Right." Connie froze in place, one hoof lifted in a delicate arabesque. "Serious," she said, hurriedly assuming a solemn expression, made somewhat less effective because her hoof was still in the air, and her tail was still dancing, though with much less intensity.

Lucy could tell when her friend was trying her best. She turned back to Ember, who had her ear pressed to the tin. "What is the bat saying?"

Ember's eyes narrowed. "I'm working it out. It's not easy. I think it's eating the leftover applesauce, and talking with its mouth full makes translating difficult. It's saying… Go—"

"Go where?" asked Lucy, eagerly.

Ember carefully translated: "A…"

"Go A…?" said Connie. "This is like charades, only with sounds. Go….A-questing. That's it!"

"Way." Ember continued

"Way?" asked Connie. "Go A-questing Way? Where's Way?"

"I …"

"Go a-questing to way I…nvisibly. Go to questing way invisibly. Oh, oh, this is such a fun game!"

"Am …"

"Am. Am. Am. Invisibly Am. Are you sure it's not 'And.' I bet it's really 'and'. Go a-questing to way invisibly and…"

"Bu …"

"Button your overcoat!" said the triumphant unicorn. "Questing riddles are so much fun!"

"Sy…"

Connie paused. "Sea?"

"Sy." said Ember.

The other questors gave Connie a little more time to puzzle it out. The bat in the tin also paused.

"Go a-questing to way invisibly and button your overcoatsie?" Connie put on her thinking face.

Everyone hesitated, and it was Lucy who broke it to her gently. "Yes, it could be that, or it could be, 'Go away. I am busy.'"

Connie considered the two alternatives for a moment.

"Yeah! Lucy figured it out."

Lucy looked to Ember with a clear now-back-to-business attitude.

"Can you find out if it used to be a dragon?" Lucy asked. "If it is, we could use the flashlight-dot-thingy to play with it and make it change back."

"I don't think bats like to play with red dots," said Ember. "But I'll ask." She tilted her head down to the applesauce tin and began to carefully squeak and eek her way through what Lucy supposed was a complicated series of questions and answers in bat. It took a minute or two, but then Ember said, "It's a girl-bat, and she was starving. She says," Ember looked up at Lucy with a grim expression in her big eyes. "She says she doesn't remember flying, but she does remember living in a castle."

"A princess?" said Lucy.

"It seems likely," said Ember.

"Hooray!" said Connie. "We found a princess. Now we just have to change her back." She danced in a little circle, tail and mane swinging, and suddenly stopped, realizing: "I don't know how to do that."

"Neither do I," said Lucy. "But if she's anything like my sister Dana, no matter how hungry she is, she's not going to be happy about having all that sticky applesauce in her fur. I'd better wash her off."

Ember made a few squeaks at the upturned tin, presumably to warn the bat what was about to happen, and Lucy soaked the shoe insole over again and began to daub the applesauce-smeared bat gently to clean it.

"Oh, no!" Connie said. "You're rubbing the fur off!"

Lucy gasped in horror, but it was true. Where the soggy insole touched the bat, the fur came away, but not only that. The wings seemed to be shrinking and the tiny bat limbs were expanding. "No, it's not hurting the bat!" Lucy said. "It's changing! It's transforming!" Because the bat-shape was swiftly becoming a girl-shape, a young woman, hardly more than a girl. She looked bewildered and very tired, but was definitely a princess, complete with a sacrificial gown and a shroud.

"It must be the water and the applesauce combined," said Ember.

"Plus the gooshy insole," said Connie.

"My name's Lucy," said Lucy to the princess.

"I'm Alisandra," said the princess. "Um, where am I?"

"It's kind of a long story," Lucy said. "Maybe you'd like to sit down for a minute while we figure out how to tell it to you?"

"Is that a dragon?" asked Alisandra, looking at Ember, in surprise. She turned her head and found Glowerflorious watching her curiously from the other side. "Is that… another dragon?"

Lucy said, "Yes, they're my friends," but any further explanation would have to wait. The overwhelmed ex-bat-princess gave a little sigh, closed her eyes, and fainted. Lucy looked up. "I guess we'd better give her a moment," she said. "I think we should give her some water, but I don't want to use the bottled water, in case it's part of what's working, you know? Connie, could you see if there's a creek or a stream or something fresh-water-y over the hill?"

"You bet!" Connie sprinted over the green, grassy rise, clearly delighted to have a concrete objective and a way to be helpful.

"Why don't I go look in the other direction?" said Glowerflorious. "I thought I heard running water a little ways back, but I was a little distracted by trying to come up with a rhyme for the song."

He grinned.

"I'll stay with Lucy," said Ember. "And the other princess."

"Alisandra," said Lucy, watching the girl drool attractively into the mossy ground. She looked like the sort of princess Lucy always felt her parents wished she could be. But here she was, sacrificed for the good of the kingdom. Maybe there wasn't a right way to be a princess after all.

A thunder of hooves interrupted that train of thought. It was Connie, coming back over the hill at top speed, but she didn't look nearly as cheerful as she had been a minute ago. She looked more worried than Lucy had ever seen.

"Guys, you have to come see this!" said Connie. "I found something, and it's important."

Lucy and Ember exchanged a glance, but the little unicorn's tone made it obvious she was in earnest. "Is there water?" asked Ember, as she and Lucy followed Connie up the hill.

"Yes," said Connie. "There's a pretty little babbling brook, and it's very fresh and will be good, but you have to see..." She ran to the top of the hill, and pointed.

For a long moment, Lucy and Ember just stared. The softly rolling hill they had climbed dropped away steeply on this side, and on the far side of the road, the same road they had been following since the Valley of the Maids and Butlers, the green forest had been completely cleared away. They could hear the brook Connie had told them about, but that was on this side, still in the forest. On the other side…

The ground was flat, and though there was grass, it was cut short. There was a broad, level area, with pea-gravel and chalked stripes. It was bordered with a lot of barrels, which seemed to make up a sort of fence. Or maybe they were storing something; Lucy couldn't be sure. The gravel area itself was empty, not a car or a wagon or a carriage in sight, but Lucy knew a parking lot when she saw one. Shrubs and flowers were planted at intervals in the lot, as if to break up the space, and at the far end stood a building, big and dark, made of some heavy, dark wood, and smooth, concrete blocks. There were windows, but they were of a strange, dark glass that didn't let anyone see inside.

"Are those satellite dishes?" asked Ember. The dragon nodded to four enormous saucers set at the corners of the lot, each one turned to a different point of the compass. On the roof of the building, a fifth dish was spinning slowly, like a lopsided ballerina.

"I guess?" said Lucy. "But I don't know what—"

"Never mind the creepy building, guys," said Connie, impatiently. "Look at the road!"

Lucy and Ember looked down to the line of dusty road that divided the forest from the strange building and the gravel park. It was the same road they had been walking along almost since they began their quest. Straight, well-maintained, although it was unpaved. Except that all along it, every few steps, were little dots. Brown, black, grey, white, some of them striped.

"Bats," said Connie.

"Sacrificial maidens," breathed Lucy.

"And kittens," said Connie.

"Beach-cleaning dragons," said Ember.

"There must be a hundred of them," said Connie. "And they're unhappy. Bad kitties hurting like Glowerflorious was, and bitty-bats, flopping and miserable like the princess we just found."

"Look how the lines are drawn on the ground," said Ember. "Those little stripes leading from the road to the barrels? This is what Glowerflorious was talking about. Don't you see?"

"They're taking something from the kittens and the bats," said Lucy.

"From the dragons and the maidens," corrected Ember.

"Whatever it is, it's hurting them. The ones closest to the barrels aren't even moving anymore," said Connie. "This is bad. This is what bad wizards do. We have to help them."

"We're going to need more applesauce," said Lucy.

They heard a roar, and turned to see Glowerflorious coming their way from the opposite direction. He landed at the top of the hill, next to Ember, and said: "There's a car coming. A '67 Chevy Chevelle with the 350 small block v8, I think. Cool car, but it has knights inside."

"Hooray!" said Connie. "Knights to the rescue." She began to dance.

"Connie," said Lucy. "They are not necessarily friends. They are knights."

"Aren't knights the good guys?" asked the unicorn.

"Knights are people who go about the kingdom and make things right," said Lucy. "At least that's what they're supposed to do."

"Well, we are people going around and making things right," said Connie. "And we're nice to us, so…"

"But knights have these rules they have to follow," said Lucy. "They don't get to make things up, and they have a tendency to think that following the rules is the same as making things right."

"That's just silly," said Connie, as an expert.

"And one of their rules is to slay dragons," said Ember.

"Bad knights," said Connie, with feeling. "Ember and Glowerflorious are our friends." She considered the dust-cloud indicating the car was approaching, and began to lower her horn ominously. "Should I go down there and be cute at them until they give up?"

Ember and Lucy exchanged a glance. "I think this is the First Rule of Questing situation, Connie. We should all stay together," said the Princess.

"I think whatever happens, you'll be cute, Connie," said the dragon.

"That's true," said Connie, managing to be adorable without also being obnoxiously smug. "Cute is my thing."

"Let's not rush into any decision," suggested Lucy. "We don't know what rules they'll want to follow when they meet us. They might want to just talk."

"They have a wolf with them," said Glowerflorious. "I heard it howl."

"For their sakes," said Connie, ominously. "I hope it's a good wolf."

Chapter Twenty-Eight
Gathering Intelligence

"You know," began Agent X. "When you said you had a pack in mind for the wolf, and we all said, 'Good job,' I'm not quite sure any of us were expecting this." He made a vague gesture to the wolf sitting in the back seat next to Chip. The wolf was hanging his head out of the window on his side, and giving the occasional howl of delight.

George said, "Explorer Scout Alfie" —the wolf chose that moment to let out another howl —"will not only provide us with potentially valuable expertise when we have to deal with the lupine community, but he is also the only member of this team to have seen Princess Lucinda in her current 'situation'."

He had to take one hand from the wheel to make the air quotes. 'Situation' was the tacitly agreed-upon euphemism they were using. It encompassed all the many degrees between, 'kidnapped,' which was George's preferred term, and 'flown the coop', which was Chip's. It saved time and friction to use a bureaucratic word, and Agent X congratulated himself for having suggested it. There were times one had to use the spineless language of bureaucracy to just get along.

"He might provide valuable insights," George said, to the accompaniment of another howl of joy from Alfie. "Insights into the dynamics of forestry and tracking and so on. Plus, he's so happy. I couldn't say no."

The wolf pulled his head back into the car. "How long have cars been around?" he asked. "This is brilliant!" He gathered breath for another howl.

"Alfie, inside, non-singing voice please," said George, hastily.

"Ah, right. Any one got more of them Bunnie-Bits left?"

Wordlessly, Chip held out the tin. Now that he wasn't starving, Alfie's table manners had improved. He emptied the tin before he spoke, for one thing.

"Whatsit say on the can? Party-sized, my bushy tail," he scoffed. "The pack that dared serve those bitty bits of rabbit at a party would lose all face. Never mark a tree in that part of the woods again, let me tell you."

"Way to scarf, old bean," said Chip in full aristocratic host-mode.

"Sorry," said Alfie, surprising them all again. "Where's my manners? Did you want any?"

"No, not at all," said Chip. "Quite happy with my cooked meat, thank you. And cooked carbohydrates. And processed liquids. Carry on." Chip seemed to be taking a perverse delight in his new uncouth companion.

"Anyone else? Right, then." The wolf seemed pleased to be fulfilling human social conventions. The humans were, in turn, pleased to see the last of the Bunnie-Bits.

"Listen up," said Agent X. He had confiscated George's helmet and was acting as their navigator and general strategist. "The tracking device has us almost right at Princess Lucinda's location. When we left the Valley of the Maids…" he hesitated and his gaze became softer. For a moment, he paused, reminiscing about the high quality of the maid service, which had caused them to linger for several more hours, truth to tell, than was strictly called for by Knight protocol. "I got information from Suzette that should cut the lead they have by half. They're on foot, or wing, and we have the car. We should catch up to them in just a few hours."

"What then?" asked George.

"First we need Princess Lucinda's signature on the non-consumption-within-the-agreed-time-frame affidavit," said Agent X.

"Then we slay the dragon and rescue her!" said George.

"Then we slay the dragon and arrest her!" said Chip at the same time.

"Err, that is not entirely clear." Now that they were almost to the crux, Agent X had to confess some the holes in the plan they'd been following. "Apparently, we are supposed to bring the affidavit, along with the Princess, back home, without necessarily 'making a big deal' about it to the dragon community."

"What do you mean, old chap?" asked Chip. "Do we hack away at the scaly beast, or what?"

"The way I see it, the first step is to not slay the dragon; let's call that Plan A. It leaves human/dragon relations as they are intact, and doesn't invite wholesale retaliation of fiery doom upon the kingdom if it turns out Chip is right and the Princess has kidnapped the dragon rather than the other way around. If the Princess comes quietly, we'll go with Plan A."

"And if she was kidnapped?" asked George.

"Or if she attacks you with a loaded unicorn?" asked Alfie.

"Then," said Agent X, "we go to Plan B."

"What's Plan B?" asked George.

"Tried and true. Slay the dragon."

"Not really a whole lot of leeway between the two, is there? Sort of flying without a net, don'cher think?" Chip said. "Jolly good thing George brought that spear of his along!"

The car was quiet for a moment or two, and then they came 'round the bend in the road as it topped a small hill, and George applied the brakes.

"Well, there they are," said George.

"What ho. No one said anything about two dragons," Chip protested.

"They're smaller than seems usual for the breed," said Agent X.

"Still, two of them," Chip said. "That seems unfair. We only have the one spear."

The tension in the car ratcheted up a notch.

"Easy boyos, no need to sing and dance just yet," Alfie said softly. The hackles on his neck were rising, though. "Even if they have got themselves a unicorn up there."

"I think Alfie is quite right, gentlemen," said Agent X, swinging his door open. "Easy does it. Let's first start by getting her signature on the form."

The three Knights and the wolf eased out of the car and walked up the hill until they stood face to face with the Princess, the unicorn, two dragons, and three horses. The air between them was decidedly tense, if not actively confrontational, and the silence stretched out, as if each side were waiting to let the other speak. George looked over at Lucy, in the attractive glasses and sturdy, warm coat, and was conscious of a pang of something like disappointment. She didn't look like the Princess he'd been imagining all the way. She was looking back at him, shoulders back, confidently standing with one arm around one of the dragons, and her other hand resting on the unicorn's snowy flank, but when all was said and done, she didn't look like a real Princess at all. She just looked like a skinny girl with some unusual friends. And the glasses were pretty unique, too.

Agent X, never shy, was perfectly willing to step up and take charge. He had already pulled the necessary paperwork from his utility belt, and he held this out like a lance: "Princess Lucinda, by the authority—"

"If you're going to say my name, say it correctly," said Lucy, in a tone that would have quashed a minor rebellion, had one been handy. "Her Royal Highness Lucinda Merrie Periwinkle Grottweiler Rotunda Doorstop." George mentally scored her up another notch in his princess rankings.

"She prefers to be called Lucy," said Ember.

"What's this?" said Chip in astonishment. "You dragons can talk?"

"We can," rumbled Glowerflorious. "When we have something worth saying."

The knights were not quite sure, but it seemed that the dragons were somehow growing bigger. George was suddenly wishing his spear was not still packed up nicely in the trunk of the car. Instead his hand tightened into a fist. He and Chip did have their swords.

Agent X looked at his companions. "I think we can live with 'Lucy', right, boys?" he said. He started forward, but Connie intercepted him, and confronted with a serious unicorn, and the business end of her very sharp horn, he came to a very abrupt stop.

"I understand you're Knights," she said. "But are you good Knights? Or bad Knights?"

The three men exchanged glances, surprised by the question, or maybe by the unicorn herself. "My very dear Miss Unicorn," said Chip, giving a bow. "I promise, we mean to be good Knights."

"But I see you have a wolf with you," Connie said, and her horn pointed in that direction.

Alfie crouched down a little in response. He was obviously more than a little nervous, and looked ready to run.

"Are you a good wolf?" asked Connie, taking a step closer. "Or a bad wolf?"

"Ah, hell," cursed Alfie. And then, without warning, the wolf flipped over onto his back. He began to roll and to rock, like a puppy, kicking his legs into the air harmlessly, and giving cheerful little yips.

"I say," Chip said. "Are you quite all right?"

Indeed, everyone was staring in surprise as Alfie got to his feet and, in spite of being a grown wolf, began to chase his tail with all the single-minded intensity of a three-month-old pup. Connie began to laugh.

"Oh, what a good wolfie. He's being so cute!" Connie said, and her tone was definitely one of approval. She began to play a song on her horn, not just a twitter, but a melodic tune made just with her horn, and to that tune, Connie began to dance, to prance, and to frolic around the playful wolf.

"Connie, you're tootling!" said Ember.

Lucy smiled, and so did George. Alfie's play time and Connie's dance began to sync up, almost coincidentally, and the tension leached from the scene. The dragons grew smaller, and less smoke billowed angrily from their nostrils. Chip was full-on belly laughing at the sight of the wolf and the unicorn, and even Agent X found his toes tapping to Connie's tune.

So, Connie and Alfie began the first recorded instance of wolf/unicorn interaction that did not result in corpses, and when the dance was done, all the humans applauded, and both the unicorn and the wolf, side by side, took a bow.

"That was very cute," Connie whispered. Of course, she had recognized him from before.

Trying to hide how winded he was, Alfie gasped back, "Chuckers, no one ever told me being cute was this much hard work."

Connie giggled and was pleased someone else had finally recognized how much harder it was to do what she did than it seemed. "I'll give you some pointers, later. You're adorable and fluffy, but you're working much harder than you have to."

"Thanks." Alfie said, and he wagged his tail.

Connie gave the wolf a wink. "I always knew you were a good wolf," she said. Then she turned to face the Knights and her friends as one. "Now what are we all going to do about those bad wizards?"

"A bit of dancing, I suspect," said Alfie. "And maybe some singing, too."

Chapter Twenty-Nine
All We Have To Do Is Everything

THE FRIENDSHIP BETWEEN CONNIE AND ALFIE BUILT A bridge of trust between the two groups, but it soon became apparent to Lucy that having to negotiate who was going to do something and how they were going to do it meant it would take forever until anything got done at all. She tried to be patient, but it had never been her strong suit.

"Listen, Agent X," she said. "Can we at least agree that something has to be done to help all these bats and kitties?"

"I feel there's a certain regulatory laxness in letting stray animals roam this close to habitation," Agent X admitted. "Provided there's historical precedent and a firm understanding of procedure."

"That means he's willing to listen to reasonable suggestions," translated George. "But he doesn't want you to get crazy."

"But they're really enchanted dragons and princesses!" said Lucy.

"That's right up your alley, Agent X!" said Chip, cheerfully. "You've been disenchanting ladies ever since we left the base! You're practically an expert. I say," he added, oblivious to the look Agent X shot him, and turning instead to Ember. "This flashlight with the red wrapper on it is ingenious! Dashed clever of you to have come up with it."

"Thank you," said Ember.

"Chip can release the dragons from their kitty-prisons, while

Agent X is freeing the princesses," said Lucy.

"Good plan," said Glowerflorious. He and Ember had become pretty chummy with Chip, which Lucy didn't understand at all. The dragons were so smart and subtle, and Chip was so dim and blunt, but somehow they understood one another perfectly.

Agent X didn't seem to want to understand anyone. "I never agreed to do anything with bats," he said firmly.

"But they're really princesses and maidens!" Lucy said, for what felt like the four-millionth time.

"Do they have a certified identification card verifying that claim?" asked Agent X, skeptically.

"I hope they do," said Chip. "Because they've been em-battered, rather than devoured. You'll need them to sign one of those forms of yours, eh, old chap?"

Agent X brightened up at that. "I hope I brought enough copies," he said. "I do have an extra pen. All right, I'll make the supreme effort to get those signatures."

"They'll definitely need hands to sign," said Chip.

"Enough signatures," said Agent X, thoughtfully, "and we might have grounds for a class action suit. I'll have to contact the base when I've collected and counted them all."

Glowerflorious seemed amused. To Ember, he said, "I'm going back over the mountain to the Valley of the Maids and Butlers. I think they're going to be the only force capable of handling as many princesses and dragons as I estimate will be in need of good, solid care. Try not to do anything to dent those pretty scales of yours while I'm away."

"I'll try," said Ember. "Try not to get yourself enchanted."

"I'll try," said Glowerflorious.

"Alfie and I are going to break up the lines from the road," said Connie, with another experimental toot of her horn. "He's going to dig them up and I'm going to dance them to smithereens. Nobody is going to drain life force or magic or anything else into those big barrels ever again! Hooray!"

"And while you guys are doing that," said Lucy, "Ember and I are going into that building and deal with the wizards."

"You can't!" said George, who had been (in Lucy's opinion) pretty sulky and unhelpful during all of this.

She gave him a look, a long look with a great deal of irritation behind it, and said, "Why can't we?"

"Well, I'm sure the dragon is entirely capable and ferocious," George conceded. "But Lucinda… Lucy… You're just a girl."

She looked at George, looked at Ember, looked at George again, and then threw up her hands. "I'm not just a girl," she finally said. "I'm a princess. In fact, I'm a heroine. I used to think I couldn't do anything when things were difficult, but I've done a lot since that day on the beach. I made it all the way to parts unknown to try and help people who needed it, and I'm going to help. What I'm not going to do," she added, glaring at him through her new, very cute glasses. "is argue with you about it."

So saying, she turned on her heel and started marching across the gravel lot towards the big, hulking fortress. She only got a half-dozen strides away before Ember was at her side. She heard all sorts of noises behind her. Alfie and Connie were dancing and digging. Agent X was explaining the importance of getting notarized signatures to Glowerflorious, who was explaining the essential importance of applesauce before he left. Chip was openly admiring the ingenuity of the red-dot-light, and then yelping in pain when one of the kittens attacked him at the knees.

There was also the sound she'd been listening for, the scrabbling of George's boots in the gravel as he hurried after them.

"He looks worried," whispered Ember in her ear.

"I don't care," said Lucy, heartlessly.

"He's gotten something out of the back of that car. Oh, it's a spear. I hope he doesn't intend to go dragon hunting after all," said Ember.

"He wouldn't dare," said Lucy, more confidently than she felt.

"'Scuze me," said a gruff voice at her knee, and Lucy looked down in surprise to see that the wolf was there, and with an expression on his canine countenance that indicated he really wanted to speak to her.

"Alfie?" she said, not sure whether that was really his name or just what Connie was going to call him for eternity.

"Just had a thought, see?" he told her. "You might not be coming back, and I wanted to say sorry for before, that night in the forest. You're good people."

"Thanks, Alfie," said Lucy.

"Just that… the song your unicorn friend was playing…" He sat in the gravel and looked back at where Connie was dancing in circles around one of the barrels. "…reminded me we had a song, too. Not my pack," he added. "Before that. My mother used to sing it to us, when we were pups. It was about wizards, she said, and I thought it might be useful for you. I'm going to sing it."

"Are you?" asked Lucy.

"Yes, but there won't be no biting," promised the wolf. Slowly, and not overly loud, he began to sing his song, and the tune, Lucy realized, was similar to Connie's favorite song.

"Surmount your burden great and small
"With slender reed, plucked from a ball
"Forsake the fire of fearsome drake
"Your point was honed in frozen lake
"Handless, strike the blow precise
"With earthborn, stone, and finest spice."

"Pretty obscure," said Ember.

"Not really," said Lucy. "It was also part of the literature that came when I got picked to be the beach litter." She spared her friend a glance.

"I hope it helps," said the wolf. "My mother told me about this place. It's a bad place, right enough, but she said the song might help someday. Never thought I'd be the one singing it to the heroine, though." Without further comment, he got up and raced back to resume being cute.

By the time George caught up with them, Ember and Lucy had crossed over the gravel and were standing in front of the big, broad double door leading into the building. It looked solid and heavy, and Lucy supposed it was probably locked. She needed to take a moment before she considered how best to go in, and wouldn't have been entirely disappointed if George had decided to barge through the door without asking, but that didn't happen.

For a long while, they just stood there, awkwardly. "It's too bad there isn't a butler," said Ember. "To open the door for us."

"Or a Maid," said George, a little wistfully. Ember and Lucy looked at him. "To offer advice," he explained. "Well," he said, holding his spear boldly in one hand, "I'm going to try the door."

"Check for traps!" cried Lucy and Ember together, and then they laughed.

George gave them a wary look, but he did bend down and examine the door from several angles. "I don't see any traps," he said at last tugging at the door. "But it does seem to be locked."

"It looks a lot like the door to the main hall at the palace," said Lucy. "That one was pretty heavy, but I remember trying to pick the lock once with a royal hairpin when I was late coming home from school and wanted to try and sneak my way in, too. Almost made it, but I couldn't see what I was doing before they caught me at it."

"Not much help, is it?" said George, trying not to look aghast at the idea of a princess picking a lock.

"Actually," said Ember, "it gives me an idea." She reached over and twisted the bracelet on her arm, and shrank. Smaller than Lucy. Smaller than one of the kittens on the road. Smaller than that, even, until she was able to fly up on hummingbird-small wings and climb into the lock itself.

"I didn't know dragons could do that," said George, still trying for a semblance of aplomb.

"They can't, as a rule," said Lucy. "Ember is special."

"I suppose she must be," George said. Lucy looked at him. "Well, you made friends with her, and got her to take care of you."

"She made friends with me, too," Lucy said. "We take care of each other."

"Listen, I'm trying!" George said.

"Yes, you are!" Lucy replied.

"Hello?" said Ember, who had emerged from the lock and enlarged herself while the Princess and the Knight were glaring at each other. "The door's unlocked now," she said, and pushed the handle, so that it swung open on suitably creaky iron hinges. "Let's try to remember that the enemy is inside, all right?"

"All right," Lucy snapped.

"Fine," said George.

They stepped inside. The doors closed behind them with a weighty "clack", and immediately truncated all sound from outside. They knew that the knights and questers were still out there, still desperately trying to charm the kitties and dragons back to their true forms, but in the darkness behind the doors, all they could hear was each other, breathing.

"I wish it wasn't so dark," said Lucy.

"You'd better let me go first, Your Highness," said George.

Lucy found herself clenching her teeth. She forced a smile on top of it. "No, thanks," she said. "Come on, Ember." And she strode off into the darkness, confident that Ember, at least, could see perfectly well in the dark.

"Ah," said George. "Right. I'll just take the rear here. You know, to make sure that nothing is sneaking up on us."

Lucy and Ember continued on together. After a little while, Lucy realized that it wasn't really pitch dark inside the building, just very, very dim. As her eyes adjusted, she was able to pick out vague shapes and details within the space. It seemed as though they were walking down a long, central corridor, which probably explained why they didn't have access to any of the windows on the outside. Lucy remembered how the central hall was set up in the palace. Once you stepped into one of the rooms, the windows let in plenty of light, but the hall didn't have any windows. Without the lamps in the sconces on either side, it would be as dark as this place.

"All clear back here," called George.

Lucy lengthened her stride. Ember kept up with her easily enough, and neither of them answered the Knight. Lucy wasn't entirely certain why she was so angry at George, except that she was also angry at herself for having wanted, in that very first second when he'd stepped out of the car, to be able to lay all her problems on his broad shoulders. Except that she was good at eventually working out her solutions herself, and he didn't seem to understand what the right thing to do really was, and the trying to kill Ember thing on the first day didn't help.

"No evil lurking wizards back here," said George.

Lucy quickened her pace, but found herself beginning to smile. She shared a glance with Ember. "Am I being ridiculous?" she whispered.

Ember pretended to think it over, but her eyes were full of laughter. "Only in the most royal way possible."

Behind them, much further back than he was comfortable with, George was beginning to breathe heavily and wish he had done more Pilates in the car instead of eating the deep-fried-party-edition Bunnie-Bits Chip had passed to him. He let out a rather weak, "Looking good from back here. Let me just, uh…"

Lucy and Ember stopped and looked at each other, grinning widely.

"First rule of questing," Ember began.

"Is that we all stick together." Lucy nodded. "Hi-ho."

They turned and waited for George to catch up.

"Need a maid to help you?" asked Lucy sweetly. He had the grace to look embarrassed, and she felt better about George, and herself, too.

George wiped his finger on a hallway table. "Well, if not a maid, they could certainly use someone around here to clean this place. It looks like it hasn't been dusted for ages."

There was a thick layer of dust on the decorative furniture, and a general sense of mustiness that suggested that it had been a very long time since anyone had been down this corridor. The sense of disuse felt oppressive, and they all became conscious again of how very quiet it was.

"So, you two have obviously found your way through worse troubles than this," George said. "I'm wondering if you'd care to tell me… Uh, what next?" asked George of the two more experienced questers.

"We were kind of hoping it would be apparent," Lucy said.

The questers waited, listening, but if anyone was lurking, listening to them, they didn't take the hint.

"Like an arrow carved into the wall, or a beckoning specter

would be nice," Ember suggested in a general sort of way in a louder voice.

Nothing.

"Hey," said Lucy,

"What?" George snapped to attention, his spear striking wildly into the darkness, so that both Ember and Lucy ducked hurriedly.

"We have a chair just like this at the palace," said Lucy. Ember and George exchanged glances, and he lowered his spear. "It's in my brother Eddie's room," explained Lucy. "It was in the throne room 'til I used it as a fort playing Defend the Castle. It sorta got chipped. I sorta chipped it. The enemy had breached the walls. We had to destroy the walls to save the walls."

"I see," said George.

"Makes sense," said Ember.

"Actually," George said. "I'm getting a little thirsty. Do you think this place has anything like a bathroom in it?"

"At the palace, every twelfth room, or one in 24 on one side, is a bathroom," Lucy said

"Really?" said Ember.

"Great-, great-, many more times great-grandfather Gustaf was quite insistent on having enough bathrooms in the palace. It is said he designed the plumbing system himself, and it was copied all through the kingdom, back in those days, for all municipal buildings."

I always wondered about why the plunger is the Royal Coat of Arms, thought George. And they tried to pass it off as an old crown with a scepter from a distant land. HA.

Ember, meanwhile, had turned her head, and began counting out the doors they had already passed, and when she got to 24, George dutifully opened it. There was a bathroom, complete with a sink and two water glasses crowned with a crimped paper lid over the brims.

"Huh," said George, after a moment.

The presence of a bathroom, of course, gave everyone the opportunity to pause and refresh themselves. While Lucy was in there, Ember and George had a chance to catch up.

"You're the one who tossed that spear at me over by the lake," Ember said, without preamble. Dragons can be subtle, but they're also dragons and can dispense with small talk any time they like.

"Yeah," said George. "Naturally, I hadn't been introduced to you at the time."

"Is that the spear?" Ember asked, waving away what looked like a looming apology with a flick of her tail. "Can I see it?"

"Sure."

"Hey, it's pretty heavy," Ember said, approvingly.

"Well, you know, it's meant to take down a dragon. A big dragon," George explained. "No offense."

"Oh, none taken," said Ember. "That was a pretty good throw you made. Good arm."

"Yeah, well, it missed the mark and ended up in the lake."

"You won't hear me complaining," said Ember. "But that lake? It was freezing! I got frost on my wings just coasting low over it on the way in."

"Yeah, tell me about it. It was freezing. I had to go swimming to get my spear back, and almost got trapped by an iceberg."

"Wait, didn't you tie a rope of something on the end of the spear?" asked Ember.

"No."

Ember was silent for a moment. "I'm guessing you didn't get the 'swallowed by the lake' coverage…"

"My Dad used to say that rental insurance is all one big rip-off," George sighed.

"Until you need it," said Ember.

The Dragon, Lucinda and George

"Thank. You. I'll keep that in mind." The conversation seemed to have lost its momentum.

"Well, here's your spear back," said Ember. "It was a good throw. Really."

"Thanks," George said. "But you were flying even better. You were really hauling ass."

"I was, wasn't I?" she preened, just a little.

"I mean, I tossed the spear, but like I knew, 'No way, man.' Totally, no one was catching you that afternoon."

"Wait, did you hear that?" said Ember. "There's something in here with us. Protect Lucy. I heard it growling."

"Oh, uh," said George. "That was my stomach, actually. I'm a little hungry."

"I have a granola bar they gave to Lucy when they, uh, tied her to the post," offered Ember.

"Really?" said George. "Thanks. Usually Chip eats all the granola before I get any." There was the sound of a wrapper falling to the floor, and the crunching of granola. "Does Lucy always take this long in there?" asked George.

"Not usually. I think she is nervous about meeting the wizards."

"Understandable," said George.

"Do you mind if I ask you something?"

"Sure."

Ember hesitated, and then gave a smoky sigh. "What exactly is an asswipe?"

George choked the last of his granola bar. "What?"

"Well, at the lake, both you and Lucy called me an asswipe. She likes me too well to tell me anything that might hurt my feelings, but you barely know me. I think you will be honest. I probably already know," she added, as airily as a dragon could be. "I inferred a meaning from context, but I just want to make sure I am correct,."

"Err, what did you infer?"

"Well, as you no doubt already know, dragons have been charged to keep the shoreline clean, and I do know that Lucy was staked upon a private beach with restricted access. I assumed it was a beach reserved specifically for the Royal Family, and that an asswipe was an official charged with maintaining the pristine quality of the private parts of nobility," said Ember.

"Err," said George as he squirmed slightly.

"Naturally, they wouldn't want to get sand anywhere uncomfortable."

"Close enough! Yes. Absolutely. Dragons, more than just huge flying lizards, but smart too! Oh, look! Here's Lucy! Hi, Lucy! Ready to go, Lucy?"

"Yeah, thank you for waiting," said Lucy.

"I'll take point," said George, and set off at a clip into the darkness.

Lucy gave Ember a look, and Ember shrugged eloquently. They followed after the Knight, and overheard him singing softly to himself:

"The first rule of questing… Hm-hmm… Hi-ho, hi-ho, down the hall we go. Hmm… Questing."

Lucy and Ember just looked at each other and with a laugh started to sing along, but after a little while, the song died out. The darkness and the silence were too oppressive, so that they were too conscious of their footsteps, their own breathing. The musty air made it seem as if anything could be lurking in the empty spaces, could be listening to their footsteps, too. It was creepy.

Suddenly, Ember said, "Did you hear that?"

Lucy froze. George tried to freeze, too, but he shifted to put the wall at his back, and ended up tripping over his spear, which went crashing through an over-decorated side table. There was a vase on top of it that did not survive the encounter.

"Oops."

"Don't worry," Lucy said. "I break those all the time. Vases. Lamps. Suits of armor. They've probably got a bajillion of them around here."

"They are bad wizards," said George with half a smile, remembering how those words had sounded when a unicorn said them. "And they never dust. I guess we don't have to be too considerate of their decorator's feelings."

Off in the distance, a sound like a school bell, a single ring. Then, a muffled voice. The sounds of vaguely industrial activity grew louder, and a pair of doors on one side of the hall were flung open. Light poured into the hallway, so bright that the questers had to squint from the sudden glare. They were surrounded by people, all wearing headsets, and these began ushering Lucy, George, and Ember into the overly lit room, primping and fussing and attaching a bewildering array of things to their clothing.

"We found them, Frank," said one of them into a microphone he held in one hand.

"Uh, sorry about the vase," George began.

"You're late," said another of the people. "Where have you been? They can only vamp for so long." She sounded harried and exasperated. Her headset made a small, buzzing sound, and she spoke into the microphone again: "Yeah, I know we go on in 60 seconds."

She began to push George towards a door, over which glowed a bright, red light.

A glance was enough to tell George that Lucy was being pushed along in the same way. He couldn't see Ember through the crowd of assistants. Possibly, she was more difficult to push. Another bell rang. "Hurry. Hurry. Yeah, Frank, give us 15 seconds. All I need is 15 seconds. I will have them there, I swear! FIFTEEN SECONDS, Frank."

Behind the red-lit door, an enormous room was even more brightly illuminated. In the center of the room, where all the light was focused, was a table, behind which sat a man and a woman. The lanterns gave off enormous heat, and stood half again taller than George's head, but what did that matter, when the ceiling loomed so high above, it was lost in the shadows, beyond even the reach of the light. George could just about make out a set of wooden catwalks on the very edge of the lanterns' glow.

"Their coffee. Coffee! WHERE IS THEIR COFFEE?" Someone screamed.

Coffee cups were slapped into two hands and one claw. Two hands clenched their cups, in spite of the heat of the brew. The dragon's cup fell to the concrete floor and shattered.

"I NEED THESE PEOPLE ON THE SET RIGHT NOW, HARRY!" boomed an amplified voice from above.

"It's done!" said the lady still urging George forward. "Go, go, GO!"

Helping hands became pushing hands and George, Lucy, and Ember were shoved forward, stumbling over the lip of a raised platform, somehow, now, in the center of all that light. Someone was smiling at them.

"Good morning, viewers. Welcome back to Morning Time Daily Report. I'm your host, Artifice Draught."

Somewhere in the shadows at George's elbow, someone had a machine in front of her. She twisted a dial, and the room filled with the sound of applause and cheers. George looked around, but there was no audience. There were the men and women who were wearing headsets and carrying microphones who were clearly busy, and also, clearly not applauding. It made no sense.

The woman at the desk said, "And I'm Ambrosia Waters," and the room filled again with the hollow sound of no-one enthusiastically cheering and applauding.

"SIT DOWN IN THE CHAIRS," Harry hissed at them, pointing, rather confusingly, towards a sofa.

"Well, Ambrosia, I understand you have an extra special treat for all of us this morning," said Art.

Half led, half pushed, George sat, and Lucy sat beside him. Ember flapped her wings, but remained near the sofa, and the people who were trying to force her down gave up, and fled out of the light.

"Why, yes we do, Art. As you know, we here at the Morning Time Daily Report have been providing continuous coverage on the Princess Lucinda Survival Day Surprise, and today, we have here as a Morning Time Daily Report exclusive, Princess Lucinda herself with the Bold Knight who rescued her and the Dragon who caused all the trouble."

Accompanied by boxed sounds of wild delight and applause, a camera rolled towards them, larger than any other camera George had ever seen and topped with a little red light. It stood half a dozen paces away and stared at them. They could feel it. The big lens was just like an eye. George didn't dare move. After a moment of frozen terror, the red light went off.

Ambrosia said, "And I'd like to remind everyone that all guests on the Morning Time Daily Report in-studio guest line come here courtesy of Morning Time Coffee, Where Every Morning ..."

"... Deserves a Great Moment," said Art.

In a unified gesture, the two hosts raised coffee cups in their hands. Their cups were identical to the ones Lucy and George held. Ambrosia and Art looked over at their guests, who dutifully, if not enthusiastically, each took a sip of coffee.

Art grinned endearingly. "Princess Lucinda, you have led us all on quite a merry goose chase this week." He chuckled, and so did Ambrosia, and so did the boxed laugh track.

The red light came on. "Well, I guess you could say that, Art," said Lucy. She gave a rueful chuckle. Under the lights and in front of the camera, Lucy seemed far more polished than she had on the hillside. There, she had been terse and tense and suspicious, but here, on the sofa, she relaxed and took another sip of coffee.

"I must say, Princess Lucinda, I love the glasses you are wearing today. Dare I hope it's the latest thing in eyewear?" Ambrosia said, and her tone was half teasing and half admiring. George watched the assistant at his side press the switch and slide another dial to achieve an artful combination of applause and admiring "oooh"s. He had to admire the skill it took.

"…And I think everyone here today is going to go home with a pair. Am I right, Art?" asked Ambrosia.

"Right as rain," said Art.

The sound of the imaginary crowd increased, but they were only imaginary. George wondered, as he took another sip of coffee, how they were going to find that many pairs of imaginary glasses to give away.

The red light went on in front of Lucy, who smiled and waved, to the sound of renewed applause.

"Tell us, Princess Lucinda, where do you get all these wonderful ideas for all these brilliant eyeglass frames? We simply cannot get enough of them," gushed Ambrosia.

Lucy twisted in her seat, and took another sip of coffee.

She said, "Oh, I don't know, the ideas just come to me.

It's like they are dancing circles 'round my head, and I just pick the one I like." Lucy smiled and gave a charming, self-deprecating giggle.

"Well, you certainly have picked well thus far, Princess Lucinda. You have a real flair for what people want to see when they see," Ambrosia simpered a little, obviously proud of the wordplay.

Lucy took another sip of coffee, then leaned forward and began to talk earnestly, "Well, I just want people to feel good about their eyewear, as you know Ambrosia, 'Glasses make the Lasses' and pretty on the outside makes you feel pretty on the inside and so if I can make people feel pretty I know I am making them happy which makes me happy. But we have to be responsible too, Ambrosia. That is why the all eyeglasses are that are produced by the Lucky Foundation make frames from recycled plastics, and then uses sustainable production techniques and workers trained from underserved communities so that each pair of these glasses gives back to the planet." Reclining back into the comfortable sofa, Lucy smiled in response to the enthusiastic applause, and drank some more coffee.

Artifice Draught leaned forward, and his handsome brows and smooth voice both lowered. "But on to more serious topics, Princess Lucinda. You have made some members of the Royal Family a little bit uncomfortable in recent days …."

"Oh, Art," Lucy bantered, seemingly no longer conscious of the camera's glowing eye. "You know what they say, 'You can't pick the family you're born to, but you can make your own.'"

George sipped his coffee, as the technician pressed a couple of switches. Bantering laughter, sprinkled with light applause. Yes, he thought. Just the right response.

Then Lucy turned, put down her coffee cup, and reached for George's hand. George, who had been mechanically matching Lucy sip for sip, took another quick gulp, put down his own cup, and clasped her hand. He had a fleeting thought that he ought to be holding her one hand in both of his, but his other hand still held the spear, and his fingers were wrapped, white-knuckled, around it. He would have had to pry them free, and the red light was watching.

They faced Ambrosia, and the technical expert at the box pressed switches that made the imaginary crowd react with surprised delight.

"Oh, you two, what is going on?" Ambrosia began in a wheedling voice, that suggested something dirty but wholesome at the same time. Normally, that sort of thing would have made Lucy cringe and snort in derision with Ember. She had called it the "Look whom I am breeding with voice."

And Ember could take it no more.

"I don't know what is going on here, but that is not the Lucy I know. The Lucy I know never liked coffee!"

Twisting the bracelet on her wrist, Ember grew. Her tail whipped out and delicately ripped the coffee cups out of Lucy's and George's hands. They both stared at her, dazed.

"Arrrrgh," roared Ember, truly angry. "Where is Connie when we need her?"

"Why didn't someone give the Dragon some God damned coffee?" Art also roared, anything but endearingly. He rose from his chair and leveled his microphone at the technician. "And turn off that stupid sound effects spell!"

The sound of an audience's reaction, that rising "Ooh!" suggesting someone was getting into trouble, was suddenly cut off, without a fade.

"UH, ART," said the big amplified voice. "WE DIDN'T EXPECT THEM AT THE SOUTH ENTRANCE, AND WHEN WE FINALLY FOUND THEM, WE WERE SO RUSHED, WE COULDN'T COME UP WITH A CUP TO FIT A DRAGON'S

CLAW IN TIME TO GET ON THE AIR."

Art snarled, "I am surrounded by incompetents!" He lifted his microphone into the air, and out of it shot a bolt of violently bright light. The bolt soared upwards and struck something on the catwalks above. There was a scream, the sound of tripping circuit breakers, and a shower of falling sparks.

The red light went out.

"OUCH," said the big amplified voice. "THAT HURT. YOU REALLY SHOULDN'T HAVE DONE THAT, ART."

"Wait, the Morning Time Daily Report?" Lucy was shaking, one hand on her head the other supporting herself against the coffee-stained chair she'd been sitting in. She looked dizzy, but she was recovering quickly. Ember was proud of her. "You are wizards?"

"Number 1 in our time slot for the last 45 years," Art said, with pride.

"Sponsored by Morning Time Coffee," said Ember, putting it together. "Even my parents drink that stuff. You were brainwashing families all through the kingdom every morning."

"What a sucky moment," said George.

"Before that, we were the Morning Daily Press, the newspaper with the highest circulation in four kingdoms," said Ambrosia.

"One of whose major advertisers was Morning Time Coffee," said Art.

"Morning Time Coffee tastes like crap," said Mindy Maxim-Fnort, snarling into the studio with a grand entrance worthy of Suzette.

"Mindy!" Art gasped in horror. "This is the studio. You know you are not allowed in the studio."

"Especially not without makeup," said Ambrosia.

"Neither was I allowed in the press room," said Mindy, who had a century's worth of scores to settle. "Do you realize that I have been in the field for more than a hundred years, Art? Almost two hundred years of playground openings, bake sales, lost puppies, and returned wallets, while you two sat here in the studio, chuckling and simpering and delegating, and twisting it all to fit your sick schemes."

"Mindy, darling, we have guests," said Ambrosia, in her best "not in front of the children" voice.

"Who cares?" asked Mindy, who didn't. "If they are here and the coffee's spell is broken, they'll have figured it out anyway."

"I don't think they have," Ambrosia started.

Mindy raised a microphone up and pointed it at her. "Shut up, Ambrosia. Shut up! Some of us have had to think to get where we are. Of course, they figured out that maidens and dragons are a source of potential magical energy. Of course, they know that by converting them to kittens and bats you can channel their anguish into a source of power. From there, it obviously follows that you would need an uninterrupted flow of dragons and maidens to feed the addiction."

"The clever part," said Ember, "was where you got us to offer ourselves up every year, to make it a tradition, so that even our families pushed back every time we tried to explain how we didn't want to disappear forever."

"You're clever," said Mindy.

But enraged at being challenged, Art had leveled his microphone at Mindy. "You're so self-righteous, Mindy. Do you also think that they figured out that the big voice up there is the voice of the big wizard who keeps the whole thing going? Do you think they figured that out, Ms. Smarty Pants?"

"No," said George, quietly. "We actually hadn't quite gotten that part yet."

"You know," said Lucy. "I remember a certain poem I heard."

"A poem?" said Ambrosia.

"Yes, a poem. It was rumored to be a riddle that makes this whole thing go away forever," said Lucy.

"OH, CRAP" said the big amplified voice.

Lucy cleared her throat, and in her best public speaking voice, as if the red light were on and recording said:

"Surmount your burden great and small

"With slender reed, plucked from a ball

"Forsake the fire of fearsome drake

"Your point was honed in frozen lake

"Handless, strike the blow precise

"With earthborn, stone, and finest spice."

"Hey," said George. "What do you know? I have this pointy spear here, and I'd say it was honed pretty well for battle when I threw it into a frozen lake not long ago."

"Hey," added Lucy. "Ember doesn't have to breathe fire, she can forsake it!"

"And I have claws, not hands, so it looks like I get to deliver yon spear," said Ember, holding out her claw.

"WAIT," said the big booming voice. "JUST WAIT A SECOND. I CAN MAKE YOU FAMOUS, YOU KNOW. I CAN MAKE MILLIONS OF PEOPLE LISTEN TO YOUR VOICES. ARTIFICE AND AMBROSIA? WE CAN GET RID OF THEM. YOU COULD BE THEM. EVERYONE COULD WAKE UP TO YOUR VOICES, YOUR IDEAS. YOU COULD MAKE THE WORLD SO MUCH BETTER!" The voice spoke with the desperate tone of someone looking for a last-minute reprieve.

"No thanks," said Ember, flapping her wings. "We've had more than enough attention already."

"ALL VERY CLEVER, YES," said the voice, reclaiming its tone of snooty archness. "BUT YOU SEEM TO HAVE FORGOT THE KEY PHRASE OF THE PROPHECY! BWA HA HA!!!"

"You mean the one about earth and stone born with finest spice?" asked George as he wiped the uneaten half of his granola bar across the tip of the spear. "UH, YEAH, THAT WAS THE ONE-" said the voice. "FINE. BUT YOU'RE STILL JUST A PIPSQUEAK OF A DRAGON. YOU WILL NEVER BE ABLE TO FLY UP HERE CARRYING THAT HEAVY SPEAR! BWA HA HA!!!"

George looked at Ember. Ember looked at Lucy. Lucy looked at George.

"Surmount your burden great and small, with slender reed plucked from a ball," said Lucy.

"Reed as in thread," said Ember, reaching for her bracelet. "Plucked from a girdle."

"You are so screwed, asswipe," George said, with a grin.

"OH CRAP."

A twist, and mini-Ember became full-sized Ember. A second twist, and normal-Ember became Ember-the-Giant. Lucy scrambled backwards, because at this size, Ember was filling the entire room, crushing the desk where Ambrosia and Artifice had sat for so long, sweeping the lights aside with her wings and tail, and shattering them. The cameras toppled and fell. The red lights faded into darkness.

"That make you feel better?" asked Lucy, sweetly.

"A little," said Ember, bending down. "I'll take the spear now."

"I think I'm gonna miss this desk, you know," said Art.

"Yeah, and I'm gonna miss weather and traffic at eight and sixteen minutes after the hour."

Art took a sip of coffee. He looked at the cup. "What do you really think of this coffee, Ambrosia?"

Ambrosia took a sip. Grimaced. "It's OK."

Art looked at his cup, and gave his charming smile, wrinkling his eyes "Yeah, it's good enough, I guess." For some reason, their banter did not have their usual zing.

Ember began to flap her wings, rising up towards the source of that booming, lonely voice in the darkness above. The wind was torrential.

After a bit, George asked: "Mindy, you really want an anchor job?"

"Well, yes."

"I have a feeling there's going to be a new morning show in the capital, GMC."

"GMC?" Mindy echoed.

"Good Morning Carolia. They will be needing a new host. Someone with a wealth of experience but a fresh, new perspective. Interested?"

"Sure," said Mindy.

Lucy had been looking up, trying to make sure with the force of her will that Ember was all right. The sparks and flames up above told her nothing, and she was feeling sick and exhausted from the tainted coffee. "Mindy," she said. "Did you know about this? The princesses and the dragons and the draining?"

Mindy Maxim-Fnort did not look as young as Art and Ambrosia, but she was still much, much older than she seemed. The difference was, she had learned something in her years.

"I knew," she said. "I didn't participate, but I didn't say anything, either. You have no reason to trust me, but I swear to you, Princess, I will never let anything like that happen again. When I was an unpaid intern, in the mail room at the Morning Time Press, my mentor said to me that a wizard's job was to pursue truth and knowledge. I want to bring that back to Carolia."

Lucy stared at her for a long time, and decided she might just be telling the truth. "If you mean it," she said, "I want to talk with you about it."

Mindy met Lucy's eyes, and nodded. "After," she said. "There's going to be a lot for you to do next. But we'll talk. After."

Lucy looked up, where a particularly violent and fiery explosion hinted that Ember was either doing very well, or very poorly for herself. She held out her hand, and George took it, as a friend.

"She'll be fine," he said.

After a few more moments, there was heard the cry of a fighting dragon. Their hands tightened. Above them, the catwalk burst into flames and began to fall.

At the remains of their desk, coffee cups clutched in their hands, Ambrosia and Art set their microphones carefully aside. They looked at each other and began to recite: "8"

"16"

"24"

"32"

"48"

"52"

And then everything went black.

Chapter Thirty
After The Fall

Sometime later, Lucy emerged from the smoking ruins of the wizards' former stronghold to find that the tide of angry kittens had gone out, and the battleground in that wooded space, before the forbidding but empty-eyed fortress of the wizards, was a horrifying mess of tangled yarn and scorched earth, dragons and princesses.

So many princesses.

They stood alone, and in groups, tall and short, thin and plump, and Lucy, looking around, saw herself in all their frightened, confused expressions. These were girls like herself. Some of them were older and some were younger, but they had been chosen, she knew, in her aching heart, that it had never been a real lottery of chance. They had been chosen by their families as expendable.

She found herself walking, in her comfortable, unicorn-made shoes, out into the wasteland. It was a wasteland because when dragons were confused, they often breathed fire or spewed jelly or spit acid, and the smoke and smell and residual burning only added to the confusion and dreamlike horror of the scenery. She knew what she looked like: not quite clean enough, and too skinny, with mousy hair and very pretty glasses. She'd fallen down on the way out of the collapsed fortress, and both the knees of her pants had been torn open. Both knees, her own knees, had been skinned, in the same place they always ended up skinned. She didn't look

particularly capable or wise or grown-up or regal or anything else.
She just looked like them.

Normal.

A little nervous, a little clumsy, with a watery smile. "Hi," said Lucy, reaching out to touch first one, and then another princess by the tattered sleeve — some of those gowns were old! These ladies had been enchanted for a long, long time. "Hi, I'm Lucy. Are you okay? Do you want to come over here? We've got a unicorn. She's really very good at conjuring up ice cream cones, which doesn't sound like much, but comfort food is where you find it, right? We have bandages. Do you need a bandage? Come on. Let's move away from the mess. It's all right."

Most of what she said didn't have much meaning. Most of it was, frankly, no better than the sort of small talk one made at parties with a bunch of strangers one hoped would be friendly, but had to be nice to no matter what. It was the tone that mattered, and the fact, Lucy realized, that all these women and girls had been educated in exactly the same way she had, by parents who had hoped they would someday "come around" to a more comfortable way of thinking. But these were girls who, like herself, were uncomfortable by nature.

"Are you hungry? We are going to start a campfire and make some dinner, there's fish in the stream, but there's granola if you can't wait. And ice cream. Our unicorn is working on macaroni, does that sound all right?"

And Lucy realized, as she walked around — it had been a hundred years, and there was literally a century's worth of princesses around, even accounting for the horrifying thought that some of the ones who had been enchanted were simply gone, and no one would ever know if they had been destroyed by the discomforts of the journey, eaten by dragons who were too obedient for everyone's good, or if they had just faded away, a battery that had been unable to withstand the drain. Lucy understood that what had made these princesses thorns instead of roses in their parents' palaces was the same thing that would make them amazing parts of the new world that she, Lucy, had only just decided she wanted to build.

It was going to be a world where dragons and princesses worked together to make everyone's lives better, by talking to each other and asking useful questions, instead of waiting for strange and anonymous form letters to arrive out of the blue.

"Hi, I'm Lucy," she said to Alisandra, and Jennifer and Norina and Etaine. "Come join us over here. You've been gone a long time," she said. "And we have a lot of catching up to do."

Charrtonio woke up with a tremendous headache. His muscles ached, and he had a sneaking suspicion that if he had been sleeping as long as it felt like, he'd probably been drooling. He was woozy, and the bright sunlight through the trees hurt his eyes. Tentatively, he tried to flap a wing.

Holy tendervitals, that hurt. And what was that little sound he made? Small, weak, and pathetic. He wasn't entirely sure what sort of sound he should be making, but kittenish mewling did not sound at all right.

"I say, dragon," said a voice. It belonged to a human sort of person, wearing shining armor.

What the? What were knights doing around here? Wait, the dragon hesitated in the middle of his indignation, trying to remember whether knights were good or bad. The dragon remembered that knights were an integral part of what he was supposed to do, but for the life of him he couldn't remember what.

Maybe this will make more sense after a nap, the dragon thought. I am just going to lie back down here under this tree.

"Dreadfully sorry," said the human, giving him a friendly tap on the ankle, which reminded him of a flea. Except that dragons didn't have fleas, did they? Where did that idea come from?

"I imagine you feel awful about now," said the human. "But we're supposed to keep you awake. Oh, what's that, Alfie?" he turned his head, and the dragon saw that there was some sort of canine-type creature at the knight's side. "The script? Of course, well done!" The knight held up something, not the sword the dragon was expecting, but a sheet of paper, and he smiled. "They wrote it all down for me. Explains everything much better than when I go off on my own. Never much of a free former, don'cher know." The dragon closed his eyes. "Now, where do I start? Ah, here it is. Oh, and a bullhorn, too. Well done, Alfie." There was the click-buzz of a mechanical device, an excruciating feedback whine, and the knight's voice was suddenly much louder.

"Welcome, dragon," said the knight, managing to sound friendly even at top volume. "It is springtime, in the dragon year 1784. You are a dragon. You were a small cat. You have been enchanted. You may feel some disorientation, but you are now safe. The wizards who enchanted you are not able to enchant you anymore. Would you like some rabbit?"

"Ugh, no," said the dragon. The thought of food rolled his stomach and made the dragon shudder.

"Still a bit queasy, are we?" asked the knight, sympathetically. "No worries, the bunnies will keep. 'Welcome. It's dragon year 1784. You have been enchanted. You are now safe.'... Sounds familiar, oh yes, safe."

The knight's speech became a murmur. The dragon risked opening one eye. The light was slightly more bearable this time, and he could see the knight was looking over his piece of paper for more instructions.

"Wizards gone. Were a kitty, back to dragon, well done, not hungry." He glanced up, saw the dragon watching him, and smiled. "My name's Chip, by the way. Ah yes, here we go." He lifted his bullhorn and read from the page, "You were enchanted to eat a maiden. Maidens, and humans in general, are neither food nor litter, so please do not eat or otherwise dispose of humans. Important fact, that," Chip added, as if to himself. He pressed the button on the bullhorn again.

"Soon, another dragon will be by to explain things in more detail. You might experience feelings of kitten-ness. This is completely normal and will go away in time. In the meantime, to get your paperwork started, can I have your name, please?"

Although his voice was oddly soothing, Chip really wasn't making sense to the dragon. He let loose with a low rumble.

"Head hurts?" asked Chip. "Your name is Head Hurts? Oh, I get it. Connie," he called, and a unicorn pranced cheerfully into view, looking expectant. "My dragon friend here might need some water. Would you please send someone to bring a barrel or two over here when you get a chance. There's a good unicorn."

The unicorn gave a little fancy-dance step with her twinkling hooves and a clear single note floated over the plain.

He was thirsty. At the mention of the word "water", the dragon's head snapped up, and his eyes popped open. He smelled fresh water in the barrels a powerfully built knight was rolling around the clearing, and lunged forward, snatched one up in his claws, and drank. "Ah!" he sighed. Part of the woolly feeling in his head was going away.

"Not bad! You didn't squish any of us, quite good actually," the human with the bullhorn, Chip, said. "A drink helped, did it? Good. We're almost done here. Those psyche chaps, dreadfully smart fellows, seem to think that keeping the hands – or claws, as the case may be – busy is a wonderfully clever way of reconnecting those burnt out synapses, don'cher know? You know what they say: 'Idle Claws are the Wizard's Workshop,' Ha Ha."

Chip lowered the bullhorn, and said to the wolf at his side: "No need to roll your eyes so dramatically. I know you might not think it's funny, but this fellow's spent who knows how long as a kitten. It's a new joke to him." He picked up the bullhorn again.

"To help out with that, we'll be leaving you this huge ball of yarn. Here, now, not that way!" Chip protested, as the dragon immediately pounced on the ball, rolled over onto his back, and began tossing it between his claws. "That's just the sort of thing I thought would happen. Too many years as a kitten, is what it is. My good dragon, listen. What you do is, you pick up a few of those tree trunks we have set aside here. They should fit like sticks in your claws, and we have this fascinating brochure, 'Knit Your Way Back to Dragonhood.' Oh, and one last thing. We will leave another barrel of water, and a pile of Bunnie-Bits, Super-Family-Sized, for when you get hungry."

There was a click as the bullhorn was turned off; however Charrtonio's acute hearing could still quite easily pick up Chip's voice as he spoke again to the wolf. "Actually, I don't care what the company calls 'em, these Bunnie-Bits aren't bits at all, just bunnies.. Ah, all's fair in love and advertising, I suppose. Whoop! There's another dragon-y fellow waking up. No rest for the wicked, eh, old chum? Onwards, MacWolf!"

What an odd, yet basically nice person a knight is, the dragon thought.

The water had helped, and the dragon sat there, a ball of yarn in one claw, and a pair of pared saplings just waiting to be used.

Dragons are by nature a solitary species and puzzling things out on their own was par for the course. But this was more puzzling than a Hovels and Humans boss level. He remembered being on a beach, performing clean-up duty, but the beach was nowhere near. Instead, he was on a rolling hillside, surrounded by other dragons. Hundreds of them, some asleep, and some awake. A few of the dragons, like himself, were holding yarn and knitting. There were dozens of knights all around, but no one seemed to be fighting. In fact, the knights seemed to be helping.

The dragon felt the oddest urge to lick his claw and then wash his face with it. Instead, he popped a Super-Family-Sized Bunnie-Bit in his mouth. And then another. It tasted like rabbit. Who'd have thought?

He picked up the brochure and began to read. The boot cuffs looked like they could be fun. He was still reading when he picked up another Bunnie-Bit. Without thinking about it, he let out a little jet of flame, and roasted it, then popped the toasty snack into his mouth: much better! He picked up a tree and looped some yarn around it, and started to knit.

It wasn't Chip who figured it out, or so he told everyone. But he was there, and he helped.

It was three days after the wizards had been defeated. The spells that could be broken, had been broken. The princesses were princesses again. The dragons were dragons. The wizards who survived the destruction of their production center had chosen either to swear loyalty to their new leader, Mindy, or had given up their microphone-wands and any hope of casting magic spells again. A semblance of order had been established.

Glowerflorious arrived back soon after the questers emerged from the wrecked studio, carrying carts well loaded with supplies and a bevy of maids and butlers. No sooner did the dragon set them down, than they began unpacking and distributing the supplies with the same ruthless efficiency and skill they had shown to their guests in the Valley. The Maids and Butlers, with terrifying efficiency, had everyone fed and bathed, and bandaged and primped and polished to boot. Lucy had been organizing things, and that had left Chip sort of aimlessly wandering about.

On the morning of the third day, Chip sat down on an enormous tree stump, which served as a bench for a very quiet princess whose dress was very old. Chip had seen a number of maidens like her wafting about the place, waiting to be told where to go or what to do. It was as if even though they were human again, they were missing some essential part of themselves. Chip had wondered whether it was because they had been among the first ones transformed. Maybe being a bat for all those years made it difficult to adjust to being human again. Maybe the light was too bright. All Chip knew for sure was that it wasn't right, and he wanted to help.

Alfie, who had adopted Chip as a source of Bunnie-Bits and ear-scratches, flopped down on the ground in front of him. The Princess shifted over, ever so slightly, though whether she was trying to edge away from Chip or Alfie, there was no clue. She was still staring straight ahead, her eyes focused on nothing in particular. Chip, as usual, was oblivious.

"Ah," said Chip quietly. "Plenty of fresh air now that the magic's gone out of it, eh? Here Alfie, fetch." Chip produced a bright red squeaky ball, squeezed it and gently tossed it a few feet. Clearly puzzled, but willing, the wolf good naturedly retrieved the ball and put it into Chip's well-manicured hand.

The Princess flinched, ever so minutely, as Alfie approached. She continued to stare straight ahead.

"Good boy." Chip said, and scratched behind Alfie's ear and then tossed the ball, again just a few feet. Alfie sighed, but in answer to a look from Chip, went to bring the ball back again. After a couple more rounds, he began to rather enjoy himself. It was almost like hunting, this "fetch" game, but without the screams. Chip and the wolf played gentle fetch for several minutes, until the Princess came out of her reverie. She began to look over and watch the game.

Chip said, "This is Alfie." The Princess jumped, startled at having been addressed, but nodded.

"He likes to play," he said, and she nodded again. Chip was glad to see she had a grasp of the obvious.

"Would you like to toss the ball for him?"

The maiden shook her head fiercely, no.

"Quite all right," said Chip and tossed the ball a little further away. "Ah," said Chip as Alfie obediently trotted after the ball. "Where are my manners? Mater would have rapped my knuckles for being so rude."

He got to his feet, a young knight from a good family, and formally presented himself to the wilted maiden in a fashion not seen in the society for almost a century.

"My lady, my name is Henrique Fusmantioff Bottomslebarron Clydness Blitherington, 5th Baronet of Streypia and 7th Earl of Pennstopinia." The sound of his heels clicking was almost as audible as the sound of Alfie's jaws opening. The wolf had returned, unnoticed, and in surprise, opened his mouth wide enough to drop the ball.

Unconsciously, the girl straightened her spine as she held out her hand. "How do you do, Your Grace?" she said with poise. "I am Princess Pamtolia Tannfessberry Clydness Newbuton Ephansia

Greenstone."

Chip took her hand and bowed over it with a flourish, and she drew a breath, as if coming to life.

"A pleasure to meet you, Princess Pamtolia Tannfessberry Clydness Newbuton Ephansia Greenstone." The names rolled out of his mouth effortlessly. "They call me "Chip", he added with a smile as he clicked his heels again, releasing her hand.

"Patti," she said with a giggle.

"May I join you on the bench, Princess?"

"Oh course, but please, call me Patti."

"Very well, but I insist you call me Henrique Fusmantioff Bottomslebarron Clydness Blitherington," he said, loftily. She giggled even longer. "No need for the titles, though."

That got a genuine laugh.

"Clydness, eh? Must mean that we are some sort of cousins, I suppose," Chip sighed. "Feel like I'm related to nearly everyone I meet, don'cher know?

Patti giggled.

"Yes, rather."

Chip offered her the ball. She took it and tossed it.

"Good arm," Chip said.

"Thank you."

Alfie came running up and waited till she put out her hand, then deposited the ball gently in it. He then sat and looked at her expectantly. This got another laugh from the Princess.

"He likes a challenge," said Chip, blandly.

"Oh, he does, does he?" said Patti. She hopped to her feet and let loose with a tremendous throw.

"CHASE THAT, ALFIE!" she roared

The wolf took off, with only the slightest hint of "Oh-thank-you-very-much'" directed towards Chip.

"Good boy," he said mildly when Alfie returned and gave the ball back to Patti.

"CHASE THAT, ALFIE!" she shouted again. "CHASE THAT ONE, TOO! BETCHA CAN'T GET THAT ONE! Oops! I beg your pardon. Would you be so kind as to retrieve the ball, Alfie?" she giggled "Thanks ever so much."

When Alfie came back, he gave Patti the ball, and rather dramatically flopped to the ground.

"Oh no, Alfie is tired," said Patti. "He needs some water. I will be right back." She dashed off.

"So, I likes a challenge, do I?" asked Alfie with just a trace of belligerence.

"It could be said that it looks that way from the outside, old chap, don'cher know?" Chip seemed to find his fingernail fascinating at the moment.

"How come I don't sees you chasing after any ball?"

"Sometimes it's good to be the Earl," Chip replied, evenly.

"And this Earl business," Alfie gave Chip a suspicious look. "How long has that been going on?"

"Oh, ever since Mater and the Earl-present did produce the heir nasty bit, yours truly. Though I suppose, technically Mater would be the only one to actually be sure. Still, I believe the punters gave it at about 80% that Pater was Pater. Oh good lord, look at that." Alfie and Chip turned and watched Patti hurrying over to the two of them, holding a large bowl in front of her.

"I remember Grand-mater saying that in her youth, that's how they were trained to walk," said Chip, with a tinge of compassion under the usual mildness of his voice. "'So still you never spill.' Poor dears had it drilled into them since they managed to get up on their hind legs, look at that. Everything drilled in, just like the introductions, eh?"

"There you go, Alfie. Nice water so you can play some more," Patti said, triumphantly.

"Say Patti, while Alfie drinks, care to join me on the stump here?" Chip asked.

Alfie drank from the bowl, and Patti settled herself decorously on the opposite side of the stump from Chip. They sat quietly for a while, looking out over the yard, and Chip and Alfie both noticed how the Princess began to droop again. Her gaze became abstracted, and she lost the lively, energetic air she'd had a moment ago, and seemed to drift, seemed to fade.

Chip motioned over to where they could both see Lucy, organizing something. "She's bossy," he said, softly.

Patti should have been shocked, but she was lost in her fog again, and only said: "Mhm...."

Chip was still watching Lucy. In his gentle way, he continued, "That's fine, though. She's still angry. Being bossy gives her something she can feel in control about, even if it's just where to place the latrines."

Finished drinking, Alfie got up and stretched, then flopped back down on the ground, this time on Chip's feet.

"He's not too close?" Chip asked Patti.

She shook her head, and managed a semi-smile. The wolf put his head down between his paws and began to doze.

"Oh, I say, Princess, I have a bit of a problem. I was wondering if you could help me with it?"

With the use of her title, Patti sat up a little straighter, and tried to focus her eyes. "If I could," she said, clearly doubtful.

"Of course, Your Highness. Only if you want to, and only if you feel able. Goes without saying, that."

Patti nodded.

"There's this fellow, see," said Chip. "He's had a bad time of it.

Not doing at all well with this magic stuff. Doesn't seem to want to talk to anyone. Doesn't want to play. Doesn't even seem to know where he is half the time. Ever since he changed back. Just seems sort of lonely, don'cher know? Does nothing but knit."

Patti just nodded, but Alfie's ear was twitching and he was clearly no longer dozing.

"He's really not doing well at all," said Chip. "But here I am, just seeing how well playing ball with Alfie helped you. I was wondering if we invited the chappie over to come join us, it might not help him, too."

Patti sat in silence for the longest time. Chip exchanged a worried glance with Alfie and was about to retract his suggestion, when all at once, Patti gave a sigh.

"OK."

"Excellent." Chip got to his feet, and smiled. "If you feel ready, I think there's no time like the present. Alfie, go and see if Sparktonius can put down his knitting for a moment. If he's up for it, escort him over, will you?"

Alfie got up and stared at Chip, trying to convey in a number of subtle ways that this was in no way on Lucy's list of approved princess activities.

"Please, Alfie, I have a good feeling about this. I think he's over there." Chip pointed to his left.

After a beat, Alfie sighed and dashed in the opposite direction.

"Other left," Chip sighed.

Patti giggled.

Soon, Alfie could be seen returning. With him was a dragon. It wasn't ravening or breathing fire. In fact, it looked hesitant. With the dragon also came Lucy. She was looking... less hesitant. In fact, she looked furious. About to say something to Chip, she was cut off by Chip's most oblivious tone.

"Ah, there's the fellow. Sparktonius."

Chip stood and extended a hand to Patti, and as he did, she rose to take it. It was natural enough, for Chip had resumed his Earl-ish manners.

"Princess Pamtolia Tannfessberry Clydness Newbuton Ephansia Greenstone, may I present the most noble and flameworthy Sparktonius?"

As if she had been trained in greeting people since childhood, and she had, even if that childhood had been almost a century ago, Patti held out her hand as Sparktonius approached. But they never actually touched. When they were only a few feet from each other, both gave a jolt, as if they had been shocked. They shook themselves, and seemed to blink with new-waking eyes at the world around them. Though no one knew it, the distance when this happened was precisely the distance they had been from one another when they'd originally been transformed.

"What just happened?" demanded Lucy.

"Ah, they still need each other, thought so," said Chip, with a nod to himself.

Later, he managed to explain it to the others, "Well, it just made sense, that sort of thing. Brain-fried at the same time to be bats and kittens. Horrid. Has to affect the both of them. Clearly, they weren't getting better, so you know, hair of the dog and all that."

He stopped and looked around expectantly, and his friends understood him, perfectly.

Agent X asked to meet all the maidens, and it was not surprising that this raised a few eyebrows, notably Lucy's and George's.

Everything was in flux, however, and the general air of the place was one that focused on phrases like, "Well, let's see," and "Benefit of the doubt," so no one protested.

Then again, by the time Agent X made his request, the dragons and the princesses had been reunited. Some of them were still quite clingy, actually. No one was surprised, not even Agent X, when at the meeting, there were as many dragons as maidens sitting at the desks he had laid out in front of him.

Agent X had staged his meeting in the remains of the big production room at the center of the ruins of the wizards' stronghold. It was no longer dark and gloomy. Though the electric spotlights no longer glared from the walls, Ember had torn the roof off the building, and most of the dragons had helped, and once the smoke and dust cleared, there was plenty of natural light.

Now that the noble maidens were clearing away their own, magic-induced fogs, their personalities were beginning to emerge. Some chose to sit up front of the improvised classroom, ankles demurely crossed beneath their elegant sacrificial gowns, their pencils held ready. Others chose seats as far back from Agent X as possible, and slouched in their seats, while managing to project aggressive boredom with a surprising strength of will.

Agent X moved 'round the room, asking each maiden her name. In front of each one, he placed a folder from a stack he carried. Each folder was marked with a young woman's name and the date of her sacrifice.

"Good morning," said Agent X. "My name is Agent X, of the Profundia Survival Day Reconditioning Coordinator's Commission. The purpose of our time together is so that when you finally decide to return home, you will be able to make the transition to normal life smoothly. I know you have all been told that you have been enchanted for a long time. Today we will take a look at some of the practicalities involved. Yes, Princess Engelbertina Marie Campbell?"

"Why do we have to do any of this? We'll go home and back to life as usual. Why is that supposed to be a challenge?"

"An excellent question, and one I think we can best answer with a little exercise. If you will all please open the folder with your name on it. Inside is a PSDRCC file containing a chronological record of everything that has happened to your city, your neighborhood, and your family since the date of your sacrifice. Please, take a moment and review that material."

There was a rustle of paper, even from the reluctant readers at the back of the room. Each of the girls had been curious about just this, and for several moments, all was quiet as the girls read. Some of the maidens, those whose clothing was the most old-fashioned, had more pages to read than others, but it was clear that everyone found something in the list that disturbed them. Agent X knew what the reports said. He had compiled them himself, from easily obtainable research. The timelines he had provided were succinct, without poetic language of any sort. What was on the page was simple, bald fact. For some of the maidens, parents had died. For others, siblings had died, too. Some had siblings who were now grandparents. A few maidens had sweethearts who had chosen other brides. Others had sweethearts who had lived and died alone. In all cases, the news was clear: While they had been trapped in enchantment, time, and people, had moved on.

Agent X raised a hand, and though not every eye was dry, all the maidens waited to hear what it was he had to say.

"If you have finished, please take the report you've just read in one hand," Agent X held up a few pieces of paper as an example. "And with your other hand," he said, "do this." He ripped the papers in half.

A few maidens gasped. A few more laughed nervously. Only a few girls, the most compliant, actually did it. Without missing a beat, Agent X continued. "Now this part; tear it in half."

There was more laughter at seeing a teacher destroying class property, and several more tore their papers in half.

"Again."

Rip. With increasing enthusiasm, the girls began to make confetti. The laughter was increasingly genuine as the pieces of paper got smaller.

"Ladies, what you are tearing up is the past," said Agent X. "It happened, but there is no reason to let it define the future you are about to build for yourselves. Please make a pile of the paper on the floor."

There was some enthusiastic energy as the girls made little piles, each her own pile in front of her own desk. Agent X then asked the ladies, when they were ready, to raise a hand and invite the nearest dragon to burn the scraps of paper.

The dragons were certainly willing, and Agent X walked 'round the room to observe as in her turn, each maiden saw her report reduced to ash.

"What is the matter, miss?" Agent X paused before one reluctant maiden.

"I understand the importance of the exercise," she said. "But I hate to think of what the fire will do to the parquet floor!"

"Milady," said Agent X. "I'll have you know that this floor belonged to the same wizards who caused this dilemma for all of you. Do you really care what happens to their floor?"

At once the maiden's manner changed, and Agent X walked onward, making a mental note to watch his step when he came back that way. The maiden was chanting "Burn-burn-burn!" with such enthusiasm that he guessed there wouldn't be any floor left.

When the burning was finished, and the maidens had taken their seats again, Agent X resumed his place at the front of the room. "Well done," he said. "But only half done. The next step is to re-enter the world. You are not ciphers in history. You are here, now, and the present world needs to take notice!"

One of the ostentatiously bored maidens at the back jeered: "And now how are we going to make them do that?"

Agent X allowed himself a small smile. "Ladies, I give you the department's most infamous form, the DDS-1020." What he held up was essentially a blank piece of lined paper. "You are going to write down everything that happened to you, from the moment you were tied to the post on the beach until now."

"What good would that do?"

"It will establish a record of what happened to you, in your own words, while it's still fresh in your mind. That is good for you. It will also be good for the world. No one but you has any idea what it feels like to be transformed, to be enchanted. It's good for other people to know what sort of sacrifice you really made. You all were very brave to have survived this long. Many maidens never made it this far," he added grimly. That had been a particularly troubling discovery in his research. "Your stories need to be recorded. By you, in your words."

"Our lives as bats?" The young women looked at each other.

"Mosquitoes are not very filling," said Engelbertina.

"Even when there are a lot of them," agreed the bored girl.

"Sonar was fun," said the girl who liked parquet flooring.

Agent X smiled, and stepped back. He had a pencil sharpener ready, but it was time for the maidens to talk, to write, and to bear witness.

The Dragon, Lucinda and George

Chapter Thirty-One
Lucy's Homecoming

Princess Lucinda sent a message to her parents. It was notable for its terseness, but it did detail the amount of space to be cleared in the Grand Plaza for a celebration.

"My friends and I will be flown to the plaza by dragons. The dragons are my friends," concluded the message.

While he read, the King's face betrayed no emotion. He merely said, "Make it so, all of it," and passed the message to his Queen, who also read it. Her face also betrayed no emotion, and she offered no comment, but silently passed the message to the retainers. There was nothing of a private nature contained in that single page. The King and the Queen said nothing of a private nature between them.

The day the Princess arrived would be remembered as "The Homecoming". It was a clear, cold day for spring, the sun bright, and a stiff breeze coming off the lake. The people of the kingdom shivered in the plaza, wearing their finery and watching the skies for the sign of dragon wings.

Someone shouted when the first wings were sighted over the lake. One dragon, then two. Suddenly the sky was filled with dragons flying, silently, in an intricate aerial pattern over the city. It was beautiful. It was terrifying. People smothered screams, and a few actually ran. Most held on to one another and remained, standing exposed as great predators flew overhead. Most eyes were turned to the King and the Queen, in their thrones upon the Great Dais, for some sign of how to behave. Their Highnesses sat motionless, outwardly calm, if not at ease. With their eyes alone they watched the skies. Their hands rested with very confidant firmness on the arms of their thrones. The royal princes and princesses sought to emulate their parents, but the youngest were visibly trembling.

There was a place of prominence reserved for an honor guard formed by the entirety of the crew of the recently christened HMS Lucinda, who stood at rigid attention, eyes focused straight ahead.

The television crews captured it all. The red eyes of the cameras never even blinked.

At some pre-arranged signal, the dragons folded their wings and dropped toward the plaza. Several people cried out, and one particularly sensitive woman fainted.

"Stand firm!" called the officers to the soldiers.

The dragons landed. They exhibited skill and restraint, but the rush of wind from those mighty wings was considerable, and the crowd was inevitably showered by debris. Fortunately, in this case, the debris was mainly confetti, and the overall effect was festive.

The King and Queen stared at the dragons, and the dragons and princesses stared at the King and Queen. The red eyes of the cameras watched everything.

The dragon closest to the Great Dais was Ember, and as the festive detritus stopped falling, she opened her two foreclaws and out of these stepped Connie and Lucy. The unicorn's coat was smooth and shining brighter than a sunbeam. Her sharp little horn was adorned with a delicate, ruby tiara and her gleaming hooves were covered with discreet, but unmistakable hearts and sunflowers drawn in nail polish.

Lucy was nowhere near as impressive a sight, but for once, she didn't care. She had been offered a dozen gowns to grace the occasion, but chose to wear the simple traveling clothes given to her by the Queen of the unicorns. Her ruby bracelet was a splash of color at her wrist, and her glasses were new, too. The frames, red, blue and gold, were the national colors of Carolia.

Connie looked at Lucy, and whispered: "You can ride triumphantly into the city, if you want," and knelt down.

Lucy knew a big honor when it was offered to her, and accepted her first-ever chance to ride a unicorn, with: "Thanks, Connie."

Glowerflorious, on the opposite side of the dais from Ember, opened his claws, revealing George and Agent X.

George casually strode across the plaza, carrying his spear with a laconic attitude. He ambled over to Lucy and said so only she and Connie could hear, "So that's the family?"

Lucy gave a terse nod, and he said, "You've so got this." She was still astride Connie's silvery back, so George nudged her leg with his shoulder. Lucy looked down and smiled, and knowing that she had the support of her friends made it easier to go on with the plan.

Agent X in his black jump suit caused a noticeable ripple of interest and admiration to pass through the crowd. As had been arranged, he quickly found a functionary to whom he passed an impressive array of forms. The clerk quickly glanced through them and nodded to the King and Queen. To this day, no one has ever ascertained with certainty whether the wink that Agent X gave the Queen had been returned, certainty being such an elusive thing.

The King and Queen continued to watch the unfolding tableau with regal dignity.

The red eyes of the cameras watched The King and the Queen.

Charrtonio then opened his claws and from one of them stepped the wolf, who had also been groomed to perfection, his grey coat rippling like silk in the breeze. From the other stepped

Chip Blitherington, resplendent in his gleaming armor.

"Here already? Handy that. Thanks for the lift, old chap," said Chip to the dragon, who nodded acknowledgement. "Looks as though we're meant to be over there. Come on, Alfie." Together they came to stand at Lucy's side, and if no one could tell whether Alfie or Chip was leading the way, it went unremarked.

Lucy and her friends stood in front of the Great Dais, just a hair's breadth from where the security guard would have to register a threat. Like a princess, Lucy calmly, almost gently, raised a gloved hand.

At the signal, all the dragons shrank. They had been giants, enormous presences filling the open space, awesome and dangerous. As they shrank, they seemed much less frightening. They became only as big as the human beings in the crowd, and each of the dragons, as they shrank, released from the protection of their claws, something surprising: Maidens, wearing garments decades out of fashion, emerged like butterflies from scaly chrysalises.

The people gasped at the sight of so much power, so quietly and precisely delivered. But the solemnity of the King and Queen, and the careful formality seen from the dragons themselves lent a surreal sort of acceptability to the scene. Plus, the people reasoned, there was the beautiful unicorn. They would wait and see what happened next, before they started in with the screaming and running away.

The red eyes of the cameras never wavered,

Princess Lucinda sat up even straighter on Connie's back, and pushed her glasses more firmly onto her nose. She had never given a public speech before, but when she spoke now, her voice was cool and clearly audible in the hushed plaza.

"People of Carolia, Father, Mother. I'm back. I've returned with the maidens who had been eaten, and the dragons who ate them. There were wizards, you see…" but she was interrupted by a small struggle at one side of the open space.

"Let go of me, you great oaf!" A middle-aged woman, plump and grey-haired was struggling with a soldier who was trying to keep her from rushing into the middle of an important, historic moment. "That's my little sister. Margaret!" she shouted.

A man at her side, perhaps a husband, perhaps a brother, simply swung a heavy fist and knocked the soldier off balance. The man was swarmed by other solders, but the woman, freed for just a second, sprinted into the midst of the maidens, shrieking, "Maggie! Mags! It's me, Maggie!"

One of the maidens, a girl of maybe sixteen in a gown forty years out of date, opened her eyes wide and turned. "Martha?" she called. Other maidens parted for her like reeds in the wind, and she ran forward, arms outstretched just in time to be engulfed by her sister's embrace.

At the King's sign, the soldiers released the man who had swung at them, and he raced to join the sisters.

There was a release of tension in the crowd, and the sound of other people calling names. "Louise?" said one.

"Annabelle?" said another.

"Daphne?"

And then the solemnity was over. Heedless of the dragons, the crowd rushed forward, seeking the faces of long-lost aunts and sisters and cousins among the sacrificial maidens.

After which, it seemed as though things would quite simply fall into place.

There was a formal state reception to welcome Princess Lucinda home again, which was (Lucy informed her friends) political code for "fancy party with not enough chairs". Everyone was invited, even the dragons, and Ember and Glowerflorious spent half an hour with Lucy's father and eldest brother, drawing out the official peace treaty that would exist between dragons and humans going forward. This could have been a complex document with many "wheretofores" and "howsomevers" dotted over the page, except that neither Ember nor Glowerflorious were lawyers, and their terms were simple:

"Dragons promise not to eat humans, nor regard them as litter. Humans promise not to kill dragons, nor to leave maidens out as litter."

There was a tasteful band, and Connie (rather less tastefully) taught them all her favorite songs. The knights, in formal clothes, danced with any maiden willing to take a turn around the floor. Agent X didn't have anyone to interrogate and actually enjoyed himself anyway. There were dainty finger foods, and Alfie (having no fingers) enjoyed following after the clumsiest guests and eating anything they happened to spill.

Returned maidens, and their families, if their families were still alive, and the dragons had been the guests of honor, and if Princess Lucinda seemed to studiously ignore her family in favor of her guests, that was certainly understandable, given that in all ways that mattered they were her guests. The maidens and their families were certainly impressed to be at the palace, and the rest of the Royal Family had been schooled in being caring and gracious, to outsiders, at least. The Royal Family seemed especially solicitous towards maidens who had no living family, drifting graciously away only when Princess Lucinda approached with her frozen smile. That smile only relaxed when her family members departed Lucy's orbit.

The King was in full "King of his People" mode, and all who later remembered that day thought how forcefully cheerful he was. He was, in many ways, the perfect host, circulating, listening, charming and engaging. Only occasionally would he share a glance with his wife, and even less occasionally would he look at his daughter, the reason for the occasion. As for the Queen, she too was doing her duty diligently, and if it was with a trace less enthusiasm, that was certainly understandable, given the circumstances. You would have had to know her very well to have noticed it.

There was no one there who noticed it.

Well, there might have been one, but she was busy at the moment.

The state reception was considered by everyone to be quite successful.

After the public part, the family retired to their private living quarters, and the sitting room where they always used to gather together. The private family affair started off strained and quickly got worse.

"Out!" The king barked to the servants.

"Your Majesty?" asked the chamberlain.

"All of you, out. Family only."

This had never been done before, but the servants at the palace, from the lowliest chambermaid to the chamberlain, were nothing if not well trained. Some glances were exchanged, but they exited without debate.

"The rest of you," said the King to the lords and ladies in waiting, the governesses and nannies, "Out." The retainers who were not quite servants, including the newest members of the older children's households, looked nervous and stood, unsure whether they were really being sent away.

"Out," The bark was shorter and angrier.

"Papa!" began Princess Dana. "Surely, you can't mean Philippa. She's like..."

"Out," said the King. "Everyone out, especially Philippa." It was the voice of a monarch.

Taking their dignity like a coat, the retainers and members of the royal entourage left the room, too.

Lucinda felt a rather savage surge of joy to see Dana rebuffed and Philippa ejected, and as she had been doing all night, she hid this under her frozen, neutral expression.

"We are a family," said the King, her father. "It's high time we started acting like one."

The children were looking at their father as if he had grown a second head. The Queen was looking at her husband as if he still had just the one, but it was growing into a different sort of head and she was not quite sure how it would turn out. From her expression, it seemed she was beginning to feel the tiniest bit hopeful that it would be a better head.

Unfortunately, being commanded to act like a family did not produce the desired results. One of the princes was clearly wishing there had been more detailed instructions. Only two of the sisters seemed at all at ease. Pacifica, with her customary quiet smile, sat with Edwina, the youngest princess, on one of the sofas, holding hands. Lucy didn't see any reason why it should be her job to break the strained silence, so instead, she watched her siblings shift uncomfortably.

They are so helpless without the servants, Lucy was thinking mercilessly. Can you imagine them on a quest? They wouldn't last a minute if they saw a little kitten or a pack of wolves by themselves. Look at them fidget. They have no idea what to do.

"Lucinda, dear, did you like the soup?" Her mother's question abruptly derailed Lucinda's bitter train of thought.

"What?" asked Lucinda. Her voice came out harsh, almost a bark. Almost, she realized her father's sort of bark.

"At the reception," said the Queen with gentle persistence. "Did you like the soup? I had them make cream of potato, just the way you like it."

Lucy felt unreasonably annoyed. She shrugged, the gesture awkward and nowhere near as graceful as a dragon's. "It was OK."

Her father looked like he was about to say something corrective, which probably would have started with, "That's no way to talk to your mother," and likely would have ended with, "as long as you live in this house," slammed doors and tears, but her mother looked at him and he subsided.

"Did you notice your spoon, dear?" she asked, turning back to her daughter.

"No."

"It was the Delftian pattern that we collected together. Do you remember when we got it?"

"No."

She did. She remembered the little antique shop almost on the very edge of the capital city, a dusty little place, and how she and her mother had laughed about the dust on the shelves and the crazy collection of things tumbled together in with the spoons, how they had both seen the Delftian spoon at the same time, and said, "Ooh!" almost reverently. She remembered they'd gone for pancakes afterward.

"And I polished it myself using the Staffian fur and the Throndish polish," the queen said.

"Oh. I didn't notice," said Lucy.

She had.

"But thank you."

That was not a thank-you voice.

The Queen took a deep breath. "You're quite welcome, dear. You look very pretty this evening."

"Thank you."

The tension in the room was not dissipating, not even a little.

Lucy snapped.

"Why are you being so nice to me all of a sudden? Is it because I am famous? Because I did something? Because I saved all those maidens? Because I made the dragons friends instead of enemies? Now that I am famous and if someone said you had to give me away, would you do it now?"

She wasn't sitting any more, but standing up, clenching her fists at her sides.

"Would you just give me away like some worn-out rag? Would you tie me to a post and then just walk away? Leaving me? Leaving me? Leaving me to be eaten by a dragon? You were probably grateful to see me go. I'm sure that you were happy when I was the one picked. No more clumsy Lucinda! No more ugly Lucinda! No more awful, awkward Lucinda! Whatever are we going to do about Lucinda? Oh, it's so sad but at least they didn't take one of the good girls. Yes, it's probably for the best that she got picked. Now we don't have to deal with her! I know that's what you were thinking even if you didn't dare say it to my face. I know it! How am I different now? WHY ARE YOU BEING SO NICE TO ME, WHEN YOU THREW ME AWAY BEFORE?"

Lucy was rigid, but not crying. Her family on all sides had frozen as well, wearing various expressions of horror and guilt, with one exception.

"Lucinda," growled her father. She subsided.

"I'm only going to say this once," he began. Then he stopped, sighed, and Lucy was aware how much older her father looked. His hair seemed to have gone grey overnight, and there were deep shadows under his eyes, as if he hadn't slept in a long time. He held out his hand to the Queen. Wordlessly, she took it.

The children stared. Their father had grown two heads, and they both were talking.

The King took a deep breath. "No, that's not true. I will say what I have to say as many times as it takes for you to believe me, I suppose, and maybe a few times more, for good measure. Lucinda— Lucy— the day we received…" His voice broke, and Lucy realized that he was crying. So was her mother, silent tears streaming down her face. The Queen squeezed the King's hand. "The day we got that letter," he continued. "It was the worst day of our lives. Whatever else you believe about us, I want you to know that much."

Lucy was stunned by her parents' display of raw emotion, and a glance showed her that her sisters and brothers were equally shocked.

"Show her your locket," said the King to the Queen.

Lucy's mother took the locket from around her neck, and pushed a hidden catch. Inside was a small photo of Lucinda, taken when she was about seven years old, studiously polishing a piece of silverware. It wasn't a particularly attractive picture. Lucy's glasses were big and crooked. Her mousy hair was askew and her tongue was slightly sticking out.

Lucinda looked up from the photo to meet her mother's eyes.

"You were the only one who seemed to care," the Queen said.

The King reached inside his pocket, pulled out his royal wallet and opened it. The officer of the checking account handled all the money. This wallet existed solely to carry photos for each royal child. The King turned the pictures one by one until he reached Lucy's. The photo was not a posed or premeditated portrait. Instead, it had clearly been taken from security footage. It showed her running down one of the corridors of the palace with a gleeful grin. In her wake, a toppled chair and broken vase testified to the havoc she had wrought along the way.

"No one ever said anything," Lucy said, softly.

"I told them not to," he replied. "I loved that grin of yours, and I never told you. You are my daughter." He shook his head. "And ever since I saw them put that damnable shroud over your head I have been going over in my head the hundreds of things I should have said."

"As have I," said her mother, once again taking her husband by the hand.

"Both your mother and I have made mistakes with you, Lucy. With all of you," he added, to the rest of the princes and princesses. "I realize now we failed you. I truly believed that, if we had…fought for you… showed our emotion for you…how would that make the families who had already sacrificed feel? How would that make the next family feel? We are your parents, but we are also the monarchs and we thought… We were told… There was nothing we could do. We thought it was the duty of those in the palace to be stoic, to be stern, to try and make it better for everyone else.

"But pain is pain. Ours was no more noble because we wear crowns. I have just spent the last three hours looking at other families, families the world might consider lesser than ours. They did their duty, and they suffered their pain, and still they were happy, in the palace. They hugged each other, even in a palace. They were at ease with each other, even in a palace. They were allowing themselves to feel, even in a palace. And they did not seem to find it at all strange to do so. Indeed, they seemed to take comfort in it."

The King looked around the room at all his children, at his wife.

"I'm sorry," he said. "I will try to do better." He turned to Lucy. "And you, Lucinda… Lucy. I'm so proud of you. You succeeded in making this kingdom a better place for everyone. This family will be better because you are home with us. Lucy, we are going to make so many mistakes, but we are forever grateful to have you here to make them with us."

The Queen opened her arms, and Lucy stepped into them. Then the King hugged them both together, a warm circle of the sort Lucy had always wished for. In their chairs, the princes and princesses held back, until Edwina, the youngest, jumped out of her seat.

"Thank you, Lucy," she said, lunging forward, and throwing her arms around her favorite sister. "Thank you for making the dragons nice so they won't eat me, too."

Lucy found she was crying, and didn't care. She just pulled her sister into the hug. Pacifica joined them almost at once, and Tracy, and Eddie and Samson, and even Dana came to the circle, where the family hugged itself whole again.

Chapter Thirty-Two
One Hero Prefers To Remain Unsung

WHY, AFTER AN EMOTIONALLY AND PHYSICALLY exhausting day, she went looking for him, Lucy didn't know, but look for Chip, she did. He wasn't all that hard to find. Lucy only had to ask one of the maids, and she indicated the second-smallest-bookroom in the east wing.

"There you are!" Lucy said, exploding into the room.

Chip looked up from the book he'd been reading. He had been quite relaxed, with Alfie lying at his feet in front of the amber glow of a fire, but when he saw Lucy, Chip changed.

"Scarcely could be any place else, don'cher know?" Chip said. "Party over, food all et, cheers given, and there you are, the maid of the hour."

Lucy glared at him and threw herself dramatically into the chair opposite his. She folded her arms and glared some more. Chip waited politely to see whether there was any more, and then bent back to his book.

"You're really not fooling anyone, you know!" Lucy flung at him.

Chip looked up from his book. "I beg your pardon," he said with mild surprise. "Fooling whom?"

"Anyone. Everyone. But not me. Not anymore!" Unable to contain her agitation, Lucy jumped up from her chair and began to pace.

Chip went back to his reading. Carefully, he turned a page.

"You are SO not an idiot."

"High praise indeed," said Chip. He didn't even look up. "Mater will be delighted to hear you say so."

"See?" Lucy pointed at him. "That is so like you! You say the most inane things and everyone thinks you are a dolt, a nincompoop, a buffoon...."

"I certainly hope there is a 'but' coming up soon, because otherwise Mater will become upset. She might even suggest I find other friends," Chip said, but he didn't seem bothered by Lucy's tirade. Instead, she got the impression he was quietly amused, which only infuriated her more.

"But," she said. "You aren't any of those things. You're smart. You were the first to figure out I wasn't kidnapped. You're kind. You figured out what was wrong with the maidens and dragons and how to fix it. You're even Alfie's best friend!"

"Well, that's nothing to be upset about," Chip said, mildly, his finger marking his place in the book. "Alfie's learning to like you, too. How's it going, Alfie?"

The wolf opened one eye, sleepily. "Ruff," he said.

"But everyone calls you all kinds of nasty names behind your back. I've heard them. It's just not fair!"

She finally seemed to have his attention. Chip closed his book. Softly, he said, "Well, that's on them, isn't it?"

Lucy didn't hear either the peaceable tone or the sensible words. The bill of indictment continued. "Chip the Drip. Chip-chip-double-dip. Chipster the unhipster—"

"Ah," Chip sighed. "I had rather hoped that one had died out." He scratched Alfie behind his ear.

"—The Earl of Blitherington," Lucy's rant continued.

"Can't argue with that one."

"—If Chip had to tie his own shoelaces, he'd tie one shoe to the other and then spend 20 minutes apologizing to the laces left out."

"Always embarrassing when that happens, don'cher know. Poor little lace. Meant to support its mate, instead of flopping about and getting trod on. Used and worn out, not doing any good to any one. Like those little pencils at miniature golf. There they are, primed and ready to go in their little boxes. Born to keep score, but instead the golfers decide they are not gonna keep score and all they get is chewed up, and tossed. Never get to do what they were meant to do. Sad, actually."

"ARE YOU EVEN LISTENING TO ME?" shouted Lucy, but her question must have been rhetorical, because she didn't wait for an answer. "They are talking about Alfie, too," she said. "'Have you seen Chip's new nursemaid? I imagine he could eat an entire cow in the time it takes Chip to open a granola bar.'"

"That seems a bit harsh," Chip protested, mildly. "Maybe a chicken."

"More like two," Alfie countered, from where he still lay at Chip's feet.

"Yes, I suppose you would know. Certainly closer to two than one," Chip nodded.

Lucy blinked, Chip's comments were finally registering. "Wait," she said. "You mean, you know what people have been saying about you?"

"Of course," he said. "As you so masterfully pointed out, I am not really an idiot."

"And you don't care?" Lucy was shocked at his indifference.

Chip hesitated. "Do you want to know what I care about?" he asked. She nodded, and he said, "Then please sit down, Lucy. I would like to have a conversation with you, Earl to Princess."

Lucy's rage had temporarily run out of steam, and so she let herself sink into the chair again, watching Chip warily.

He had put aside his book and was leaning forward, elbows resting on his knees. "There are two kinds of nobles, Lucy. The ones you hear about most often are the sort that like to lead from the front, fussing and gesticulating and ordering people about. They get things done, but with all their shouting and waving, they don't do a lot of listening and thinking. They don't like surprises and they don't like being overlooked. When the spotlight fades and they run out of reasons to bellow and roar, they feel lost. They never learned how to do anything else, and in frustration, they become all sound and fury, ranting about how they are always right and no one ever pays any attention to them."

Chip waited until Lucy had figured out just who he was talking about. She blushed, but when she nodded, Chip continued. "The problem is, once you start ordering people about, it's too easy to forget that they are people. They become orders, see? You forget that they might have plans and wishes of their own. Even worse, sometimes they forget it, too. If you're very good at ordering people about, you'll find some of them will just stop moving about on their own. All they do is look to you, waiting for you to come up with all the answers."

Lucy opened her mouth to say something, but then closed it again with the words unspoken. Chip nodded. "It doesn't mean you're an evil wizard," he said gently. "You can want the best for everybody and still not leave them any room to make their own mistakes and learn from them, and I'm the last person to deny that sometimes the world needs big personalities up at the front of events, to do all the shouting and waving."

He smiled, shrugged, and leaned back in his chair. "But there is another approach. As Grand-Mater used to say, 'When you stop expecting yourself to be perfect, you can be what you really are.'"

"What is that?" Lucy asked.

Chip shrugged again. "Imperfect, I suppose. People are more likely to be themselves when they are not over-awed, you know. I can make suggestions, certainly, but I prefer to let people make their own choices. If they choose to think I'm unintelligent, or uneducated, that's their right. They might find themselves mistaken, and it could be a lesson for them. The point is that what they think doesn't have to change my opinion of myself, or what I know I can do, and I can do what I think is right whether people admire me for it or not."

"But then other people don't ever know how you helped them. They don't know you're a hero."

"True," Chip agreed, amiably. "My way doesn't work if that's what's really important to you."

Lucy sat in silence, frowning at nothing as she mulled this idea over, and Chip waited patiently for whatever thoughts were simmering in her head to let one bubble to the surface.

"Can I ask you something, like, for real?" Lucy said at last.

"Yes."

"When my mother invited you to the palace, and you picked the flowers from the garden…" Chip waited. She sighed. "What would you have done?"

"If you hadn't kicked me in the shin, and run away screaming bloody murder?" he asked.

"Yeah."

"I would have given you some flowers."

"And then?"

"Polished some spoons, I expect."

Lucy pressed her hands against her burning cheeks. Chip grinned. "Ah, you are wondering about the maiden thing, I expect."

Part of Lucy wished the ground would open up and swallow

her to spare her the embarrassment, but another part was the girl who had defeated the wizards, so she met his gaze (it was understanding, rather than mocking) and nodded, "Yes."

"Well, it never seems to do much good one way or the other," Chip said, gently. "And you deserve someone to look after you while you're busy looking after everyone else."

"But I did run away, and you still fluttered about acting like it had all been a done deal," Lucy protested. "In front of all the other knights."

"Ah, yes, those fellows," Chip shook his head. "If they're your type, you only have to say."

"They aren't," Lucy said.

"Truthfully, Lucy, there's things men and boys sometimes say to each other when they think girls won't hear them. Some of what I heard made me think one or two young men were just the sort of blusterers I was talking about, too busy thinking of maidens as prizes to be won to think of them as people with feelings and hearts. Would you want someone like that to come courting?"

"I don't want to see that sort at all," said Lucy, firmly.

"Excellent good sense," said Chip, with approval. "I say, Alfie?"

The wolf lifted his head from his paws. "Yus?"

Chip said, "If you should happen to see a Bryce fellow, padded shoulders, good teeth, awful sword he has no idea how to use, and not nearly as charming as he thinks he is, that sort. If you see him out wandering the halls, feel free to escort him out again as soon as possible."

"Rrright," said Alfie, with a wolfish grin.

"And if it happens you should find your teeth around his ankle as you are trotting along, don't worry over-much if you should happen to sneeze."

"You mean a dancing kind of sneeze?" asked Alfie, carefully.

"Most definitely. A Royal Ball dancing kind of sneeze," Chip nodded.

"You got it," Alfie said, and one got the decided impression that the tendon was as good as severed.

"Wait, you were protecting me?" Lucy's voice was rising.

"The only way I could figure out how. You wouldn't let me get close enough to talk to you, because of my dreadful reputation, I suppose. I could have warned you about him during one of your sister's soirees, but I really am a horrid dancer. Comes from not knowing my right from my left, I suspect."

"Oh."

The room was comfortably quiet. The dying fire was still warm, and glowed companionably. Chip picked up his book again, and opened it to the page he had left.

"Thank you," Lucy said.

"You're welcome," he said. Alfie lowered his head drowsily back to his paws again, and Lucy got down from the chair to the floor, the better to scratch the wolf behind the ears. Chip turned a page. "Oh, good job with the wizard business. Dragons and maidens. Well done. Something to be said for sound and fury, when it's done well by the right person."

To the end of her days, Lucy remembered the way she felt at that exact moment, her heart full, and her mind, for once, at peace.

Chapter Thirty-Three
Herd Is The Word

BECAUSE SHE LOVED THEM, AND THEY KNEW ALL THE WORDS to her favorite songs, Connie invited all of her friends to come along and see her grand homecoming, and they accepted. "Human receptions are pretty cute," Connie said. "But the Herd works a different way."

They stood at the head of the valley, almost directly opposite the place where Connie had galloped away all those days ago. Though she'd never seen it from this angle, Lucy recognized it by the singe marks Ember had left on the meadow and half the trees, though it looked as if the unicorn vale had received some springtime rain since then. New grass was peeking up through the ashes, and it was clear the hills would soon be as fresh and green as before.

"When you come back from your quest," Connie said. "You stand right here on Judgment Rock and you toot your horn as loud as you can. When the sound comes out, it lets everyone know that you are home, and then everybody comes to see you, and then you tell Daddy what happened, and he says you are wise and then everyone has a big party with cake and ice cream." Apparently, the idea that she might not be deemed wise had never crossed her mind. Traveling had not dimmed Connie's self-confidence in the slightest. "At least I think my party will have cake and ice cream," she continued. "Because my parties always have cake and ice cream." The little unicorn's tone was very solemn, because parties were, after all, serious things.

She drew a deep breath.

"You've so got this," Lucy said.

"We know you'll be great," said Ember.

"OK," said Connie. "Here I go, guys!" Carefully, Connie climbed the remaining section of the hill, to where a slab of bare stone projected out over the valley. The wind picked up her mane and tail and waved them like a banner. The sight was enough to take someone's breath away.

"Cute," Ember murmured to Lucy. "But not cutesy." She apparently meant that the polish on Connie's hooves added a touch of gravitas.

Lucy got it right away. "Just perfect," she said.

Connie gave a nod to her friends, then took another deep breath and tootled her horn. It wasn't a twitter or a squeak this time. A single note, clear and perfect, came forth. The purity of the tone surprised Connie as much as anyone. She hesitated, then blew again, with even greater confidence. The note gathered in intensity and began to echo and rebound against the hills.

"Listen," gasped Lucy, whispering in surprise. Because the perfection of this landmark and the natural shape of the valley caused Connie's single note to echo and reverberate, it multiplied and the harmonics built a chord from the solitary tone, and the magic in Connie, or in the valley itself, made the entire valley resonate. Connie's single note was magnified, until it sounded like an orchestral chord.

"Wow," said Lucy.

"Awesome," said George.

"I'm guessing she passed," said Ember.

Connie's chord had just started to dissipate when it was replaced with the thundering of hooves. As one, dragons and humans took a discreet step away from Connie. When the ground began to shake, they were much less discreet.

Connie, on the other hand, was prancing with excitement on the rock.

"Oh! Oh, there they are! There are Mummy and Daddy!"

Unable to restrain herself, Connie leaped off the rock and raced towards the Herd. Her parents were in the lead, but it was clear that every unicorn in the valley had come to welcome the filly home again. Now, instead of the massive collision simple physics would have mandated, Connie and the Herd initiated an intricate circle dance at full gallop. They weaved in and out, tight curves and narrow misses. Horns slashed high and low at incredible speed, while tooting a beautiful harmony incorporating and celebrating Connie's original note.

It was a dance of welcoming and homecoming and of trust, and the other questers were amazed at the display of pure power and control. They were also glad not to be anywhere inside that melee.

When the dance ended at last, Connie was back on the rock, quivering with joy. Her father said, "Connie, how was your quest?"

"Daddy, it was so much fun!"

Her mother said, "And did you learn anything while you were gone?"

"Mummy, yes I did! The first thing I learned was the twenty-seven rules of questing. You wouldn't think there could be so many rules, but Ember and Lucy helped me to figure them out, and every time I learned a new rule, I put it in a song. The chorus went 'Hi-ho!' and that chorus can go on for hours, if you want it to! I will sing it for you later, Mummy. You will like my singing."

"Do you know," said Frank to Nell, "I have heard some parents complain that their children never talk to them."

"I also learned that lots of sad bitty bats and mean little kitties were not bats and kitties, but bewitched little girls and big dragons. Ember and Lucy found out that it was because they were being sucked up like batteries, though I didn't find out what those are, only it doesn't matter, because the bad wizards (boo!) who were doing the bad things (also boo!) got defeated by Ember's amazing lance (hooray!)."

"I wonder what those parents did right?" Nell murmured to Frank, her tone one of mild curiosity.

"And I helped turn the bats and kitties back, but then they were scared little girls and big dragons. Glowerflorious and Alfie and I were super-duper cute to cheer them up. This is my new friend Glowerflorious, and he is a dragon that I met when he was a kitten. He was mean, and I was bewitched, which felt all woozy like it was bad cotton candy in my mouth, which is funny, right? Because how could cotton candy ever be bad? But it was."

"They actually seem to think it's a problem when their children don't talk," said Frank. Nell raised a queenly eyebrow skeptically, and Connie resumed her tale.

"Lucy and Ember told me to think of you, Mummy and Daddy, and Boots, Scoots, and Skipper stomped their hooves and I thought of the Herd, and once we got him to stop being a kitty, Glowerflorious became my friend, but not like boyfriend slash girl-friend because he really likes Ember, and Ember likes him too, but it took Ember forever to be cute to him. Finally, Lucy had to tell her, like 'Hello, he does so like you,' and Glowerflorious called me a bad-ass little unicorn. What's a bad-ass unicorn, Daddy? Because I don't think I have bad any part of me and Daddy, have you even been listening to my epic tale of adventure?"

"Bad-ass," said the King of Unicorns. "Yes, dear. I'm keeping up. Why did he call you a bad-ass?"

Lucy realized it was the King's calm tone and supernatural ability to track his daughter's thought process that made him so beloved by his daughter and wife. Those traits in general probably proved useful in his kingship, as well. It was no wonder he was loved and revered.

"I think it was what I did to the bad wolfies," Connie was saying.

"And what did you do to the bad wolfies?" asked Queen Nell.

"I forget," Connie sighed. "So many things happened."

"Connie defended her friends against eight ferocious wolves and sent seven of them to their just rewards," said Alfie. Frank and Nell looked at Connie's new friend, who, as a wolf, had never been on the receiving end of that kind of stare before.

"I kicked them, too," Connie added, reclaiming the focus of her parents.

"How did you know they were bad wolves?" her mother asked politely.

"I asked them," she said. "And when one of them started biting me, I thought that might be his answer, so I started kicking," Connie said solemnly. "And poking."

Her parents looked at each other. "Sounds pretty bad-ass to me," said Frank, judiciously, and her mother gave Glowerflorious a nod of approval.

"What else did you learn, Connie?" asked her father, courageously courting further narration.

"Well, one of the wolfies actually is a good wolf," said Connie. "This wolf. And he can be really cute. He does a great chasing his tail. Show them, Alfie."

"Erm," said Alfie, providing an example of the textbook definition of an embarrassed wolf.

"We'll take Connie's word for it," Frank suggested.

"Thanks, Sire," said Alfie, in the textbook definition of gratitude.
"Anything else, Connie?"

"I learned what it is Maids and Butlers do in the Valley of the Maids and Butlers, and it isn't actually very much fun, because it's laundry (boo!) and saying shush all the time (also boo!), although I do like bubble baths and having my hooves painted. They asked if I wanted to stay, or go home, but even though I wanted to stay, I thought about it, and went on with Lucy and Ember, because they needed me. Oh, and Daddy, I was thinking it over, and I just now figured out why they don't make bouncy-houses for unicorns!" she said. "The horns would totally poke holes and deflate them!"

"Ah, would they?"

"Oh, and one time, Lucy was sad, and being cute just made it worse."

Queen Nell tilted her head a little in polite enquiry. "And what made it better?"

"Nothing but hugs."

Frank and Nell looked at each other, and as King and Queen gave a pair of regal nods.

Connie gasped. "Oh Mummy, Daddy, was that my test?"

Her father nodded.

"Oh, Daddy, you are the smartest Daddy, ever!"

The King lifted his head, and in his most majestic voice, intoned: "Connie, the Herd sent you on your first quest, leaving the safety of the meadow, the security of home, and the certainty of answers. You have come back knowing that sometimes it is best to act, and sometimes it is best to think. You have made decisions and lived with the consequences. You have demonstrated justice without losing the capacity for mercy, and retained the core of your joy. You have kept and nurtured the bonds of friendship.Herd! Let it be known that Connie has returned to us wise."

The Dragon, Lucinda and George

One hundred unicorn hooves lifted. One hundred unicorns stamped. Th e valley thundered its approval. Connie became very still and her eyes wide. For once, she was rendered completely speechless.

"Herd," said the King of Unicorns. "Welcome Connie home." A massive shock rolled through the meadow, followed by the sound of every horn lifted in praise ringing from the hills.

Later, everyone agreed that the cake and ice cream were the best ever. The new unicorn-proof bouncy-house was pretty neat, too.

Chapter Thirty-Four
Disenchanted Dragons

THERE HAD BEEN THE RECEPTION, PEACE TIME negotiations, then the parade, and after Connie's party, Ember and all the disenchanted dragons returned home.

Home, if you were a dragon, was on the far side of the lake, where the cliffs were high, and the mountains were ominous and rumbly and ice-slick, and occasionally, if you were lucky, there was a stream of lava inside the caverns, to make guarding your hoard pleasantly toasty. Dragons were naturally solitary creatures. They might cluster together because of geography, but they didn't have leaders or chieftains, per se.

Ember's family were two of the chieftains they definitely didn't have.

When they arrived, her brothers went straight to their hoards, possibly to count them, and make sure everything was still there, or more likely, Ember thought, to escape the burning, solemn silence of their parents' combined stares. Her brothers were possibly still feeling fragile from their kitten days, anxious to curl up and play with a ball of yarn for a while. Not everyone had been as quick to recover as Glowerflorious, but she thought they'd be much more themselves after a few days spent bickering over what had become of their hoards, which had been redistributed among the family members when each of her brothers had been presumed killed-by-knights.

Ember winged into the cavern and settled gracefully at the base of her parents' hoard, which was as close as dragons got to furniture. Her parents had been hoarding for a long time; their combined pile was like a glittery mountain inside of a mountain. She could tell they had thought she was never coming back, because she recognized pieces of her childhood hoard scattered in the foothills of theirs.

Her parents were watching her. Ember knew how intimidating a dragon's stare could be. She'd learned dragon staring from experts. She told herself not to be nervous, but old habits die hard.

"Esmeraldavinia," said her father. "Explain the meaning of this."

Her mother said nothing.

"Well, Father," said Ember. "Mother. I found Scorchander and Charrtonio and six dozen other dragons at the very edge of the kingdom, where they had been enchanted by evil wizards, and brought them home safely. As you can see, they weren't dead after all. Almost none of them were." She had been practicing the speech for most of the flight, and although Glowerflorious had suggested she include the parts about how difficult and dangerous it had been, she thought it was best and more modest to stick to the bare bones, the facts.

"You shouldn't have," said her father.

As usual, Ember couldn't tell whether her father was kidding or not. Even among dragons who take pride in their enigmatic expression, Ember's father could have won prizes for his deadpan delivery.

Her mother said nothing.

Ember could have spent hours trying to decode the flicker of her father's tail, or the way her mother's glance took in the girdle-string wound in and around the ruby bracelet Ember still wore, but she was feeling a little tired, and honestly, just wanted to know the answer. "What do you mean, Dad?"

Her father growled.

Oops. That was not a happy dad sound. Ember looked from her father to her mother. She realized that help was not going to be immediately forthcoming from that quarter. Mother crouched on top of her particular part of the hoard, as solid and unmoving as if she'd been carved out of diamond, and her gaze was just as hard.

Suddenly, it occurred to Ember, after her recent in-depth experience in the outside world, that her parents, and dragons in general, were entirely unsuited to the service sector. Nothing in their body language suggested even the slightest desire to be helpful, subservient, or accommodating. They were exhibiting a bit of curiosity, perhaps, but no dragon business mission statement, and certainly none written by her parents, would ever include the phrase, "Our customers are our business." Or "We exist to provide our clients with 110% support 100% of the time."

Ember filed that thought away to be examined later. She was good at it. She'd been filing inconvenient thoughts away most of her life.

"Well, Dad, I felt it was important. There were just some things about Clean-up Day that didn't make any sense."

Her mother's eyes narrowed. Her father said, "Such as?"

"It started with the form letter," Ember said. "It said I was being sent out for the 472nd Beach Clean-up Day."

"I remember," said her father. "It has long been our right and responsibility to keep the shores of this lake clean, and to maintain the dragon way of life."

"But Dad," said Ember. "I couldn't help but notice that this letter supposedly written to and for dragons was in a human language. And last year, we had a big ceremony for the tricentennial anniversary of coming to these mountains, when the volcano first blew. We haven't been at this lake even four hundred years. It didn't sit right, so I went to my DALSED station and started doing some research."

Her father looked at her mother. "I knew getting that thing was a mistake," he said. Her mother said nothing, and her father glared at Ember. "I thought all you did on that terminal was play your Human-sympathizing Mystery Game."

"It has other functions, too," said Ember. "Like a research library, databases full of dragon history. I used it at the ceremony to write my report about the volcano. But this time, I went back 472 years. There was nothing in the records back then about a new Beach Clean-up Day, not here, and not where we dragons were actually living at the time. Nothing about whether it was one specific beach or if not, why it suddenly needed to be done on all the beaches. Not whose idea it was or anything. In fact, the first time Beach Clean-up Day was mentioned was only 87 years ago. And it just... starts. Wait, I can show you."

Ember reached into the foothills of the hoard, and after sorting through childhood knick-knacks for a moment, found the DALSED terminal, and gave a little sigh of relief: It was actually plugged in.

She booted it up, and with claws typing rapidly, pulled up the data she'd uncovered.

BEACH CRISIS MENACE — ANOTHER THING SO- CALLED "EXPERTS" MISSED

SITUATION INTOLERABLE — Ocean Life at Risk!

DRAGON WAY OF LIFE IMPERILED

HUMAN MAIDENS AND/OR 3.5 OUNCES OF SHAMPOO LEFT ON A BEACH IS GREATEST THREAT TO

DRAGON WAY OF LIFE SINCE, LIKE, FOREVER

Ember looked up and said, "Nothing at all in the records until 87 years ago, then all of a sudden, there are hundreds of studies claiming that the rate of human littering, especially with regard to maidens, had increased exponentially, and that coastal reclamation projects needed to be expanded. Not begun, Dad. Expanded, as if they'd already been going on, but they hadn't."

"I see. Let's see your search strategy," said her father, in the same patient tone he'd used when she got upset during her homework.

Ember's claws clacked on the keyboard as she pulled it up.

Her father studied the results. Her mother's long neck arched as she looked at the results over his shoulder. Then they looked at each other, and her father sighed.

"I'm sorry, Ember. You did not consider the possibility of synonyms or changing word use over time with 'or' statements," her father said. The sadness in his voice, owing to her failure at such a simple task, stung.

Ember flushed with embarrassment. "Sorry, Dad, but actually, I did. See?"

Another series of clacks, as Ember keyed up another document.

"Here it is. This is the final search string, and the entire search strategy. You can pull up the history of my search evolution here."

Breathing heavily, partly from nervousness, she turned the monitor around so that her parents could study the screen. By this time her parents were sitting side by side, and together they silently read Ember's search history and the search string as it had evolved. When they came to the end, they looked at each other for a long moment. Her mother blinked.

"Is good," she said. Ember blinked in surprise. For her mother, this was pretty much her quota of words for the year. She didn't usually waste her time with praise, either.

Her father nodded. "This is an extremely clear search strategy, Ember, well structured, skillful and imaginative in its manipulation of the data. It's forcefully executed. Well done, Ember. A master work."

"Yes," said her mother with a hint of exasperation at having to repeat herself. "Is good."

"And so what did you do with your result, once you determined Sacrifice Day and Beach Clean-up Day were not as old as had been claimed, Ember?"

Ember blinked again. Her father hated nicknames. It was very well known. Calling her by one was a huge concession.

"It made me think about the other things 'everyone knows' about Sacrifice Day. Like the elaborate lengths the humans supposedly went to in order to litter. Chaining maidens to posts covered in rags? It's illogical, even for humans. And then, when we performed a civic environmental duty, cleaning up their mess, why were they upset enough to try to kill us? I had to take knight-fighting lessons? Why would knights care about trash?"

Ember's father seemed to have recovered from his fleeting brush with emotion. Or at least, he had returned to his watchful mode. Her mother simply continued to stare.

"I thought about what you said, Dad, about following the money. Lessons, training, flavor aids, moisturizing spray? Who was paying for all of this? And why? I knew it couldn't be for the good of dragons. Each year there were fewer dragons. The humans didn't seem to be getting much out of it, either. So I decided to ask one of them what she thought, instead of eating her first."

Her parents continued their impassive motionless staring.

"And so Lucy and I—"

"What is a Lucy?" said her father, sharply.

Ember blinked, and realized for the first time how much she

had changed since leaving home. "Lucy is the litter. Was the litter. No. She's NOT litter. She is a being. Like a dragon only with gooshy parts. Lucy and I compared notes and we both decided to find out what was really going on, and put a stop to it because it was so illogical. So off we went and that's what we did. And so now I'm home. We did it."

As concluding statements went, Ember knew that hers was never going to win any human or unicorn prizes, but Ember knew her parents. Ember settled in to wait for their verdict.

"Is good," said her mother.

Ember exhaled. She hadn't even realized she'd been holding her breath.

"I think your mother, as always, has managed to say it all."

Ember was proud enough to give off sparks at that compliment, but now was the hard part. "The thing is," she said.

"Yes?" her father asked.

"I'm not done with my searching yet," Ember said.

"What do you mean?"

"The truth is," said Ember, "I don't know if I'm actually all that into hoarding. I'm glad you and Mom like it, and I know it's what Charrtonio and Scorchander were looking forward to, but I actually like flying. I like traveling and seeing new places."

"With Glowerflorious," growled her father, casting a baleful glance outside the cave.

Ember blushed, but lifted her chin just a semi-rebellious notch. "Yes, with Glowerflorious," she said. "I got to know him pretty well while I was on my quest, and what I know I like. He's trustworthy and kind, and he makes me laugh. Plus, no one makes a bigger splash in a lake. We were talking, Glowerflorious and I, and neither of us is ready to hole up, just yet. Then we remembered. There was one part of the form letter we received that mentioned a valley, no volcanoes, but snow-capped mountains, caverns of gold, and fat deer running around, and he and I, we…"

"We want to go together," said Glowerflorious. He must have felt her father's glare and come inside the cavern to answer it. He didn't seem intimidated by her parents at all, and gave Ember half a smile, and a friendly wink. "We want to discover for ourselves whether it really exists."

Ember held her breath as her mother looked at her father, and her father looked at her mother. They exchanged nods, and then her mother turned and looked at Ember and Glowerflorious where they stood, side by side.

"Is good."

Chapter Thirty-Five
Journey's End

THE UNICORNS, SO DELIGHTED BY THE RETURN OF THE youngest member of the herd, had been very generous. George and Agent X rode the rest of the way on horseback, traveling in a leisurely fashion, taking time, as they hadn't been able to before, to appreciate the lush forest and the peaceful surety of having completed their assignment. George, in particular, was feeling at peace with himself. He didn't mind camping on the ground, especially without Chip's snore as a constant buzzing in his head. He didn't even mind when the here-and-there of springtime weather resulted in a downpour just as they came to a crossroads above a familiar little town.

In one direction, the road led off into the rest of the kingdom; in the other, it led down to the town itself. From here, they could see the civic center of the town, with a fountain, a police station, and a little library. A little further on was a hotel, and behind that, a small cottage, with a lantern in the window.

"Well, this is it," said Agent X.

"Reckon so," allowed George.

"I expect you've got someone waiting down there." Agent X gestured to the town, and the distant cottage.

"Hope so," said George. "I wouldn't be surprised if her sister would be happy to see you if you happened to show up at the inn looking for a dry place to sleep and a warm bite."

"You're probably right. But I'm thinking I might end up leaving town a mite early tomorrow morning."

"Wouldn't be the first time," said George.

"No, it wouldn't be," said Agent X.

They sat in silence while the rain fell on them. If the rain meant to get them any wetter, it failed, since they were both already as soggy as men could be without dissolving.

"I've been thinking," said George. "I might stick around here a while longer, if it's all the same to you."

"Your call," said Agent X. "But they'll come after you, you know."

"Who?"

"The auto dealership. They're going to want paying for the dragon-sized dents in the fender." He shook his head, and adjusted his hat. Rain sheeted from the brim down the solid black collar of his coat. "You should've gotten the insurance."

"I did this time," said George. "Hindsight's 20/20, remember? Don't worry about me, X." He hesitated, while the rain came down on both of them, and said, "You might want to consider a little hindsight yourself."

"About what?" Agent X looked at him.

"Lingering," said George.

"With the sister down there?" he nodded down towards the Inn.

"You might want to consider it," said George.

"Might come down to it someday. Maybe tomorrow, maybe never." Agent X shrugged.

"Just sayin'."

"Don't worry about me," said Agent X. "You're the one burning courtin' time. Get a move on, and say howdy to that little lady for me."

"Been a pleasure riding with you," said George.

"Pleasure's been mine," said Agent X.

He did linger, though, watching through the rain as George touched his heels to his horse, and rode down into the town, past the civic center and the hotel, and up the smaller path that led to the cottage. The lantern was flickering in the window. George rode past, and stopped in the barn, where he made sure his horse was put away properly.

He wasn't long about it, and the moment his boot hit the front porch, the door flew open. Rachael stood framed in the doorway, with a shawl wrapped loosely around her shoulders, and a paintbrush in one hand. She wasn't as cute as her sister, but what she was, was strong enough, and real enough, to bring a man back home again, even riding through the rain.

Agent X was too far away to hear what words George and Rachael exchanged there in the doorway of the front porch, but he was plenty close enough to see it when they came together in a powerful embrace. Rachael pulled George inside the cottage and closed the door behind them. Pretty soon, the lantern flickered out.

As he nudged his horse down to the town with a slight touch of his knees, Agent X knew that there was soon going to be a lot of hard editing ahead, but he also knew just how he'd record the moment for posterity: ***"At the end of the journey, our heroes lived as they deserved to, happily ever after."***

THE END

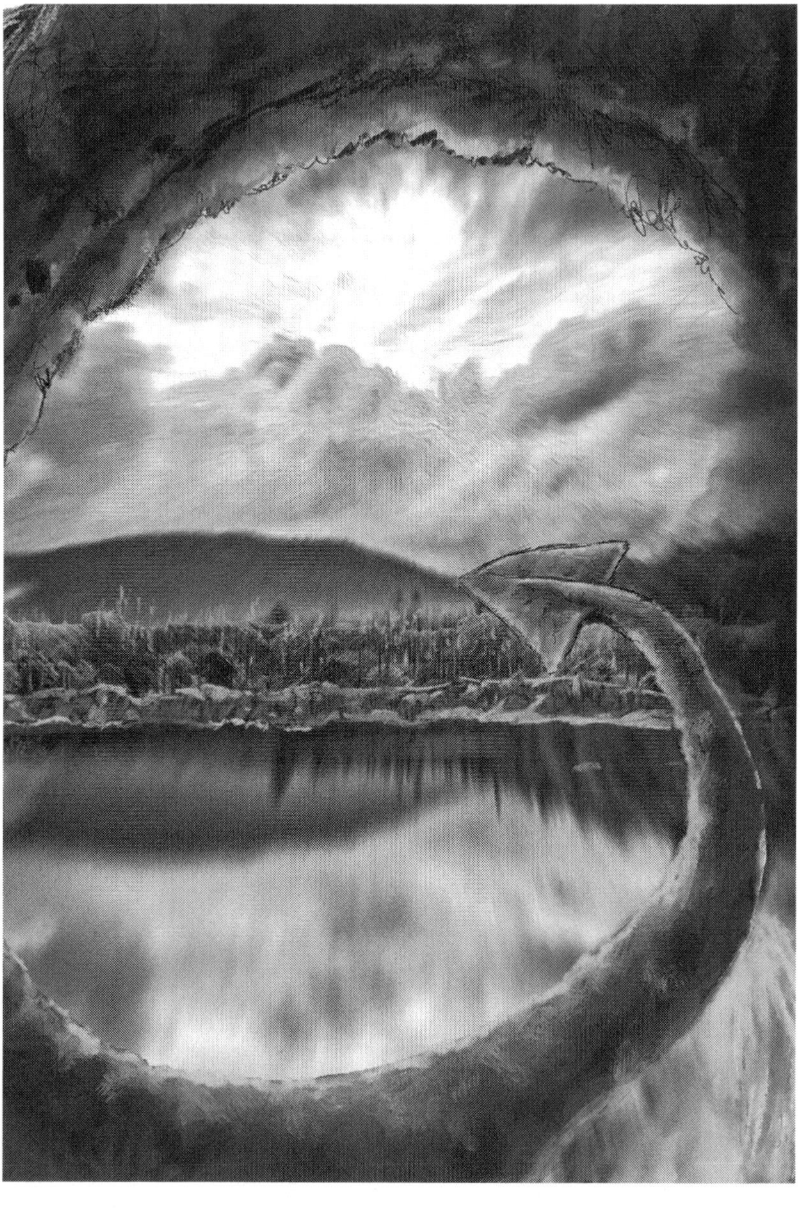

About The Authors

Margit Elland Schmitt

Margit Elland Schmitt is the author of several short stories, including "Sparrowjunk" (about childhood illness and a fairy's dangerous addiction to stories) and "Under Janey's Garden" (about gardens, weddings, and wizardry). In the hours she's not writing, Margit works in an elementary school library, carefully cultivating the reading habits of impressionable young people. Before becoming the library lady, Margit embraced such diverse careers as teacher, editor, actor, singer, and kitten-whisperer. Fun Fact: When Margit was in sixth grade, her teacher informed her that she lacked enough imagination to ever be a "real" writer, which inspired her with ferocious determination to get real. Is this book the result of expertly applied reverse psychology? Well played, Ms. Wilson. Well played.

Dan McLaughlin

Dan McLaughlin was born in Hollywood during halftime of a Rams - Colts game. Although the Rams scored a touchdown soon after his birth to tie the game, the Colts then scored 17 points to win. This, along with multi-decade stints at UCLA and as a government bureaucrat, has given Dan an appreciation for the subtle and sometimes capricious agency of wishes, words, actions, and consequences.

Among his philosophical influences he cites Thomas Kuhn,

David Springhorn, Paul Feyerabend, the Reduced Shakespeare Company, and Bullwinkle the Moose. Recently retired as the local history reference librarian at the Pasadena Public Library, Dan can be found working merrily in the garden, pacing nervously during any UCLA game where the lead or deficit is less than 25 points, or walking sedately the beloved puppies with his even more beloved wife, Vendi.

Dan has written five novels, two nonfiction works on the history of Pasadena, one musical, and a play. In reverse chronological order, his works of fiction have been: WereKitty, a work which considers what happens 20 years after a torrid love affair between a normal human and a member of the differentially animated community when the WereKitty's father is trapped in a Chevy Cruze; Gott Mit Uns, a play that tells the story of an 8-½-foot penguin, a goddess pursued by two bureaucrats through today's America to keep her paperwork correct; Mime Time, a murder mystery about a mime about to be nominated as the Republican Presidential candidate of 2012 and the people who want to kill him; Gott Mit Uns, the novel which is the source of his recent play; Pass the Damn Salt, Please, a novel which explores the importance of language and politeness in relationships, told entirely in dialogue; ICE Girls, an award-winning novella which examines the story of the Little Match Girl from the point of view of management; and the award-winning musical Oh No, Not Emily!, an operetta in which a modern fake Emily Dickinson poem is sold to a post-modern college English Department.

Two of Dan's works have been nominated for Just Plain Folks awards: Oh No, Not Emily! for Best Theater Album, and ICE Girls for Best Storytelling Album.

Before that he and Mark Sellin were "2 Guys from the 70's". Also with Mark and other friends, Dan wrote, directed, and acted in several plays at the Renaissance Faire in Southern California, including their greatest hit, Ye Olde Tale of Goode King Arthur. He also has created radio play versions of The Trojan Horse, AKA The Big Horsey Ride and The Odyssey, AKA Going Home and Getting Lucky.

In terms of his nonfiction, Dan has been the local history librarian at the Pasadena Public Library for over 25 years. He has designed and contributed content to two local history resources: the Pasadena Digital History Collaborative and the Pasadena News Index. His two nonfiction works are Pasadena History Headline Quiz, which consists of 690 Pasadena history trivia questions with online clues on how to answer them, and Pasadena: A Mystery and a History You Can Explore, which presents the reader with literally thousands of mysteries taken from Pasadena history and the means to solve them. These two books both provide a fascinating look at the history of Pasadena and give the reader the instruction to research online topics in Pasadena history that interest them.

Most recently he has edited Animation Rules!, a two-volume work written by his late father, noted independent filmmaker and head of the UCLA Animation Workshop, Dan McLaughlin.

Margit and Dan

Margit and Dan met at the Renaissance Faire at Black Point in Northern California, about 30 years ago. Dan really doesn't remember the event, but apparently he accosted Margit and her friends in the guise of a peasant huckster selling pieces of the New World real estate with his friend Mark Sellin. Time passed, and Margit began to be on the huckster end of accosting people at the Faire. Dan took note of Margit's talents as a performer, writer, and director, which he liberally exploited when he cast her as the lead "Molly Writerblock" in his operetta Oh No, Not Emily!, and as the lead (and only) Penguin "Great Goddess Bo" in his play Got Mitt Uns.

The inspiration for this book came after Margit had spent too much time rereading the legend of St. George and the Dragon. Margit and Dan talked it over, and both agreed that the dragon was treated unfairly. She complained about having an idea but not enough time to write. He complained of having time to write, but not enough of an idea. There was enough of a spark to make them give it a try. Somehow, both of them found time and inspiration enough to put an entire story together. The result is here.

Made in the USA
Lexington, KY
04 June 2019